DIRTY DUBLIN

Yvonne Fitzpatrick-Grimes

I dedicate this book to my darling Dave,

four extraordinary children, and a host of family and friends.

Acknowledgements

For the editorial skills of Carrie, the tenacity of Lynda, and the work and friendship of Margaret ... I am eternally in debt. And warm thanks to Edward for the opportunity.

About the author

Yvonne Fitzpatrick-Grimes was born in Dublin in the 50's. Writing isn't her only passion. On a good night, she drinks whiskey and red lemonade; dances gigs and reels with wild abandon; and sings ballads in parts of Dublin and London to which only the demented or delirious would venture. By day she isn't idle either – she wrote the Homily in the opening scenes of Lasse Hallström's film *Chocolat* and has contributed to various reputable Irish magazines and newspapers. She is also involved with Irish Heritage.

Fifty per cent of all the author's royalties from this book will be donated to the charity Dogs for the Disabled (www.dogsforthedisabled.org)

One

'What in the name of Jaysus are yeh up to now?' Concepta stopped, mortified by Fatama's contortions in the middle of Stretham Street. Fully aware of the peeping Toms camouflaged behind net curtains, Fatama was less than concerned. She was bent over double, rummaging deep in the lining of her leopard-skin coat.

'Would yeh ever come on? I want to get finished early. Get me order in for me Christmas turkey before Billy Atkins locks up and goes off to deh slaughter house.'

'I'm gummin' for a fag,' Fatama snapped, becoming increasingly bad-tempered with an elusive butt. 'There it is, the little bastard.' The flattened fag appeared with a flourish. 'It was far from turkey yer were two years ago. So less of yer cheek. Don't ever forget who's puttin' the food on yer table.'

'Isn't it time yeh took a needle and thread to that auld hole?' Concepta rattled with the cold as she waited for Fatama's brown fingers to knead life back into the battered butt.

'Sew up me auld hole,' Fatama spluttered and coughed as she started up again. 'We're not shaggin' seamstresses, Concepta, we're whores for Christ's sake.'

Stepping gingerly in through the back door of Adam and Eve's, she didn't give Concepta as much as a backward glance.

'What de yeh tink of me colour?' She was swinging right and left of a picture of the Blessed Virgin. Trying to get a better view of her beehive. 'Musha the chemist mixed it special for me – Baby Blush Two.'

'In the name of Jaysus, Fatama. That's a snap of Our Lady yer usin' as a mirror.'

Having found just the right angle at the Blessed Virgin's ankles, Fatama's blunt hands were proudly patting the platinum tower. 'Swears it's the same mix as Marilyn Monroe.'

Without batting an eyelid, she traipsed on through the church, took their usual short cut. Keeping up the rear, Concepta counted the number of pins and clips in the hairdo. She was about to make a joke about the perils of passing a magnet when they were both distracted by the funereal tones of a priest.

A wedding in Ireland in Christmas week would be suspect at the best of times. But a wedding during the Holy Hour stopped the two prostitutes dead in their tracks.

'Begod, someone must have bribed the Bishop.' Fatama cocked the remains of her left eyebrow. A bare side altar and not a flower or a friend in attendance. She surveyed the wedding scene.

'I don't know about bribin' him – they look more like they're here to bury him,' Concepta cast her own septic commentary on the skeletal wedding party.

The bride stiffened at the double indignity. Scrutiny and mortification heaped on top of this marriage of convenience was the last straw for Muriel Grey.

'She's right der, Father. Yid whip a better reception up in a morgue.' Fatama heaved her heavy breasts back up to where they once belonged.

The spluttering inside the bridegroom's head was only by the grace of God refused exit by his mouth. Stuck to the altar like a comic caricature, howling embarrassment screeched around Fonsie Duggan. He looked up at the priest for some glimmer of guidance. But he might as well have been idle. Caught up in this web of deceit, the priest had as much chance of controlling the two prostitutes as he had of controlling the antics of Barclay O'Rourke, the Bishop of Dublin.

'That's more like a marriage made in Ireland than a marriage made in Heaven,' Fatama's cheek continued to confound her captive audience. Her gaudy dress – as short and as cheap as her commentary – sent a frisson of consternation through the congregation.

Just as quick as one of their tricks, they were off. Their steel-tipped stilettos boldly beating a retreat whilst their low-cut lurex, promising more mischief than it could produce, ballooned and subsided in convulsions. Brazenly banging the heavy church doors behind them. They put the heart crossways on the wedding party, leaving their mouths hanging open like stunned mullets.

Muriel Grey's stomach heaved from the smell of hops and yeast creeping into the church from Guinness' brewery. Morning sickness. She was marginally more impressed by the two prostitutes than she was by her hastily convened marriage. Displaying every ounce of these feelings, she stared straight ahead at the Christmas crib.

'Jesus, Mary and Joseph. What have I done? Acquired a name for my unborn baby, a husband for respectability. And freedom, freedom for my Bishop.'

Well, at least one of us is free. She stroked her dress, the only thing in her wardrobe wide enough to accommodate her little gift from His Grace. More seasonal than stylish, the dress too seemed to

8

lend its own brand of ridicule to this pathetic production. Delaying the ceremony, she'd waited and waited. Delayed taking the marriage vows that would bind her hand and foot to a man she barely knew. But Barclay O'Rourke wasn't coming to any church, wasn't coming to any wedding. He wasn't the one weighted down with a belly full of baby. Wasn't the one weighed down with a wife.

Riled by the frozen face on his new bride, by the ridicule and impotency of the occasion, a new rage began to boil inside Fonsie Duggan. If I could only reverse the promises, the platitudes; take the hands of the clock and turn back the pleadings. But he couldn't – something in Fonsie Duggan always cowered, always kowtowed to the Bishop of Dublin.

In high spirits, the two prostitutes took up their respective positions on the church doorsteps. For a Christmas week, there was plenty of bustle but no trade.

'A green dress with a splash of red on it. She looked more like a Christmas tree than a bride.' The smoke circling Fatama's lungs made her choke.

'She's the right shape for it, anyway.' A fit of coughing took the end of the sentence with it. Concepta didn't catch what she said.

'It'll be cold comfort that auld fellah will be getting off his frigid bride this side of Christmas.' She threw her head and her remarks towards the church.

'Still an' all, we should be grateful for are small mercies. She won't be takin' the bread out of our mouths anyway.'

'Pity he wasn't as careful with his auld man as he was with his feet. Some fancy footwear for a weddin' – galoshes!'

Fatama wasn't listening. She wasn't much older than the girl in the church when she was married off to an auld man herself. Married and maimed by a country bull. Before she was twenty, her womb and her will battered and broken.

She was freezing. She never wore any knickers. Superfluous to requirements. She never knew whether it was overexposure to cold or to cocks that left her feeling permanently frigid. Some said she was barren. She was barren all right – barren in her heart.

'A little drop of mothers' milk.' She was scanning the street as she pulled the baby powers out of her bra. Latching her lips around the bottle, she sucked greedily. In a voice that was none of her own, she began to mock the local midwife. 'It's always more desirable drunk at body temperature.' She was wagging her finger, assuming the authoritative stance.

9

Concepta preferred Guinness. The rich dark colour, the soft silky feel. She had two black babies. She had had them in the dark. She never knew the Da's, just the colour of their money. 'Get a belt of that brewery into yer lungs; it will do yer heart a power of good.' She inhaled deeply, the smell of hops and yeast wafting free over the Guinness wall.

'Get a grip on yerself,' Fatama roared above the sound of the factory siren. 'What's Guinness got to do with the price of whores in Dublin? It's more than the hops and yeast in yeh. Yeh'll be wantin' to pay the rent.'

Fatama had pulled her first punter. Hitching up her skirt, she hauled herself bold as brass into the cab of his lorry. As it pulled away, her peroxide head shot out of the window, her green eyes alight with mischief. 'Just remember one thing, Concepta: there's more prostitution in the marriage beds of Ireland than there is on the streets of Dublin.'

It started to snow. Averting his gaze, Fonsie Duggan drove his unhappy bride home to Leixlip. Up Aran quay, past dolls prancing and dancing in McBernie's Christmas window. Over O'Connell Bridge, taking the long way home to Leixlip. Because he'd never mastered reversing. It should have been his epitaph.

He took a sideways glance, not that it needed confirmation. The atmosphere in the car was as thick as ice. Finding second gear with some difficulty, Fonsie lurched and jumped his car through the crowds at the foot of the Ha'Penny Bridge. Seventeenth of December, leave it to you, Fonsie, to pick the worst day in the Christmas calendar: the day they come up from the country to do their annual shop.

Back down the quays, he could almost feel the festive lights strung alongside the Liffey winking and jeering as he left Dublin behind. Shaking, nudging each other in disbelief, questioning the sanity of the recently widowed man. Making him feel like the fool at his own wedding.

With very passing mile, Muriel's hurt eclipsed Fonsie's pride, with the prostitutes' coarse words grating in her ears – *that's more like a marriage made in Ireland, made in Ireland, made in Ireland.* Stiff as a poker, she sat beside her new-found husband.

And she wasn't the only one the Bishop betrayed.

In the still of the sacristy, the celebrant laced his stomach with the spirit he so badly needed. He'd seen it all today. Mischief, mayhem and madness. Sealed and sanctified by his own holy hands in the sacrament of marriage. Jezebels, all three, trawling their filthy wares through the house of God. His faith haemorrhaged. Filling with hate he'd never known before, he cursed and spat. *I saw three whores perform today, I saw three whores perform today*, over and over like a thing possessed. Terrified, he made the Sign of the Cross and begged God's forgiveness.

An end had to be put to his gallop. Someone had to stop the Bishop of Dublin. Reaching into his pocket, he felt the letter.

Two

Like a whisper, fear stalked her as she crept down the bare corridors of the Bishop's Palace. Past the porous silence that lay in wait outside the other servants' rooms. Tiptoeing along by the bad auld bitch's bedroom. Every church in the city pealed out its warning. Guts slipping and sliding, she avoided floorboards that creaked and told. If she could clear the hall – God, it's long – before the other servants woke, she'd have a head start.

As she slipped up the Bishop's back passage, not a soul stirred. The only sound she heard was the thumping of her own heart. Feeling the well-oiled bolt, she slid it silently back. Leaving a trail of wee-wee in her wake, she was out the door, racing down a pitch-black avenue before she took her next breath. It was midnight in Dublin.

Fuelled on a frenzy of fear and freedom, she sprinted like a thing possessed. Stopping and starting, she used the trees that lined the avenue as cover when the headlights of an odd car or bicycle appeared out on the main road. Past the stout pillars, through the cast iron gates, she ran as if all the bats in hell were after her. Chasing her down Drumcondra Road. Her heart raced her heels as she pounded Dorset Street, Bolton Street, Capel Street.

Not daring to stop; like the dancing dolls in the Christmas window, she ran on and on. Somewhere in the distance, she saw the lights of City Hall. Covering more ground than she expected, she was over Capel Street Bridge and up the side of Adam and Eve's. As the stench of the Liffey hit the back of her nose, Attracta Rafferty let out a whoop of relief. She was home. Home, amongst her own, back, safe in the Liberties.

Her Ma wouldn't be cross for long. Her tempers didn't last. Money would be the biggest problem with Nel Rafferty, and Attracta could solve that. But auld Sexton, the auld bitch she was fleeing from, now that was a different animal. Eighteen months under her roof and never once did I hear a kind word, let alone see a smile. Not a word to throw to an auld stray. If a stray dog had the misfortune to land up there. Attracta reassured herself as she prepared the opening lines for her Ma.

She'd put her in the picture about Sunday right away. The deep shite, the big lump of a county one got her into. How she couldn't take her hand off her arse till they were in it up to their red necks.

An' all because of a letter. A fukkn' auld letter. If the big gobshite hadn't sung like a yellah canary, we'd have got away with it.

We were bored outa our skulls. Not a sinner would have been any the wiser if the big fat country lump of a one hadn't started gruntin' and grovelin' to auld Sexton. And it was all her idea.

It was her showin' me how to steam a letter open. Holdin' it over the spout of the kettle. Sayin' that Mrs Sexton always steamed letters open this way. Puttin' ideas into me head. Accusin' poor auld Humphy of lookin' shifty. Poor stupid auld Humphy. Accusin' him of skulkin' around the Bishop's backyard of a Sunday. That's how she put it. Sayin' it was our duty to open it.

Oh! she had plenty to say. But not as much as a word of warnin' when she heard auld Sexton comin'. Passin' the sodden letter to me. Starin' as if butter wouldn't melt in her mouth. Caught red-handed.

Attracta rehearsed the lines for her Ma. Adding bits, subtracting more. It was only a bit of crack, Ma. Bursting to tell her side of the story. She turned into Smock Alley. She hadn't realised how long or how narrow the alley was, or how high the walls either side were.

New sounds and shadows were slowly replacing her fears. The grunts and groans of stinking drunks in shop doorways amplified the still of the night. Jumping past St Audeon's Arch, she heard a woman scream. Indoor sounds – outside. She thought she saw her Da. But the arch was darker than the night.

By the time she saw the lights of Mercy Mansions, the fear that had her wings dissolved. With tears tripping her, she beat her way through lines of freezing washing that festooned the long hallway. Liberties bunting. She was home.

'Shut up for Jaysus sake, Attracta Rafferty, ye'll waken every child in the house.' Nel could just about make out her daughter's face in the glow of the Sacred Heart lamp.

'Yeh put the heart crossways on me. Burstin' in on a body like that. It's one o'clock in the mornin'. What in Christ's name's possessed yeh? Yer blue with the cold. Half the country riddled with TB. Yeh'll catch yer death if we're lucky.' Nel took the cardigan off her own back and pulled it round Attracta's shoulders.

Between her Ma's chattering teeth and her own rattling bones, Attracta couldn't get a word out.

'Pull yerself together, child.' Her Ma tipped a cup of water into a saucepan and set it to boil over a glimmer of gas. 'Yer bladder was always behind yer eye. Did anyone hurt yeh?'

Attracta managed to shake her head. The hiss from the gas made a comforting sound.

13

'Did anyone touch yeh?'

Sensing her Ma's terror, Attracta pulled herself together.

'No, Ma,' she simpered. 'It's that bloody Mrs Sexton, Ma. She's a mean auld bitch.' She wrapped her fingers around the mug of boiling water, heating herself as much on the outside as inside. She took a tiny sip. The water burned the tip of her tongue, her lips. But it didn't stop her making her case.

'And a two-faced one at that. Treatin' us like dirt. An' as soon as the Bishop comes near the place, all smiley, mealy-mouthed. I'm tellin' yer Ma, it was eighteen hard months, hard labour in hell!'

'Keep takin' sips, don't lose the heat.' Nel didn't want disease in the house. She'd enough to contend with – poverty.

'Sure, the Bishop of Dublin hates her guts. Yeh can hear it in every word he has to say to her.'

'But why in the name of God, why the middle of the night? Could yeh not have waited till daylight at least till yeh decided to bolt?

'Are yeh mad? On the edge of Christmas, she'd manacle me to the sink if she got as much as a sniff of escape. She has spies everywhere. Feckin' little tittle-tattles.'

In the month since she'd been home, her Ma's belly had thickened, grown awkward and round. In stark contrast, her face was grey, her arms and legs gaunt.

Nel saw Attracta's pupils narrow. Yeh couldn't be up to Attracta Rafferty. There was more to this than met the eye.

Nel's sigh was weary. She was resigned to failure. Seventeen years married to Jemser Rafferty was a great apprenticeship.

'I didn't do it, Ma.' Nel went ashen.

'Yeh didn't do what?,' she eventually said.

'I didn't read the letter. Humphy Hadlum only handed it to me because he knew me. It wasn't me that held it over the kettle and steamed it open. Sure, how would I even know how to get into a letter like that?'

'What letter? What are yeh rawmashin' about?'

'You know it's the truth, Ma. You know I never could read joindy-up writing. I was only lettin' on. Pretendin' to the others that I could read.'

'What letter could be of any concern of yours?' Nel couldn't understand why Attracta was getting herself in such a state about a letter.

'But Ma, yeh don't understand. Mrs Sexton said that I could end up in prison.

Said I'd be lucky if I didn't end up in Mountjoy for Christmas. For interferin' with the Bishop's post.'

'Did she now, indeed. Well, rest assured child, yeh won't be goin' near any prison. An' if she puts either a foot or face across Nel Rafferty's door, I'll break it in two with me bare hands. Now would yeh have a titter of wit, child, and save yer tears for when yeh need them.'

Nel's thoughts distracted her as she felt for the remains of a Woodbine. Stashed behind a clock that told all but the time. I thought it was too good to be true, one workin' at Christmas. Maybe I was just short-listed for happiness. She blew smoke towards a stained ceiling.

'This wouldn't have anything to do with the butcher's young fellah?,' she eyeballed her daughter. 'Because I'll tell yeh somethin' for nothin', Miss, I see precious little signs of him missin' you, madam. He has his father's heart scalded.' She stopped for a minute. 'He'd tip a cat through a skylight, the same article.'

'Jaysus, Ma, give us a break. It's out of the fire, not into it, I'm tryin' to get.' Even as Attracta lied, she filled with a strange sort of excitement.

'Nel Rafferty's not as green as she looks.'

But Nel was puzzled. What class of person could put the fear of God into a scrap of a girl like that? And for what? Was there more to the matter than Attracta was letting on? She could be a minx, the same little madam. For once, it wasn't man trouble. She saw them watching her daughter. Since she was twelve, young fellahs trailing after her like dogs on heat. She prayed it wasn't man trouble. She could cope with anything, but she couldn't cope if her daughter was pregnant.

'Ma, look I've seventeen and sixpence, Ma.' Attracta's hard-earned savings turned her Ma's head around. 'I won't be under yer feet for long, I won't be a burden. I'll get another job. Yeh know I will.' She kept her mother distracted.

'The auld fucker will never find me in the Liberties.' Attracta's confidence was coming back. 'An' if she does manage to smoke me out, I won't be backwards in comin' forwards. I'll swear on a Bible before the Pope of Rome himself that it was auld Sexton that read that letter. Not me; I didn't.'

'Couldn't,' Nel corrected. 'Couldn't read the letter.'

'She was like shit boiled white, whatever she saw in it,' Attracta revelled in the housekeeper's horror. 'Housekeepers, me arse. Glorified spies. Leeches livin' off other people's lives. That's all

15

they are. That's all they're fit for. The big fat country one was shakin' an' stutterin' like a lump of liver when she threw it at me. I could only catch some of what she was sayin'. Cute country whore.'

'Yeh caught none of what she was sayin', was readin' or what she saw! De yeh hear me, Attracta Rafferty?' Her Ma's voice cut through the codology.

'What yeh don't know, yeh can never repeat. And what yeh don't repeat, yeh don't slander. De yeh see where am drivin'? Steamin' open other people's post is serious. And steamin' open letters addressed to the Bishop of Dublin is no laughin' matter. So as far as we're concerned, you can't read. So you know nothin'. An' yeh saw less.' Her Ma looked and sounded more serious than Attracta had ever seen her.

'An' where, tell me, does Humphy Hadlum fit into the picture?' Her Ma's tone had changed back to its old self. As if the previous minute never existed. Attracta was visibly relieved.

'Nowhere. He was just the taxi.' She wasn't sure how much she was supposed to say now, how much she was supposed to know.

'Bejaysus, isn't it royal too? An' all we have is an auld postman on a bike.' Attracta felt safer with this Nel.

'Oh, one half of the world...' The rest of her Ma's sentence hung in mid air.

In all the commotion, the youngest Rafferty had woken. As Nel bent to pick him up, pain ripped her belly like a serrated knife. She turned her face from the child and took a couple of breaths.

'Yer soakin'. What am I to do with yeh, Joe? Five of yis in nappies – and the weather pig ignorant.' Talking over the pain, she sat under the child and tried to ignore the hurt. It couldn't be labour. It wasn't her time yet. 'It'll be good to have an extra pair of hands around the place.' She disguised the odd catch in her breath. Still, hands come on the ends of mouths, and now I've twelve to feed. But the pain in her belly was overriding her concerns.

'Wet a few leaves of tea there, daughter, before the arse is burned outa that pot.' Nel sat on the edge of the chair, waited as the pain subsided.

She hadn't added in the child on the way. Couldn't bring the count up to thirteen. She'd get Christmas over first. Then let January throw at her what it liked.

'With the help of God, I'll last that long.' Her thoughts became words.

They both heard Jemser. Careering up the hall, he fell through the door headlong on to a bockety leatherette sofa. Its fourth leg, a mineral crate – Jemser's contribution to carpentry – creaked furiously with the fall. He was snoring before his second foot left the floor. Putting her finger to her mouth, Nel Rafferty shepherded Attracta and Joe past their father and into the bedroom.

'He's that drunk, he wouldn't recognise his self in a room full of mirrors,' Nel spoke softly to the frightened child in her arms.

Attracta was disgusted. From the fryin' pan into the fire; she gritted her teeth as she felt round a contingent of bodies. Feeling for the pissy pool, hoping and praying the bed would be dry. Straightening up the two army great coats that kept them all warm, she shoved into a tangled nest of brothers and sisters.

On the far side of the room, Nel Rafferty lay in between half a dozen more of her children. She thanked God for Attracta's seventeen and sixpence. Peeping through a crack in the door, she made sure Jemser was sound asleep before she put the windfall under her pillow. Over and over again, Nel's fingers felt for the security the seven half-crowns brought. Reassured that they hadn't slipped down by the wall, she spent them ten times over. If Jemser Rafferty found out about the money, he'd have her heart scalded. A born toucher, it'd be pissed up every alleyway in Dublin.

She'd never hear the end of it when he discovered Attracta was back. Nel let out a long sigh. There was never any love lost between Attracta and Jemser. Attracta had his mark. They were the head of one another, if the truth be told.

Still an' all, there was silver lining in every cloud. The money would make a great difference. She'd pay a few bob offa Biddy Mulligan's slate. Buy holly with red berries on it to decorate the place up. A couple a little wind-up toys for the younger ones in Moore Street. Some guns and caps for the older boys, a spinning top for the younger ones an' maybe a mouth organ they could get an' auld tune out of on Christmas day. A chicken an' a bit of mutton to throw in beside it from Billy Atkins. And a big bag of monkey nuts, a few tangerines, and maybe a bit of mistletoe over the door for the crack. Sure, they were on the pig's back. She slid into sleep, her fingers curled tightly round the big silver coins.

Attracta woke early on Monday morning, the bells of Adam and Eve's ringing out the hour of six – auld Sexton's time. Her chin rubbed against the coarse material of the army coat. For a second, she panicked. A pissy horse blanket if yer lucky is all that yeh'll find in jail. The slanty words came back to terrify her. Smothered in shank loads of stinking toes, she stuck her head up for fresh air. A wave of pure relief swept over when she realised she was home.

Thanking God for Rafferty piss, she nipped out of bed and checked that the waxy red note was still in her shoe. Gripping the cold lino with her toes, she remembered how warm the Bishop's Palace used to be. Winter and summer. She hurried back to bed and burrowed deep. In the still of the early morning, she had time to think.

They'd be searching high and low for her now, in the basements, the attics, the bell tower, all the priest's hideholes in the Palace. The big country one, staring at empty spaces, grates and empty plates. She'd be doing her biddin' in the shivery silence, if she was still there now. Cleanin' out coarse cinders, sieving and saving large pieces until her knuckles were raw. Have every waste not, want not hearth set, upstairs and down. Scuttling out of sight before the great white light himself could set eyes on the unclean. Before a drop of tea passed her tonsils. Before Mass, and Communion. And a feckin' priest dronin' on and on. Before she was allowed a bite to eat, pounced, scrubbed and peeled pounds and pounds of spuds. And when the older servants sat down to a hearty breakfast, until she was told the differ she served them in silence. Served my arse; this mornin' they could wait and wait.

Attracta began to plan. She'd given her Ma the seventeen and sixpence. That left ten bob for her. Sight of January could be lost in the run up to Christmas, and she wanted herself sorted and out of Stretham Street as soon as possible. She'd go down to Biddy Mulligan's first thing this morning and pay a few bob off her Ma's slate.

Biddy sweet, she'd be more inclined to part with gear she kept for her stuck-up customers. If Attracta had learnt nothing else in the Bishop's Palace, she'd learnt that poor might get sympathy but the well-dressed get the job. She'd seen it all herself at the back door. Fine feathers made the right impression.

She hadn't seen the Butcher's Boy for three weeks. Something skimpy would turn his head. Jaysus knows, it didn't take much. Somethin' tight and temptin'. A shiver from her head to her toe. She knew he was a heart scald. But he was her heart scald. Well, he would soon be. He'd given her the glad eye often enough. Asked her out often enough. But she could never get the right time off. That wouldn't be a problem now.

No more than her excuse to be in Atkins' butchers shop. Billy Atkins made the best bit of brawn in Dublin. Her Ma loved brawn. And she could take her place with pride with the paying customers with the right clothes on her back and money in her pocket. She would take her time choosin' too. Let him get an eyeful. His father wouldn't be runnin' her when he heard the few bob janglin'. Runnin' her like he'd run her an' others before, for hangin' round the shop. Hangin' round his son.

That was as far as her dreaming and scheming got when the bed erupted. Heads, limbs, torsos and toes appeared out from every crease and crevice.

It was a cross between madness and mayhem when the Raffertys first woke up. Fighting and farting, scrapping and scrambling for shoes, shirts or shorts. It was the survival of the fittest. First up, best dressed was the war cry coined in Raffertys' kitchen.

Attracta hugged a dozen brothers and sisters. The thought of having her home for Christmas put their heads in a spin with excitement. Attracta always has a few bob; the speculation mounted in the older ones over what Santa was going to bring had the young ones chittering.

Attracta felt as if the weight of the worlds had been lifted off her shoulders. It was a great day to be alive. An even better day to be free of fussy auld fukkers and farters. She sprung out of bed. Stuck her foot in her shoe before she put a stitch on her back. It's one thing to be back amongst yer brothers or sisters. But another to see them wearin' yer shoes and yer money heading out the door in the toe of it.

Commotion and conspiracy thickened. If the wind was at her back, she might just catch Father Benedict in the afternoon. He was the best man in Dublin at gettin' yeh a job. She'd have to tell him why she was on the run. Tell him about the mix-up. Just in case he got wind of it on church tom-toms. Cover yer back. She buttoned up her cardigan.

'Shut to fuck up,' Jemser Rafferty's roar exploded above the bedlam. He thought someone had taken a hatchet to his head.

'Oh that's charmin'. Lovely fukkn' language for childer to be listenin' to.' Nel Rafferty looked down at the crumpled mess. She knew he'd had a skinful the night before. The sickly smell of cider and smoke was turning her stomach. And she knew exactly where and who he'd been drinking that lunatic soup with.

Flicking a dishcloth like a lion tamer's whip, Nel caught him on the side of the head with a sharp wet corner. 'Who the hell do yer think yer talkin' to?,' she snarled, lashing out again and again as Jemser cowered and covered his head. Trying to protect himself with his bare hands from her slaughter and slander.

'Why don't yeh shag off back to where yeh were last night? Yeh little scum bag. Shag off back to Fatama Fagan.' Her blood boiled till it raged through her arteries and scalded her heart.

'Jaysus, don't start that Fatama Fagan shite again, Nel,' he pleaded for his life.

'Don't ever mention that whore's name and mine in the same breath.' Nel lifted her foot as high as her unobliging belly would allow and kicked him as hard as she could. 'Yeh lousy faggot.' She was panting with pain and exertion.

It was the last straw. He was up and running like a whippet when he spotted Attracta.

'What in the name of Jaysus is that one doin' back here?' The sour note in his voice said it all as he skidded and shuttled out the front door.

'Mind yer own shaggin' business. Yeh cheat, yeh traitor, yeh fukkn' fornicator.' Nel flung the remark with the same gusto as the frying pan, nearly taking the head off their long-suffering next-door neighbour.

'I told yeh she'd try the patience of the fukkn' saints. It was only a matter of time till Attracta Rafferty was sent back to dement us. But would any fukker listen to Jemser Rafferty?'

'Tell the auld whore at number ten; she can listen to her heart's content.' Nel slammed the door so hard it flew open again.

'I wish he'd bloody well stay with her and leave me alone.' She stopped to take a breather. 'I'm beat just carryin' his kids. And that bitch's with every Tom, Dick and Harry up every arch an' alleyway in Dublin. Tell me how the fuck does she never get up the pole? Once, just once, let that whore get pregnant.'

St Audeon's Arch: the smell, the screams scuttled through Attracta's head. Outside sounds inside.

'She's neither a heart nor a womb.' Attracta put her mother's hands around a hot cup of tea. You're going to have to do somethin' with yerself, Ma. You're almost thirty-two and this'll be your thirteenth. Yer too thin, too pasty, too old, too impatient. Yer not up to it.'

'If six childer in the bed between doesn't stop Jemser Rafferty, what in the name of Jaysus will? Up with it, in with it, out with it, that's about the height of it. It doesn't take long to leave a child in a belly.'

'Well, somebody must know somethin' about stoppin' the startin'. Because Protestants don't get pregnant. Not as often as us, in anyway,' Attracta persisted.

There was more than prayers said at the Bishop's Palace. There were always snippets and titbits carried down from the big table. She'd hear the older servants whispering. Ballyraggin' some doctor or other who was going to stop the women of Ireland having babbies. If she knew where he lived, she'd take her mother there herself and have her doctored.

'If he ever goes near that whore or her apprentice again, I swear to God I'll cut his auld lad in shreds. Strangle her with the sinews. Sort both me problems at once.' Nel sat back on the creaky settle. How had the wildness she loved so much when they were courting turned to such weakness as soon as they married? Nel had never felt so lonely in all her life.

***

The best laid plans of mice and men. By the time Attracta had got her mother calmed, her brothers and sisters sorted out, it was late afternoon when she arrived in Dublin.

A clock in Mortie Goldman's pawnshop at the top of Capel Street put a stop to Attracta's gallop. The rich and the Raffertys pawning their wares in the one shop. The thought struck her as comical as she stared at a blue and china clock with a delicate beauty all of its own. She could tell by the jitters of the little hand that it was working. Some Christmas, she'd buy her Ma a clock like that for the mantelpiece. Plotted round the dead-pan faces of its companions, time stood still. As still as it stood last Sunday. A stab of terror seized her.

Sunday hadn't left her yet. Slow and silent Sunday, it had dragged itself into the wet afternoon. Devilment was in the damp air. God knows what possessed them. Auld Sexton's snorin', bad-tempered Bishop's roarin'. Rain, boredom and bullshite all collaborated to put them astray in the head.

Attracta stared at the timepieces through the dirty window. The array of blank faces, staring back at her. She was always in the wrong place at the wrong time. The stony silence of the servants visited her again. Her face stung. Traitors. Cowards. Bloody Sunday. When time dawdled, time stood still. And every clock in the Palace told her to run, run, run.

Cold shifted Attracta from her hypnotic state. Ticking ghosts. Feckin' auld clocks give a body the willies. The Raffertys can do their bidden to the bells of Adam and Eve's. Never did them any harm before. Who needs clocks anyway? She set off at a cracking pace down to the Customs House docks. A bitter December wind blowing in off the Liffey cut her journey in half. Sawdust and porter curling up her nose from pub cellars put her in mind of her Da.

There'd be no Jemser till well after the Holy Hour. Her Ma would be all right after a few hours sleep. She left the kitchen with a shine and a polish that would put a smile on her Ma's face. They'd be as thick as thieves by mornin', Jemser and Nel. She'd seen it all before. He'd be back cajolin' an' canoodlin' tonight. The trouble with you, Nel Rafferty, yeh never jumped to the whip. His slobberin' mouth makin' her giggle like a girl. Makin' its black slimy promises. Wooin' her with words that paralyse and praise. But something in her was worried. Her Ma wasn't well.

Biddy Mulligan brought colder comfort. Come back next Thursday. She was sure Biddy had clothes stashed under the stall. That she didn't do business with her because she thought she'd be looking for tick. Attracta felt the power of the ten bob note in her fist and decided that Biddy's slate could wait. And so could the Butcher's Boy. She wouldn't be seen dead in the auld-fashioned cardigan her Ma had insisted she wear out.

Disappointed but not disheartened, she turned for home. The row, the ructions this morning between Nel and himself had delayed her. She'd start again tomorrow. Start earlier.

She could see the ambulance outside the flats as she turned into Stretham Street. She knew it was her Ma. They were carrying the stretcher down the narrow hall. She pushed her way through a galaxy of gawkers. The crowd surging forward with her, the ones in front passing the word softly to the ones at the back.

'Get out of their way.' The imperious voice of the midwife cut a path straight through the centre of the crowd. Sensation-seekers infuriated her with their need to mass, to stand and stare.

'What's all the commotion?' Concepta was hanging out of Fatama Fagan's window.

'It's own'y that auld sow Nel Rafferty – in her usual condition.' Fatama craned round Concepta to get a better gawk.

'Well, and there'll be no shaggin' fear of you ever having trouble in that department,' Mrs Mooney, who could hear the grass growing, shouted up from the crowd. 'Yeh can't even get yerself a husband.'

'Shut up and mind yer own business, yeh auld busybody. Why would I lumber meself with a husband when I could have yours any night of the week?,' Fatama spat.

22

Attracta grabbed her Ma's hand. She could feel her mother's nails biting into her palm. The dark part of her eyes huge, staring. A groan rose from the crowd as the stretcher was shoved awkwardly into the back of the ambulance.

'What happened, Ma?' She climbed in beside her.

'I don't know. I got out of bed, tried to use the lav and a big warm lump, like liver, slithered down me leg. The pain in me belly was terrible. Then the bleedin' started and wouldn't stop.'

'Will the baby be all right, nurse?' Nel Rafferty asked the midwife as she tried in vain to stem the haemorrhaging. She wasn't sure if it was the placenta or a large clot that Mrs Rafferty was describing. She just wished she had got a glimpse at it before the neighbour had got rid of it.

'We're doing the best we can, Mrs Rafferty.' She slid back the small window and spoke urgently to the ambulance driver. 'We'll be at the hospital soon,' she tried reassuring Nel as she struggled with the blood-soaked swabs. The two-tones wailed as the driver wrestled with icy streets.

As they lifted her Ma out of the ambulance and on to the trolley, Attracta saw the pool of blood. Her Ma's chest shuddered as it laboured for breath. Tiny beads of sweat spread across Attracta's top lip. She tried to steady herself on the corner of the trolley. The midwife gripped her arm.

'Wait here,' a voice bid her.

It seemed hours before anyone spoke to her. 'There's nothing you can do,' a young nurse said kindly. 'And yer mother's in the best place. So go on home, pet, we'll look after her now.'

It was midnight by the time she reached home. The streets were dark. She was too worried to be afraid. Mrs Mooney had the children washed and fed, and most of them were asleep. The others settled as soon as they heard Attracta's voice.

'Well, luv?' their next-door neighbour asked.

'They told me to go home. They took her straight down to an operatin' room. They were talkin about a serious section, or somethin' like that, in anyway.'

'Oh, Sacred Heart of the Crucified Jesus,' Mrs Mooney blessed herself with the sign of the cross. 'They're goin to knife it outta her.'

The thud in the doorway was Jemser fainting. They'd heard him come in but weren't interested enough to interrupt their conversation.

'Jemser Rafferty was always squeamish,' Mrs Mooney said in a self-righteous voice. 'He's as pissed as a fish, luv.' And nice as ninepence, she stepped over him and let herself out the door.

Attracta promptly followed suit, and went to bed.

***

As he opened the heavy front doors of the Franciscan friary, a mop of white hair nearly swallowed up Father Benedict's eyebrows. A raw wind blew Attracta in with it.

'It's me Ma,' she burst out as soon as she saw Father Ben, one of the kindest priests in Adam and Eve's.

'In the name of God and His Holy Mother, Attracta Rafferty, what are yeh doin' out in only a cardigan in the depths of December? Come in, come in child. You'll perish with the cold.'

'I don't feel the cold,' she lied to the priest as her gizzards and guts shivered and shook inside her. Even with her jaws clenched tight, her teeth cha-cha-cha'd to the beat of the huge rosary beads that circled and circled Father Ben's belly.

'Follow me,' Father Benedict bid Attracta. The benevolent brown of the Franciscan friar contrasted starkly with the embroidered vestments that she'd washed and ironed for the Bishop of Dublin.

Licking and smacking the soles of his feet, his open-toed sandals led the way to the warmth of the kitchen. There was always plenty in the pot after lunch. And always plenty happy to eat it. Lifting the lid of a noisy pot, Father Benedict forked glistening slivers of chicken into a bowl of hot clear broth. His ruddy face roused to a steamy glow, he placed the bowl gently in front of Attracta.

'I never knew a growing child yet that wasn't hungry.' He busied himself with the food. He'd heard all about Nel and the little babby.

Attracta found her eyes straying to his sandals in spite of her troubles. His big yellow toenails bore more than a striking resemblance to a set of false teeth on Biddy Mulligan's stall.

Setting a small dish out for himself, 'to keep her company', he asked quietly about her family, her age, her job.

Answering between mouthfuls, Attracta filled him in. Her father's passion for the porter and prostitutes, she blurted it all out. Me mother's difficult pregnancy. The fistfights. The hungry mouths. The cold. Christmas. The dead babby. Sure, they didn't even know that the babby was dead. Fukkn' auld doctors and the midwife had to

24

tell them. Translate the fukkn' highfalutin' Latin words. She repeated verbatim what Jemser was roaring and bawling about.

Father Ben was more than familiar with the Raffertys. And indeed guilty, if guilty was the word, of slipping Jemser the odd few pence for a pint. Sure, it probably insulates him from the slum, the old priest reasoned as he listened in part to Attracta's tale of woe. He made a mental note to send the League of Our Lady round to the Rafferty's before Christmas.

Father Benedict's powerful brown eyes watched as Attracta exhausted one subject. Slipping effortlessly to another, chapter and verse of Mrs Sexton's cruelty were relayed in the marathon. Nodding in sympathy, he maintained a diplomatic silence.

Who in God's name sent a young innocent so far out of her depth?, the old priest asked himself as Attracta babbled on. No doubt some busybody's contagious notion of kindness. Sure a scrap of a thing like this would only be feeding fodder for auld Sexton's furies. The Bishop's housekeeper was well known as a begging ass around Dublin. Her tantrums were legendary. She'd terrorised archbishops and bishops alike, and more than one poor parish priest in her day.

And Attracta's good looks would do her no favours either. Jailbait – he'd heard the confession too often. He struggled to bring his attention back to the subject so sore on Attracta. His thoughts distracted him as she glossed over the bother with the Bishop's letter.

'Sure, yeh know yerself, Father, I wouldn't have taken a blind bit of notice if the taxi driver wasn't Humphy Hadlum. An' him stutterin' an' sweatin' an' goin' on about the grand woman. How anxious she was that the letter was placed in the Bishop's hands. An' to be sure, it was delivered as she just might come lookin' for her money back.'

'The road to hell is paved with good intentions,' the old priest suddenly said aloud.

The warmth of the kitchen had started to dry out Attracta's cardigan, and the smell of the wool disgusted and embarrassed her.

'Sixteen on Christmas Day. What a privilege to share your birthday with our Saviour, Jesus Christ.' He rose from the table .

Attracta smiled. She didn't know what privilege meant.

'Don't worry your little head about a thing. We'll do what we can for Christmas. And what we can't do, we'll leave in the Almighty's capable hands.' Father Benedict let Attracta out into the cold night air.

'You can bring this back in your own time.' He wrapped his cloak round her thin shoulders. 'God will provide – and sure, maybe a word in the right ear.' His powerful brown eyes communicated what he couldn't say. Attracta knew they were going to be all right.

Father Ben reminded himself to contact the League of Our Lady. Mrs Grey was the very woman for the Raffertys. She had neither chick nor child to disturb her now that the husband was buried and her daughter married. The Countess, she liked to be called in the Liberties. He made a note in his diary.

Three

Christmas spirit was intoxicating Dublin. But the Countess was having none of it as she trekked through the Liberties.

It comes earlier and earlier, she grizzled, as she hauled bags and belongings up slippery steps, down endless hallways. Disinfectants, dusting powder, catechisms, miraculous medals and rosary beads hung at her elbows, wrists. All her statutory requirements cracking off hips and shins. She offered up her struggle for her daughter's sins. She nodded and squinted alternately at early morning risers and late home-goers. Making a mental note of the latter; she wondered where Muriel had done the dirty deed.

She must learn to travel lightly. Sixty-six was no age to be going loaded like a donkey. Yet there wasn't an implement or a pamphlet on her person that hadn't been tried and tested over decades. And centuries. She gave a combatant sniff as number 44 fell into sight.

Nine o'clock sharp, she presented herself, full kit and caboodle, on the Raffertys' doorstep. Children of all makes and shapes dived for cover. Only the Garda knocked that loud and that early. Possessed of a strong will, a sharp tongue and a sturdy constitution, Mrs Grey strode straight into the bedlam. You could hear a fly fart as she dispensed her credentials. In a blinding flash, Jemser Rafferty understood that Father Benedict's rendition of a woman around the house and his own were poles apart.

Mrs Grey set to work immediately. Armed with carbolic soap, Jeyes' fluid and an indefatigable sense of commitment, she scrubbed and scraped from dawn till dusk. The reformation of the Raffertys had begun.

In the time it took Jemser to get up and out, the Countess, with Attracta's help, had a full complement of Raffertys out of bed, breakfasted, powdered, polished and shoved out the door. Within days, they were to be found wide awake every morning after a good night's sleep, on time and concentrating in the convent school. Within two weeks, they were virtually free of head lice, snot, scabs, scalds and other antisocial diseases for the first time in Mother Mary Joseph's records. They are a credit to your charitable regime. Women like you are the backbone of our struggling society. It is truly a modern-day miracle, and I am privileged to witness it, she had taken the time to write to the Countess. A copy of this, Mother

Mary Joseph informed her, would be sent to Bishop Barclay O'Rourke, His Lordship the Bishop of Dublin.

Mrs Grey read the Reverent Mother's letter before she left home. That the Bishop hadn't crossed her door since her daughter Muriel had dropped her bombshell was as big a blessing to the Countess as it was a cross. She hadn't told a soul, let alone the Bishop, about her daughter's shame or the marriage of convenience that mortified her daily. The Countess had developed palpitations from the stress of it all. It had been a very traumatic time in her life, between her husband's death and her daughter's disgrace; it had been hard to hold on to her sanity.

But one day, one day under the seal of confession, she would entrust the Bishop with the cross she carried; yes, she'd tell him the uncut story. Familiarise him with the twist in her husband that she couldn't satisfy the recklessness in Muriel, the same bad seed.

Days before Christmas, a team of dedicated elbows arrived to help the Countess with her momentous task. If they couldn't supply a Mammy on Christmas morning, they could make the place sparkle and make some of the Raffertys' dreams come true. With all the zeal of flat-earthers, they set about the task on hand. Attracta was in her element sharing in their sanctimony. When they were satisfied that 44 Mercy Mansions was fit for human habitation, the solidarity withdrew to collate and collect necessary and unnecessary requirements for Christmas.

Under these strange and sterile conditions, the Rafferty household settled into its new routine. Attracta was sewing and mending, learning how to cook economical and nourishing meals, to keep a home fresh and free of disease. The key to which was sanitation, the Countess preached, as she bustled and busied herself with the unfortunate's business.

She'd taught Attracta well. Reinforcing her demanding standards at every available opportunity. 'The chameleons' Jemser christened the brigade of women who had commandeered his home. 'I hope yis are as enthusiastic in the bed as yis are in the kitchen,' he'd mumble as they swept under and around his feet.

'Turncoat,' he'd taken to calling Attracta. Her ability to blow with the wind he blamed squarely on Nel's Protestant granny.

'Sure, when the Reillys were offered the bowl of soup, they dropped the O quicker than a nun's knickers.'

He managed to send an entire chapter of women packing in one afternoon. But not the Countess. She persevered and persevered.

Tireless in her pursuit of perfection, the Countess preached as she polished, polished as she prayed.

'She's not so much a promise as a threat,' a more sober Jemser told Father Benedict. 'Three days to Christmas and me house is a cross between a convent and dispensary. An' don't think for one minute I don't know what her game is. She's her beady eye on me daughter. A skivvy's apprenticeship's happenin' under me own roof. Jemser Rafferty didn't come up the Liffey on a bike, yeh know, Father.

'Stickin' to timetables and targets regardless of the festive season. She's not a normal woman. If she's not disinfectin', she's desecratin' sacred Dublin coddle,' he groaned like the north wind every time he bumped into Father Benedict. 'At least let me have Christmas in peace.'

Jemser's pleading less than a week after Mrs Grey's installment fell on cloth ears. Father Ben knew only too well what the deranged Jemser was complaining about. The Countess' aversion to alcohol and laziness was legendary in the Liberties. There would be no fear of the Countess complaining though. She had won her nickname with flying colours; challenges were the blood and guts of her crusades.

Father Benedict had turned avoiding Jemser and the Countess into a high art. But for the sake of the season that it was, he broke his golden rule and telephoned the Countess. Told her as gently as he could that what Our Lord and Saviour would want at this special time was peace and harmony in a household such as the Raffertys. It was Christmas week, there was no Mammy, no promised babby. What they needed now was lashings of goodwill. Not timetables and targets. She'd listened patiently; she'd meet him half way but wouldn't be swayed on the matter of alcohol.

***

There was only one place on earth to be on Christmas Eve and that was in Dublin; Jemser had left early that morning with a twinkle in his eye. The Holy Hour had come and gone and there was still no sign of him. The Countess could deal with him when he returned. Attracta made her excuses and left just after two o'clock. The Liberties were bursting with an energy that came around only once a year. In spite of the Countess' proclamations of squander and excess, overindulgence and bad debt, it crept in under doors and through windows.

A smile as broad as the mouth of the Liffey smothered Attracta's face as she swept out. Some of the women would have begun boiling their Christmas hams already; others would have started cooking the spiced beef and Christmas puddings. Rich spicy smells as old as Christmas itself were beginning to fill the halls. No one in Dublin was poor at Christmas.

Attracta shivered with excitement. Though she was long past believing in Santa Claus, she still believed in the magic of Christmas. Don't dilly-dally, Attracta. The Countess had wagged her finger at a list as long as her arm of unfinished chores. Auld Nick was in her knickers since early today. But neither the divil nor the Countess would deny Attracta Rafferty her yearly right. Dublin on Christmas Eve.

'Take as long as yeh like,' the next-door neighbour who'd been listening outside for any news of Nel had told her. 'Get whatever yer Mammy wants, whatever fills the hole left in her heart by the dead babby. Sure, wouldn't yeh pull the stars out of the sky with yer bare hands?' Every sinew and nerve stretched as she dramatised her horror.

'Biddy Mulligan's lookin' for yeh, while I think of it,' the neighbour slipped into another role seamlessly. 'She said to be sure to tell yeh to come down teh day. She says it's important. An' if its money she's after,' she squared up to Attracta, 'we've had a whipround amongst ourselves.' She threw her eyes around the tenement as she shoved five bob into Attracta's hand. She nodded in Attracta's response, and when none was forthcoming she nodded again, slowly now, at the sensitive silence. The magic was beginning. Dublin was beguiling.

The wind blowing up off the Liffey offered Attracta no such compassion. In spite of all the good spirit, her cardigan couldn't save her from the chilling. She took the short cut through Adam and Eve's as much for warmth as for comfort. 'Sacred heart of Jesus, don't let me Ma owe Biddy too much,' she genuflected before the exposed Blessed Sacrament as she made her prayer. 'I know I promised Nel I'd buy holly with red berries and brighten the place up for the little ones. And sure, I'd love a real Christmas tree standing in the corner meself. But even with the ten bob note and the five that's fallen from Heaven...'

Rotating on the piping hot radiators around the walls of the church, she was bartering with the Blessed as she took the free heat.

'Yeh can't eat decorations, when all's said and done. As it'll be a toss-up between toys and turkey. To say nothing of Nel's slate. And that could be as big a pound.' Biddy was always too flahulach with Nel. Attracta was holding the money so tight in her hand that she was too afraid to let it go even to bless herself.

McBernie's Christmas window was a wonderland. Attracta stared at the dancing dolls. Reindeers laden with a calamity of presents parcelled up in tinsel ribbons and big red bows. She wished with all her heart she was part of the fun and festivities in the moving Christmas display. But the people around were dressed for the weather and they could afford to stand and stare. She moved on.

Dublin was on the move as she turned into O'Connell Street. Revving up for Christmas Eve. Men running late. Women children in their wake, taxing shopkeepers' spirits. An enormous yellow star shone high above the crowds. Its flashing light, dispensing good will, lit, lost and lit again Attracta's excitement. Red, white and yellow lights swung from lamp-post to lamp-post, bestowing a cheerful air all round.

On street corners, traders rang out their seasonal hymns. Get yer Christmas crackers. Sparklers over here, luv. A penny a piece. Ten for sixpence. They belted out their bargains above the din of toy monkeys marching up and down makeshift stalls to the beat of their tiny drums. Turkeys, geese, game and fowl dangling from butchers' gallows hung round waiting for their Christmas fate. *Adeste fideles* rang out of the mouths of well-wrapped carollers capitalising on seasonal sentiment. Attracta eyed the bulging collection boxes. What would Christmas be like with that sort of money? She squeezed the fifteen bob in her hand. The money felt small. Her heart felt like lead in her chest.

The outline of the Customs House sent a shiver through to her bowels. Biddy Mulligan's stall was laid out opposite the city morgue. The cold near the basin of the river would have frozen the brass balls off a monkey. How Biddy braved the dockside in the depths of winter was a national mystery. She wished her Ma wasn't so free with the money. Drums, guns, dolls and marbles didn't keep the cold outa yer bones. Nor fill yer belly. Her spirits plummeted as she came closer to reality.

Losin' the babby had made her Ma soft in the head. She'd need a magician to finance Nel's notions. She'd have to make some hard decisions.

'Filthy weather, yeh wouldn't put a milk bottle out on a day like that – what?' Biddy Mulligan greeted Attracta as she made another spidery entry to her slate. She could always do ten things at once. Attracta eyed the mistletoe and tinsel as she gathered a few bits of children's clothes in her arms.

'Ignorant weather, isn't it, luv? Yeh wouldn't know what clothes to pawn! What more could yeh want for Christmas?' Biddy was bantering, trying to sell a set of false teeth to her next customer: 'an' yis could share dem an' da turkey.' Two shrunk and shrivelled faces folded softly into a smile.

The dead pluck, the auld ones called her secondhand ware. Yeh'll get scabies offa that stuff, they'd say. But scabies was the least of Attracta's problem. She'd need a rolling pin to stretch the money at the rate she was stockpiling.

Attracta was trying to be practical. But it was hard to be sensible and exciting. So far, she hadn't a sprig of holly, never mind a Christmas decoration. She'd rooted deeper than death in Biddy's reject box. Yeh couldn't get much lower than secondhand rejects. Some of it was stained, some of it was in tatters. She'd seen her Ma give away better stuff. She could buy streams of coloured paper and plait it together – make their own decorations. Her mind raced. They'd done that before. She was doing somersaults with sums and promises.

'I thought you'd be bakin' the Bishop's Christmas Cake.' Biddy's voice made her jump.

'Me Ma's in hospital. I'm home lookin' after the young ones.'

'Soooooo.' The long 'so' said, 'Try pulling the other leg.'

The voice was generous, the signs were good. Attracta felt herself relax.

The man beside her was testing a pair of spectacles on faintly pencilled prices. 'Are yis managin' all right up there? Try them on yeh, they read grand.' Biddy's all-seeing eye saw him giving Attracta the once-over. She winked in exchange for his shiny sixpence. 'Take dem off yeh now, don't waste dem lookin' at unimportant tings.' Dropping the money into a thick leather pouch, she turned her attention back to Attracta.

'Wait 'til I have a quiet minute; I want teh talk teh yeh.'

Attracta's heart went crossways: her Ma's slate. She could feel the money hot in her hand melting down. 'I know exactly what I want.'

'Well, isn't that grand for ye?' Biddy struck up an independent pose. She liked Attracta Rafferty. There was something about her that reminded her of herself. 'There's an overcoat over here that

32

might keep the chill offa yer bones.' Biddy jerked a plump thumb in the direction of a huge box.

Attracta's lips were getting bluer by the minute but she was trying not to shiver as looked Biddy hard in the eye.

'It's yer Christmas box.'

Attracta waded in a wealth of warm clothes, leather shoes, woollen socks and toys. Dolls with eyes and hair: guns, caps, holsters, jumpers, coats, wellingtons all spilled out onto the pavement. 'Oh how?' She could hardly speak for excitement.

'Oh, how deh yeh tink? Father Ben himself. A livin' saint.' Biddy's voice broke up.

'An' a clean slate for Nel when she is back amongst the livin'.' She saw the weight of the world slip off Attracta's shoulders. A tear ran down Biddy's cheek. 'The cold does make the auld eyes run riot.' Attracta didn't hear her; she was trying to get her arms around the box.

'Humphy Hadlum will take it round tonight. Put that coat on yeh now, the weather is droppin' fast.' Biddy tightened the shawl round her shoulders. 'Yed tink it was tailored to yeh. Did yeh ever think you would see the day Attracta Rafferty's back'd be swathed in cashmere and her feet shod in soft kid leather? Would yeh ever have believed there was a time when Biddy Mulligan could slip her foot into such a tiny shoe and her waist was only nineteen inches round? And look at the cut of me now.' Biddy couldn't get over the style of the young girl.

'Deh know what, Biddy Mulligan? I'm goin' now while the goin' is good up to Billy Atkins to buy as much turkey an' bacon as five bob'll buy.' Her eyes shone with pride and pleasure.

'Well, yer dressed in the best, well turned out for the Butcher's Boy.'

Attracta's face turned the colour of a big bleeding beetroot.

'Keep yer wits about yeh and yer two feet in the one sock.' Biddy watched a terrible beauty walk away. Saw the smile and the swagger. Jail bait since yeh were ten. She tipped her chin and her concern to the sky as she turned to her next customers.

***

It was six o'clock by the time Attracta arrived back in the Liberties. Home with a turkey under one arm, and a ham under the other. A

33

shiny shilling for the meter and a heart that was beating faster than the tin monkey's drum. Between the coat and all the money still in her purse, she'd strode into the butcher's shop. With an independent air, she placed an order with the best and the rest of them.

He couldn't take his eyes off her. Couldn't get over the size of the order. Giblets, offal, bones and scrag-end were all the Raffertys ever bought. And now, begod, she comes home and they're all livin' like lord's bastards. She didn't stop. 'I'll have more time when Christmas is over.' She stuck her parcel under her arm and headed home. Left him with his tail between his legs. She hoped with all her heart that he was looking after her, but she was too proud to turn round. If yeh want the boys to notice yeh, just look the other way. Keep going, keep going, she'd headed high as a kite for home.

She couldn't count the amount of times she said Happy Christmas to cold black strangers. She was that excited she forgot all about Nel's Christmas tree and her holly. 'If I had extra arms they'd be getting' tangerines and bananas too.' The Rafferty children could hear her coming the length and breadth of Stretham Street.

As the door of the flat swung open, the decorations nearly dazzled her. There was a Christmas tree as tall as Nelson's Pillar standing on a turned-up tea chest in the corner. Floppy red and gold decorations covered the ceiling. A big paper star hung from the light in middle of the room. And holly, her mother's holly, laden with the reddest berries tucked in behind every inch of the picture rail. Attracta's eyes stood out like stalks in her head. Suddenly everything looked grand. It was going to be a magical Christmas after all.

'Give me the ham and I'll put it on to boil. And maybe you'd ask Mrs Mooney to put the turkey somewhere cold?' The Countess asked Attracta so politely that she went without a word.

'The style of you, and no bell on yer bike.' Mrs Mooney turned her round and round. In all the excitement of the moment, Attracta had forgotten about the coat.

'Come in here quick and look at what Santa left for the childer.' Mrs Mooney took the turkey from Attracta and led her in by the hand. The wonder in her eyes told its own fairy tale.

Bicycles, tricycles, prams, spinning tops, wind-up soldiers, snakes and ladders, comic-cuts and brand new yearly annuals. Tins of biscuits, sweets, trifle, plum pudding and a huge Christmas cake, and a chalk Santa with a bag full of presents trying to get down the chimney. And to top it all off, there were tickets to the Gaiety Pantomime. Tickets for the whole family to celebrate in the New

Year. Mrs Mooney almost exploded with excitement when Attracta added Father Ben's presents to the kindness.

'An' all the names yer Mother and me called all them holy men and women. I'll feel the shame till the day I die.' She blessed herself with the sigh of the cross and added a prayer to her plea: 'God send her home to us safe and sound from that auld hospital soon.'

It was midnight before the youngest fell asleep. Tiptoeing their way round, Mrs Mooney and the four eldest Rafferty children turned what space there was left of the flat into a wonder world. 'Hollywood has never seen the likes of it,' Mrs Mooney greeted a delirious Jemser. The bells of Adam and Eve's were ringing Christmas Day in loud and clear.

'Cut a slap of that ham for yer Father. For a man that's fathered such great childer deserves to be fed like a fightin' cock.' Jemser, sitting proud as punch on his battered auld settle, saw Christmas in – in style.

'The Countess is comin' in the mornin', courtesy of Jemser Rafferty.' Five shocked and stunned faces stared at their father. 'A pre-dinner drink, I believe they call it in the better quarters of Ballsbridge.' Their hands were over their mouths trying to stop the giggles.

'No, no, when Jemser Rafferty has plenty, why should anybody stay hungry? I've invited Mr and Mrs. Mooney as well. If I can't have me own wife with me for the festive season, I might as well have someone else's.'

Attracta wasn't too sure about the Mooneys. But she could bet her last five bob that the Countess wouldn't be spendin' Christmas with the likes of the Raffertys, here in the Liberties.

But at ten o'clock on Christmas morning, the Countess was standing at the door. With half a dozen bottles of stout for Jemser, a bottle of port for herself and a dozen bottles of lemonade for the dinner. It was the closest thing to an apparition Attracta had ever experienced. She blessed her good fortune not to have placed a bet.

Somehow they managed to feed sixteen people and still have a mountain of food left over for St Stephen's Day. The table groaned nearly as loud as their bellies and backsides with turkey and ham, spuds mashed up with butter and green brussel sprouts. The Countess was the life and soul of the party. Questioning everybody about their business, but telling nothing about herself.

Attracta never knew a woman who asked so much about other people's lives and gave so little away about her own. The poor Mooneys had been mortified into telling her how they could never

35

have children. Something her Mother wouldn't even ask. She found herself getting annoyed with the Countess's questions. She wasn't one of them. She was a cuckoo in their nest. She hadn't the right to intrude.

'Have yeh ner a chick nor child yerself?'

The baldness of the question took Countess by surprise.

'I'm a widow.' The answer made it through the tight lips. Attracta noticed the stark absence of emotion.

The Countess could have slit her throat as soon as she parted with the information. The least anyone knew about her personal business, the better. Considering the state it was in, she needed – and would take – her time until she came up with an acceptable version of events. Muriel's visits had been few and far between since she'd acquired the flat. Her absence wouldn't be missed or noticed for many's the long day. So she'd be wise to hold her breath. The least said, the sooner this whole charade would go away. The Countess's troubles caught up with her once again.

Seeing the shudder, Attracta thought the better of her next question.

'Will yeh partake of another?' Mrs Mooney was showing off. The Countess held her glass out till it was overflowing.

'I think the pair of yis have partaken of enough.' Attracta was pulling on her coat, heading off to see if Humphy Hadlum would take the Countess home.

Mr Mooney had taken a leaf out of Jemser's book and was snoring softly beside him on the sofa.

Disconcerted by the queer silence that filled the space between her and the Countess, Mrs Mooney drank her port down all at once.

Wallowing in her own sorrow, the Countess looked for comfort. But Mrs Mooney was as drunk as a skunk.

'I never had a child,' Mrs Mooney was crying quietly.

'That any woman would willingly subject herself to such a bestial act outside the contract of marriage offends my most private parts.'

'Not one word, not one, did I understand. I couldn't even say for sure that she was talkin' English,' Mrs Mooney was sobbing by the time Attracta returned.

Humphy Hadlum hauled the Countess into his taxi.

'One day, one day, I'll confess her sin and then maybe he'll understand the hurt his isolation is causing me.' The Bishop's absence cut again to the quick.

It was all the same to Humphy. He wiped the beads of sweat off his top lip and swung the starting handle again. Between mad auld ones, bollixed engines and Fatama and Concepta pissin' like Heaton's horses at the back of his car, it was just one more miserable fukkn' Christmas.

Four

Late into the night, Archbishop Ennis' light blazed. He read the contents of the letter again and again. His brow buckled. 'The ruination of one of his Bishops.' The sentence burnt into his brain, but which bishop? And who was the author of this salacious gossip? The words danced like the devil before his eyes. One thing he knew for certain, the writer had access to facts and figures that could put a man of Civvy Street in prison. And that the writer's frame of mind at the time of committing his concerns to paper was far from serene.

So given all he had and all he hadn't, he gave himself time. Obeying his cardinal rule, he put the incendiary document under a pile of books and lent distance to his perspective. He'd thought long and hard about his maverick bishop and his wayward desires. Considered his informant. A priest, he knew from the language. And his possible motive?

He pondered his own position, his own spiritual paralysis. He detested tensions within the Church. Dreaded the rumblings of gossip. It was the worst possible scenario, the worst possible end to the old year, the worst possible start to '47. Lamenting the senseless waste of it all, he took himself to bed. Reflected how fast dignity flew out the window when a prick took over the running of personal affairs.

An irritable man aided and abetted by his gift of oratory, Archbishop Ennis lorded above his peers with remarkable ease. But his gift for speech did nothing to redeem his short temper. The knowledge that he was soon to retire did less for his tolerance and his present predicament. He wanted to retire quietly, slip away gracefully. Not be flagged up on the eleventh hour, taken down in a blaze of scandal by some hapless fool.

Two options opened themselves up to Archbishop Ennis over the course of the next few weeks. One, to ignore the anonymous letter. Two, to throw the letter open to the College of Bishops due to convene in Maynooth in January to discuss issues of dogma and moral import. The latter had a certain appeal and the added element of surprise that might just smoke out the offender.

Paradoxically, one of the more pressing issues waiting to be debated at the convention was the new Minister for Health and his proposed Mother and Child Act. Neither the irony of his dilemma nor the contradiction was lost on the Archbishop: Doctor Noel

Brown's magnificent obsession with educating the women of Ireland in matters relating to sex and maternity. The Archbishop wondered, as he poured the stiff whiskey, how the topics included would translate themselves in the document sent as a matter of course to the Pope at the end of these conferences. Wondered what scandalous part of it the Pontiff would or wouldn't use in his next episcopal letter.

***

The third Friday of January was bone-cracking cold. Stepping briskly into Maynooth College, Bishop Barclay O'Rourke found the temperature inside about as clement as the weather he left outside. The Archbishop's face was his barometer, and any clergy worth his salt knew how to read it.

'Dublin, it's good of you to join us.' The face was set at freezing. He didn't turn round. His curt salutation, born of an older imperial order, rankled the collective body of bishops. But these frustrations paled into insignificance when faced with the contents of the document laid bare before them.

'After full and mature consideration.' The Archbishop stayed at the window, his back turned firmly to the assembly. He fiddled agitatedly with his episcopal ring. The obscene amethyst clenched and unclenched in his fist marked time with Barclay's mounting panic. His mind raced for cover as he scanned the paper for names.

'I have placed before you a copy of a document, which I received ten days ago. It carries no names, not even the signature of its sender. Why then, gentlemen, does it strike such a deeply disturbing chord in me?' Small droplets of white spittle were foaming at the corners of his mouth. 'Is it because, for all it lacks, it doesn't lack credibility? Evil is amongst us, gentleman. The vile stinking evil of sex and money. Sex? Where are our vows of celibacy? Money – our vows of poverty?'

His tone was one of incredulity. 'Misappropriation of Church funds? What else is there to sin against? Is nothing sacred? Is it some paralysis of mind?' The Archbishop spun round and addressed the astonished collective as if he were addressing the guilty party himself.

'Have you any conception,' his left eye squinted in an involuntary spasm, 'of the damage a document like this could do to

Our Holy Mother, the Church? The hurt it could wreak on us? A bishop is the father of the diocese, for Christ's sake. He's in a position of power and privilege. His personal life and religious life are inextricable, indivisible.'

Barclay couldn't bear to make eye contact with Archbishop Ennis, fearing that, deep in the eye of the prelate, he'd see some scandalous tableau of himself and Muriel Grey. Vows of celibacy rang round his head as the Archbishop raged. This I promise, this I vow, this I swear. Why did I do it? Risk everything; handpicked, reared, crafted by the clergy. Risen to become Bishop at the early age of forty-two. A Cardinal's seat not out of the question. Why, why, in God's name, had he risked losing it all?

In the past month, he'd asked himself the same question a hundred times. But it was futile now. Archbishop Ennis was playing cat and mouse with him. Dangling him on the end of a rope, for the sport of his brothers in Christ. Playing with his sins, privately persecuting him, publicly hanging him. Nothing could save his fall from grace now. He hung his head.

He had often wrestled with the proposition that his vocation was manufactured, not a sacred calling. The answer, he suspected, lay somewhere between the two. He'd wondered if his weakness for sex was a byproduct of one or a direct product of the other. Perhaps it was some awful side-effect.

When he was a younger man, he had wrestled with his weakness and won. Banished it to the parish of the meek and mild. Why now, why, when he had achieved so much and wanted so badly so much more, had he seized the opportunities for sin with such open hands? Was the truth simple? Did he lack the strength to spurn? Was he chronically incapable of walking from occasions of sin?

He was jarred back to the harsh reality by the final blast of the Archbishop's fury. 'We must learn to mutate these unhealthy feelings. It would be wanton of me not to cut this canker out of my bishops, out of my priests out of my parishes. And that, my Lords, is exactly my dilemma. Where exactly must I make my incision: in you, in you, in you?' He swung wildly from one bishop to the next and the next. 'You tell me.' He was standing in front of Barclay, his fury right alongside him. Not looking at, not addressing, just standing.

'But before I do anything so radical, before I subject good organs as well as bad to the rough cut, find me this sick Bishop and find me his feeble scribe.' There was a pitch to his voice that wasn't becoming. 'For what one lacks in morals, the other lacks in fibre.

40

And we, gentleman, are as well rid of one and the other – as we are of his sickness.'

'We are one body. Either we carry this cripple or we cut him out; for the good of the body, for the health of our Holy Mother, the Church. And that, gentlemen, I believe, covers in practice what we are gathered here to discuss in principle: the moral dilemma of women in matters relating to the Mother and Child Act. And as unscheduled as it is unsavoury, the celibacy of priests. God save Holy Ireland.'

Archbishop Ennis rounded on his heel and left them with the stinging sarcasm. In private, more spiritual moments, the entire episode left him feeling cheap.

A haughty grimace masked Barclay's relief. He had witnessed his own trial and execution, glimpsed the future. The length, breadth and depth of the reprieve settled round him like a lucky caul.

Five

Limbo wasn't somewhere else. Limbo, with all its Biblical bells, was located in Leixlip. Had Barclay O'Rourke not found the perfect hiding place for her unborn child? She could have lost her mind, let alone herself, in the godforsaken place.

It had been the bleakest Christmas that Muriel had ever known, not an iota of cheer or choice. They were still officially grieving, Brigit, the old retainer, had silenced Muriel. She'd eaten what she could of the Christmas fare. In a lifeless dining room opposite a frosty-faced Fonsie, she fought rising and falling vomit. Sitting, standing or lying, her morning sickness now lasted all day.

Brigit had declined the invitation to join the newly married couple. Without the schooner of sherry that she'd taken the liberty of serving herself, Muriel might just have gone down to the end of the garden. And thrown herself into the troubled waters, where the Liffey meets the Rye. Thrown herself. Instead of which, she vomited the sherry and the Christmas dinner into her lap. Nostrils flaying, Fonsie had left the table looking more delicate than Muriel. The ill wind had cut Christmas unceremoniously short.

Life in Leixlip revolved around routine, and routine revolved around domesticity. Every physical fibre in Muriel's body strained to run. Every mental skill strove to stay in the straitjacket existence. Caught between desperation and destiny, she struggled for her sanity. Side by side her delicate state of mind, long hours passed themselves relentlessly on to the other. Days started, nights ended at the bidding of a black bog-oak clock.

As the monstrous clock struck a quarter to eight every morning since she'd arrived, Fonsie's ablutions began. Brigit, dressed from head to toe in black, stepped out on to the main street, turned left and headed off for eight o'clock Mass. By nine, Fonsie was severely shaved. Brigit was back. Wrapped in a dark navy apron that covered her back and front equally, she cooked the morning breakfast.

Muriel wondered what marked the difference in their days. Fonsie appeared at nine thirty and ate a piping hot breakfast. Not too hard, not too soft, the yolk of his egg – fried, boiled or poached – never varied, never changed.

And neither did Fonsie's demeanour. His newspaper propped on a sparkling blue milk jug, he screeded himself from his new wife. By ten, he'd disappear to an office located in the front of the house.

Well away from domestic smells and sounds, he began his day's work.

Even the infant appeared to understand the regime. When all the breakfast dishes were washed, dried and put back on the kitchen dresser and the table reset for lunch, he was brought out from his bedroom. Then, and not a minute before, the child's bath, breakfast and bowels were attended too.

At twelve, the house, indeed the whole village, came to a standstill. As the Angelus bell rang out its appeal, they stopped what they were doing, faced the chapel on the hill, genuflected and recited the age-old prayer. Any time other than noon and six, the bells were sounding the death knell. Brigit had tutted her when she saw her blessing herself at an odd hour.

Lunch at twelve thirty was followed by the baby's walk. This allowed Fonsie the absolute silence he needed to listen to his clients' legal needs and deeds. Dinner was served after the evening Angelus, after which Brigit and Muriel would wash up the dishes and set the table for breakfast the following morning. The child was tucked up in its cot by seven. By eight o'clock, all three knelt on the stone floor and recited the rosary.

Fevered clock-winding followed this nightly ritual. As the keeper of time, Fonsie appeared on the appointed hour with an assortment of keys and began to coil up and measure out the course of the next day. By ten o'clock, the house was as black and quiet as Muriel's frame of mind.

If she had had any conception of how desperate 'this blessed convenience' – Barclay's words – was going to be, she would have taken her mother's cold comfort, left Ireland and lost herself and her bastard in London. Or taken herself off to a home for unmarried mothers and put her mistake up for adoption. And at least there she'd be spared Fonsie's attentions.

Night after night, Fonsie demanded his entitlements. Every clock in the house heralded the nocturnal hurtle. She loathed his advances with extraordinary repulsiveness.

But rejection, revulsion and the ructions that followed each and every attempt didn't deter Fonsie Duggan. It wasn't the contract of marriage, as he understood it. She didn't care what he said or how many times he said it. She wouldn't betray Barclay. Wouldn't defile the infant hidden safely under her heart with another man's seed.

The rituals, the expectations supporting the Duggan household, were sucking the lifeblood out of Muriel. Days dragging into evenings, nights manacled to monstrous mornings. There were times she thought she was in purgatory, persecuted by timepieces marking every miserable moment. Locked away in an asylum for the insane, being nursed by Brigit and abused by Fonsie. Some days, she'd plan her escape to England. Take her chances with the hundreds of other women in the same pregnant predicament.

But she wasn't just another woman, and it wasn't just anyone's baby she had the privilege of carrying. His power, his promises, his proximity, all collaborating would sedate her. Every clock in the house quartered and halved slow time. Strange how there were never enough spare hours in the day for Barclay. And now all she had were spare hours.

It was eight o'clock as they knelt to say the rosary. She'd excused herself from giving out the decades: she hadn't said the rosary since she was a child so she might forget or worse – mix them up. As always, Muriel's thoughts rose above the rattle and hum of the prayers. She bowed her head and pretended to pray.

She'd broken her promise to him the day before her wretched wedding. Desperate, she'd sent a note begging him to come to the chapel. He could trust her. She wouldn't betray him or their baby. Not by a word, not by a whisper. She'd shield and protect him. Marry this man she hardly knew. She wouldn't renege on her word.

Sealed but unsigned, she'd placed it in the driver's hand. Even in her desperation, she'd been careful to take all the necessary precautions. She'd marked the envelope private and confidential in bold letters on the top right-hand corner. She knew the system. Private and confidential letters were left untouched. Given priority. She'd paid the taxi man two shillings to deliver it to the Bishop's door.

Please God, don't let him be angry with me. I know I promised I wouldn't make contact. Please let him understand the desolation. She lowered her head, hid her hurt. She couldn't understand his silence.

She'd waited and waited before she finally took her marriage vows. And when decency wouldn't let her wait any longer, she made a pact with God. Silently: a voice inside her head drowned out the marriage vows. No matter what anyone absent or present believed, she was making her marriage vows to her Bishop. Not to the stranger standing at her shoulder. Not to this marriage of convenience or this hastily organised husband. The Bishop's silence was acute. Her hurt transcended Fonsie and Brigit's prayers.

She rubbed the dents in her knees as she straightened herself up. The praying had gone on longer than usual tonight. She had the New

Year to thank for the respite.

As Fonsie began his clock-winding, she bid them goodnight and made her way up to bed. She couldn't bear to watch him winding what was left of last year into the next. Maybe tonight, as a gesture of goodwill, he'd leave her in peace. The clock in the hall struck a quarter to ten. It would be at least a half an hour before he appeared for bed.

Pummelling the feather bolster that divided the marriage bed, Muriel began her own secret rite. Feeling for the soft leather pouch hidden in her handbag, she pulled out a relic and held it in her hands. Idolising his photograph. Adoring it with the same prayer-like obeisance with which Fonsie adores his clocks. 'Consecration of Bishop Barclay O'Rourke 1932' is inscribed on the back. The thick black ink. His hand – heavy on the up-stroke, light on the down – she knows by heart.

Muriel ran her fingers over the shiny surface – feeling for life. Kissing his hands, his face, tasting him in private. Dressed in the finery befitting a Prince of the Church, he looked resplendent in robes of scarlet. He's looking straight at the camera, his potency evident even on paper. She held the photograph up to the light just as she did night after night. Examining it like a doctor would an X-ray. Searching for something she might have missed. Searching for their secret.

Fonsie's foot on the stairs put an end to the ritual. Monstrous confidence replaced in an instant by abject misery.

She smelled the drink as soon as he came into the bedroom. Without as much as a breathing space, he whipped back the covers.

'Muriel,' his voice syrupy as he reached over the bolster.

'I'm not feeling very well.' It would take more than a feather pillow to stop him tonight. Her stomach lurched as he squeezed her breast and the sour smell of whiskey hit the back of her nostrils.

Oblivious to her protests, Fonsie mounted the barricade. His sour tongue slipped into her mouth. Taking frigid silence as consent, he lifted her nightdress. In a hopelessly obscene gesture, his erection penetrated her thighs. Trying to calm the screaming rage inside her chest, she heaved him with unnatural force to his own side of the bed.

'It's not going to happen. Do you hear me? A physical reality separates us; I'm carrying another man's child for God sake.' She'd gone further than she had gone before. Said too much.

The malice shot straight through his chest, pierced a reservoir of complexities. In the long silence that followed, Muriel thought she was safe.

But in a rage that knew no bounds, Fonsie plundered his past. He called on his late wife. The sour side of that marriage. The accursed sex there too. He physically recoiled from the memory of the conception. The agonising birth. The painfully slow death. He wondered how many more couples were trapped in miserable marriages.

He grunted loudly as he recalled Barclay's bargain. A mother for your son. A wife, young enough to keep the chill off your bed, your bones. Healthy enough to give you more children. To dull the pain.

He took advantage of me at a particularly vulnerable time. Indentured me for life with a warped donation. Rounding on Muriel, Fonsie mumbled low and slow. Then his voice, his anger, rose and ripped through the silence.

'Don't you ever forget, madam, who's accommodating who here. Women without men are outcasts in society. They don't fit in. They're objects of pity. You would be wise to reconsider your marriage vows and to understand your wifely duties. There's nothing for nothing in life. Your Bishop found you a husband, madam. Not free board and lodgings.'

Muriel burned with humiliation. On the far side of the bed, Fonsie's anger spent, he snored and sucked at the saliva that dribbled from the side of his mouth. Slept the sleep of the just. She wondered how much alcohol it took to affect these juxtapositions.

Coiled round her unborn child, she tried to pray. In a bid to open her soul, she recited the Our Father. But it was useless; she was too distraught. She was in an awkward situation with God. She hadn't prayed properly in a long time. Neither had He listened when she'd begged and besieged.

How, how, had she fallen pregnant? How did He let it happen? They'd been so careful. Always interrupting. Always frustrating hands and handkerchiefs ready to catch the seed. She'd coughed and coughed, nearly torn her pelvic floor, when he'd been unable to stop himself coming.

She rocked silently. Rocked her baby, rocked herself. She was tired looking for reasons. Exhausted looking for charmed solutions to solid situations. There was no magic cure; just cause and consequences and the bitter taste of reality. As every clock in the house rang in the New Year, Muriel fell into an uneasy sleep.

In sleep, she's an older woman observing herself through a two-way mirror. From the vantage point of age, she strains to stop the inevitable disaster. But her wisdom is lost in the divide that separates

46

them.

They're alone in her father's library. I've fallen in love with you, she blurts out. I'm going away. Going to university in Cork. She's crying and laughing. The thought of your absence haunts me. Surprised by her bluntness, he's rebuking her boldness. Twenty years and many miles of silver hair between us, he's teasing. I'll be older and greyer by the time you've mastered your commerce. And you, my precious child, will find a young handsome man who will listen more carefully to your hopes and dreams than an old man like me ever could.

Turning an adolescent scene into a compliment, he takes her hand, looking into her eyes and telling her she's beautiful. Leaving her with all her hopes and dreams intact.

Enthronement lends powerful potency. Time scrolls on – she can see the degree in her own hand now. The soft light of a late summer lighting the scene. The sensuous pleasure as he turns her around is shocking still, a woman not a child any more. Hears his whistle low and slow. The chemistry in that blinding second, instant, tangible. There is no question of who wants whom. They are both culpable. She's putting her fingers to his lips. Him blessing the kiss that blows life into their love.

***

Stoking the early morning embers, Brigit tried to keep her misgivings at bay. But her thoughts were as black as the marriage she was daily witnessing. Things were not well in the private quarters, and there was no denying them.

Sometimes she wondered if the ghost of the old missus had come back to haunt them all. To punish him for a pregnancy that nature itself should never have allowed. She clacked her tongue. To have a child at a time in their lives when they should have been grandparents was an awful land. She wondered if she had a word with the priest, if she had Mass said for the late missus' soul, whether it would shift the congealment of misery that hung over the house.

She'd heard the commotion the night before. Worse than usual. The New Year offering: more of the same. The same short shift to his lumpy love.

Sure, yer nothin if not predictable, Mr Fonsie. Yeh could set yer

47

clock by yeh, sir. Brigit scratched a sweaty patch on the side of her head. Lamented the past and the future. 'Tis an unnatural coupling to say, the least. A duck and a kangaroo. A duck and a kangaroo.

Six

Only three weeks since Christmas and all traces of it had disappeared. Attracta Rafferty looked at the bare streets, the blank faces. She wished that the spirit that transformed everything and everybody wouldn't desert so starkly. She missed the magic. She wondered when her Ma would be back home. The Countess' regimentation was all right in its place, but there was nothing warm or welcoming about it.

Attracta was outside the Coombe Lying in Hospital fifteen minutes before visiting, kicking her heels. She'd more on her mind today than her Ma. She was bidding her time, savouring the flavour of anticipation with the smell of the soup the Countess had boiled and bottled up for her Ma. She'd left Stretham Street early today, strutted down Thomas Street, past the butcher's window. Teasing him. Laying down the scent. She'd be back this afternoon to collect more marrowbones.

She hadn't seen hide nor hair of him over Christmas. She'd felt like a complete eejit when her sister Gorette had found the tie she'd stashed away for him. Jemser thought she'd lost the run of herself when she'd pretended it was for him.

She looked behind; the queue of visitors was getting longer. She wondered if she was backing a losin' horse. She transferred the parcel she had for her Ma from one cramped arm to the other. The heat from the bottled soup warmed her. He had plenty of young ones and auld ones hawking their wares for him. She wouldn't join in the parade. What she had, she prized. And so did he. She felt it in her waters.

And it would be rare and wonderful when he got his hands on it. Until she had his ring on her hand, he wouldn't get his hands near her. And he better make a move soon. She was on the move herself. She just might tell him that today. Put the skids under him.

She just might tell her Ma her good news too. But that could depend on the humour.

Some at the back had started a shove that was feeling its way up to the front. The visitors' bell rang out above the scrum. The hospital doors swung open. Attracta wondered what her Ma's mood would be like today. She was like a shit in a swing swong this weather. Yed need a fiddle under yer arm to keep her sweet.

49

It must be a sign she was gettin' better. She had had neither the energy nor the inclination to fight four weeks ago when she was admitted, roarin' in agony. Nor in the weeks that had followed when the babby was buried up in the Holy Angel's plot in Glasnevin and infection had laid her so low; she neither knew nor cared.

Attracta didn't blame her, losin' yer babby was one thing. But losin' yer womb, and the hope of ever havin' another babby, was enough to send the sane around the bend. Some things were unforgivable. God shouldn't let cruelty have a double edge. He shouldn't. And there not even an empty bed in a ward away from the other women and their babbies. A cryin' shame and constant reminder.

She could see her Ma slouching in the bed. Nel saw Attracta laden to the gills with lotions and potions, waving as she weaved her way past patients, beds, cots and other people's visitors.

Between rubs, remedies, cures and backfires, she was nearing the end of her rope. Every lunchtime, every afternoon, a delegation of Raffertys were trouped into the hospital. The nurses suggested relays. But Jemser wasn't about to be landed with ten kids.

'Did yeh hear him to Matron?' Attracta hadn't time to take her hand off her arse before Nel started. He was doing his best, as any right-minded person could plainly see. And as such the visits would continue, he blathered, blagged the entire troupe past the toughest matron on the south side of Dublin.

'I'm not able for the disruption, let alone the disgrace. A feckin' circus, they turn the ward into. Every shiny, scrubbed one of them, Jemser included, makin' a holy show of me. The little ones shoutin' at the top of their voices. Still roarin' like gullets that they'd never had a Christmas like it before, a dinner like it before, coats, shoes, socks, shite like it before. I almost suffocated with mortification tryin' to hide me face under a blanket.

'Nothin's secret or sacred; the world and Garret Reilly are privy to private details. We're lice free, Timmy announced only last week, to the terror of the women in the surrounding beds. Now I have strangers giving me advice. The shame has set me back a good week.

@Tellin' on themselves, that's all the Raffertys were ever good for. Not an ounce of savvy between them. Or consideration. And as for that vulgar spectacle yis called Christmas. If I never see another one like it, it will be too soon. How am I supposed to give an encore next year? Where, bejaysus, will all this, all seein', all dancin' Santa Claus be by then?'

Nel didn't know which threatened her more – last Christmas or next. Mornings and afternoons were made bearable only by the promise of a sober Jemser slipping in on his own. Attracta couldn't get a word in with a shoe horn. Nel was up to ninety.

'What's in the paper bag in, anyway?' A grudging inflection.

Attracta opened the brown paper parcel slowly. 'Soup from the Countess. Rubs for yer rash for down the hall. An' a green scapular for the League of Our Lady's.' She announced each item with a pride and pleasure that sickened Nel's stomach. Her life had been overtaken and over run by do-gooders.

'Poor man's penicillin.' Attracta poured the beef tea, still warm, from the sparkling milk bottle. 'Marrowbones and shin beef,' she declared proudly. 'Between this and the invalid Guinness they give yeh here, yeh'll be leapin' like a hare before yeh know it. Aren't the Countess and her cronies only a blessin' in disguise?' Attracta put the paper cork back in the neck of the bottle.

Nel's face fell further than her spirits. Her own flesh and blood blowin' and crowin' the praises of the sufferin' upper crust. Ten of them it took to replace one good woman. Did nobody even stop to do the sums? Where in God's name was the justice? She drank the Countess' cure, begrudging every mouthful.

'She has another order of bones ready for me to collect from the butcher's later. There'll be more soup tomorrow.' Attracta laid the foundations for her early departure. Nel's bitterness could be turned on yer coming as easily as yer going. She watched, waited for the smart remark.

'That'll be sore on yeh. A trip to Billy Atkins shop.' Nel couldn't let an opportunity to caution at her daughter pass, even if it came out crooked most of the time. But Attracta couldn't be told civilly. She was hell bent on destruction. And destruction was waitin' with open arms in a butcher's apron in Thomas Street.

'Why they bother with the likes of us, and them all such great swanks, is a mystery to me.' She wouldn't be sucked into Nel's humours or sarcasm.

'They judge themselves by lookin' down on us. That's their problem. We judge ourselves by lookin' up at them. That's ours.'

The sniping wasn't lost on Attracta. But she was too busy sowing the seeds of her own good news to get swamped in sour grapes.

'The Countess will be there now.' She checked the face on a big black clock that ticked and tocked the comings and goings of the maternity ward. 'Scrubbin' and rubbin' spuds, gettin' grub ready for feedin' time at the zoo. You could set Greenwich Mean Time be

51

her. I'm tellin' yeh, Ma, the militia couldn't mount an operation like it. Yeh have to take yer hat off to the Countess. She's there when she says she is, hail, rain or snow. Nothing puts her off her routine. Yeh could see yerself in the lino and hear a pin drop when the childer are sat down to do their homework.

'Oh, you can roll yer eyes, Ma, but Mother Mary Joseph says that some of us is actually intelligent. That Gorette could go on to bigger things, higher places. She could be on the stamps one day Ma, she's that bright. She can read and write without stoppin'. And they say she had a photo memory. Yeh remember without ever lookin' back. Did yeah realise that, Ma? That sort of skill is a lifesaver. Where there's knowledge, there's power.'

'That's the sort of shite that sends good men reachin' for a pint.' Nel's bitterness fell on deaf ears. She liked Jemser sober, and for that matter her children schooled, but that another had succeeded where she had habitually failed – that riled her reason. 'Gorette the dark horse, Gorette the brain box, tell Nel Rafferty something she doesn't know.'

'They've divided the bedroom into four. Curtains separatin' the boys from the girls. They managed to get three single beds into the same space you had two.' Attracta's face went bright red.

'Bejaysus, they've the cheek of the devil. Segregatin' the Raffertys.' If Nel could have, she'd have signed herself out of the hospital there and then.

'Some of us is too big to be sleepin' together. When yeh think, Ma, Christy is fourteen, Kevin isn't far behind. Just because they're small doesn't mean....' Her words tailed off.

'I wonder if they'd jump in me grave as quick.'

'Yeh won't know the cut of the place when yeh come home. Honest the god, the two rooms look twice the size.'

Her news could wait. All efforts at congeniality were lost in Nel's consternation.

'Ma, listen an' I'll give yeh a laugh.' Attracta was determined to lift the atmosphere if nothing else before she left.

'Didn't the Countess write off to Radio Eireann for free tickets to a recording of classical music, when Jemser told her he liked Handel. Only tryin' to get the right side of her, he was Ma. Sure it could have been the handle of a brush for all Jemser knew. Packed off last night he was with the four big ones. Off for a taste of culture.' Nel's eyes began to smile at the good of Jemser landing himself at a concert.

'And when the Countess turned on the wireless and heard him cough in the middle of the broadcast, she confiscated his tin of tobacco and roll-ups. I'm tellin yeh, Ma, people would pay good money to see the same performance in the Gaiety. She frightens the shit out of him.'

Nel was fuming. It was the last sentence that swung her into a fit.

'Once she has her swanky arses outa my house before I return home, there'll be no problems.' Nel sniffed hard. She wasn't amused. She'd heard enough, had enough of auld wans with time on their hands making monkeys out of the Raffertys.

'Sure, she's scalin' down already.' The swanky sentence grated further on Nel's nerves.

'That in itself. I wouldn't like it to come to blows.' Nel had spent more than one long night lying in her hospital bed, imaging sending the Countess flying with one good puck.

'I think they're arrangin' for one of them to call in for an hour or so every morning. Get the kids off the school and Jemser out of bed. They say yeh'll need time to find yer land legs.'

She didn't dare open her mouth about her Ma's and Jemser's bed been moved and screened off in a corner of the kitchen. She had said enough for one day.

Nel snorted. 'They've about as much hope of helpin' Nel Rafferty as they have of doin' the polka with the Pope in the Phoenix Park.'

'Well, yeh won't have me around for much longer, Ma, an' yeh'll need a hand, even the midwife said as much. So I'd think twice before I got too choosy.'

It came out of her mouth in spite of the warning bells in her head.

Nel was visibly crestfallen.

'They take more than they give, the same articles never lose sight of that.' Nel's hurt manifested itself as anger. Do-gooders were riddled with suspicion in Nel Rafferty's eyes. 'Stickin' their noses up everyone's hole but their own.' The whites of her eyes had turned red.

'Did yeh hear a word I said, Ma?' Attracta didn't know whether her good news was ignored or overlooked. 'I start work for the Countess in Ballsbridge as soon as you come out of here. Ten bob a week. Half day Wednesday and every third Sunday free. Me own room and me own uniform; to keep, Ma.'

'It didn't take them long to loot me house.' But she was too proud to tell her daughter how much she wanted her to stay at home, now more than ever. Nel turned her face to the wall.

'Come on now, Ma, sure yeh nearly died when I ran home from the Bishop's place. Just think of the space and peace. Meself and Jemser, not at one another's necks. And don't forget the money, Ma.'

When Nel wouldn't be plamassed, Attracta tried another tack.

'Ma, here's great gossip around the street.' She dropped her voice to a conspiracy. She needed to make tracks but she wouldn't leave Nel on a sour note. 'Are yeh listenin?' She poked her Ma in the ribs.' Nel made half a turn. 'There's a doctor up in the dispensary dolin' out tings called French letters. The Guarda raided the dispensary last week.' Attracta continued in spite of the look on Nel's face. 'Priests, bishops, archbishops even, are all callin' him out from altars.'

'What in the name of Jaysus is French letters?' Nel couldn't wait for her to finish.

'Rubber things, ah come on now, Ma.' She tucked a disbelieving chin in to her chest, pretended she was familiar with the contraceptive that Concepta had told her yeh could buy in the Chinaman's pub. 'That stop yeh getting' pregnant.'

'How?' Nel was lost to this world.

'The man shoves them on his mickey. Like skinnin' a sausage.'

Ears were flapping the length of the maternity ward.

'Where the hell are yeh getting all this from?' Nel picked up her ears and her bottom lip. She didn't want the women in the surrounding beds to think her tearaway daughter was a prostitute as well as a problem.

'I heard the auld wans gossipin' on the saggy steps. They say if they'd raided the right pubs in Dublin, they'd find half a ton of them in the cellars,' Attracta laughed like a dirty drain.

'Well bejaysus, isn't it rich? Three weeks after Nel Rafferty loses her womb, they find a cure for pregnancy.'

'Yis could all be still virgins – if'n only yis learned a few Protestant tricks,' Attracta addressed the sensational silence behind her.

'It's that Minister for Health, that bousey Doctor Noel Brown, that's behind this, I'll bet me life of it,' a heavily pregnant country woman's voice to the challenge. 'Can none of yis see beyond yer noses? There'll be no youth to look after yis in yer dotage, if yis follow like blind fools after every messiah that offers yis his short-sighted solutions.'

It didn't take long for the row and the ructions. 'Mind yer own shaggin' business, yeh bloody auld busybody. It's all right for the

54

likes of you, with yer big farm at yer arse, to be havin' babby after babby. Yer too well watered and fed to dispense advice to the rest of us eejits,' another die-hard threw her hat into the arena.

In a voice loud and clear, Nel addressed to the ward: 'I'm just skin and bones draped over an empty hole now: but bejaysus, I know common sense when I hear it. It's time women took a hand in runnin' their own affairs. Learned that men fillin' ere holes doesn't make us whole.'

Attracta didn't know if it was the past, the present or the future her Ma was rantin' on about.

She slipped through the war of words. She could see her Ma swinging her legs out of the bed, giving out the exact location of the dispensary and the quickest route to the Chinaman's public house.

***

The siege gave Attracta the cover she needed to leave the ward before her Ma had the time to deliver her habitual harangue. Don't let yerself fall into the kind of trouble yer poor ignorant auld Mother did. In the family way at fifteen, bound hand and foot to a bousey by the age of sixteen. Lumbered with a baker's dozen of childer in the same amount of years, in what architects call vertical villages and the enlightened fertility flats. Attracta knew it so well she could have pressed it on vinyl and sold it to the Yanks.

She felt for the make-up at the bottom of the brown paper beg. Nel would have her guts for garters if she saw her with lipstick and eyeshadow. To say nothing of the hair.

Downstairs in the toilets, well away from prying eyes and proclamations, she backcombed her hair into a more grown-up style. She'd seen Concepta with the new hairdo, and although she had little in common with her old schoolfriend these days, she thought she looked dead sexy. Rubbing a bit of rouge into her pale cheeks, she began to feel like the film stars that she saw looking slick day in and day out on the cinema billboards.

With her departure from Stretham Street near at hand and looking this good, he was bound to ask her out. Dolled up to the nines, she'd hold her own with any of the ones she had seen swinging out of him.

She winked at the image in the mirror. The pasty pallor replaced by rich glowing colour winked back at her. She felt rich; the hue from Biddy's navy cashmere coat added its own allure. She had just put a lick of pale pink lipstick to the final come-on when she heard her father's voice echo in the hospital foyer.

Peeping through the crack in the toilet door, she could see Nel, raised from the bed like Lazarus, and Jemser, newly lit fags in their gobs, holding hands right outside the toilets. The feckin' soup, the poor man's penicillin, must have got her up and runnin'. Attracta cursed the cure that was coming between her and the Butcher's Boy. Caught between the devil and the deep blue sea, she sank down on a lavatory seat and listened to her father's rant.

'Lunatic's logic, that's what I'm tormented with in me every wakin' moment. There's childer in corners I never knew existed, and prams. Prams in fits of sobriety I've pushed all over Dublin. Jemser Rafferty, a lady-boy, a legend in Dublin.

Me guts are in spasm, vegetables stewed to the point of exhaustion, grey greasy coddle that would put yeh on the lav for a week. She must have learnt to cook in the Curragh. God be with the days when a pint and a simple night out would be washed down by the luxury of coddle made by yer own fair hands.' Attracta didn't have to look: Nel would be fool for Jemser's flattery.

'Attracta's a turncoat. I don't know where we got her from; she must be a throwback to your Protestant granny.' She had heard the comment a hundred times. 'An' yer lucky to be sleepin' with me any more at the rate beds is trundled in and out of Jemser Rafferty's home.'

'Not the pissy mattresses for all the neighbours to see?' Nel's plea was lost in Jemser's confusion.

'Sectioned off we are, in a corner of the kitchen.' He was at full throttle – at this rate of repeatin' and rawmashins she'd be there all day 'Where does a man go for privacy, Nel? The sooner yer come home and get the sleepin' arrangements sorted, the better. Even the lovely leg I fixed on the auld settle – replaced by some Holy Jo of a carpenter.

'Oh, they're a shower of lachichos, the same ladies. Feckin' faces like the foreign missions. Scourges. Bejaysus, I didn't know whether to congratulate or commiserate with me own flesh and blood.'

Attracta couldn't hear her Ma's reply but she could guess at it.

'I'm astray in the head. Banned from drinkin', and banished from me own bed to find gainful employment. Ordered to visit me own wife. I'm exhausted when I get into bed and exhausted when I get up. An' I suppose yeh heard about the big job in Ballsbridge?'

Attracta pressed her face tight to the crack of the door. She could see her Ma and her Da. Deep in cahoots, one eggin' on the other. He was like a man demented. The tie, the Christmas present, looked as if it was half stranglin' him. He must have sponged the price of a pint or three somewhere. If he didn't move soon, the Butcher's Boy would have bolted again.

'And here's another ting. She keeps all the children's allowance, Nel. She made me sign the book – said I had no need for money. I had no expenses. What price does she put on sanity? I nearly said it to her face. I'm tellin' yeh, Nel, not a word of a lie.'

Attracta was about to make a run for it when she heard the change in her Ma's voice.

'Would yeh ever go home, Jemser Rafferty, before I burst me new stitches.'

'It's no joke, Nel. I haven't had a drop to drink since she crossed the door. And God alone knows, anyone of that contingent could lead a good man to drink and destruction. It's not natural, Nel, when a man can't sit easy in his own home without a pioneer pin being brandished under his nose. If them kids wash their shaggin' hands any more, they'll get dermatitis. Oh, you can laugh, Nel Rafferty, but sure didn't me own mother get it from workin' in the laundry! When are yeh comin' home, Nel?' He was pleading like a little boy.

Attracta could see her Ma stroking the hair on the nape of his neck as they stubbed out their cigarettes. Love's young dream, walkin' hand and hand back up to the ward. She didn't hear her telling Jemser that she'd be home next week.

She headed at high speed for Thomas Street. She didn't know what cashmere was, but with each passing day she liked the feel of it more and more. It was a long way from the auld horse blanket that went with the job in the Bishop's Palace. She was double-delighted she hadn't fekked the hairy auld regulation issue now. Biddy would have never given her a coat if she had had one already.

From time to time, Attracta checked herself in shop windows, gathering more confidence with each step. She was on top of the shop before she knew where she was. Trying too hard to look as if she was used to the swank, she put an extra wiggle in her walk and sauntered in.

After all her contortions and conversions in the toilets, a wan twice the style and double the experience was standing behind the butcher's block.

'Are you new?' Attracta wouldn't keep the envy out of her voice. She'd have traded her grand coat, her big job in Ballsbridge to work side by side with the Butcher's Boy.

'To what?' An evil eye gave her short shift.

Attracta had cut her first teeth on sarcasm so she wasn't that easily put off by some upstart from the north side.

'I'm here to collect a parcel for Raffertys.' She scoured the back of the shop as she spoke. There was neither sight nor light of him.

The parcel plonked unceremoniously in front of her. 'Is there any other particular variety of bones yeh'll be wantin'?' The wan took another swipe.

Attracta wished with all her heart that she was collecting the fillets of beef the Countess so often treated herself to.

'Tell Mr Atkins junior that Attracta Rafferty is lookin' for him.' She staked her claim. 'And while yer at it, can you ask him to have two of his best fillets of beef ready for the Countess on Friday. And to make sure it's been properly hung. We don't like to eat it tough.' It was worth it just to see the astonished eye widen in the wan's face.

Attracta swung her cashmere coat round her, stuck her nose in the air and swept out of the shop. She didn't know where the bullshit came from. But she was relieved it came to her rescue.

She might have got the better of the one behind the counter, but the satisfaction did little to lift her heavy heart as she trudged back to Mercy Mansions. Sinking into her boots, she faced into a bitter January wind.

'Isn't well for some that has a decent parcel of meat to anchor them down on a windy day like tehday.' An auld woman's harmless remark nearly got her a belt of bones in the gob for her trouble.

He was coming out of the bookie's. She was still looking after the auld woman. He bumped straight into her.

'Yer in a fierce hurry.' She tried to sound casual.

'I haven't got long. The Father will be clock-watchin'.' He was very fidgety.

'Long for what.' She could see he didn't like to be teased. 'I've just come from there; there isn't sight nor light of yer father in the shop.'

'I'm feckin' freezin', I'm not hangin' around the street. I'm goin' into the Chinaman's.' Attracta caught him completely off the hop.

He followed her in. She wondered if he had any swallie, the speed the black stuff slid down his gullet.

'Who's the wan, by the way? She's not the sharpest knife in the box. All I wanted was marrowbones. I was lucky I didn't leave with fillets of beef. She's as thick as hobbyhorse shite. Yed want to employ a better class of skivvy.'

'I have to go.' Foamy yellow rings still round an empty glass. Attracta followed him out a side door. Left her Club Orange untouched on the table.

'I'll take yeh to the pictures on Friday night.' Strong hands pushed her into a doorway.

'It's broad daylight.' She flushed royal red as he pulled open her coat. Sloe-black eyes wavered between her face and her blouse. What he lacked in height he made up in presence. There was somethin' animal, somethin' tantalising about him.

'Will it make a difference when it's dark?'

He pushed himself against her. She thought a marrowbone had come loose and stuck in her. A shudder shot straight through her. She felt something elasticy snap deep inside her. Her embarrassment ran scarlet and deep beneath her clothes

She was different. Different cows, different milk: and not properly broken in yet, he'd bet a week's winnings.

'Friday at seven outside the Big Stamp House.'

Attracta's heart pounded in her chest pounded with a pleasure that lasted all the way home.

***

Jemser was ahead of her. Peloothered, tearing along the hall.

'That auld table'll be bald if yeh don't stop rubbin' it. Yeh can give me a rub down if yer feelin' that energetic.' He was ballyraggin' the Countess by the time Attracta followed him through the door.

The whiff of Nel's homecoming had filled him full of Dutch courage.

'We won't be troublin' yeh much longer for yer services.'

The sneer, the slithery vowels, well oiled with Guinness and glee. A plume of blue smoke wafted up the Countess' nose. A month living under a new dictator had shown his wife in a complete new light. Attracta saw the anger coming seconds before he emptied both barrels.

The Countess's face, flushed red, clashed with pink lipstick and an alarming stripe of vivid green eyeshadow. Attracta tried not to look too closely at the annihilation.

'Matt Talbot will have to find another cause. Yeh can take this pioneer pin an' stick it up yer tight arse.' He dismissed the patron saint of drunks and the Countess in the same sour breath.

'And that, Attracta, is how you talk to the servants.' He bowed low in mock grandeur and faced his mortified daughter.

You could have cut the atmosphere in two as the Countess' back disappeared at the speed of a tinker out the door.

'If you've cost me me job in Ballsbridge, there'll be fukkn' hell to pay.' Attracta's fist followed her anger straight into Jemser's face, sending him with disturbing ease back over the settle.

Seven

A thin place, Muriel Grey called Leixlip. Straddling the borders of Dublin and Kildare, belonging to neither, beholdin' to both. She had staked her location and her peculiar predicament in one short sentence.

She was out in Leixlip. Keeping His Grace's secret under wraps. Muriel touched her stomach, hard and swollen. How could such a blessing become such a burden. The child fluttered inside her; tiny butterfly's wings. The uneasy guest. What have we done? Guilty by association. Oh, the sins of the Father. She straightened her spine as she entered the kitchen and tried to greet the day and Brigit Murphy with some class of civility. Was it morning sickness or mental sickness? Muriel didn't feel well enough to answer her own question.

She dragged herself to the toilet. Fonsie had left the bedroom without as much as a backward glance this morning. Would that he was as inattentive at night. Her bladder was full to overflowing. She couldn't use a po in daylight. Hatch like a hen in the middle of a bedroom. These ablution arrangements would have to undergo severe changes. Like the sleeping arrangements.

She ran past him over wet cobbled stones, drops of heavy rain hitting the crown of her head and back as he came out of the lavatory. She held her breath, her nose, until her eyeballs bulged, her lungs almost burst. Fighting through a fog of smoke and shit, she vomited with rare gusto. She was deliberately late for breakfast. She'd seen enough of him last night; she could do without looking at his grey face again this morning.

The postman waved as he threw his leg over the crossbar; dream-stealer. Rivets of rain ran down his moleskin cape. Something sore twisted inside Muriel when she'd realised the letter was addressed to Brigit.

And then the deluge came. The sky filled with a demonic energy, and it raged. It was cleansing; Brigit had given her knowing look. Slippery streets, back yards, birds' feathers slicked back to the bone, were all credited with the blessed properties. In the disquieting atmosphere, everything seemed unsettled. Caught between a jagged longing for Barclay and rabid pish-terouge, she floundered. And while the mind flayed for outlets, the body offered no such respite.

The changes were evident daily. Her breasts, once pretty and pert, were swelling and sore. Her stomach bulged, her waist resolutely refused to stop spreading. The sharpest of pain caught her under the rib whenever she bent to put on her shoes or pick up the small child. Fonsie's son: a ray of sunshine in this dull place. But there were good spots in the bad times. The sickness in the early hours of every morning was less vicious and less frequent. And there were times in the day when she actually felt normal.

Ironically, the more the baby inside her grew, the more acutely she felt Barclay's absence in her body. The want that filled her every waking moment. It was bad enough to suffer, but to think about the suffering brought a whole new monotony. Coupled up with this burgeoning reality, it was almost too much to bear.

In the end, Muriel was so sick of thinking, of talking, of theories, of downpours, of mirrors with their faces turned to the wall every time lightning struck. So sick of it all that any company other than her own and Brigit's seemed irresistible.

Her foot had been stuck to the floor for a fortnight. She picked up her pen and paper and began to write. Real or imagined, her list got longer. She was determined to get out from under Brigit's feet; to get away from her own dread.

Muriel eyed a window of blue sky, reading it as an omen.

'You could be lucky.' Brigit read the same opportunity differently.

Baking soda bread for the evening tea, Brigit wondered what Muriel was doing with the list. Wondered what more she could want from Komiskey's shop that wasn't already in the larder.

The basket was to cover the belly. She knew that auld trick of old. But she wasn't going to keep herself to herself for much longer. With her build, sure yeh could see the makin's of a big dinner, let alone a babby.

And what pray does she think the early mornin' vomitin' is all about? Does she think a body has no ears? Bookkeeper me backside; yeh might be bright at figures, but yeh haven't got much common sense when it comes to calculations. Brigit plumped the dough into a tidy mound as her thoughts shaped up.

She's beginning to burst out already, breasts, belly and backside. Eatin' for Ireland. Cabin fever couldn't help her condition either. Ah sure, it's the first decent day we've had in a fortnight, who could blame the girl making an excursion?

Brigit lifted a jug of fresh buttermilk and poured it slowly into the concoction. 'Now up yeh can pop, son.' She balanced Jack on the low stool between her belly and the table. Suspended between teasing and thoughts, the child played with surplus dough.

'I'll be as fat as a fool if you don't stop making and baking delicious food.' Muriel sought to confuse. She'd already fielded intolerance for fat when Brigit found her vomiting. She was only ten weeks gone. Time, if nothing else, was on her side. Besides, if faces needed saving later, she could always claim the baby was premature.

'We'd all want to watch the waistlines,' Brigit humoured her. The women in her own family were all strappin' like herself. Broad shouldered, wide hipped. They could have carried children for the full nine months and not a soul have been any the wiser.

She compared Muriel. Five foot five inches high at the most. Narrow at the waist, slim hips. Muriel was slipping a foot into a shoe that would fit a child. Brigit took stock of the tiny frame; forecast for the birth wasn't lost in the calculations.

She'd helped at her fair share of deliveries, and little women were lumbered with the big problems. The size of the foot is equal to the width of the pelvis. That's what the local midwife said. There was something disturbing about the sight of a woman in a child's body. Brigit hadn't put Muriel's age in its proper place – she had her at five years less than her twenty-five.

Yer belly will tell yer business, long before yeh mouth, she nodded at Muriel. She's never seen a hat set at so many right angles. All business and no trade; she dismissed the manoeuvrings but not her concerns. Yer a lonely little petunia in an onion patch. All talk and no tellin'. Stone-cold secrets sit in dark places. Brigit could almost feel Muriel's pain. She rolled her shoulders and tried to shift some of the stiffness that was settling in the back of her neck.

Death is double sore when it happens durin' childbirth. And marriage, when the widah's not cold in the grave is another sin on the soul. Brigit had often put up with auld busy bodies in Komiskey's. *An' the likes of us trusting him with our private affairs when he can't trust hisself. Is he right in the head? Is he up to the job? Don't judge anyone in his or her grief.*

The odd few had tried reason. In the end, rumour and reason condemned both of them. Its weight added its own load on Brigit. She was glad she had nipped the role of confidante in the bud. She'd been down that thorny old boreen before. Once pricked, taught twice about pluckin'. She had heard too much from the old missus to be giving her senses to the new one. Besides, she had enough on her plate at the moment.

Her sister's face in all its malevolence bolted before her mind's eye. Her neck stiffened, and she realised her knuckles were kneading bare board.

Muriel was trying to get a neck scarf to sit right. 'Never mind fashion, make sure yer wrapped up warm.' She's as broad as she's long in the big swanky coat. She was hoping that Muriel had the wit to keep the coat pulled closed. For as sure as there was a god in heaven above, some shitehawk would see the seed's of another story.

A movement in the yard caught her eye. An old jackdaw picking over the remains of a field mouse. Brigit welcomed the fickleness of the distraction. The ground was still damp. There'd be no drying yet. No point in putting the washing out until the winds were strong enough to dry the ground.

'Can I get you anything at Komiskey's, Brigit?' Something about Brigit was bothering Muriel. She'd seen another side in the past week, a solemn side. She was more comfortable with the blather and skite Brigit.

'Its children's allowance day. There'll be crowds out there to beat bannaher.' Brigit was talking for talk's sake. 'Throwing money round Leixlip like men with no arms.' She didn't tell Muriel what the women in Leixip called the weekly allowance. Mickey money; Brigit enjoyed the boldness of the words on her lips. Mickey money, she sighed; sure the rich vulgarity would be lost on the likes of yeh.

'Will I take the little man, here?' Muriel saw the tiny fingers footer and flick wet dough.

'Its damp out there, still there's no point in testing fate. The chest's the best its been in an age. Leave him to me. When the wet winds blow over, we'll start the walks again. Besides we might have a baker on our hands. Isn't that right, son?' She blew a puff of flour off the child's nose. 'A Butcher, a Baker, Candlestick-maker.'

Muriel pulled the door behind her. Her childhood raced alongside the familiar nursery rhyme as she headed for the shop. She marvelled at Brigit's patience, and perseverance prayed it would stretch to two. A sharp east wind hit her in the face. Brigit was wise to keep the child indoors. Cold or no cold, Muriel was glad to be out. Glad of the break in the weather and the routine. She tucked her chin tight to her chest and took the main street at a brisk pace.

Figaries, Brigit called her notions for fig rolls and aniseed balls. Sure an' it's better than last missus' figaries: coal lumps. The slip of tongue startled her. Set her wondering if the coal had made any contribution to the late Mrs Duggan's demise.

Brigit felt the familiar stinging in her bowels. The letter was still causing ructions with her constitution. She whacked the latch on the bedroom door, just made it to the commode. Yeh'll be fine, yeh'll be fine; this pain will pass. And so will all the shock and confusion. She tried to talk down her concerns. Her nerves were in tatters since the arrival of her sister's letter. A fortnight now, and not a sign of the ructions letting up. She jumped with the force of the fart and skitter that shot the sides of the bowl.

Not a hello or how are yeh, not a please, thanks or kiss me arse. A word of warnin' wouldn't a went a miss. The Bishop of Dublin is to father a child, the first line of the letter was seared on her brain. Her sister's frustration had risen off the page. I saw the letter meself, with me own two eyes, I'm nearly sure I recognise the hand.

Brigit's heart went out to the poor unfortunate; only a personal appearance by the Angel Gabriel himself would save her from Maggie Murphy's wrath. For if I know Maggie Murphy, she won't rest 'til she's found someone to blame. For as sure as there's a head on a ha'penny, it wouldn't be the Bishop of Dublin's fault. Bad cess, teh yeh, Maggie Murphy, for bringing more trouble on this house. Brigit scoured the inside of the commode with boiling water, swilled it round and round and tipped it out the back door. And he won't be the first Bishop in Ireland to father a child: sure, there's worse things between Heaven and Hell.

Brigit never called her sister by her married name, Sexton. Sure, she was never married long enough to be a missus. She flung a bucket of soapy water after the first, rinsed away the remains.

Brigit rubbed her stomach, tender and distended. 'Begod, she's surpassed herself this time.' She spoke to the bewildered child as she dried red-hot fingers in a snow-white towel. Mischief-makin' Maggie. Couldn't take her hand off her arse till she terrorised someone else with gossip the Blessed Virgin must have hung her head and wept about. She sipped the bitter solution of bread soda and milk she'd made up to settle her stomach.

Impatient sucks between Brigit's tongue and her palate signalled more distress. The child's imitation was lost in the milieu. The thing that unsettled Brigit the most was that her sister's gossip was never far from the truth.

She could have kilt a body. And soul. No suggestions on how to hang on to yer reason in the face of such treason, leave alone a body's faith. How she's so highly prized by the clergy is as big a mystery as the Blessed Trinity. Brigit was talking out loud.

The child was wagging his little finger, shaking his head, shouting alongside her. Our Holy Mother the Church has survived worse slanderers. She took comfort from the received wisdom as she put the finishing touches to her baking. She'd seen the letter burn in the fire all of a week ago, tried to bury the scandal deep in the folds of her brain. But as was her wont, her body hadn't disposed of the terror and tension quite so easily.

Brigit had shown Isaac Komiskey the letter. It was Isaac who lifted the lid of the range and burned the calumny in a roaring fire. It was him who told her not to tell to a living soul, not even Father Maloney. To have such scandal thrust upon a simple parish priest was a sin in itself. Better to bear the burden than put it on to another's back. Maggie Murphy had committed blasphemy.

That's what Isaac had said, and that's what Brigit accepted. He'd put a shot of whiskey in her tea and sat silently beside her until she steadied herself. Maggie Murphy was always a confusionist. That's what Isaac Komiskey had said. She cut a deep cross in the dough. It always takes yer belly a week or two to catch up on yer brain. She held the child back as she slid the soda bread into the red-hot range.

***

A bell that would wake the dead refused Muriel any hope of a quiet entry into Komiskey's Grocery and General Hardware Store. Isaac watched from the back of the shop. There was more to this particular madam than met the eye. More still to the marriage that was daily making Fonsie Duggan as miserable as hell.

Muriel pulled the basket tight to her stomach, stepped back in time. The women's chapel: it provides a venue for women to gather and gossip, bargain and borrow. With seventy-five years' trading in Leixlip, there are few habits, trends, credit rationings or consumptions that the Komiskeys aren't aware of, Brigit marked her territory for her. And she was probably right. She was certainly right about every dog divil and child being out and about today. The queue snaked round the shop and went back on itself in places. No one seemed to be in the slightest hurry. Least of all me.

Muriel nodded at the women in front and to her side. She'd seen some of them at Sunday mass. No doubt, more had seen her. The sideshow: the local solicitor's substitute wife. On the odd occasions when she'd accompany him, she'd felt their eyes boring holes in her back. Morning sickness had been a godsend the following Sunday. And the Sunday and the Sunday after that. On high days and holy days, she made an appearance. But it was neither comfortable nor comforting.

Kathleen Komiskey was as busy serving as she was at settling up old accounts. Isaac's sister's routine was as good to watch as she was to witness. Two stout counters, worn shiny from elbows and echoes of the past, stood at either end of the shop. The shop was the scene set in childhood, her grandfather's magical stories. 'I'll be with yeh in a minute;' she could hear Kathleen Komiskey. Take yer time. A woman's voice seemed to answer for them all.

Kathleen spoke as she scanned the shelves, taking selected items in one hand, passing them without by your leave to the other. Stacking, tidying, lining up the different varieties in her own peculiar way. Making notes on the back of a pile of paper bags. A running account. She worked with a mix of speed and dexterity, stacking, packing, keeping a running total. I'll be with you in a tick. She swivelled a big black ledger and showed a customer the extent of her credit. Muriel noted the differing cadences, the propriety.

At the far end of the shop, Isaac Komiskey worked as methodically as his sister. Mouth drawn down hard to the left, he redirected an irritating stream of smoke. Over the years the steady stream had caused a permanent blink. Muriel could see him lifting and weighing out potatoes, flour, chicken feed and, at a guess, sugar soap. The clatter and bang of his huge scales set a hum and buzz of expectation. Flat Kildare vowels rose high above the din.

Muriel noted the abundance of confidence. Contrasted it to the times she'd stumbled across some poor person asking for credit. But today was different. There was a lilt in the women's voices, a lift in their step. She could hear Isaac discussing some forthcoming football match. See the smile on the man's face as he picked up a refilled battery for his wireless. Men were happier down Isaac's end of the shop. From time to time, she could hear the rattle of nuts and bolts as they searched for a replacement or a tighter thread, hear small drums of stove paraffin being rolled out to the front of the shop.

The energy when there was money to trade was marked. She welcomed the normality, the distraction. Reality raised its head: sore points pricked at the ideal world. Muriel was a pretender not a participator in their world. The whispered warning: the unhappy seek distractions. Maybe they were right.

Miss Komiskey lifted her head for a second and nodded at Muriel. I'll just tot up. There it was again, the changing tone. Hard cash falling deep into a drawer told its own tale. Every transaction was transferred to a bound ledger, all the soft colours of the rainbow displayed on its deckled edges at odds with its harsh reality. The current of concern shot over the counter when an overdue debt was pointed out was a further source of distraction for Muriel. Some accounts covered two and three pages. A tune whistled through the wide gap in Kathleen's front teeth accompanied every disclosure. The exclamations, the excuses, the silences. Muriel noted the natural rise in decibels when the silence became too loud to bear, the fall when the transaction was completed. A butt of a pencil whipped out from under Miss Komiskey's tight black perm signalled the end of the phase.

'Why did the big story book frighten yeh, Mam?' Embarrassment filtered through the shop.

'Out of the mouths of babes and sucklings.' Nods and shuffles accompanied the sympathy.

Muriel shifted her weight from one foot to another. She thanked God she wasn't beholden to man or beast. That she was a woman of independent means. Not indefinite means. The pinched look on Muriel's face told more than she could know. She had enough savings to keep her going for the next year or two, if she was careful. And if she needed to, she could always work. She had all her qualifications, and good qualifications they were too. She wouldn't like to be beholding to Fonsie Duggan.

Nor for that matter, would she want to be holding her breath for Barclay O'Rourke's contribution. In all the dealing and wheeling that went before, money had never been mentioned.

Wouldn't yeh hate to have to ask a man for the price of a pair of drawers? Brigit's opinion, more by accident than design, managed to describe the situation. The thought unsettled Muriel.

'Shopkeepers age in different places.' Kathleen Komiskey was stretching awkwardly from the top of her steps, reaching for a box of candles. The queue didn't seem to be getting any shorter. The clippity-clop of Miss Komiskey's slow descent made Muriel smile. Nothing happens in a hurry here. Still, if she had nothing else to squander, she had time.

And time was getting easier to pass. She took her walks at night, slept all the better for them and had imposed a structure of sorts to her days. And she was fitting in better with Brigit's routine. If no one else's. The frown was back on her face again. Still, it would be time enough to carve out a niche of her own when the baby came. Her role as a mother would lend her more credibility; it would establish her place in the house. Presently, she was treated like a house guest, and for now she had no complaints. But she'd only play second fiddle for so long.

The queue shuffled along. She was beginning to feel like a fraud in the midst of all the exchange. A blow-in: if she had a bill to settle itself. Suddenly, her requirements seemed shamefully trivial. She looked around. Nobody was taking a blind bit of notice of her. They were too busy clucking and clacking. Cluckin' and clackin' – the couplet rolled round her tongue as she slipped into another daydream. The women in the shop didn't talk to her, or she to them. Smiles and nods were sufficient onto the day. Leixlip people are slow to accept blow-ins. Twenty-five years me own father was here and they still called him a blow-in, Brigit had told her.

The pace suited Muriel. When she had something to say, it would be time enough to talk. Keep yerself to yerself and yer opinions closer. For whatever's yeh say, it will have doubled by morning. You'll be a great source of wonder to them to be sure. Keep them guessin', keep them guessin'. Brigit was always describing, divulging the nature of the beast. Muriel wondered, but not for long, what was bothering Brigit. She'd been out of sorts for the past couple of weeks.

Unaware of their judgements, Muriel stood in their midst. She could hardly see Isaac now for thick blue smoke. A Dante in his own Inferno. Brigit's voice. He sees the whole village in a different light. We started national school on the same day, Isaac and meself. It would have been easy to fall in love with Isaac Komiskey. To invest him with all the wonders and wants in a husband. But sure, fallin' in love with love is fallin' for make-believe, as the fellah says. Brigit's voice was always liquidy when she spoke about Isaac.

Familiar feelings crept up on Muriel as she dallied and daydreamed. Her senses filled with old sights and sounds, smells. Events jostled for pride of place. She could almost feel the texture of the battered brown hat her grandfather would slap on his head; feel the big hoary hands sweeping her along as he headed into town on pension day. Smell the smoke that had filtered through fibres of his clothes and skin. There was something about the smell of old Clan tobacco that surrounded her with uncomplicated love. Unconditional love that always was and always would be.

Silent and unbidden, a cacophony of memories fired off in all directions A Jameson and red: she could feel the vibrations of the bell on the public house counter. Hear the swish of bubbles as the red lemonade invaded the still of the whiskey.

From a forgotten tale came the sound of sweet fiddle notes. Muriel could see coarse stubble caressing the instrument, the bow sweeping across high strings of the bridge, the fingers of the left hand feverishly finding just the right note. The heartbreaking exchange between music and master. No, no, a stor the music never dies, it's handed down note by note, a gracious gift from yesterday to today, velvet tones, sounding his pride.

In an instant, the past became the present, and Muriel lost all sense of time and place. She could smell the sawdust and porter rising up through the floor. Feel rough whiskers on the base of her grandfather's chin as he lifted her up on the counter.

The long view where the pub ended and the shop began is back as plain as a pikestaff. The sparkling sweetie jars that made her mouth water are back in her mind's eye. Barley sugar twists, bright orange or black, liquorice strips, bulls eyes or bonbons, aniseed balls sucked to the seed, macaroon bars licked to the death. Hot clover sweets she'd never select; sticky brown lozenges stuck fast to the lining of her pocket. Butter fat toffees. The jelly babies, red, yellow or green or her favourites, the black fellows, kept in their own jar. Segregated.

The hank of boiled ham hanging from a hook in the ceiling of the public house, its translucent fat smothered in yellow crumbs. The yeast from the batch loaves rising and filling their noses with the smell, with hunger. The tap, tap, tapping of the hammers as a man in full view made coffins that nobody felt obliged to explain or excuse. Where dying was as natural as living.

Then home after dark, big as a bull on her grandfather's broad shoulders. The pipe lighting the road. The smoke in his hair, her mouth and nose. Home to Granny. With the parcel of ham, a Spanish onion and a loaf of fresh white bread. Muriel's memories were coming so fast her lips were wet with spit.

'Move along there, missus.' Harsh Kildare vowels couldn't break the spell. Reconnected with the nuts and bolts that riveted her life together, Muriel found peace in the past. Her grandfather's shadow. That's what they called her.

Milking cows at the crack of dawn. Setting off to the creamery in Scotshouse, milk churns splashing warm milk against their steely cold bellies. The resonance when she pressed her ear against the milk churn. As close to Heaven as she could get. Searching for stray hens' eggs with the sun on her back. Running home through fields of

70

barley, hens' eggs still warm in the palms of her hands. Yolks running wild on a plate of warm soda bread. Afternoons filling churns full of cool clear water from a well sunk all the way down to Australia. Days divided divinely into what was regarded as their stations in life, until death stole them away. One after the other. And left a hole gaping and wide.

Until Barclay. Barclay.

A jab of red-hot memory took her breath away. She almost called out his name in an outburst of profane joy as he passed through her soul and possessed her. In an instant, she was lit by the power of him. She feasted on stored sensations, on every tiny fragment. This was her world: not the gruff reality she was surrounded by, not the Fonsies or the Brigits.

Agony and ecstasy; she was caught between the two thorns. She missed his physical presence. No one could fill a room like Barclay O'Rourke. No one could hold a light to his mercury-quick mind, his smile, his disarming charm. But the space between love was cold. The cold almost too much to bear.

She straightened her back. There was fog between herself and the rest of the world. The women's voices filled the vacuum around her, but she had no interest in what they were saying. She would never have anything in common with ordinary women. She put her hand on her stomach and felt for her tiny bump, their sacred secret. She'd keep his secret safe. Keep it submerged deep beneath her loyalty.

'I was sayin', Missus, could yeh move along there before we take root.'

Private feeling visiting her in public places: her face became transparent. She shuffled along more aware than ever of the difference than the distance that separated her from the crowd. Sorry, sorry, she went through the pantomime of pretence.

She realised she was being scrutinised even as she was being ignored. Lips set in prim lines were moving with the minimum of effort. A child's eyes told her more about their whispers than she needed to know. For a split second, her eyes met theirs, then fell below the line of vision. A vulnerable feeling crept over Muriel.

'My fellah didn't wash for three days after the Bishop of Dublin shook his hand.'

The conversation was settling, shaping itself around her. Words wet with excitement were tumbling out of the speaker's mouth. Every head and heart was in agreement with her. The mention of his name brought her up short. She realised in an instant that they were eulogising about Barclay.

Talk centred on a visit to a local school. The elevated event had taken place not a stone's throw from her front door, and as far as she could gather, within the past week.

'Grand! Sure, you'd travel the roads for many's the long mile to meet the style and grandeur like of him.'

'He's a man-made mountain.' There was unison in them, a drive.

'Six two in his stocking feet. Not to be crossed: he boxed for Kildare when he was a gossoon.' Reverence and envy mixed in equal proportions.

'Talk about a pair of sparkling eyes. Isn't it a shocking waste, all the same?' The syllables sounded indecent. A change, a primal energy, skittered and spread itself around. Leaked out of eyes under skirts and blouses. Muriel's blood boiled.

Above their elegies, she heard his proximity. Pain seared her heart as she realised how near and yet how far he was from her. In an instant, her longing turned to frustration. She wanted to lift the basket from her stomach and scream out that his child was amongst them, listening to them singing his father's praises. She wanted to expose him. But she'd only expose herself. A thief, who'd stolen their hopes, raped their god, plundered their religion. Her only recourse was self-inflicted paralysis.

In this harsh new light of reality, feelings of isolation and desertion were creeping into Muriel's bones. Her arms, her legs felt heavy. She had stumbled across something sore. Deep in the heart of her, she knew that love could mutate, be chiselled away by loose talk, lame excuses, empty promises. But it was early days yet, and her vision was blurred.

The air in the shop was getting scarcer. Muriel's knees buckled.

Brigit saw the mob coming down the side of the house. She flung the baby clothes she'd been examining to the back of the hot press. In case two and two would be put together and become twins.

Isaac carried Muriel feet first into the kitchen. For one barren moment, Brigit thought she was dead.

'What in God's name's happened?' She opened her own bedroom door and pointed towards the bed. Half the village was crowding into the tiny bedroom. She thanked God and his Holy Mother that her commode was spotlessly clean.

'What's wrong?' Brigit tried to pull the coat around Muriel to save her dignity. But they were already whispering, wondering when Fonsie had done the bold deed.

'Will yeh get himself. And get rid of this shower,' Brigit gestured to Isaac.

From his office window, Fonsie Duggan saw the crowd carrying his wife's limp body. Terrorised at the prospect of becoming a serial widower, he'd poured a large whiskey and prepared for the next death sentence. Isaac left him to his own devices and went his own way home.

'What came over me?' Burrowed deep into the soft comfort of Brigit, Muriel's eyes beseeched like a child.

'Nothing wild or wonderful. Yeh only fainted. A commoner church garden faint.'

'What's to become of me, Brigit?' Muriel's shoulders went up and down in a series of hopeless gestures.

'Take a sup of sweet tea.' Brigit's kindness augmented her solitary state.

Eight

Spring wasn't quite in the air, but it was certainly in Attracta Rafferty's step.

She hummed as she buttoned the tiny white gloves that had seen better service. Set her hat at a jaunty angle and headed at a cracking pace for Adam and Eve's. He'd said he'd see her after Sunday Mass. But then the Butcher's Boy said more than his prayers.

Me weekend off, maybe he'll make it up to me. Well, he can try. There's bigger and better than him that could have stood Attracta Rafferty up; so he better be talkin' fast and tryin' hard. He'd be waitin' a long time before she'd let him near her again. He could cool his heels an' his ardour outside Adam and Eve's this mornin', google with the rest of them, before she'd dain to talk to him.

She'd allowed herself an hour to walk the two and a half miles to the church: to walk through Stephen's Green to cut a dash in Dublin. There was no point dressing up for the people Ballsbridge – they wouldn't know the difference. In the Liberties, she'd be noticed; every item lock, stock and smokin' barrel be taken notice of. Amongst her own she'd get the return on her investment. Between Biddy's coat and shoes and the Countess' accessories it would be tuppence to talk to her soon.

It had taken elbow grease and perseverance to get back the lustre that the hat and gloves lacked. But it had been worth if for the finishing touch. She'd steeped the cotton gloves in a pot of her own piss until they were whiter than white. A good steaming and brush up lifted the jaded nap on the velvet hat. Steam, piss and prayer. You could almost smell the white. Where would yeh be without essential elements? She'd never let good clothes get into poor condition.

The admiring glances she got going through the Green were second only to the wolf-whistles and stares as she strolled down Grafton Street. Heaven: high as a helium balloon, she marched through Temple Bar, down the quays and straight up to the front of Adam and Eve's. She took her time genuflecting, easy and slow. Gave those who wanted time to get a good eyeful. She could hardly pray for pride.

Father Ben thought he saw a vision, as the waif who had haunted the Liberties only six months previously knelt before him at the communion rail. Dressed in such finery, she could have passed for a Protestant.

And he wasn't the only one watching closely. Standing at the side altar ready to catch her eye on the way back from communion, the Butcher's Boy was relishing every detail. And making no bones about the pleasure it was giving him. She'd felt his eyes burning holes in her back during Mass. She didn't look back. She was busy trying to impress his Mother and Father.

Suddenly all the steeping and boiling, the brushing and airing, were worth their weight in gold. The Atkins were shop people: they would expect respectability, to see any company their son was keeping dressed in the best. Head up, chest out as she paraded past by without as much as a sideways glance. Piety pays. Time enough for niceties when she was formally introduced after Mass.

Mass for the first and only time in Attracta's life seemed hopelessly short. She genuflected and left ahead of the congregation. She didn't want to miss him. Didn't want to be missed by anyone. Outside the main doors, she took up pole position, let those who wanted give her the once over.

Crowds cluttered the foyer and the church steps. She tried hard not to look anxious. He'd promised he'd see her after ten o'clock Mass. Doubt clung in a sheen of sweat to her back. She'd been vexed with him since he'd left her stranded outside the General Post Office. The big stamp house he called it. The big stamp house me arse, the big culchi. The whole of Stretham Street had the story by the time she pitched back up home. A laughing stock.

She took a sneaky look around. Not hide nor hair of yer man. *Cross me heart and hope to die.* He'd sworn holes through a tin can that a cow had got into trouble in the Liffey. But even as he took his tin can oath, her stomach had chundered the warning. Maybe he's forgotten it was this Sunday. More to the point, maybe he was only avoiding a scene in the shop. She would have had his guts for garters the same day. And he knew it. She should learn to take heed of her leanings.

Lifting her head, she peeped out from under the brim. She couldn't have missed him? Well, he couldn't bloody well miss you, the shout inside her head rattled her reason. There'd be a sob story. Another cow calfin'. He could tell lies to a band playin'. Well, he'd had his last chance. Once was once too often with Attracta Rafferty – but twice. Fuck him.

And to think she nearly lifted her skirt for him. Lifted her skirt in the Odeon cinema. Nearly. Jaysus. The rims of her eyes tightened. Well, yeh can shag off, yeh big bollix. Better then the Butcher's Boy had given her the glad eye.

Father Ben tapped her on the shoulder. She nearly jumped out of her skin. 'Well, somebody's looking mighty. Would the young lady have time for a cup of tea with a parish pump priest like meself?' His voice, his eyes, delighting in the transformation. He saw her hesitation. 'Perhaps another time?'

She thought on her toes. He just might turn up yet. Maybe all wasn't lost. Now was as good a time as ever to let him have a taste of his own medicine. To teach him a lesson. A lesson in public. She could still take advantage of the Sunday style. Lord it over him. Tell him he must be mistaken. The wrong Sunday. She had another date. An important date.

'I'd be delighted.'

'Could you wait five minutes?'

She couldn't have been more pleased to oblige. There wasn't a soul coming out of the church that missed a stitch on her. A young fellah was giving her the glad eye. Attracta lapped up the attention. A slithery shiver took her by surprise; she sighed, she was enjoying the ride. Every auld wan in Dublin was bendin' the priest's ear as he made his way back to the vestry. Take yer time, Father. I've got plenty of it.

The Atkins passed at close quarters; they looked particularly distracted. Still no sign of their son. Were they looking for him, too? She'd nodded to them in the curt way she seen the auld wans in Ballsbridge nodding at one another.

From his vantage point in the vestry, Father Ben could see the Butcher's Boy kicking his heels at the back door of the church. Auld gobethewall. He knew what he was up to. He'd seen that look in his eye on too many occasions and on too many women. Heard too much and too many confessions about the same article. Some from married women. He blessed himself; he shouldn't recall sins. But the same buckooh was an occasion of sin if he ever knew one.

Heavy clouds were gathering over the Liffey, hurrying in from the west. A good dousing will do you a power of good and just might cool yer ardour into the bargain. He shut the tiny window, stopping the rain blowing into the vestry.

Attracta's bottom lip was on the ground by the time Father Ben swished around. He smiled to himself. Me bold Butcher's Boy is at the wrong door. It's seldom he misses a trick. He didn't make her any the wiser. Attracta Rafferty could do a lot better than the Butcher's Boy.

'They must be paying some money in Ballsbridge these days.' The big bushy eyebrows lifted high, a straight line of admiration.

Attracta blushed. 'The Countess. She's been very good to me.' She touched her gloves, her hat, almost apologetically. The twinkle in his eye gladdened her heart. He could charm the birds off the bushes, the same Father Ben. Wasn't it a shame priests didn't marry? She was smiling from ear to ear. A shame bishops don't marry. Another slither. Attracta Rafferty, yeh should be ashamed of yerself.

All thoughts of the Butcher's Boy were replaced in an instant by the thoughts of the gorgeous Barclay O'Rourke. The Bishop of Dublin had recently graced the Countess' drawing room. She swelled with pride as she passed looks and nods of appreciation from his brothers in Christ. Down, down long passages into the kitchen. To sizzling bacon, eggs hoppin' off pans, freshly baked bread straight out of the oven. Another world; down under Dublin.

'Can we have another plate over here for our distinguished visitor?' Father Ben pulled a chair out for Attracta and with one great sweep of his hand bade her sit. He took her coat, the hat; the gloves stayed put. She was showing off to all 'n sundry. And why not? He smiled to himself at the good of it.

Attracta looked around the kitchen and was glad she didn't know anybody. She sat ramrod straight like the ladies in Ballsbridge. She wondered what the serving women were making of the great style. She could almost hear the comments. About the swanky young one the priest was entertainin', when they got home.

'Now,' Father Ben pulled his chair close and sat knee to knee. 'I'm all ears. So tell me all your news.'

Flattered to have his full attention, she didn't spare breath.

'I have a room and a bed to meself.' She nodded vigorously. 'A dry room, Father, in the basement. It hasn't exactly what yeh call a view. Still...no change there. What yeh never had, yeh never miss', she winked. 'But it has a Belfast sink in it, a mirror, a wardrobe and a tallboy. Did yeh ever hear the likes of the names? Me bed's wedged in beside a huge chimney-breast – it keeps the mattress bone dry. Meself as warm as toast.'

Father Benedict hoped summer would be as good to her as winter, but he didn't get a chance to voice his concerns.

'The Countess had the clothes ready and waitin' as soon as I set me foot in Ballsbridge.' She smoothed her dress down over her knees and stroked the sleeve of a virgin-blue cardigan. 'Dressed for the location and occasion. She wouldn't be the object of her neighbours' indignation. Word for word, Father, that's how the Countess put it to me.' She drew her lips into a tight knot, wiggled the tip of her nose.

'An' there was me worried about disgracin' meself. Hadn't I little to worry about? Isn't it a far cry from the girl yeh saw sittin' here before Christmas?' A second's silence marked respect.

'What few belongings the Raffertys ever owned before hung from a nail on the back of the bedroom door. Now I have empty drawers and hangers to spare. I've a uniform with starched cuffs and collars, a frilly apron and cap that I take home to wash. I have me own special recipe for getting tings whiter than white. There's one to spare in the event of spillage, sweat or stains.'

'She calls me Miss Rafferty, I call her Countess.' Attracta nodded in harmony with his nod.

It was a caution to the Priest how the disingenuous Mrs Grey could be so seduced by Dublin wit. He'd heard her called a few other names in his day. Less formal and flattering. Interesting how none of them had been allowed to slip into the vernacular.

'Wasn't she cute, all the same, not producin' the likes of this' – her hand gestured to the clothes – 'while I was still at home?' Attracta threw her eyes and her concerns to the back of the church in the general direction of the flats.

'Can yeh imagine, Father, a trunk load of this clobber arrivin' in Mercy Mansions? Jaysus, my family would have thought they'd found treasure.'

Father Ben smiled. He knew exactly the type of currency the clothes would generate in the Rafferty's hands. And they wouldn't be exchanged for compliments either.

'Yeh know yerself, Father. Wall teh wall in the Jew man's, like the rest of the stuff she found in the house when she came home out of hospital. Didn't last kickin' time. No more than the money she got for it. And there'll never be the price of it to buy it back.'

She searched the old priest's face. Said a silent prayer he hadn't heard about the punch Nel threw at the Countess. Below the belt.

'Are you comfortable there?' Father Ben sensed discomfort.

'Comfortable, Father?' She grabbed his lifeline with both hands. 'Comfortable, sure I'm on the pigs back.

'Carpets overlappin' carpets, not a bare board in the house. Red like the ones yeh sees in snaps of the Vatican. It has rooms with only chairs and tables sittin' in them. Rooms in reds, greens, yellows and blues – colours that would take the sight out of yer eye. Rooms called by colour. None of yer corporation greys or greens there, Father. An' all lit up like the Kish lighthouse. *Electric.*'

She waited for a comment, and when none was forthcoming she continued.

'There's indoor toilets and outdoor toilets, not one or two, three of them. There's posh for yeh, Father. Can yeh even imagine the comfort? None of yer buckets or out runnin' like hell from rats in dark hallways. Kickin' the feckers out of yer way, before yeh even get yer arse on the seat.'

She didn't see the surprise on the priest's face. She was in full spate.

'Or hoppin' from one frozen foot to the other because some bousey was too ignorant or too drunk to come out. The Countess even has a lav off her bedroom. I think it's a bit too close for comfort meself, but every one to his own, Father.'

She held her nose for a split second. The gesture wasn't for Father Ben's benefit.

'There's a garden there that yeh could hold an All Ireland in, an' not a soul in it, not even a clothes line. A gardener keeps up appearances. I'm allowed use a little side garden. A little sun trap under the kitchen window, where we hang out the washin'. It's that well protected, yeh could sit out in yer nip in all weathers.

'Yeah should see the neighbours, Father: spring summer and winter clothes. Dressed for all seasons. Sober as judges, and all as fat as bishops. She shook her head, like an old sage. 'They're a different breed than you and I, Father. Better lookin' too. A better pallor.

'I'm tellin' yeh, Father, whatever Saint yeh prayed to for me deserves a medal. I'm livin' like a lord's bastard in a house the likes of which I've only ever seen on a cinema screen. Take the number nine bus out there yerself, Father, get a look from the upstairs. I'm tellin' yeh, it would put the sight back in sore eyes. Let yeh see how the other half of Dublin lives. It was an eye-opener for me. I didn't know houses like that existed in real life.

'An' sure with a bit of spit an' polish and a good dose of elbow grease, I have the place lookin' like a new pin. Mind you, it took the best part of two months and half a stone of sugar soap to shift the dirt. Gas isn't it, Father?

'When yeh think of all the declarations an' exclamations in an' about the Liberties. All the swoonin' and the sniffin' salts, and it was them that was dirty all along. It was far from exact standards, the Countess house was. Say what yeh like about Nel Rafferty, there was never a dirty stitch in our house. Still fit for a prince of the Church, it is now.'

Attracta threw out a sprat to catch a salmon, watched him carefully to see whether he'd taken the bait. Did he know about the

Bishop's hideout? Poker-faced. She throttled back. She'd say less till she heard more. She'd been warned.

'You find yourself in a very sensitive position here, Miss Rafferty,' the Countess' voice mimicked to life. 'My house is what's known in clerical circles as a safe house. It's a rare thing, a house where a priest will not be compromised. You will meet people you're not used to meeting. Hear, see things that mustn't be repeated.' She had more airs and graces than the King of England. She had Father Benedict laughing out loud.

The Countess had chosen the austerity of the study to lend gravity to Attracta's induction. When the Bishop brought the new Minister for Health round for afternoon tea, the Countess' excitement was no match for Attracta's curiosity. You're a very lucky young woman to have the privilege of serving a Prince of the Church and a Minister of State under the same roof.

The Countess' speeches were always the same, always laced with the same syrupy reverence. Only names changed. If it wasn't Lady suchabody, it was Lord suchabody that she had the privilege of serving. Attracta didn't know whether they were invited by the Bishop, for the Bishop or because of the Bishop. But he was always at the top of the Countess' table. Always holding court.

She'd a faraway look in her eye. Father Ben refilled her cup and thought of his own nieces. Cosseted and protected. There was no comparison. Attracta took the cup in both hands and gulped the hot tea. She was parched.

In the past month, things between herself and the Bishop had taken a quare turn. It was hard to say who was more privileged to serve whom. Attracta had never experienced attention from the likes. Or the likes of the attention. She'd come across priests with roving eyes in her day. Once even with roving hands. But never a Bishop.

And while Attracta had found priests' attention peculiar, she was experiencing no such peculiarities with the Bishop. On the contrary. A man in his position. A man of his power. Her head spun. She bit her bacon sandwich with gusto. The devil himself got into her knickers every time she saw him. Every time. He'd brushed up against her accidentally on purpose not once nor twice. An' the look in his eye. Jaysus wept. The elastic in her knickers twanged. Brazen Bishop. The slithery shiver; again.

She hoped Father Ben couldn't read minds like some of the saints she learned about at school. But Father Ben suspected nothing more than hunger. He was comfortable with silence. Welcomed it even. She'd been chewing on the same piece of bacon for so long it had become tasteless and stringy. She swallowed the mass in her mouth and continued with the more acceptable face of her monologue.

'Yeh'll never believe who's a regular visitor.' She touched her finger to her lips nodded reverently. 'The Bishop of Dublin hisself.' She took the sentence like an oath. 'There yeh have it. The very same. That's the class of caller we have where I do work. Oh yes.'

Father Ben straightened himself up at the mention of the Bishop's name. She'd managed to impress him. 'It's only the likes of yerself I'd be tellin'. Brings his important friends and work', she added.

Father Ben spoke with a certain confidence. 'Oh, Bishop Barclay has his hands full these days; he needs all the peace and quiet he can find, and prayers too. God gives him strength.' He made the sign of the cross. 'For it's hand to hand combat he's in with this new Minister for Health. There's those in the government that would see him felled, if they had their evil way and their evil bills passed.'

Attracta wasn't listening to a word; she was way ahead of him. Waiting for her turn to tell more to impress the priest with more of what she was privileged to hear.

'Oh, the Countess does have a leg to spare when the Bishop's comin'. An' he's always comin'. And he wants for nothin' when he comes to Ballsbridge. A woman is summoned to do the cooking on these high and holy occasions. And there's no ends to the entertainin'. Missus come and do, she calls the cook. It's all fancy French food. Oh la la to the likes of you and me. Irish stew wouldn't be up to his Holiness' palate. They put more food in the bins than the likes of us put on our plates. Wouldn't it make yer head all spin, Father? Brings big wigs from the government too.'

Father's Ben's eyebrows and ears picked up. Attracta took another sup of her tea. Teased out the tension. It wasn't often she had the floor.

'There was hell to pay last week between the Bishop and the Minister. Something about Mothers and Children. How they'd be lookin' for a licence to kill the old, the sick and the unborn soon. Oh yeh, you'd have thought I was too thick to pick up the consequences of that.'

She could have cut his curiosity with a blunt shears. 'I made a point of rememberin'. It all got very ugly. Like a pair of fightin' cocks up at the Red Barn, they were. They fought freely in front of me, Father ,because they thought I'd be to thick to understand.' She could see the question framed on the priest's lips so she answered before he asked.

He lifted the pot of tea and refreshed her cup. She had his undivided attention. Her ability to retain and reduce such incidents to street comedy level worried him. He felt uneasy.

'Not a word to a sinner of what I'm not supposed to be tellin' yeh now, Father.'

'Nor you either.' It was the least he could say.

'Sometimes I do think I was just born in the wrong mansion.'

In the vacuum that followed her pronouncement, Father Ben had an awful feeling. Dull thuds right the way through to his bones. What had he done pressing her on the Countess, pushing her, and her in such a quandary? Oh, the road to Hell is paved with good intentions. He should have read the warning signals when she was run out of Drumcondra. Attracta Rafferty was far from the little innocent. On the contrary, she was something of a loose cannon. And an irreverent one at that. He tried to think of something to say.

'But the biggest blessing of all, Father.' She leaned closer. 'I don't have to share me bed with another living soul. Even in the Bishop's Palace, I had to share a bed with a big fat country lump who snored and farted and stank the room out. But that was before I knew the differ, Father; never again.' She touched his sleeve, but her appeal was at odds with her eyes.

She couldn't explain to the priest or to anyone for that matter the simple blessing it was to be out from under the blankets to be able to see what yeh were puttin' on in the mornin'. No more blind man's buff.

Or the Godsend it was not to have to listen to yer father and mother pantin' like things possessed. To have to suffer yer ma's muffled sounds or smelling the secret fishy smells. The good riddance to sharing beds with brothers and mickeys that stood up like men's. Up and down. Disgusting details she'd never divulge to anybody, not even Father Ben. He wouldn't understand the seedier side of life in the Liberties.

The priest grasped the silent moment. 'Well, I certainly hope your employer appreciates you half as much as you appreciate her.'

She followed his big brown eyes to the clock. Two o'clock. She nearly died.

'God, I'm sorry Father, why didn't yeh stop me mouth runnin' away with yer day like that?'

'On the contrary, it's I that have detained you too long.' Father Ben's stomach was rumbling loudly. A sirloin roast was resting on the table. He thanked God for the cook's foresight as he eyed the sliced prime beef, the creamy horseradish. Attracta picked up her coat and made for the door.

'I'm off to see me Ma and back out to Mallards by four. Or Duck House as the Bishop calls it. It's our private joke.' The familiarity left him with his mouth hanging open.

Stepping out into blinding Dublin sunshine, Attracta hoped that someone she knew would see the style and the respectability.

***

Picking her way round the filthy puddles on the Money Mile, Attracta saw them a split second before they saw her. The bones in her head felt as if there were separating with jealousy. Concepta and the Butcher's Boy. Standing so close he could have seen what she had for his breakfast. Mortification and temper mixed in equal parts. Gazumped by a slapper.

Attracta marched straight up to him. With a short sharp punch, she hit him hard in the chest. 'Keep your fukkn' nose out of this, if yeh want to be wearin it tahmarrh.' She stopped Concepta in her tracks.

'As for you, mister, don't ever try to lie yer way out of this one. Don't!' she roared when he tried to open his mouth. 'Don't ever waste my time again. You're nothin but a fukkn' little mickey twister.' She didn't give him the satisfaction of a reply. Stung beyond belief, she put speed and distance between herself and them.

Risking life and limb, Concepta ran after her.

'Will yeh hold onto yer horses. Yer pickin' up the wrong end of the knife.' Concept's pleas were lost to the thunder in Attracta's ears.

'Where did yeh get the gear?' Concepta tried ingratiating herself. She'd never seen such finery on a shop dummy in Dublin, let alone on the Money Mile. Breathless, her question fell on deaf ears. Blind with frustration, she attempted one-upmanship.

'I hear yer scrubbin' floors in Ballsbridge.' Attracta smiled smarmily. She had no intention of engaging Concepta in conversation, let alone enlightening her with updates.

'Fuck you, Attracta Rafferty. What would the like of the Butcher's Boy want wit the stuck up likes of yeah? Yeh were always only a bitch, always scrabblin' above yer station. Well, the higher yeh rise, the further yeh fall. Why should I bother to tell yeh what he wanted. He'd be better off without yeh in anyway.' The hurt shot from Concepta's stomach and struck like a knife between Attracta's fast-disappearing shoulders

'I can earn more on the flat on me back in ten minutes, than you could earn on yer hands and knees in a week. I knew yeh when yeh thought knives and forks was jewellery. When yeh hadn't a pot to piss in. Yeh stinkin' little stockin' full of shite.'

Concepta turned on her heel. She could rot in hell before she'd tell Attracta he was tryin' to find her. He was better off without Attracta Rafferty.

***

Attracta stuck her nose in the air. It was three weeks since she had been home. Three weeks since she taken a swing at the Butcher's Boy. She wondered would there be any word of it or him at home. There wasn't much missed in Stretham Street. She stepped out the style for all to see. Would he ever look at her again? Maybe Concepta was right, she was only a stocking full of shite, but she wasn't a whore. When she gave herself to a man, it would be for love not money.

'Haven't yeh got the build for the swanky clothes?' Nel was strung out between pride and prejudice.

'Look at yer daughter, Jemser; not kickin' time in Ballsbridge and like a mirror image of the high and mighty. It'll be tuppence to talk to yeh soon,' she taunted her daughter as she baited her husband.

'It's only the clothes that's grand, Nel, only the clothes.' Jemser didn't even lift his head.

Attracta walked into the bedroom. Stuck her gloves down her sleeve and hung her hat and coat on the nail as she tried to compose herself.

'Pride goes before a fall.' Jemser was still spoutin' when she walked out. 'Dressin' up like the gentry. Yeh won't know whether yer shit nor shite. Falsifyin'. If anyone from the corporation sees yeh comin' in an out a here, they'll put up the rent. That's where all yer airs an' graces'll get us.'

Attracta eyed Jemser with contempt. Afternoon and he'd already had a skinful. He was drumming a spoon, pontificating, waiting for his Sunday lunch. The table was covered corner to corner with

84

remnants of an *Evening Herald*. Tattered, it served as a reminder of Nel's old ways and wants. There wasn't a sign of the tablecloth or cutlery that the Countess had installed in the house. Nel was shaking salt and pepper with great gusto into a simmering pot. Putting the final seasoning to Jemser's weekly treat. Attracta prayed it wasn't the usual. But whatever it was, she could rest assured Jemser would have the pick of it.

'Would yeh look at the sit of him, like a Lord's bastard.' Nel wiped a plate with the elbow of her cardigan and set it before him.

Attracta regarded the sheep's head. Jawbones clenched in manic rage, it sat in state on Jemser's plate. Watery offerings gushed from eye sockets, nose and ears. No matter where she looked, the apparition followed her.

'There's more meat on a butcher's apron.'

Jemser's head snapped up. He eyed his daughter hard, dared her to repeat her cheek.

As soon as she uttered the word 'butcher', her stomach lurched. She saw the look of hurt on his face again. She was sorry now she'd been so hard on him, so hurtful to Concepta. If she played her cards right, she just might catch him on his way home.

'Illustrious people does prefer it plain,' Jemser's eyes challenged her again as he mashed carrots and spuds with the back of a dessert spoon.

'There's no good sheep left in Ireland accordin' to Billy Atkins.' Nel was swinging and swaying like a sixteen-year-old around him.

The young fellah's message had left Nel's head as conveniently as it came into it. Twice he'd called, twice he'd reminded her not to forget to tell Attracta that he waited.

'While I think of it, there's a parcel of stuff there from Biddy Mulligan. Her hole must be open. It's not like Biddy – nothin' for nothin'' Nel was talking in half sentences and thoughts. She was too busy trying to do two things at once, to tell Attracta the clothes in the brown paper parcel were fit neither for bath, ball or pawn shop.

'Eyeballs or snout?' Jemser stuck his fork in the boiled eye and held it up for auction. A scrum of kids jumped for the opaque offering. Jemser popped the eye into his mouth and sucked like a connoisseur.

'Eyes or brains. Be god, I can never make up me mind which yeh makes best.' Nel ladled a little more pearly barley onto his plate.

'Take them out to Ballsbridge with yeh. They'd probably suit conditions out there better not here.' She was talking to Attracta about the parcel, but her eyes never left Jemser.

He was as thin as a rake. Her time in hospital had left him skin and bone. Fretting. Nel blamed the weight loss fairly and squarely on the Countess.

'Yer as light as a jockey, Jemser, eat up the starch; it'll put a bit of meat on dem bones.'

'Well, yeh know what they say about jockeys, Nel.' He had his arm around her waist.

'No, tell us, Jemser,' she led him on.

'Little jockeys does have big whips.' He slapped her hard on the backside.

The Raffertys guffawed as if it was all original. Attracta never felt further removed from the hilarity. They were all as common as muck.

'A feed fit for a king.' Jemser stood up from the table. The rest of the family piled into the remains.

He'd sleep on the settle for an hour, then it would be back to the pub. With my money lining his pocket, no doubt. Week after week, it was the same old stories. A born toucher full of slimy black words and sheep shite. Butterin' up Nel, an' her lappin' it up like a teenager.

Attracta didn't know which one of them was worse. She hadn't eaten a bite. She scraped the contents of her plate back into the pot. The sheep's head picked clean lay in greasy water.

An atrocious smell filled the kitchen. Every Rafferty's eye lit with delight.

'That's a new flavoured fart,' noses twitched the air. 'It must be Attracta's, Ma; it's too rich for us.'

Attracta looked disgusted.

'Don't be stupid, kids, they don't fart in Ballsbridge,' Nel sneered.

Attracta took her little brother and lay him across her knee. Distraction was better than derision. Not that that would work either. She was in a no win situation. The nappy was full to bursting. Her brother's backside was raw, his little mickey worse.

'You should think about having him circumcised,' Attracta's voice sounded above the screams. 'The Countess said boys should be done at birth.'

'Circumcised, circumcised! Me child's mickey shint like a Donnelly's sausage now, is it?' Nel Rafferty stiffened

'Jesus was circumcised.' Attracta inclined her head; not too low, not too high, just as the Countess instructed.

Shades of the Countess brought Nel up short. She squared up to her daughter. 'Well, they crucified Him as well, in case yer Countess didn't know; maybe she'd like us to get a hammer and nail him to a cross as well.' Her nostrils fought for fresh air. 'Yer a pot walloper in Ballsbridge, madam, not a medical student in Stephen's Green. Don't ever forget yer station.'

Attracta had started to irritate the hell out of her recently. She had a sister just like her over in England. Not kickin' time in the place and she was talkin' like the Queen. Attracta was a born ringer for her.

'Two months in Ballsbridge an' yer full of shite an' onions. Struttin' round here with a face on yeh like a smacked arse. Lookin' down yer nose at the likes of us. Isn't that right, Jemser?'

She looked over her shoulder. Jemser was stretched out on the sofa. It crossed her mind to tell Attracta that the Butcher's Boy was lookin' for her. But she was too annoyed with her to tell her anything that might pump her more full of her own importance. Go to blazes and wait. Wait like he could, wait and wait, cool both their passions.

Jemser wasn't listening to a word being said. He was dreaming about last night. He had been good all the time Nel was up in the Combe. The repentant sinner. He'd sworn his fidelity. Then last night, he'd wrestled with the weakness and the want that made his promise impossible. That neon smile spread in hot pink across her face. The breasts, wobbling pelts full of lust. The curves, perfect in leopard-skin lurex, yards of mortal sin. The towering platinum beehive that put Fatama head and shoulders above the rest. The teasing, the torment. The smell of her Cote l'Amour. The wall, the frenzy, the shuddering. He stiffened with pride.

'Jaysus,' he said and sneezed.

A snail trail of snot on his sleeve revolted Attracta. Consumptive spit. Little git.

'Wash your hands before you sit at the table,' she ordered the last relay of Raffertys. 'And where's the toothbrushes yis got for Christmas?' She grabbed her sister by the hair and yanked open her mouth.

'Get off the shaggin' stage, Attracta,' Nel Rafferty's voice rose like a fighting frigate. 'Where de yeh tink yeh are? And who de yeh tink yer talkin to? It's far from a toothbrush you were reared, and it doesn't seem to have done your mouth any harm.'

Attracta turned the colour of a big beetroot. She was raging to be called out in front of the young ones. She'd enough on her mind without Nel's caustic mix. There was no pleasing her mother these days. Even the extra few quid she shoved into Nel's bag every third week was taken for granted. Expected, no less. Nothing, not even a please, thanks or kiss me arse. Probably given to Jemser to get rid of him.

'Is there ere a chance of a lend of a loan of the mickey money?' Jemser was stirring. It was time for another a pint.

With a face on her that would stop a number ten bus, Attracta rammed Biddy's parcel under her arm. The door slammed behind her as she ran the length of the tenement hall. She hated her days off. Riddled with ridicule. And now she was too early to even catch a glimpse of the Butcher's Boy. It would be weeks before she'd set eyes on him again. Three whole weeks. He'd have forgotten all about her by then. Found something else to distract him.

Pulling the brim of her hat well down over her face, she shut out reality, the filthy streets, the long grey faces, the jeering and sneering. She sniffed the cuffs, the collar of her coat. Fags, stew, piss and shite.

Cursing every saturated stitch, she picked up her step: left behind the crowded rooms, the quarrelling, the misery, the sheer paralysis of it all. Blinkered by bitterness and blinded by the brim of her own hat, she very nearly missed him. Hunched over his pint in the Chinaman's, he jumped when she tapped him on the back.

The awkward air filled with relief.

'Now's it's me that's in the hurry,' Attracta smiled.

'I was goin' home anyway. I'll walk yeh to the stop.'

She had a leg to spare as she walked beside him.

'I'll miss me bus.'

'We've ten more minutes.' Her back was to the wall. He slid his tongue back into her mouth. Went about his pleasure with a terrible ease. A shiver ran up her. He didn't take his hand off her nipple as he backed her back up against the hot bakery wall. She didn't resist. He rubbed himself against her up and down her thigh. Deep inside her, something quickened. Useless to resist, she rode the waves. She didn't know whether she was wet with sweat or the heat off the wall when she got on the bus.

Women are whores all the same; the Butcher's Boy slowly tapped his empty glass. She's better down than an acre of hay that one. Back in the Chinaman's, his thoughts pleased him nearly as much as the creamy fresh pint.

88

***

A contrariness of colours filled the frame of the door. A vivid red dress, hideous lipstick and an alarming slick of green eye shadow, cheeks painted like a parody of the past, sent a disturbing message to the Bishop.

'I sincerely hope I'm not intruding?' Barclay tried not to look too closely.

The first Sunday day in months he'd turned up unannounced, and the Countess was committed to a tiresome four. She seethed.

'On the contrary. Is there anything you need before I go?' Her words were saying one thing, her eyes another.

He studied her face. Bloated from excess. Should he tell her that her absences were eminently occupiable?

She'd telephoned at least six people. She had told him that not one of them was willing to oblige her. Frustration growing out of her like her bad perm as she'd tried to impart this useless sentiment to Barclay.

Her dilly-dallying was irritating him.

'I'm just off, Your Grace.' She viewed Barclay over the top of her tortoiseshell glasses. 'Miss Rafferty should be back by four.'

'I hope to be long gone by four,' he lied easily.

She gathered up her car keys and her gloves and left the house more than a little disgruntled.

Barclay shook his head. Strange how he had chosen to return to this particular place after all that went before. He settled himself in the cosy upstairs study. Where else would he find such peace, such creature comforts? Where else would he find a tonic like Attracta?

But today was about survival. He had more on his mind than the licentious Miss Rafferty. He'd travelled out to Ballsbridge today to formulate a strategy, to bridge the dangerous gap that was developing between him and Muriel Grey. The nuisance letters, the attempted telephone call. The near-calamity in Leixlip last week when he'd seen her from the corner of his eye. He felt the mounting panic. He needed to redefine the boundaries. He needed to prevent disaster.

The first letter was dangerous, wholly irresponsible. The last brazen, blatant. He thanked God he had opened his post himself on both occasions. That little madam was turning into trouble. He had to put a stop to her gallop. He did what he always did when he was at war with himself or others. He put his anger down on paper before he attempted polite address. The exercise never failed him.

He outlined his concerns in bold sharp strokes. Committing his thoughts quickly to paper, the rough draft brought with it, along with the release, the benefit of clarification. Yes, her position is frustrating. He sought reason. But domestic invitations bring their own complications. She makes my position impossible. We made our beds. Muriel more than me. Now we must lie in them. I did what I did to salvage the situation. Fonsie did what he did to feather his bare nest. Now we must all live with the consequences. He rubbed the ink dry with a tight fist and rested his pen on the telling tale.

Maybe I could take a drive out to Leixlip, assess the situation on the spot.

Struggling with the frailty that had made this thought futile, Barclay searched through a packed diary. It was an empty gesture. He had no intentions of putting his holy head in the lion's mouth. Less of forfeiting one of his prized racing days in the Park. In the final analysis, he decided on compromise. He picked back up his pen, scribbled a quick note. Upbeat, non-specific, it bore little resemblance to the harshness of the original draft.

He was due out in Maynooth before Easter. He would do his utmost to call and see Fonsie, baby Jack and, of course, the woman of the house herself. It was a holding tactic, but it should keep the vixen from his door. He pressed the wet ink gently on the sheet of blotting paper. Folding the finished letter, he slid it into a white envelope. Placing it securely in the side panel of his briefcase, he took out another sheaf of notes.

A matter of national consequences needed urgent attention. The need for inspiration and discernment was paramount. He wouldn't, he shouldn't, be distracted by domestic irritations.

With boundless capacity for self-deception, he picked back up his pen and addressed the latest proposal of the Joint Episcopal and Cabinet Committee. The proposal to establish a new National Health Council needed urgent attention.

Congregations needed to understand the bounded duty of Catholics to obey their bishops. The Catholic Church needed to reinforce the scope and authority given it in the Irish constitution. To irradiate once and for all any confusion caused in minds by the new Minister for Health between Church and State. To impress upon the faithful the need to beware of false gods, and their evil messengers; to exterminate any evil influence or deviation from the proven path of the Church. To punch the Minister for Health's contorted immoral

Bill, with its cowboy constitution, its maverick morals for Irish mothers and their infants, once and for all into its proper place. Oblivion.

Barclay was as good on paper as he was in the pulpit. He numbered his pages and banded them together. But his thoughts were tailing off. The fight running out of him was slowly being replaced by a luxurious sensation in his loins. He put his pen down and looked at the gold fob watch Muriel had given him for Christmas. He had wondered about bringing it to Weir's; they were very accommodating. It would have made a tidy little return, nice little wager on a horse. He snapped the watch shut, stood up, stretched himself and opened the study window. *Miss Rafferty will be back by four.* He felt the stirring in his loins.

***

Sunday, bloody Sunday. She slid in through the kitchen door. Nothing but the birds and the breeze were stirring in Ballsbridge. She'd seen the Countess on the road as she walked home. Off to her bridge. She was as bad for the cards as Jemser was for the booze. Not as much as a nod or a wave; she never showed her any respect any more.

Attracta opened her wardrobe and hung her coat and hat back up. The smell of Stretham Street hit her nose. Would she ever be rid of the stench? She'd hang that coat out, give it a bit of a freshening up when she'd had a cup of tea. Let a benign Ballsbridge breeze blow the smell away.

It was one of those days. When nothing satisfies. When Attracta knew that the rest of the world and the Butcher's Boy was out there having great fun and her foot was stuck to the floor. Biddy's parcel was on the kitchen table; she'd pass a bit of boring time with the contents later. She stared out the kitchen window. Stretham Street, for all its faults and frustrations, was suddenly alive. Even on a Sunday, there'd be something stirring.

The house was as silent as the grave. Not even the bonus of the bold Bishop to distract her. A sly smile crossed her face. He was a flirt. And a tease. The Countess was always skinnin' his heels. On the prowl sniffing and scowling an' still she missed it all. The winks, the sly smiles, the quick brushes and touches when they passed in the hall. A game of chance made all the more exciting by the vigilant Countess.

She'd never realised that inside a Bishop there was blood and guts roaming around. And hands. He wasn't the Butcher's Boy. Hadn't the power to pull at her like that boy had. But his flirting was a bonus when she was bored. She could have done with a bit of diversion today; it would be another ten days before she saw himself. And he better be there this time. Something deep inside her told her he would.

The afternoon was slower than usual. Skull boring Sundays. She undid Biddy's parcel and looked at it through new eyes. Maybe there was something she could unpick and stitch. Where did Biddy think she'd be goin' in the stockin's and the purple garters. Let alone the feckin' dresses.

She pulled out the first dress, tried it on and watched it unfold light as a feather around her. Twirling and turning like a demented doll, she swung round in a swirl of chiffon. Soft, flowing clothes. She stroked the other dress. 'A year's wages in the Liberties,' she said out loud. She loved the cut, the look, the feel, of expensive clothes. The power they had to transport to another world. Champagne tastes and lemonade pockets.

She threw her head in the air and took herself to a grander place. Shimmyin' round the room, the luxury of silk petticoats close to her skin. Colours reflecting off her face brightened her humour. Rich reds and blues. No mean measure of dyes here.

'Fine feathers make a fine bird. And they feel feckin' fabulous as well,' she screeched with delight. 'Sure, where would you be going with no bell on me bike, Attracta? Yeh never know, I might have found meself a secret admirer.'

Like a child with a dressing up box, she talked and answered herself as she dressed up. The second dress was pulled out of the parcel; it clung like scales to a fish. Full of the strange sight of herself in the wardrobe mirror, she picked up the stockings, the purple satin garters. Ran the silk across her top lip.

Filled with new vigour, she rooted, looted, the Countess' trunk. The stockings went perfectly with the shoes that she'd found at the bottom. With the toes stuffed with newspaper, they fitted now. Any shoe from a four to a seven she could make fit her foot. She slid the stockings up to the top of her leg and finished off the look with the satin garters. The slip that went under the dress was as good as the dress itself.

A strange feeling came stealing over her. It wouldn't be long before the Butcher's Boy was back for more. She could feel it in her waters. She just might wear the slinky slip. If the humour was on her, she might even let him have a feel. But only after he begged. She swung round again. And he'd be a long time beggin'. Either way, she'd be dressed in the best if the occasion presented itself. She was in high spirits. Full of herself, full of possibilities, full of life.

Sweating from all the excitement and exertion, she set a kettle of water on to boil. Stripped to her knickers and stockings, she filled a basin to the brim with hot water and washed under her arms, under her legs, back, belly and sides. She giggled at the good of her boldness as she nipped out to the clothesline with her coat. It would be a cold day in hell before she'd been seen runnin' around Stretham Street in stockin's and garters or her nip.

Barclay watched from the window: felt the vice grip: the deep-seated need for routine fornication. The release, the rush, as the dirty words spilt out of his pen and across the page.

Reaching, bending, stretching, lost in a world of dreams and reality, Attracta imagined herself strolling through Stephen's Green as she hung out the stale clothes.

The little black dress, slick as ell shin. High enough to tease, low enough to hide her dignity. Lacy garters, silk stockings sliding into soft leather shoes. A straw hat, sunglasses, her kid gloves. Drinking coffee poured from a tall silver pot in the Russell hotel, or the Hibernian or the Shelbourne. All the auld ones around trembling with jealousy. She'd passed the steps of all three hotels every day on her way to school. Unfettered by the chill in the evening air or reality. In her mind's eye, Attracta was posing in all three of them.

The daydream heightened the daring. She ran her hand up her leg; the smooth material felt sensuous. The finery made her feel frivolous; her nakedness, different, desirable. Her nipples were standing up like Mother Mary Patrick's silver thimble. She rolled the firm flesh between her finger and her thumb. They'd been more than a mouthful for the Butcher's Boy.

She felt a heat deep between her legs. The Butcher's Boy rubbing himself up and down on her thigh. A shiver deep inside her shocked her. Goin' at it like a pump action shotgun, her head batterin' out the beat again the baker's wall, makin' her groan like an alley cat. She could feel the swelling inside her knickers. Getting her all hot and bothered again.

Transfixed, he couldn't take his eyes off her. The sight of Attracta in stockings and garters introduced a whole new set of possibilities into the young maid's personality. Sex, vulnerability, virginity. His mind skittered for sanity sanctuary. But he was caught.

Stuck fast in his erotic web, his fevered pen couldn't keep up with his fantasies: *hard pink nipples invade his conscience. Ripe, firm white breasts waiting to be squeezed, her belly as flat as an altar boy's, thighs that could hold tight to a man long before and after the dirty deed was done. She's flaunting herself, tantalising me, facing me front on.*

His temples throbbed. Try as he might, he couldn't ignore these voyeuristic feelings, the surge of blood, the rogue member rising, bulging, filling the front of his drawers. Lewd thoughts slithered like a serpent around his head. *Tight as a drum I bet. She knows I'm watching; she's begging for it.*

He wrote and wrote. Eyes startling, palms sweating, he unbuttoned his trouser fronts. A flush rose in his cheeks. *A woman's unclear loins made not in God's image and likeness, but of man's flesh and desires; this paradox, this carnival of sexuality, that leads us by the horn to the serpent's prey.* She was coming down the hall. Like a dance stopped in mid air, something truncated, snapped off. He pushed his sodden handkerchief deep in his pocket.

'Is there anybody here?' Attracta pulled her dress quickly over her head.

Squirming with a residual shame, he put his pen down, quickly turned over his obscene notes…

A hostage.

He couldn't see himself as Attracta saw him.

'Are you feeling all right there, Bishop? I heard a chair rockin' an' creekin', it put the heart crossways on me, I don't mind tellin' yeh. I thought I'd the place to meself.' Attracta wondered if he looked as odd or as green as her eyes were telling her, or had she been too long out in the garden light?

The cocktail coursing through his loins made him look gawky. He looked vacantly back at her.

She had to ask him twice.

'Oh, nothing that a strong pot of tea won't fix. Let it brew.' His voice had a strange, savage note in it.

There was something similar in the Bishop and the Butcher's Boy. Maybe there's a bit of the Bull in both of them. Aware that he hadn't taken his eyes off her, she sashayed out of the study.

Alone, he tried to comprehend this latest round of infatuation. The ball-breaking desire, the senseless, useless torture. He recognised the basic instinct. Ranked it as low as his other sins. His libido was dangerously out of his control around her. Why did he expose himself to occasions of sin? He tried to relegate blame, to rationalise a vocation where he'd staked his liberty and lost his freedom.

But even as he strove to rationalise, he foresaw the inevitable. It was futile, he had never seen such perfection. She had the sexiest body. He almost imploded with desire again. Pregnant and swollen, Muriel's spoiled body bobbed before his eyes. How could any man contemplate such misshapen offerings after such a feast? Barclay shuddered, left that memory out in Leixlip where it belonged.

She was back laden with tea and biscuits before he had time to compose himself.

'Yeh could trot a mouse with hobnailed boots across this tea.' Attracta set the tray on his desk. 'I'll close this window. It's getting a bit chilly now, it was glorious earlier.' He has a bird's eye view of me little sunspot from here. Excitement saturated her again. Had he seen her in the nip?

She caught hold of the sash window and brought it down with a bang. A trick wind lifted his papers and sent them flying to the four corners of the room. Scrabbling on all fours, they managed to assemble the unruly bundle.

'Well, I never thought I'd see the day when the Bishop of Dublin would be on his knees before me.' They were laughing like dirty drains.

In the delirium of the moment, neither of them noticed the two pieces of paper – his callous dismissal of Muriel, his course observations of Attracta – gliding gracefully underneath Countess' ancient bookcase.

Nine

Every passing month, Barclay's silence grew louder. And still she waited. Waited, desperate for the next lie, the bigger lie. She wished some of the harmony that Brigit had brought about in the house could find its way into her heart. Amongst her crosses, Muriel counted Brigit Murphy as a blessing. Rituals and routines that once only irritated brought with them now a certain security.

Although there was still no accounting for washdays. Brigit was taking a seasoned advantage of spring. Muriel looked around. Nine thirty in the morning and the scullery floor was littered with sheets, pillowcases, bedspreads. The range groaning under the strain of boiling buckets. Coarse grey underblankets, buffers between sheets and mattress were taking up two chairs. A wringer, its rubber rollers wrapped in sort cotton cloths to protect them from perishing, had been dragged in from an outhouse and was standing ceremoniously in the middle of the kitchen floor. She must have been up at cockcrow to assemble this production.

Muriel stood the breakfast dishes into the bowl and began filling it with boiling water from the kettle.

'I'll wash the blankets and wring them.' Brigit had been adamant that the weight would swing Muriel's womb out of kilter. The threat had done the trick.

'How on earth will we shift the volume?', Muriel had asked quite genuinely.

'What? Two strappin' girls like us, and winds out there that would sail the Queen Mary. Yeh'll be surprised how far we'll have got on by midday. And we'll reward ourselves well.' Her wink was as good as her word. She wondered what the twinkle in Brigit's eye promised.

'We'll go like the hammers of hell. Get the big stuff as dry as we can and pack it off the Nuns for airing, ironing. The small stuff we can handle ourselves.'

Buckets of water were filling quicker than the new Leixlip Dam. Brigit was in her preferred element. Nappies, tiny baby gowns, all hand-embroidered, were appearing from the back of the hot press. All in the name of spring-cleaning. 'It might be a bit previous and presumptuous,' Brigit agreed with Muriel, 'but you could never be too ready for babies.'

In Dublin, even the poorest families sent out some of their weekly wash. Muriel had tried to reason with her. 'Sure, don't I see the same racket round here.' Her protest was as loud as her disdain. She wouldn't have her clothes lumped or likened with the hoi polloi's. 'Oh no, begods'– she was nothing if she wasn't particular about who's backside she shared a boiling pot with.

'If the man on the moon came down to see, he'd know it was Monday by me, me, me.'

Muriel could hear Brigit singing the nonsense ditty as she sorted out the washing. 'It's Friday, Brigit.' Her belly bounced as she laughed; the baby inside her smiled.

'Well, we treat it as Monday seen as no Monday for a month has presented us with washin' never mind dryin' weather. We'll wash what we have to and give some of our summer requirements a nice little freshen up into the bargain.' Spring-cleaning.

Muriel couldn't beat her so she joined her. She lifted the baby clothes, washed them while the water was fresh. Plunging her arms elbow-deep into the scalding water, she felt the soapy flannelette gowns slip and slide between her fingers. She wondered as the tiny garments trembled on corrugated washboard whether Brigit was being cautious or cute.

The belly was rising, her breasts and backside had both changed shape, but to a casual observer it would have been impossible to put a date to her dilemma. Brigit, and strangely Fonsie, had never asked when the baby was due. She squeezed the baby clothes and gently placed them in a bucket of fresh rainwater. Neither, for that matter, had she volunteered the information. Only Barclay knew that the baby was due in July. But for all he knew, he might as well know nothing.

Muriel pulled a sheet from another of Brigit's steeping buckets and, pounding it with raw vigour, shook off a malaise that all too often took her prisoner for the day.

'I'm tellin' yeh, if I could patent yeh, I could sell yeh for a fortune.' Brigit was admiring Muriel's thoroughness as she whacked through a mountain of washing. For a wiry woman' she had great strength. 'Yer goin' like a thrashin' machine. Keep up the good work and we'll take advantage of the weather.'

It was Brigit who had single-handedly brought about the change in the house. As Muriel and Fonsie were convinced in their own separate minds that one was to blame for the other's misery, it had become impossible for Brigit to live under the same roof as them. If the devil himself had thrown a cordon of misery over this house, he

97

couldn't have done a better job. Brigit was so drained from births, deaths, marriages, misery, all under the one roof, that, in desperation, she'd taken the bull by the horns. Her attack had caught them both completely off the hop.

'We've all walked around like the living dead for long enough. All of us is nursin' our own private grievances.' She'd had to pause to catch her breath. Muriel was surprised to hear her putting herself in the quandary.

'The pair of you can do what you like, but I won't be draggin' the remains of the past into any more of the New Year. There's a season for everything. A time to change. And lest we forget it, there's a child to nurture.' She didn't say which child she was talking about. But they knew what she meant.

'So what I propose is this. I'll see spring in and out. If there isn't a big change in the atmosphere, I'll pack me bags and take meself off to the peace and quiet a body deserves at my time of life.'

Dressed in her Sunday best she'd served her ultimatum with the breakfast.

The sight of Brigit in her going-away clothes had sent Fonsie back to a terrified place. For shock value alone, it was hard to better. And for curative properties it lacked nothing at all. Fonsie was flummoxed, Muriel terrorised. The thought of life under the one roof without Brigit put the heart crossways on both of them.

The immediate change in the household was marked. Muriel was relieved. As she started pulling her weight around the house, Brigit's load and humour had lightened. And as the tensions had eased, so had the regimes. Each in turn brought their own benefits, never more noticeably than when Fonsie was away. There were times when Muriel heard herself laughing out loud.

Now and then, Brigit took a day off and went into Dublin to see her sister. To be her own master for a day was a wonderful byproduct of the vacancy. To be left on her own with the small child was a bonus. It gave them the time and the space to get to know one another. Brigit's absences were surpassed only by her homecomings. She couldn't imagine her day without Brigit or Jack.

Muriel looked down at her feet and saw Jack beside her. *No* was his new word, and he was getting great mileage from short sentences.

'It's like the Western Front in here.' She took Jack in her arms and brought him out to Brigit. 'I'm afraid of him getting near the fire when my back's turned.'

She surveyed the scene. The battle of the buckets. She had buckets for everything. Buckets for pissy nappies, buckets for shitty nappies, buckets for boiling nappies on her big black range. Buckets of clear water for rinsing, and buckets of rainwater for softening. They were all vital to the finished product. Sure, the secret of washing is in the rinsing; she had a line of buckets along the scullery wall that would have bamboozled a seasoned washerwoman.

Muriel heard the postman laying his bike against the wall. She was out the door like a shot from a poacher's gun.

Brigit hinged at the waist to see what was holding up production. She could hear Poor Willie's nerves, he was yapping and stuttering. Brigit could have told her herself that brown envelopes meant business matters not personal matters. But she'd only be wasting her breath. She put no store on the same letters. They only ever spelt out bad news. Or worse, trouble.

But whatever news Muriel was waiting for, it had to be important for there was always a determination about her when she took the post from poor Willie's hand.

Muriel was examining the morning post, passing it without as much as a bye or leave to Fonsie. She had only posted the letter on Wednesday. It would be foolish to expect an answer so soon. Still, a letter of his might have crossed hers in the post.

Willie couldn't bear to look her in the eye. Couldn't bear her disappointment. Whatever she was holdin' out for morning after morning. He'd told Brigit so himself.

Brigit wondered if it was her mother she was waiting for a letter from. She'd said something guarded once, but that was the one and only time she'd ever mentioned her mother. Oh, there was a story there too, to be sure. But it was none of Brigit's business.

She picked Muriel's nightgown out from a pile of dirty washing. Felt the milk hard and dry on the front. Leakin' already. And sure, why not? She watched the soft material settle in one of her stepping buckets. Time's pressing on and so is the child in her belly.

Brigit burst a giant air bubble with her pouncing stick. Starting from December, she counted the months one by one as she stirred up her dirty laundry. It could be here by September, barring a slip on the wrong side of the blanket. The thought wasn't new, and neither was the embarrassment that always followed. Mr Fonsie on the wrong side of the blanket? Brigit blushed.

Muriel rubbed the ache in the small of her back as she stooped to pull a load of washing from a bucket. The hard ball of baby in her belly cramped her movements now. Six months in the making, sure

99

there's no denying you now. Muriel put her hand to her stomach. Nothing had prepared her for the activity that was going on daily inside her. She longed for Barclay's hands to feel what she was feeling. In stark contrast to her own confidence, the child inside her grew stronger by the day.

He'd have received her letter by now. She leaned on the washboard. Welcomed the chance to straighten her spine. He can't but reply. It was a simple request to have afternoon tea. Tea with herself and Fonsie. Who could comment?

It was nearly four months since she'd written before. God knows, she couldn't be accused of pestering him. On the contrary. She had been the soul of discretion. Patience. Anyone else in her position might have turned up on his doorstep. Though God knows, there had been dark hours when she'd been tempted.

What if he had misread her long silence? She manufactured the dilemma. What if he was feeling as deserted and frustrated as her? She flushed with new hope. It can't have been easy for him either. She chastised herself for not thinking of him, for not being more considerate, for being so self-absorbed.

God how she missed his physical presence. Their trips out to Blessington. Book-keeping business, he'd validated the excursion. He'd marched her boldly into the bank and introduced her as his book-keeper. *The occasion might present itself when you could be asked to make this journey on your own.* He'd announced her as a trusted member of his staff. Generating an energy and power that held the manager and bank staff alike in awe.

He'd insisted that the manager take her personally to a strong room and show her the secure box where he kept sensitive documents. She loved the power, the secrets. The Vatican boxes full of gold coins hidden in a vault in Blessington.

Suspended high above reality, when believing themselves invisible, they made love. Rare days. In the euphoric mountain air, cradled in the soft heather beds. Looking down on a dimmed Dublin far, far below their secret hiding place, Barclay had started a fire in her he couldn't put out. Caution thrown to warm winds. Rare and wonderful. Her sigh was audible.

'If dem buckets are empty, I have another and another soakin' in here.' Brigit wasn't too impressed with the stop-and-go capers in the kitchen.

Muriel hauled herself back to reality. She'd swap her life with Brigit Murphy in the morning, exchange all the anxiety and secrecy for the simplicity and peace. She wanted to tell Brigit that her breasts were spilling milk, that the baby was somersaulting inside of her. That the fluttering was magical, and made her life worth living. That she was terrified of giving birth. That she didn't know which hole the baby would come out. Couldn't begin to imagine how anything so big could come out anything so little. But countrywomen were cute when it came to matters maternal. Telling about the antics and incidents would only be telling on herself.

She'd only told her about the baby when she'd found her wandering in the small hours of the night. New life in the house will be as welcome as the flowers in May. That was all Brigit said. She hadn't asked any awkward questions. Hadn't asked her when the baby was due. And she was relived. Time enough to discuss due dates and deliveries.

She was going to give birth; it was as simple as that now. It didn't matter when or where she did it, only that she did it with the minimum of fuss and maximum of discretion. The doctor whom Barclay had sent her to had mentioned a particularly good nursing home out in Bray. It was far enough away to keep their secret safe. And near enough for Barclay to visit.

Trust no one with your business. Always take your private affairs out of your own town. Not even the local doctor. We're all only human, at the end of the day. She'd taken her vow under the seal of confession. Promised him as secret and sacred as the security box. She'd never break the seal, and he knew it.

But she'd have to ask some one about the mechanics of giving birth. Her maidenhead had still been intact when the doctor had examined her. She wasn't as surprised as him. They'd never gone the whole way. Barclay had been careful. He'd always used his handkerchief. She couldn't believe her own ears when the doctor had explained how the pregnancy could occur. She'd wanted to look at the diagram, but the embarrassment, stupidity and terror combined to tongue-tie her.

So here she was, she hadn't known how it got in, and now she didn't know how it would get out. But there were books – and Brigit. It couldn't be too difficult. Women had given birth on the side of the road and survived.

Washing waiting to be hung out piled high on the draining board. Muriel looked at her work. She wouldn't have been capable a month ago. The sickness and sadness all combined to incapacitate her. But she wasn't sick or as tired any more. Brigit had been right about the walks and the ginger.

Nightmares are a symptom of yer condition, Brigit had told her the night she'd found her wandering. She'd chosen to believe her. The alternative, the dream, that there was another woman, was too horrific to contemplate.

Brigit had advised a good walk before bedtime. And a cup of warm milk with a shake of ginger in it to stop the nightmares. It will set yeh right for the night. They got the ginger powder from Kathleen Komiskey the next morning. There's very little this combustion won't shift. Brigit had warned her in the same breath not to be drinking so much. The child that gets used to a steady supply will be on the titty day and night. Muriel had taken that thought back up to bed and slept that night despite the bovine imagery.

She'd let Brigit know more about her feeding arrangements nearer her time. There appeared to be no end to this washing. Brigit's magnificent obsession, Muriel sighed as she stuck her hands back into the suds. She'd wanted to crawl into Brigit's bed that night, lie in her big motherly arms and tell her the sorry tale. Wanted Brigit to tell her that the woman who stalked her dreams, unsettled her mornings, was a figment of her imagination. But she was trapped between her nightmares and her promises.

The silence in the kitchen was getting harder on Brigit's ears. But she held her peace as Muriel daydreamed. Little white mice ran around and round pregnant women's heads; they were always away with it, away with the fairies. She was glad of any help – glad Muriel had the energy to help with the spring-clean.

She had done as Brigit had bid her and started stepping it out. Stepping it out instead of kneeling on a cold floor saying rosaries she didn't believe in. Still, she wondered at the contradiction, for as often as not it was in the chapel that she found herself. Praying to remember him, praying to forget. Never sure which she prayed for more.

In spite of herself, she built up stamina. Before long, she was covering two and three miles before bedtime. And she had found to her delight that not alone did her reasoning improve, but sleep, blessed sleep, had started to come in earnest. And rested and reasoned, her pregnancy and burden had become easier to bear.

'I'm beginning to think that there are lightning strikes accruing in the kitchen.' Brigit's shout made her jump. She slid a pillowcase on to her washboard and made the rapping sounds that kept Brigit's heart content. The water in the sink was tepid. She must have been daydreaming for some time.

'I need a top up.' She folded a dishcloth in four and lifted a kettle of boiling water off the hob.

'I thought I needed to go back to the hiring fare and find meself another washerwoman.' Brigit's voice was light.

Muriel blew a bubble off the palm of her hand and watched as a thin breeze took it in Jack's direction. He had just begun to make a few wobbly walks between tables and chairs. They both saw the triply steps as his hands reached for the glistening bubble.

'I hope his Mother in heaven above can see.' Brigit turned her head from the wonder. She didn't want Muriel to see her tears. They were getting on well together, but they didn't know one another that well yet. 'Summer snakin' up on us an' we've hardly winter cleared out.' She turned the sentiment round more to her liking.

They were all becoming more comfortable in each other's company. Each in their own separate way had fashioned boundaries the other respected.

Fonsie's trips into Dublin, a regular Friday night feature by now, were having a marked improvement on his disposition.

But not his desires.

Believing she could outmanoeuvre him Muriel had begun to stay up later and later. But last night, double-exhausted from walking and waiting, he'd caught her trying to steal into bed. Muriel's shoulders lifted and stiffened. Revulsion – stark, automatic – ran riot through her body. Nothing was foolproof.

'I hope you're not catching a cold.' Brigit saw the shiver as she carried a bucket past.

'I think I saw an earwig.' A lame excuse. 'Let me help you hang some of these blankets out.' Muriel grasped the opportunity to distract herself with both hands.

'Not in your condition. Besides, I have me own ways. There might be confusion if yeh got me buckets in the wrong order. Isn't that right son?,' Brigit chittered away to the little soul slipstreaming her soapy moves.

'I'll get this lot out, start bringing in what's already dry.' Muriel welcomed the breath of fresh air. The sight of the line full of whites, flapping like sails in a crosswind, made Muriel's heart swell. She buried her face in the spotless clean sheets, the smells, the sounds, spiriting her back to her grandmother's knee. To the songs and singing as she sowed bleached flour sacks and made soft white sheets.

'Days made up of other days.' Muriel sat two smoothing irons on the fire when she came back, and let them heat up while they fed themselves and the child.

They worked in tandem, sharing their pleasures and dividing their chores. Ironing fiddly pillowcases or bone-dry Irish linen tablecloths that hadn't seen daylight since they were banished to the farthest regions of Brigit's hot press, was more of a pleasure than a problem to Muriel. She took her time, was careful to run the hot iron into all the nooks and crannies. Brigit's slam-dunk couldn't compare. 'I'd rather eat it than I'd iron it,' Brigit would glow with satisfaction.

And whilst washing Fonsie's socks, shirts, underpants or vests was a bridge far too intimate for Muriel, Brigit did it without question. Muriel preferred to leave that particular personal touch to Brigit.

'We could have done twice the washing with half the amount of water and accrutramonds.' Dull thudding irons accompanying the small talk.

'We very well might, but would they be half as clean?' Brigit wasn't about to abandon the habits of a lifetime.

'How do the other women in the village manage without running water just outside their door?'

'Some wouldn't be as fussy,' Brigit sniffed indignantly. 'Yeh could tell the clean ones and the dirty ones from the time they were at school.' She sat the iron back down on the fire and waited for the plate to heat up to piping hot. She didn't like cool irons. They were for fussy ironers, not for women like herself.

'Women like my mother, God rest her soul, hauled buckets full to the brim the length and breadth of Leixlip twice and sometimes three times a day. Depending on how particular they were a course. Splishin' and sploshin', buckets bangin' at their anklebones. Fillin' their shoes in fair weather and foul.' Brigit spat on the plate of the smoothing iron and waited for the hiss that would tell her it was hot enough to continue.

'Oh, roll on the new Minister for Health and his schemes to pump fresh water into every house in the land.' Brigit's voice was proud. 'Doctor Noel Brown: now there's a man who understands a women's needs.' It was an afterthought, but the statement was none the less passionate for it.

'The thorn in the government's side?,' Muriel made mischief and diversion.

'Shower of blackguards, need a rose bush stuck up their holes.' Brigit resorted to the vulgar vernacular out of pure frustration. 'It might make them get up off their arses and start listening to the women of Ireland instead of themselves. What would men know about rearin' children? Or bearin' them by the dozen? Vatican roulette, how are yeh?'

Muriel was as taken aback by Brigit's passion as she was by her own ignorance. She wondered if Vatican roulette was coitus interruptus. But embarrassment wouldn't let her ask. She winked at Jack, rested and energetic from his nap, dying for someone to play with him. But there was still ironing to be done.

Brigit watched him scramble for a foothold in Muriel's skirt. Twasn't a bond so much as a burgeoning she was witnessing. In all the sadness of the past few months, it was a sight that warmed the cockles of Brigit heart. The sight and the sounds doubled her pleasure.

'How does a trip to the pictures the marrah afternoon grab yeh? The Saturday matinee. Charlie Doran has Billy the Kid in the box, he told me so his self. I love cowboys and Indians.' Brigit sounded childlike. 'It'll reward us well for all the hard work tehday.'

The invitation took Muriel completely by surprise. Brigit had never stepped out in public with her before. 'What about Jack?'

'Under me oxter as always. And if he gets restless, sure Charlie has no objection to his chariot parked up at the back of the picture house. He's the only man that ever took Brigit Murphy to the picture house in Leixlip. Isn't that right, son?' She sluiced a bucket of silky bubbles between Jack's tiny toes.

'An' Omo bright he'll be for the occasion.' Brigit took the soapy infant in her arms and dunked his legs and bum into a bucket of soft warm rainwater.

'The only man?,' Muriel teased a story out of Brigit as she picked up the child.

'There was someone once. The ghost of a hope of a plain golden band.' Brigit's left thumb scratched the empty ring finger. 'He used to deliver the bread to the shop next door here. He had a notion of me, yeh might say.

'It could have come to somethin' until me sister started makin' mischief. Sayin' she knew the family well, every seed, breed and head of them. That they were nothing but a shower of tinkers from Maynooth. That they'd tell lies to a band playin' and steal the cross off an ass' back while they were at it.' Brigit's dander was up.

'And she kept it up 'til me ardor cooled down and he found himself some other eejit.' She hadn't stopped once for breath.

Muriel was sorry she'd been so cavalier; she'd hit a very sore spot in the heart.

Brigit stared hard out the window. It was a long time since she'd thought about that particular episode and her sister.

'Sure, maybe I don't need a man in me life the way other women need them.' Brigit took back up where she left off. 'Besides, am I not happy in me own skin? I wouldn't want a man getting' under it.'

Sex, Brigit recalled silently, was a disgusting business that married women had to endure and single women would be well advised to steer clear of. 'Still, that sister of mine made bloody sure that she got herself a husband.'

Brigit's ironing rhythm got completely out of sync, her frustrations taking her to a new level. She made sure she wasn't the one left at home lookin' after two auld parents, Brigit's thoughts ran on and on. Maggie Murphy and her manipulations.

'And she isn't beyond slander either.' Brigit spat on the plate of the smoothing iron.

Muriel was sitting at the table feeding left-over stew to her and Jack. It was five o'clock and she was weary and hungry again.

Brigit was miles away. But not one to let her thoughts hijack her for too long, she talked over them.

'A maiden aunt of mine married a man of sixty-seven when she was in her eighties. She might have been past her labour, but she wasn't past her prime. Not if the smile on his face was any measure of the marriage.' Muriel laughed at the boldness of the voice, the swing of Brigit's shoulders.

'Yeh know what, they say there's no auld shoe out there that an auld sock won't fit. So yeh never can tell. And I've a few years left in me yet.'

You could have picked sunflowers from her eyes, she laughed so loud and long.

***

They were the first in the queue on Saturday afternoon. Overdressed, over-early and very overexposed. With a box of sweets under one arm and Jack under the other, Muriel was sticking out like a sore thumb as she waited for Brigit to come with the pram. Stick a big coat on yeh and cover up yer business. She'd let Brigit talk her into a topcoat that was more suited to the depths of winter than mild spring.

The queue was getting longer, sneaking its way round the corner and backing up the Captains Hill. Women with children and shopping bags at their feet queued after a fashion. Children playing with stones in a small huddle near their mothers.

Those in the village with only a moving account of Muriel now had a glorious opportunity to view her in still splendour. A synchronised snigger ran through the heads of the crowd, their coarse practical judgment evident, she believed. Brigit nodded to some, ignored others, only passed herself with a few. 'We'll have the best seats in the house; it'll be worth the wait.' There was a new energy in Brigit as she waited for the pictures.

Red spots appeared at irregular intervals on Muriel's neck and cheeks. Itchy rash, nervous rash. She felt completely vulnerable. She wished with all her heart that she could see Barclay. Wished and wished again as she looked down the main street. She wouldn't even pretend to know him if he appeared. Just a glimpse of him would do. She promised any spare saint who was listening to a sinner. Maynooth was just up the road; a miracle wasn't beyond the realms of possibility.

The crowd had swelled to fifty or sixty before the door swung open.

'Bottles or cash?,' Charlie Doran's listless chant made Muriel jump.

Brigit told her to the differ when she thought it was a joke. 'No, no, some pay with bottles; they're worth money. Lemonades two pence, porter sixpence for six. It soon mounts up. Especially with porter. Oh, bottles are big business in these parts. Many's the time when I was young in service that I traded porter bottles to see the latest release.'

'Two admissions and two paper pokes of aniseed balls.' Brigit shoved two thrupenny bits into Charlie Doran's hand. She had a guest today so she wouldn't be associated with bottle banks or bartering.

On backless benches over fuel-splattered floors, Muriel and Brigit took their seats in the back row of the picture house. 'Stay on the end, that way we won't make a disturbance when we need to pop yer man in his pram,' Brigit told her

Muriel looked around the makeshift cinema. A converted garage, it serviced motor bikes and the odd car during the week, and the fantasies of the village women and children on Saturday afternoons;

courting couples and odd men on Sunday nights. As the film flicked into life, Jack fell into a sound sleep. 'Get yer sweets ready.' Brigit was like a child herself when she slipped back into her seat.

Sniffing a mix of diesel and petrol fumes, they gazed at the makeshift screen, stealing scenes for their dreams. Hands moved noiselessly from sweets to dumbstruck mouths, all eyes and ears glued to the spotty screen as hordes of scantily clad Indians terrorised a wagon train of besieged men, women and children. But they had to wait till the second half for the cavalry.

'If the garage has had a good week and Charlie's of a mind, he'll wind up his gramophone in the interval and play us somethin' from his record collection.' Brigit's chest swelled with anticipation.

Between the children screaming orders at generals, Brigit's whoops of delight and Jack's total acceptance of all and sundry, Muriel's trip to the cinema held a fascination all of its own. Theatre in the round; she waited to see what was going to happen next.

True to Brigit's word, just before the interval, the industrious Charlie appeared with tubs of ice cream and bottles of lemonade with straws already in them. Joseph Locke on the gramophone, already wound up and waiting to go in the wings. The singer took them all to another plane. Shoulder to shoulder, Brigit and Muriel swooned and swayed with the rest of the row as he crooned his seductive sounds.

'Now, that's a voice made for a woman.' Brigit didn't disguise her pleasure. 'Me own personal dilemma would be to have to choose between dancin' with Dinjo or listenin' to Joseph Lock.' She settled herself down again with the rest of the village and escaped into the second half. The arrival of the cavalry brought the entire cinema to its feet. Troops bugling and bungling their way up and over the hill to the rescue were greeted with an almighty cheer.

The Indians had lost before the shouting had begun. But it didn't deter the audience. Muriel couldn't believe her ears; she was standing and shouting as loud as the best of them.

'Now, where would yeh find the likes of that entertainment?' Brigit stood proudly to attention at the end of the picture. Another swell of emotions roused Muriel. She watched the selection of moods and melancholies that commandeered the makeshift cinema, as the Tricolor jumped and fluttered on a snowy screen in time to a scratchy National Anthem

They might have been the first in, but they were the last out. It was far easier getting an empty pram into the cinema than it was getting a full one out. By the time they humped and bumped the big pram over Charlie's floor and manoeuvred back out on to the main street, the sweat was pouring off both women.

'Begod, we'll have teh get yeh instructed in the art of pram-pushin'.' Brigit was as amused at Muriel's huffing an' puffing as she was by her performance at the afternoon picture show.

'Keep yer eyes well peeled for bikes as yeh cross over the main street. There's some that thinks they're representin' Ireland that speeds through here.'

But Muriel was getting nowhere. The crowd that had just left the cinema was gathered outside on the pavement. She wondered what the hold up was. 'It'll be a bicycle, I'm tellin' yeh. Some eejit will have come over the handlebars,' Brigit's voice rang out from the dough of the crowd.

But it wasn't bicycles or accidents that were causing the commotion of the early evening picture-goers. Pushing her way to the front of the crowd in an attempt to get across the road to the house, Muriel found herself face to face with her earlier wish. Sitting like a king in convoy, waving regally to the crowd, Barclay O'Rourke was holding court.

She couldn't have manoeuvred herself into a better position if she'd tried. His driver was having difficulty steering his car through the crowd. Faces pressed to the windscreen, hands shoved through the passenger window. People hopped on the runners of the car calling out for prayers, blessings, intentions.

Muriel let go of the pram, left it on the pavement.

The picture house crowd seemed to double and heave. Muriel was so close to the car that she could have reached out and touched his face. She looked straight at him. Each going in the opposite direction, she felt as if someone was tearing the heart out of her chest with their bare hands. She felt like some caricature of herself. He recognised her. In one long drawn out, grotesque moment, reality drew back its fist and punched her full in the face.

She saw the hand fiddling with the episcopal ring, the urgent tap on the driver's shoulder. Whole paragraphs of information dismayed and dismissed in one snappy gesture.

Ten

He looked at his watch: the appointed hand pointed to and past breakfast hour. If only the service in the kitchen was as reliable. Fonsie snapped the fobwatch shut.

'Well be the hokey, the things yeh see when yeh haven't got yer gun,' Brigit's voice was at fever pitch. The energy and excitement in the women's quarters was enough to send a man astray. He could hear them at fifty paces. A cockatoo's cage, screeching the praises of the Holy Man. Oh, to be a Bishop thus adored, to parade your pageantry to enthrall. Normally, Sunday brought its own rest, but even that, it appeared, was denied Fonsie Duggan today. How much of this inane babble did a man have to put up with under his own roof?

What Brigit hadn't seen outside the picture house with her own two eyes, she had liberally embellished to all and sundry. With inside information, she wasn't about to be sidelined by all the excitement. She'd missed all the finery, the waving and the blessings. Saw only the red scull cap as his car had accelerated up the road to Maynooth.

But she hadn't missed the opportunity to garner or discuss the full and finer detail with half of Leixlip after eight o'clock Mass. Had the Pope of Rome stopped and blessed them himself on the main street, it couldn't have caused more commotion.

'Well, an' I tellin' yeh, I'd have given the same fellah a piece of me mind if an' I'd a got near his fancy car.' The conversation in her head bubbled over in a steady stream as she stepped back in the door from her Sunday Mass.

Muriel welcomed the colourful disclosures that whitewashed the hurtful truth.

'Did you see him blessin' the Byrne twins, by any chance?

The blather and skite in the kitchen eclipsed the excitement at the chapel gates.

'Put the hand out the window and touched the red heads of them. An' that pair nearly kilt the mother deliverin' them.'

Muriel shook her head. She hadn't seen that.

'An' us within the ball-of-an-ass of proceedings. We might as well be a couple of bats. There was a time there last year, and everywhere I turned the same buckaroo was skinnin' me heels. And Mr Fonsie's too, bent over backwards accommodating. This year is a quarter past itself and more, and not sight nor sound of him. Wouldn't yeh think he'd have called?' Brigit's chin, high and mighty, tossed her confusion to the kitchen ceiling. 'But he'll whistle up here again when he wants somethin' else. Mark my words.' There wasn't an ounce of malice in Brigit's proclamation. It was delivered more for effect than cause.

'Perhaps it wasn't the desire that was lacking Brigit; perhaps it was time?'

Muriel codded herself as much as Brigit. Well into the small hours, she had tossed and turned: tortured truth. Twisting it until she found it easier to handle, she had passed through the pain barrier. Barclay wasn't her persecutor, he was her protector. He had sheltered her against parochial preys. Shielded their secret. Listening in the kitchen to Brigit relaying chapter and verse this morning, relishing detail, nods and winks, Muriel knew that he was absolutely right to drive on.

By dawn, she was thanking God for Barclay's infinite wisdom. Never underestimate native cunning. Damocles' sword hangs in the air on glances, shifts silences. They'll fillet with double the drive they revere. She'd recalled all Barclay's warnings, all her promises. By morning, her conversion was complete.

Fonsie checked his watch again. Every clock in the house chimed in his effrontery. But blatherskites and flibbertigibbets were oblivious to time, he found. If breakfast was running as smoothly as their tongues, it might just be on the table. Only women could make so much of so little.

Fonsie's cough summoned breakfast but brought less than a minute's lull in the conversation.

'That water will be ready teh wet the tea in a minute,' Brigit's shout bordered on the coarse.

Blather and skite: Fonsie tapped and tutted.

Aware of his disdain, the two women lowered their voices to a whisper.

Mulling over the deity's details. Pageantry and procession, it's easy to placate peasants. Fonsie threw in a few more snorts and sniffs to shift them.

They must have him picked clean. Vultures. He opened the morning paper and found himself staring at a photograph, more flattering than usual, of Barclay. He held the paper close to his chest as Muriel approached. Hid the photograph from her view. He couldn't stomach another round of eulogies.

Whipping the top of his eggs, he began breakfast. But thoughts of the Bishop dampened his appetite. Was there some divine law that explained the reign of one man over others? He laid his spoon down on the side of his plate. Some magical potion that drew energy from the weaker of his own species. Made them decidedly poor by comparison. Power, conferred by the gods to get others to do your bidding.

Fonsie wrestled with the physical truth. Egg yolk ran riot round his breakfast plate. Barclay O'Rourke, the divine spark. He was talking out loud. Mortified, he looked in the direction, but no one was taking a blind bit of notice. His bearing alone manages to make other mere mortals look like extras from the silent movies. Fonsie shook the morning paper vigorously. The Bishop's smile as broad and brazen as Dublin Bay smiled up at him.

Women and maternity. Fonsie smirked. The Philosopher Ruler and his silver-tongued lies. *Gynaecologists stepping on sacred ground. Hospitals run without the guiding hands of religious orders: unaccountable, unsupervised.* Trumpetted words jumped off every line. Fonsie searched for vision and found only staid ignorance. And rising blood pressure. *Abuse of power positions.* Words without end. He deplored the moral skullduggery. The barefaced cheek of Barclay's crusade.

He pushed his breakfast aside. Did religious rulers credit the women of Ireland with no wit? Did they really believe they would follow, without recourse to reason, patriarchal tyrants? Wouldn't recognise a moral debacle because it was camouflaged in clever language? He shook his head slowly. Had the bold Bishop and Muriel had recourse to this cursed remedy, perhaps two, three, four if you included the unborn child, they wouldn't be in the painful predicament they were in today.

Fonsie turned the page; he couldn't look at the forked-tongued Barclay another minute. We're ruled and reigned over by those guiltier, more frustrated, than ourselves. In a rare moment, the splendid irony of the crusade spun itself round Fonsie. Of all the causes in all the countries, how had Barclay been chosen to front this campaign? Was it the gods' charity, or sport?

The rattle and hum in the kitchen had settled, softened around his son. The hand that rocks the cradle rules the world; it was time religious rulers familiarised themselves with received truths and wisdom.

He listened to the women's voices, soothing and tender, pampering, nurturing the child. The morning ritual. Clutching and

112

hatching. He longed to be part of that intimacy. To belong to the sacred circle. Longed for her to light up for him the way she lit up for the child, and for Barclay's silent photograph later.

A pause in the breakfast proceedings brought Muriel up short. The set of Fonsie's jaw struck a note of caution as she came into the dining room. The morning's paper held too close to his chest. Eggs normally scraped clean overflowing their shells. She wondered if his ulcers were at him. A stark absence of sympathy accompanied the thought.

Scalding tea landing in the china cup amplified the silence between them. Oil slicking down sparse hair was glinting on the top of his head. Phlegm that would be hawked into a handkerchief after breakfast was loosening at the back of his throat. Predictability, as painful as the procedure.

BISHOP'S REVOLT. Her eye fell on a partially hidden headline. She savoured the anticipation. She'd read the morning paper when she was on her own. He was hardly ever out of the news these days. Not since he'd taken on the might of the Minister for Health and his revolutionary reconstruction of the health service. She sighed as if Barclay's burden was hers as well.

Fonsie watched as she waited on him. Pregnancy became her. Her skin was soft, silky, and her breasts warm. Shifting his body from the torment of her closeness, he crossed his legs. He envied Barclay O'Rourke's head, hands, on those full breasts.

He could feel the beast that came between them nightly stirring. Surviving the nights had become a hazardous enough state. Must the mornings be miserable as well? Surviving daily on massive doses of outrage, and nightly on outrageous doses of alcohol; a righteous voice held a kangaroo court in his head.

The scrutiny made him feel queasy. What had come over him? Staring at her body like that. It felt indecent. Had he no shame? He was an odd mixture of queer parts. Reticence, silence, fury and perversion. His fingers drummed the table as he tried to make order of an existence that bore no relation to the past or the future.

He couldn't bring himself to recount the nightly escapades. Couldn't countenance addressing the matter without retreating into searing embarrassment. How could bollixes like Barclay O'Rourke get off scot-free, while others were left carrying the burden?

Kathleen Komiskey was surprised to see Fonsie standing in the shop. Doubly surprised when he cancelled his *Independent* and changed the longstanding order to the *Irish Times*. Neither Brigit nor

Muriel noticed him walking past the kitchen window. Nor the engine of the car starting up.

The thought of Barclay paying his attentions to her full breasts set up a sensual stimulus in Fonsie that hadn't been satisfied in many's the long night.

Reeling with the injustice and frustration, the road to Dublin disappeared in straights and bumps under the chassis. Lust, pride, hate, envy, all the deadly sins lay clotted in his chest. Accelerating hard, he headed for the fleshpots in Dublin. He'd never availed himself of the services on the Money Mile, but by God Muriel Grey's coldness was making it look like a warm and inviting place. But old habits die hard, and age-old guilt is a powerful deterrent.

Like a sinner returning to the scene of the crime, Fonsie found himself kneeling at the same side altar of Adam and Eve's. Just five months ago, she'd knelt at this same altar and taken marriage vows: in sickness and in health, for richer for poorer. A kind of hopelessness came over him. *Am I one of those poor unfortunates who never seems to get beyond the starting line in life?*

A curious, tight expression crossed his face. *Why did one marriage end in such disaster and another start in such misery? What was I thinking when I agreed to marry her? Did this failed priest think he could placate God by saving his Bishop? Why didn't I see that all I was making was another thorny bed? Resentment's all that blossoms between us, feelings so barbed and vicious they'd tear a man's heart apart. Tenderness is a foreign place, hope's a stranger.* Fonsie stared blankly at the benign St Francis staring blankly back at him.

Using the short cut through the church, Concepta found herself on the threshold of Fonsie's pain. The frown that buckled his brow didn't escape her. She couldn't place him. He wasn't a regular – she knew every one of them by sight. And they her!

But she recognised hurt when she saw it, knew the troubled souls. And in her own way prayed for them. But when they were well dressed, prosperous like this one, their pain was curiously comforting. It made her feel that there was some justice in the world. That God didn't just punish the poor.

Using the pillars as protection, she continued her surveillance. Saw him wipe his brow as he stared up at the Cross. Didn't miss the lips either, going like the hammers of hell. God, or whoever was up there, was getting it in the ear.

And unless I'm becoming delusory, I think she's planning to ask him out. Out to my house, my home. Christ does the woman have no savvy? Does she intend to rub my nose in it? Must the very souls of my ancestors be made witness to my humiliation? Rage swept over him. He couldn't stomach the turmoil. How had such good intentions paved a path to Hell? In the midst of this misery, another unease came over Fonsie. He felt he was being watched. Looking around him, everyone seemed to be engrossed in private prayer. An image of himself hunched, kneeling in a candle-lit church, brought him abruptly to his feet. Genuflecting more out of habit than desire, he bolted.

The haunting air of the young girl's song lent a sad harmony. Fonsie's sigh was audible.

'Yeh might as well sing sorrow as cry it.' Concepta sidled slyly up the bar and put her drink down beside his. *'As she moves through the fair.'* She dragged due sympathy from her cigarette.

He allowed himself a nod of acknowledgement. She wasn't what he wanted, but she just might be what he needed.

'Hasn't she a lovely voice all the same?' She looked over at the stage, her face lost in a haze of blue smoke. After a suitable silence, she tried cajoling him. 'You're a stranger in these parts.' Her green eyes flirted independently.

He answered without thinking: 'My doctor lives in Dublin.'

'Oh....are yeh sick?' Concepta's voice was syrupy.

'Headaches.' He told the white lie easily.

'You should try some of Musha the chemist's Tiger Balm. It cures everything. They say it even cured a strike in Guinness once'. A shy smile gate-crashed his face.

Wound up as tight as a watch spring; somewhere in his fifties. Concepta's mind ran miles ahead of her. The kind of man her Da might have been if he were still alive. 'Now doesn't that feel a whole lot lighter than the face heavy with murder yeh lugged in here with yeh?'

Fonsie flushed with embarrassment.

He bought her a pint of Guinness, ordered another drink for himself. 'It's yer only man.' For a bold moment, their eyes met and he indulged in the delicious feeling of delusion, allowed the past to fade into a foreign place. The whiskey coursing through his veins was reaching seedy places. He found himself unable to take his eyes off Concepta.

Older than him at the game, she lifted her glass. Inhaling deeply, she spoke at last.

'I love the smell of Guinness. It takes me back and forward. The hops, the yeast.' The hurt in her voice strangled back, but he heard it all the same. She talked to him more than anyone had talked to him in a long time. Took notice too. The attention flattered.

'Life was great when me Da worked in Guinness. A fire in the grate, a welcome smile. None of this nonsense.' She slipped her foot out of her shoe. She didn't see him wince at the sodden cardboard insole. 'An Christmas,' – she lit one cigarette from another – 'the hamper, groanin' with fat rich food that had us guessin' and fartin' for a fortnight.' She could hear Fonsie laughing softly.

Concepta closed her eyes, never shared the hurtful bits. The change at home when her Da died. The desertion, the desolation, the drink, the smells, the shame. The taunts of the other children. The game, the game, yer Ma's on the game.

Attracta was great then. Me best friend. Beat seven kinds of shite out of anyone who looked crooked at me. Wouldn't let them away with it. But that was in the auld god's time. Before she went to work for a Bishop and I went on the game. They sat in silence, both drinking in their own separate worlds.

Concepta opened her eyes and smiled up at him. Wide-eyed innocence offered up a plethora of false ingredients. A diaphanous blouse was having a curiously pleasant effect on Fonsie. He ordered another round. He hadn't been flirted with for a long while. He prayed to God it wasn't too late.

He felt the sweat, the rising panic, his face pinched with reality. He was going to be sick. He scrambled past her.

'Over before it began,' Concepta shrugged her shoulders. Contented, she finished up her pint. Then, following his example, she called it a day.

Whether it was the whiskey or the smell of the Liffey that took him, he'd never know, but hanging by a thread over the Liffey wall was where she found him.

'Der yeh are again, third time lucky.' The breeze blew the sentence away. 'You're lookin' a bit green around the gills.' She leaned in beside him.

'I'm grand.' He was fully intent on going home. 'Do you fancy something to eat?' The words shot out of his mouth and shocked both of them.

'And why not? I can think of worse ways to while away a mild May evenin'.'

Concepta stuck her arm through Fonsie's. 'You're a gentleman, a dying breed, but yeh couldn't drink soup.' She nudged him. The air charged with unformulated hope. They strolled towards Phoenix

Park. Lost souls looking for a carnal encounter passed them by on the way.

How they ended up in the Lido, a chip shop on Parkgate Street, was as big a surprise to Fonsie as it was to the other customers in the queue. And it wasn't the last surprise he had that night. And he was relatively more sober, relatively, by then.

'Stop the lights,' the Flower Rafferty's skit echoed the length of the queue.

Concepta gave Attracta Rafferty's brother a bull's look. Fonsie, who was feeling out of place waiting his turn for a bag of fish and chips, looked decidedly startled.

'Don't mind him; he's own'y a big mouth.' Her vexation gave an air of seriousness.

'He got a job in the Carmelite Convent stringin' rosary beads for the Foreign Missions, and the thick he left a bead offa every mystery. A whole week it was before the nuns realised he couldn't count. Hundreds of pairs he'd strung up. Thick as hobbyhorse shite, he is. They were no use to God, man or the missionaries. He told the poor nuns he'd give them to the little children in the Liberties. Anyone under eighty in Dublin could tell yeh the same story. Feckin' Raffertys make a hames of everything. Merciful Jaysus.'

Concepta tapped her chest three times. 'Jemser flogged them to the Yanks. The only day's work he ever done in his life. An Irish miracle.' Fonsie was laughing out loud – her indignation was as funny as the story.

He hadn't enjoyed himself so much in years. 'Eat up yer fish and chips, yer like a string bean.' She settled herself down in the long grass in the Park. Looked at the emaciated profile half sitting, half lying beside her and hoped it would stand up to the service! She poked at the chips, broke open the greasy batter and picked at long strings of ray. 'Not enough salt and vinegar. With all the ballyraggin' we forgot.'

As they lost the last of the evening light, reality dimmed. She was a flower that had the moon mixed up with the sun. He wished all his encounters were so good.

Shyly trying to hide a swelling erection under his fish and chips, he began to realise events were overtaking him. His body was betraying him. They were somewhere, Concepta swore, that was called the Furry Glen.

Maybe it was the moon, her musky smell or the curiously large nipples, straining against her peep-through blouse. But clinging to her in the long grass, fumbling and floundering, he fell between her

117

legs. With deftly developed reflexes, Concepta reached down and literally plugged him in. And it wasn't one second too soon.

Perhaps it was finding his pleasure in such an obscure place that made Fonsie throw back his head and laugh. Laugh out loud in that honest-to-God way that loosens the chest and warms the cockles of your heart. And when he'd finally stopped laughing, he was crying, crying in the same open, honest-to-God sort of way.

Overexposed in every sense of the word, ascending shyness crept back into his chest. Buttoning up his trousers, he slid back into his old skin. Absurdity, painfully familiar, rushed to fill the vacuum. He searched for his glasses in the grass, saw his left shoe lying on its side. Such was the fever, such was the abandonment.

'Look at yeh now, all of a doo dah.' Sensing Fonsie's awkwardness, Concepta took him in her arms and rocked him. Lips pressing against his wet brow felt softer than sin.

'You know, Concepta, the worst feature of regret is it goes hand in hand with hopelessness.'

'Well, don't let it' She offered him a nugget of hope. 'Meet me again next Saturday night. I won't even charge yeh.' Her honesty, her generosity, flummoxed him. A broad smile filled his face as they walked back into Dublin.

'Where will I find you?'

'If I'm not on the broad of me back, I'll be on the side of me foot on the Moncy Mile. Down by Adam and Eve's.

She was a silver stitch in his big black sky. He slipped a ten bob note into her pocket. She looked him straight in the eye. 'Shoes,' he said quietly. Her face broke into a smile, a private smile.

He was struck by the simplicity of their exchange. Ten bob. A small sum to pay to wash away the gross humiliations of Muriel Grey.

Eleven

Attracta Rafferty put the final polish to the lunch that had the Countess' head in a spin for weeks.

The Bishop of Dublin and the Honourable Hillary Green at my table – I'm the envy of the bridge scene.

Attracta smelled the sherry on the Countess' breath. New in the beginning, the smell had become as familiar as it was frequent

Warm sunshine threw its charm over the industry of the day. Waterford crystal outshone Irish silver. Starched linen groaned under a weight of grandeur.

'Champagne, the champagne, check that it's chilled.' The Countess wound herself up tighter and tighter.

'The sooner the baby Jesus comes the better.' The French cook employed for the occasion didn't understand the language, but she knew what Attracta meant.

Women of all makes and shapes were arriving in flusters and flounces. The perfume and the cook's piquant sauce mingled mercilessly. A reverent hush heralded the Bishop's arrival.

The cook peeped through a crack in the kitchen door. 'How handsome, statuesque your holy man is. Such style, such a talented tailor.' Her lips parted with pleasure.

Attracta's head spun from orders and disclosures. With each course, she became more essential and more invisible. Bold as brass, Attracta swerved as she served Dublin's finest. All but Barclay displayed sublime indifference to her. The cook was taking the occasional swig from the odd bottle. Attracta followed suit but took more.

The champagne was slipping past tonsils faster than phlegm. Fuelled on self-importance, voices were rising to Liberty levels at closing hour. Attracta viewed the unfolding scene with a sort of malevolent composure.

'A culinary orgasm.' The cook handed her another course.

She nearly knew what she meant. If she could have said the words in the sexy accent, she'd have whispered it in his ear. The swigs of champagne were having an enlightening effect.

From the tips of her toes to the edge of her ears, parts of her were prickling and turning bright pink. Lust and disgust danced wild in her head. She couldn't stop the thoughts as she stared at him. She settled instead for a sly wink. Sexy and slow. Her eyelid opened and shuttered. A private picture. She heard him catch his breath. Winded him. If she'd had some of this bubbly business when they were on their hands and knees upstairs in the study, he'd have been holdin' more than his breath.

The day accelerated. The summer sun dropped low and fast, its crimson light flattering and fooling. Attracta lifted and laid. How they could fit more food, after the courses they polished off, was a measurement mystery to Attracta. In the Liberties, cheese was a luxury. Here it was a fifth course. Barclay was holding them, enthralled.

'A robust mental life is good for the soul. Yes, of course people need material comforts and satisfactions. But they also have an inherent need for spiritual satisfaction.' He parried stalls and objections between mouthfuls of musty cheese and port.

If yeh can't blind them with bullshit, baffle them with brilliance. Attracta wondered how long it would take to learn to play the word game.

'We need to think in the spirit of possibilities.' He mesmerised his captive audience.

'Witness how the women bow to the shaman. In France, we've replaced them with reality.' The cook was finished for the day, her politics were lost to the world and Attracta.

'Surely the spirit of possibility is all Doctor Noel Brown is guilty of?' A voice of dissent.

'The Minister for Health's problem is that he seizes on the hum and buzz of anticipation. But instead of gathering up the eager respondents, he allows the offensive to descend into a scrum of madness.' Barclay deliberately ignored the speaker.

'TB is rampant in the country, polio a real threat. Somebody has to take the Health Ministry by the neck before we lose our finest investment – our youth'.

The auld one, whoever she was, was like a dog with a bone. Attracta could see that he was visibly irritated.

'I've seen other sides of the good doctor's character. Worrying sides. I'm not too sure that his mental health is the best.' Barclay was getting personal.

'The last time I observed him, his phrases were perfunctory, grabbed from the mind. They weren't flowing smoothly from the heart as often before. I don't know if indeed I wasn't witnessing the beginning of his decline. He abounds with passion. But stamina and long-term solutions are more essential. That is, in my experience anyway, ladies.' Affecting a humility that was lacking, he addressed the table in general.

But the Hon. Hillary Green was not to be ignored. She was going at him again, yapping at sore heels.

'I can only say that, living in England, one is treated to a very different perspective on social and moral issues. When I compare the two countries, I for one am glad of the uninterrupted peace.

'When I am in Ireland, I am subjected to hectoring, arrogant triumphalism in our churches. There are issues here that are not issues there, which begs the question. Are the lines in Ireland between corporal power and temporal power fused? Is this marriage between Church and State wise? If you'll forgive me, Your Grace, it appears to me to be an unholy union.'

Consternation wouldn't begin to do justice to the expression on the Countess' face. She tapped the side of her glass with a hard fingernail. Attracta poured the wine in the delicate way she had been taught. Applying a steely elbow to Attracta's wrist, the Countess managed to fill her glass to the brim.

'Is not the purpose of the Church to advise the State on matters spiritual and the role of the State to advise to bring balance? What is this desperate need for the Catholic Church in Ireland to control politics as well as morals? Does the Church not recognise the weakness of her position, the conflict intrinsic in the two regimes? The long-term effects that this unnatural liaison will have on its subjects? In this light, should this union not be seen as a threat, a corrosive agent that could one day rot the Church from the inside out?

'History tells us over and over that controlling regimes are fraught with human rights issues. Can the Church, in all its wisdom, not look back, see the fight it will have on its hands in the future? Does it not understand that what its followers want is not a befuddlement of social and moral issues, but a simple road to an honest God?'

Whatever the Hon. Hillary Green's ballyraggin' was all about, Attracta noted it had a remarkably softening affect on Barclay's cough. He took a large cigar from a rosewood humidifier, snipped the end off and lit it with an expanse of exuberance. Letting bland silence mingle with blue smoke rings, he pondered the question and the questioner.

'Our stance is firmer; it has to be. We are dealing with a very different populace. Our religion isn't tempered with the temptation of romanticism. It's the cold comfort of reality that ensures the Catholic Church in Ireland's future, my dear.'

'I find your pragmatism interceptive, patronising, paternal and worrying in the extreme. If I were God, Your Grace, I'd put De Valera in Rome and the Pope in Phoenix Park for Easter, so that the people of Ireland could tell the difference.'

Visibly shaken to be tackled hard by a woman, Barclay drew deeply on his cigar.

It became increasingly difficult for Attracta to follow the conversation, but not Barclay's intentions. She got the land of her life when his hand touched her leg as she stood silently beside him waiting to replace the silver cigar-clippers. Without giving it a second thought, she dropped the cigar-clippers. Reaching under the table, she grabbed the inside of his thigh and squeezed hard.

'There yeh are,' she looked him straight in the eye as she retrieved them.

A disjointed silence followed.

'I've completely lost my train of thought.' He strove to regain his composure.

Relishing the advantage, Attracta watched as she stood by the sideboard. A sly smile covered her face. The dirty auld delinquent, he's as game as the Butcher's Boy. No wonder mad auld wans write him love letters. She wondered what he'd make of the steaming open affair. But that would be only telling on herself, so that one would have to wait. She realised that the Countess was coughing in her direction and straightened herself up.

They were still up to ninety puffin' an blowin' about politics. A spoon tapping the side of a glass summoned her. The Countess was making serious inroads into the port. Attracta filled her glass to the brim twice in the space of fifteen minutes.

'Perhaps his Grace would like to see the cheese board again.' Barclay dismissed the offer with a wave of his hand.

A bloody auld bamboozler, they'd have his cards marked in the Liberties, quick sharp. She saw him looking at her, wondered if he could read her thoughts.

'A cynic is a passionate person who doesn't want to be disappointed again. Am I not right, Miss Rafferty?

It all sounded very intelligent and very important. Attracta almost knew what he meant and nearly liked being included. But the Countess' flinty eye as she carried a heavy tray into the kitchen put paid to a smart-arsed answer.

'If you'll excuse me for a moment. It's good to stretch the legs.' Barclay made the lame excuse and followed her into the kitchen. He poured himself a glass of water.

'How's my dazzling young pick-me-up these days.' He lowered his voice. Lowered his eyes too. Attracta saw a deeper hunger in him.

'What do you make of all this?' He gestured towards the dining room.

At first she thought it was the dropped hand he was referring to; then she realised it was feedback he was fishing for.

It's hard to know the difference between shit and shite sometimes.'

He laughed so hard the water blew down his nose.

'She's blessed with bounce.' He'd spotted a reflection in the kitchen window and changed his voice and his tune.

'We wondered where you were hiding. Come and give us more of your wonderful insights.' Only the slightest of sways betrayed the Countess' demeanour.

'In the kitchen, where the heart is.' He looked back and winked as he was led away.

It was teatime when the last of the women left. The Countess had passed out in the drawing room. Two of the older women covered her with a mohair throw. Exhaustion, excitement; they bandied excuses. Can we drive you anywhere, Bishop? He wouldn't hear of it. His old car knew it's own way home. If he held tight to the steering wheel, sure it would drag him from Drumalee to Drumcondra. They laughed as if it were original.

Attracta listened to it all as she cleared up. The sooner they stopped scratching and excusing each other's backs, the sooner she could get her feet up. She checked the drawing room: the Countess was out for the count. She took off her apron and cap. Ruffled her hair where the clips had dug into her head.

'Don't you look a picture.' He was leaning on the jar of the door. Openly admiring. She'd heard the last car leave. They were on their own again. The Countess, the Bishop and Attracta. An unlikely trio.

'Your mistress is out for the count'. A cork popped smartly from a bottle made her giggle. He poured himself a glass of champagne. Inveigled his way in. 'Won't you join me? Little vices are the spice of life, don't you think?' His eyes feasted greedily. She didn't need convincing.

'I'm sure I don't know what you mean.'

'I'm sure you do.'

123

He wasn't prepared for Attracta's love.

Her kiss, carnal and cunning, woke a hunger and passion that matched his own. The Countess' snoring rose and fell above the passion. Like gluttons at a banquet they licked, slurped, grunted and groped. She suffered none of Muriel's inhibitions, limitations or accommodations. His handkerchief landed on the floor. She took his hand, put it where she wanted. She satisfied herself; satisfied him. We mustn't.

But he wasn't driving this one. It was too late to negotiate. She threw her leg over him, entry and orgasm came all at once. Full of him, she was bucking like a wild goat. She wouldn't stop. Bent shamelessly over the kitchen table, they coupled as savagely as two stray dogs. In an outburst of profane joy, his back arched and he flooded her.

She held him tight between her legs. An energy peculiar to itself came over her again and again. Her shouts startled him. When she was finished, she stopped. It was her first time to do the bold thing. Not his by all accounts. He knew his way around a woman.

Back-street girls knew how to look after themselves. He buttoned up his trousers. Different cows, different milk. Muriel was feminine, Attracta was female; one for public, one for private.

Twelve

Whether it was conscience, concern or good old-fashioned covering his back, Muriel never knew. But as the Bishop's visit came closer, she chose to believe it was love.

'Sure, he'll be as welcome as the May flowers.' Brigit blinked earnestly as she inspected the fireplace. When we used to light a fire in here regular, it could blow as much as it sucked.' She ducked head and shoulders into the huge grate. 'That stack was never stable.'

Muriel caught some of what Brigit was saying but more blew up the chimney. It was the morning of the visit, and she didn't want another debate on the safety of chimneys.

Talk for talk's sake. Three o'clock was the anointed hour. And if the past were any measure of the present, Barclay wouldn't waste a minute. He'd be as anxious to see her as she was to see him. Hope had effortlessly outmanoeuvred reality when he'd written to accept the invitation. And added the P.S. to say how forward he was looking to it.

'Here, let me help. We'll get it lighting now; it will be bedded in nicely for the afternoon,' Muriel moved the performance along. She'd heard enough huffin' and puffin' about fires and bodies burnt to cinders. Ripping and rolling the sheets of newspaper tight, she handed them to Brigit. It was eleven o'clock already.

Brigit wiped the sweat off her face with her apron. 'On your head be it,' she resigned herself as she set the fire. She'd never seen such transfiguration. Muriel on a mission – she was a different woman.

She'd seen little signs in the past week of the lethargy and apathy that made up too many parts of this young woman's week. On the contrary. She was up at the crack of dawn, energised and organised. Moving furniture, taking curtains down for cleaning, carpets out for beating, polishing musty mirrors, silver ornaments. She was like a woman near her labour.

Brigit felt a sense of unease and not just a little displacement as she looked around. She had always run a plain house herself. Muriel had a finer hand for the finishing touch. The freezing drawing room on the north side of the house that hadn't been opened in twenty years was the main beneficiary of all the beautification. Though she'd had her doubts and voiced them when the room was first opened. The smell of damp death and must, augmenting her fears.

She marvelled at the menagerie of accessories that had reappeared. Bothersome, she'd only ever found ornaments. She'd stuck them at the back of the sideboard years ago. Out of sight and out of her way. Looking around at the gracious drawing room, Brigit had felt her haste to be a bit ignorant. Dresden made at the hands of fine craftsmen that Muriel had baptised brought new life to dead surfaces. Silver, green with age, stood proud on the highly polished sideboard. Even the oil paintings that used to give Brigit the creeps had benefited from the sprucing.

'The touch of the master's hand.' She nodded her approval. It would have been nice to have time to turn her mind to delicate matters. But there was always a backside to be wiped, spuds to be scrubbed, rooms to be kept clean. Maybe in another lifetime I'll be the lady of the house, not the servant.

'Would yeh look at the style of itself?' She stroked the velvet pile on the back of the sofa. 'And it as auld as Methuselah.' It had come from an auction in the Castle, and it had seen better times even then.

'Isn't illusion everything? This room was such a favourite of old Mister, and Missus. God rest their souls. Begod, they had some rare auld times in this room. Entertain the local gentry, the Horse Protestants, the Teeny Tinys and their likes, often partied here till dawn: yer expected guests won't feel out of place here today. Nor yer bold bishop: many's a winning hand of poker he played on that very card table.'

Brigit's eyes misted. 'Mr Fonsie's wife… his recently deceased' – she blessed herself and tried to cover her mistake – 'never set foot nor face in it. Too mean to heat it she was.' It was the only disparaging remark Muriel ever heard Brigit make about Fonsie's late wife.

'We used to store perishables in here. Game, the odd pheasant handed in for services rendered. Apples spread out in straw on that auld sideboard would last for months. That will give you some idea of how cold it was.' She didn't mention the corpses that were laid out and waked.

She did a full turn. It's a pity she isn't as good at disguisin' her condition. Brigit felt her face redden. The bump was past battin' down. It was embarrassing to have to face the Bishop of Dublin with a belly full to bursting. Thank God he didn't know what she knew herself, that the child was conceived in sin. Made before the marriage. Despite what Muriel would have them believe.

'Yeh were right about the fire and the curtains. It was fortunate the sun never got its rays into the fabric. Who would have thought we'd have resurrected them? An' the pile as flat as a pancake' Brigit put her concerns and conscience to one side.

'After the hiding we gave them, did they have any other choice?,' Muriel smiled.

'They're as good now as the day old Mister had them delivered here on a pony and trap from Arnotts. I have to hand it to yeh, Mam.' Brigit was as proud as punch of the finished product.

Muriel herself was delighted with the transformation. From the day she received his letter, she'd worked with a passion. A treasure trove waiting to be unveiled, the room had lent itself generously to the labour of love. It had all come together beautifully in the end. A roaring fire in the grate, the bundles of fresh flowers added an extra lustre. She closed the door on her endeavours.

Fonsie's hat was on the hat stand in the hall. It wasn't like him to leave without his hat. Or before the Angelus, Brigit had voiced her concerns as his car turned out the gate. But in the midst of all the finery, it would have been nice to have had a man about the place. She wasn't so sure about the Teeny Tinys; the Horse Protestants could be tricky. They belonged to a different order, an old world. She'd tried to warn her, but Muriel didn't take counsel kindly. It would have been wiser to entertain the two parties separately, she'd ventured.

But Muriel saw things differently. Contrast sometimes brought colour, and she had been quite terse. Colour was right. Where the Horse Protestants were concerned, colour was guaranteed.

'I suppose I better throw a drop of water at the face. The Teeny Tinys will arrive early and leave late.'

Muriel wished Brigit wouldn't call her guests that. But she wasn't about to start all that protest over again. The church clock struck a quarter past the hour. She fidgeted with a lace blouse that had fitted perfectly three weeks ago. Stretched to straining now, it looked more like crochet than Nottingham lace. She rearranged buttons, rearranged herself. Her palms were sweating. She checked the clock for the umpteenth time. A quarter past two. The doorbell echoed the length of the hall.

'Be the hokey. Leopards never change their spots.'

Dressed in yesterday frocks, side by side in a square of bright light, the Teeny Tinys stepped into the hall. Slamming the heavy front door behind them, Brigit trapped the wind. 'That auld door swells and stiffens at this time every year, a bit like meself.' Smoke bellowing from the chimney breast. Brigit spoke over the coughing fit. Muriel tried to greet the Teeny Tinys.

127

'Are we the first?' A rustle of satin eventually settled itself down on the sofa. Restlessly, eyes searched for signs of the past and present.

'A little sherry? Their synchronised movements signalled a yes. It was to be a pattern.

'When is our boy due?' Sparkling eyes looked up at Muriel.

'Three on the dot.' Her answer sounded pompous; she could hear the nervousness in her own voice.

'And dear Fonsie?' They turned their powdered faces to Brigit.

'He left on urgent business. If he gets a good wind at his back, he could be back before the Bishop arrives.' Brigit filled their glasses up to the brim.

Relief and annoyance visited Muriel in equal measures. The one and only time she could have done with the bould Fonsie and he'd bolted.

Sinking nervous gaiety, the tiny women drank quickly. Bracelets jingling on teeny tiny wrists joined in the race.

'Have a wee scone. Soak up the alcohol.' Muriel wished Brigit wasn't so blunt.

'Don't worry about us – years of practice in a hot climate.' Nods and winks accompanied the disclosure.

'You know the Bishop well?' Muriel made polite conversation as she refilled empty glasses.

The yolks of their eyeballs rolled in hilarity and rivalry. Trouble in a silken suit. Our father taught him in Clongowes. We were working in Dublin at the time, but we used to visit Father. Barclay was a rogue then. And after. A loveable rogue. He'd have us plagued backing the ponies. Oh and sneaking post out to the girlies. He was prolific with the pen.'

Unbridled tongues delivered their version of history. His parents were killed on the way home from the races in the Phoenix Park. He was only eight. Clongowes had him from them in loco parentis. They spoke in unison.

'Father taught poor Fonsie too.' They looked apologetic. ' Poor Fonsie. No wife for years, then two come along at once.' They lifted their glasses, emptied the last drop. A double act.

Muriel looked at the mouths opening and closing in a hopeless race. They were proving more of threat than a treat. Why hadn't she listened to Brigit? An engine running in the back yard heightened her anxiety. Two blank faces stared at a blank window and then back at her. Fonsie; her heart stopped. Please God, don't let him be drunk. They were still talking, telling tales. She couldn't hear herself think, couldn't hear whether the car had passed or pulled into the yard. From this side of the house, it was impossible to see.

'He never took the vow of poverty. Did he dear?' Muriel was superfluous to their requirements. An interloper. The hour of three came and went and there was still no sign of him.

'There's a difference between and prudence and penury. Poverty doesn't cut it with the tailor or shirt-makers.' They lifted their glasses and saluted Barclay's credo with rare gusto. Muriel had heard the words herself from Barclay's own mouth. Selective memories and tactlessness both threatened her.

Strangers voices coming from the kitchen distracted her further. Her day was becoming tangled and untidy.

She could hear Brigit talking and laughing. High hooligan laughter. Barclay was in the kitchen. In the back door. After all her hard work.

Pawing the floor, tiny glitzy shoes were way ahead of her, greeting him like a long-lost cousin.

'Through the back door like a dirty shirt.' Brigit, all hot and bothered, had lost all sense of propriety.

'God save Ireland.' His unmistakable greeting. Larger than life, the walk of a king, his lackey secretary in tow, not a word about the lateness. He greeted the Teeny Tinys first, held their hands and their eyes.

Poised on the edge of their world, she waited and waited. Devouring every move, every syllable. The intimacy that bound them together was, by its very nature, pushing them further apart. She wondered if he could feel the distance between them now. The urgency to reach out and touch him was violent. Her chest, her heart, almost imploded with intensity. He moved eventually to greet her. Keeping the hurtful distance at all times. She curtsied low, kissed the ring on his finger, took private pleasure from the public formality.

'Sit over here on the previously ordained chair or herself will have a fit.' Muriel's embarrassment knew no hiding place. She'd never seen this side of Brigit before.

He swished across the room. There was something missing from Barclay, something different. Enthroned under his scarlet skull cap, he took his seat: settled the silk skirts that denoted his station in life with remarkable ease. The plain pectoral she'd given him hung around his neck. For an indecent moment she could feel her fingers ripping open the long sutane that covered his splendid body from head to toe. His secretary's eyes burned into her soul: the marriage Celebrant brought her to her uncomfortable senses.

Fonsie should be here playing his part. It wasn't so much his absence as the lack of presence that she deplored. He was always in the wrong place at the wrong time.

'And the man himself is otherwise engaged?' He threw his question open to the room. As if he were addressing a delegation.

'So it seems.' A sort of commiseration rose and froze on Muriel's lips.

'These are the sacrifices we men who serve have to make.'

A covert message? She searched his eyes but could find no trace of conformation.

All around were nodding and agreeing with Barclay. Everyone playing a part when there was no part to play. Conversation was stilted. Long strings of nonsense were followed by loud silences. The day was turning into a disaster. As the silences became deeper, his secretary spoke. About the weather, disgruntled farmers, the price of shorthorn cattle. No mention of TB. Or the polio epidemic that was sweeping Ireland. Or of Dr Noel Brown.

Muriel longed to throw a spanner in the perfectly tuned politeness. The hullabaloo about Brigit and the back door entrance had run the course twice over. Barclay was asking the women about the appointment of the new Protestant Bishop of Cork. Muriel was losing more than her composure. He was infinitely more at ease with the Teeny Tinys. She tried to realign the buttons of her blouse, but she was subject to scrutiny.

'Go on go on go on.' Brigit was sounding like something from the *Playboy of the Western World*. Stage Irish. Scones plastered in butter cream and jam wasn't quite the elegant cream tea Muriel had envisaged. There was no refusing her. 'Yis have only had a round of sandwiches. Wouldn't feed a fly. I'll wrap some scones up; yis may take them home.' Her insistence was making Muriel cringe.

He touched his stomach. 'The waistline, Brigit.'

'Is he doesn't watch it, the rest of us will.' His secretary's voice.

She remembered the register. Ah yes Miss Grey, the bog-standard retort, the sigh that followed each and every request. The same weary resignation, accusation was still there. It was probably his fault that the Bishop had been dragged through the servant's entrance. Agricultural eejit.

Was it the sin or the sinner that disgusted him more? She held his eyes until his dropped below her line of vision.. Gave him a glimmer of the pleasure she took in conceiving his Lord and master's child. She put her hand to her back and shifted her awkward bulk.

'You must be near your labour!' The Teeny Tinys heads moving from side to side like cats waiting for an answer.

Mortification poured from every sweat gland in the room. Silence from every pore. Barclay's eyes, bulbous with embarrassment, stared openly at her.

As red as the beaten curtains, Muriel turned faced Barclay full on. Suddenly the devil had her by the tongue. For a delicious moment, danger filled the air.

'We're not exactly sure of our dates.' For the first time that afternoon, she felt in control.

'Another baby in the house.' Their cooing lingered long into the embarrassment, their soft, downy chins swinging from one flummoxed party to another.

'Yes, and his Grace here has done me the personal honour of accepting the noble position of Godfather.' She held him hostage.

He was nodding and smiling at the same time. If she had held a gun to his startled head, she couldn't have brought the evening to a speedier conclusion.

Thirteen

Attracta had the 'flu. The Countess had given her two days off – she took ten.

'It must be the left-overs after the fancy lunch,' she'd tried to convince her mother and herself between bouts of violent vomiting.

'Is that yer handbag?,' The young Raffertys taunted Attracta as she hauled the galvanised bucket round after her.

Nel had never heard of food poisoning that lasted a fortnight. But she was saying nothing. The least said, the soonest mended. And this had to mend. The alternative was too awful to contemplate.

The Countess had less sympathy. A sick servant was no use to God nor man. 'Take yourself off home, Miss Rafferty. You're no use to me sniffing and dripping and drooping around the house. Besides, it might just be contagious'. Attracta was relieved to be back home. There was no pressure to provide for fat auld wans wants, no dirty auld Bishop breathin' down her neck.

She lay on the settle watching the comings and goings. It was like Amiens Street Railway Station inside and outside the flat. Gossip, the lifeblood of the Liberties, flowing and flooding the halls, stairs and landings. Auld wans' whispers, addin' it on, makin' it up. She'd missed the crack every time she had to go back to work.

Here, there was time for everything and time for nothing. There was no life in Ballsbridge, unless it was arranged. And it was all arranged around feeds. In the Liberties, eatin' was all part of livin'. There they lived for their lunches, their bridge and their bullshit. And their Bishop. Attracta pulled the bucket over beside the bed and retched her guts up again.

'If yeh ate a crust of bread, at least a drop of gruel.' Even as she pleaded with Attracta, Nel prayed fervently that the sickness wasn't what she dreaded most. 'Here, at least yeh'll have somethin' to bring up.' She handed her daughter a cup of boiled water.

Attracta Rafferty didn't lie in bed. The scourge of her life was always up and at it before the earliest of crows. Trying to accommodate Jemser and Attracta under the one roof was taking its toll. The one flesh and blood and they couldn't see eye to eye if it was to save their sight. Attracta on her own, Jemser on his own. But put the pair together and yeh had a rare recipe.

Nel pulled the cork from a half empty bottle of porter. Sat herself in by the fire. The stout kept well out of Jemser's sight was what the doctor ordered. Invalid Guinness. Build back up the iron, he'd said in a serious voice. Nel raised her glass; suffer the little servant back on to the Countess, she nodded fervently to the silent salute.

'Twenty to twelve. Five minutes since yeh last heard the bells of Adam an' Eve's.' Attracta looked out the window; she was like a bag of weasels all morning. Fightin' with herself, fightin' with her fingernails. She could feel the vomit rising up again in her. She had an hour to pull herself together. Every muscle in her back and her belly was racked. Blood vessels were bruised and broken under her eyes. She felt as if she'd done ten rounds with Jack Johnson.

But sick or sober she had to tell him today. It was shit or bust. Yeh'll be all right. She wiped the bile from the corners of her mouth. He'll be as proud as punch.

But the more she talked herself round the confrontation, the more bile she spewed up.

Wednesday half-day, finished at one, scrub up, down the boozer before the holy hour. She could hear the swish of soap and water in the outhouse as he scrubbed and rubbed his hands together. Stripped to the waist, he'd be. Up to his elbows in the big auld sink. Oxters: ears, neck and face. An' the pickin' and proddin' out the cardinal red from under his fingernails. It was a sight to behold. He was particular, the same fellah. A vain cock.

It was there that they did it first and thereafter too. In the little outhouse, against the very same sink. An' the look in his eye as we'd swing through the door of the Chinaman's after. She took a deep breath. A pint for him, a port and lemonade for herself. The perfect end to the perfect day; she'd watch for that special something as he savoured his pint. The reverent silence before he'd lower the thick black liquid down his gullet. The cheek. It's yer only man after yiv done the bould deed. No shame, just pride and pleasure. Replenishes the energy, builds back up the red corpuscles.

He'd put the glass down with a vested authority and wait for the creamy circles to cling to the sides. She knew not to speak during this studied ritual. Some things were sacred to men. There wasn't a sinner in Dublin who'd say black was the white of yer eye when yeh were with the Butcher's Boy. Swollen with pride she'd be when they stepped it out at the Liberties.

Built like a brick shithouse, that's what they said. The best catch this side of the Liberties. Slippery as a shithouse, Jemser always said about him. Ignorant culchie. But Jemser was only jealous. Auld wans an' young wans would give their right eye to be seen on his muscular arm. Oh, love is blind, her Ma always sighed when she said she was meeting him. But they'd be singin' a different song this time next year when she had a ring on her left finger. A string of kids and cattle round a fine house in the country. Livin' off the fat of the land; the Rafferty's would be braggin' all round Stretham Street. Wantin' and waitin' for nothin'. Beholden to no one.

'Yer like shite boil't white.' It was an instant reaction to Attracta's pallor as she stepped out of the bedroom. Nel was as desperate for her daughter's sickness to pass as she was for her own fears.

'Well, boiled or half-baked, I'm not spendin' another day with this contraption swingin' under me chin. Another day of me head in that bucket and I'll slit me own throat.'

'But yer a terrible pallor.' The first shift yeh see in her in a week, and you go and put yer big foot in the way. Nel hauled her mouth out of the way of her own well-being.

'It's only food poisonin', Ma. I have to shake meself some time.' Attracta hoped Nel wasn't listening to closely. 'I'm round at Concepta's.'

Nel settled herself back in the chair. She liked the temporary comfort of the lie. Taking her Guinness by the neck, she let it mingle gently with her delusions.

Attracta slapped vivid rouge and lipstick on an alabaster complexion. Nel watched her daughter change into a china doll.

'Maybe yer right. A bit of fresh air. But cover yerself up. Don't shed a clout.' She sank the rising fear with another mouthful of Guinness.

Before the next bout of sickness overtook her, Attracta reached for the door.

'Tip that bucket a' puke on skins. Billy Atkins won't know the differ when he collects the swill; neither will the pigs.' Attracta left before her Ma got any closer to the mark.

She ran the gauntlet of saggy steps, braying biddies' and prying eyes. 'Bejaysus, Attracta, yeh smell like a whore at a hockey match. You're lookin' very hot in yer leathers.' They jeered as she trouped past in her big coat.

'I'd get all yeh can outa him while it lasts. Yeh can't pawn romance when he's finished with yeh.' Their catcalls ran in front and behind her, bouncing off peeling ceilings and cold damp walls. She could feel the bile rising with the heat and temper.

'Have yeh tasted his sweetbreads yet?' Smutty laughter ripped along the saggy steps. 'Oh, the nearer the bone, the sweeter the meat.'

Surely to God they couldn't know, they couldn't have been watching. Attracta didn't know where to put her face. Now or then. She didn't like doing that. Never knew whether to spit or swally. But he could be very persuasive. Normally she'd have given as good as she got. But today she was carrying the weight of compromise. She was heavy with worry.

Cashmere might keep out the cold. But it didn't keep a body cool. She stopped to open her coat. Her belly had ballooned; her diddies were getting harder to hide by the day. She couldn't keep her condition under wraps for much longer. Her body was getting as far ahead of her as the weather.

Pressing her fingers into her thigh, she counted out the weeks since her last period. No matter how many times she counted, she ended up with the same number of weeks and the same number of fingers. The only sight of blood she'd seen in the last two months was in the butcher's shop. Whether yeah start on yer thumb or yer finger, yeh still end up pregnant. Another rush of bile sent her scurrying up an alleyway. There was nothing left to throw up, the dry retching pulled furiously at the bottom of her belly.

Her last period had been on Paddy's day. March 17th till May the 27th. By her handy ready reckoner, she was ten weeks pregnant. Another month and the whole world would know what only she knew now. Another month and the whole of Stretham Street will be markin' yer cards. Debatin' when yeh got caught. Addin' locations to their calculations.

She whipped herself up. A speck of vomit landed on her coat. She sniffed the collar: stale porter and puke. He'll ravish yeh. Her stomach turned over again.

Searching for the answer her fingers couldn't find, she gulped gallons of fresh air. Taking Thomas Street two steps at a time, she was into the final straight. The shop was a hive of industry. Everybody working flat out to finish on their half day off. A young fellah was hoisting up awnings with a rare gusto. Another swilling sawdust off the shop floor directly into the gutter outside.

Heads snapped up as she walked into the shop. She wished the ground would open and swallow her. Hiding rising panic, she put a broad smile on her face and asked for him.

'Well this is a nice surprise.' Billy senior sounded as if he was tipping someone off.

When his son came out of the back with a new shop girl in tow, she knew why. The Butcher's Boy knew by her face there was trouble. And so did his father.

135

Giving her short shift, he directed her to the Chinaman's. Told her to wait there for him.

'Order me pint before the Holy Hour.' She did as she was bid, not a peep out of her.

'Who's the wan?' She waited till half the Guinness was down his gullet.

'Which wan?' He looked straight ahead.

'Anyway.' She was in no mood for his riddles. 'I think we're in trouble.' She was trying to demolish days again on her handy abacus. He didn't bat an eyelid as she outlined the dilemma. She struggled to choke back tears, to read his silence.

'I'll be round to the house first thing in the mornin'.' Slippery as an eel. Attracta sensed it but couldn't see it.

'They'll be wonderin' what's keepin' me if I stay too long.' We slaughter on a Wednesday, yeh know how it is. Not a word to a sinner now.' He was waving like a returned emigrant when he left her.

Her relief was enormous. Sick as a pig, she still let him have his way.

She slid into bed as soon as she arrived home. Gorette was under the covers; reading as usual. She was trying to tell her something about paper that had fallen out of a pocket in Attracta's apron. Something about the Bishop of Dublin and a bit on the side and dirty words that he was writing to her.

But Attracta's head was too full of marriage and the Butcher's Boy to listen to her little sister. A firm puck in the ribs brought the business of the Bishop to an abrupt end. She didn't give a shite about any auld Bishop or his bit on the side.

Attracta was whispering, 'I'm getting married and you're goin' to be me bridesmaid.' She swore her to secrecy. 'Get rid of the feckin' auld piece of paper, dump it, do whatever yeh like with it, but don't bother me with it. Don't yeh see Gorette, I'm finished with Ballsbridge and Bishops, finished. I'm free.' But Gorette, the brainbox Gorette, the dark horse, wasn't about to dump anything.

Fourteen

Sane people send a thank you note after dinner. The Teeny Tinys sent a Nanny goat and a Billy. Muriel looked into the back garden. Tethered together and they still managed to get up to devilment. What in the name of God possessed them? Muriel asked the same question every time she set eyes on them.

'They'll be worth their weight in gold when the baby comes. It might be the very time we need them most.' Brigit had been adamant. 'What if you can't feed the creature? It was beg, borrow or steal milk for the little man here. The auld tinned offerin's had him bunged up. And meself moidered. There's nothing to better goat's milk.'

Even after they had devoured a line of washing, Brigit's defence stayed strong. 'At the very least, we have a garden now; up until they were forced upon us, we had a forest. And I warned yeh, the Horse Protestants were different. I met them in Komiskey's this evenin' when I slipped in to give Isaac the new novena. Oh, still full of the Bishop's visit. Blubberin' and bubblin', they couldn't contain themselves. A post mortician would have nothin' on the detail.' Brigit was bedding the fire down.

Beginning her nightly rituals. Sprinkling thick brown paper bags with water, she wedged them in at the back of the range. The dampened slack would keep the fire going into the small wee hours. Keep the home fires burning bright for the man of the house. Such as he was.

God preserve us from the demon drink. She blessed herself, kept her prayer to Matt Talbot as silent as her thoughts. The patron saint of sinners was her last resort, Fonsie's drinkin' had erupted, and there was something she couldn't put her thumb under – between himself and Barclay O'Rourke.

The visitation had doubled the trouble, had accelerated the drinkin' out of all reason. Begod, he could drink his parents into a cocked hat. And that's goin' it some.

A long sigh summoned old ghosts. 'Many's a time they were still partyin' here at dawn, the same pair. But that was in the auld god's time.' Brigit rubbed a grey hand round the small of her back. 'Oh, there was never a tomorrow in them days.'

Brigit was in one of her storytelling moods. A slow smile spread across Muriel's face. The rawmashins, ministrations, brought their own special comfort and helped to pass the long nights. At first, Muriel thought she was still talking about the Horse Protestants. It took sometime to realise that it was old Mr and Mrs Duggan she'd resurrected.

'I can still see Master Fonsie. Not two hands higher than a duck an him sittin' in the window, watchin' an' waitin' for them to come home. An' of course it would be daybreak before the auld horse and trap would career into the yard. Oh now, a clatter of hooves and confusion. As often as not, I'd be blowin' morning life into this very fire.'

She didn't elaborate on the misdemeanours. Herself mouldy tryin' to button him up. Make him presentable before they'd come through the door. An' the front of the trousers sodden. 'Where they got the straight-laced Fonsie from was a mystery?'

'I often heard them asking the same question. Then laughin' like lunatics. The fairies they'd say, a changeling they'd say. A changeling was right for he was never a child; sure, he was too frightened to be a child. An' now look at him. Too frightened to be a man.' She shook out the past, brought back in the present.

'Mind you, if Mr Fonsie hadn't picked up the cudgels after he left Maynooth and put his mind to the practice, we'd all have been in the poor house.'

'Was he away long?' Brigit was glad of the detour.

'Four or five years, as far as I can remember.' Muriel listened for the connection with Barclay but no mention was forthcoming.

'Is that where he became friends with the Bishop?' She wouldn't normally be so blatant.

'They were seminarians in them days.' Brigit set the scene. 'There was a gang of them would come here to tea a couple of times a year. Playin' cards, singin' round the piana. Horse Protestants included. Of course, the pair of them would have been well into their forties by then. Safe, yeh see, past their prime. Maynooth'd sanction them. Propriety found pride of place in Brigit's voice.

'Was age relevant?' Muriel was hungry for detail.

'Oh aye. Sure, a parish priest's housekeeper couldn't sit up in the front of his car with him till she was past fifty years of age. The likes of you and I, no matter how innocent, couldn't be seen in a public place on yer own with a priest. Unless yeh had special permission from a Bishop. And it would have to be a very valid reason.'

Very valid reason. She wondered if placing bonds, bundles of used notes, in Barclay's security box would qualify for the special dispensation.

'Oh, save yer breath.' Brigit lit on Muriel's sigh. 'If yeh put a clerical collar on a pig, there are women out there that would chase after him.' Every syllable was invested with authority. 'The likes of yerself or meself wouldn't understand the fascination. But the devil is always waiting in the wings for Holy Orders.'

'Oh, yer innocence is easy offended, Mam.' Making Muriel blush was never Brigit's intention.

'Some of the young seminarians were lovely. God bless us, pure as the driven snow. It was sacred just to serve them. But that Barclay O'Rourke was as mad as a March hare.' Brigit stopped abruptly. 'Sure, who am I tellin'? Didn't yeah work for the same fellah?'

Muriel's demeanour changed.

'I never found the Bishop to be anything less than reliable.' She couldn't hear the lie in her own voice but Brigit could.

Sensing the offence, Brigit changed her tack but not the advantage.

'They liked good tables, the same boys. There were very few exceptions. The Duggans here, with their partyin' and posturin', their huntin', shootin' and salmon fishin', would have been a godsend. The remnants of auld decency they might have been in the end, but they had all the class and the clout to impress. The likes of Barclay O'Rourke had their eye on the big game. Barclay was always going to be a bishop. He made no bones about it in private, however much he protested in public.'

'Ah sure, who could blame them wantin' the bit of comfort. It's better than sittin' in the poor unfortunates' company wastin' their warmth an' words.'

Her defence lacked something essential for Muriel. But tonight wasn't about arguing, it was about listening and learning. Though at times the lessons were as hard on the ear as they were on the heart.

'Drinkin' and carousin' around Kildare this pair were famous for.' Brigit pointed as if the old ghosts were round the kitchen table. 'Not a titter of wit between them. 'Twas no wonder Fonsie couldn't stay the ecclesiastical course. In truth, he was never bred to pray. But he was bred to pay. Sure, Maynooth's fees were always in the post. In the heel of the hunt. 'Twas probably pride played the final hand in Fonsie's downfall. I suppose that and the parents passing. Dead an' buried within six months of the other.'

Heaviness settled round Brigit's shoulders. There was more on her mind than she was letting out. Muriel wondered what it was.

'His departure fair sorted the men from the boys. Clergy were scarcer than hen's teeth around this house then. The buckos that watered and fed the best were the first out the door. But to give Barclay O'Rourke his due, he didn't desert as such. He disappeared. But sure they were already groomin' him. Manufactured in Clongowes, processed in Maynooth.

'Poor Fonsie was like a man on a mission. Married and a father before yeh could shake a lambs tail at him. Cash wasn't as short as credence to the newly weds. Fonsie's wife had a few bob, and a couple of well-placed contributions redressed the balance. He restocked the larder and the drink cabinet.

And paid for it all too. Oh, credit was a thing of the past. There was precious little of it left in anyway. Hell bent on reinstatin' respectability, he was. So when Barclay O'Rourke became Bishop of Dublin, well God preserve us, he crowed like the village cock.

'But it was less an' less of his Lordship we saw once he got hold of the mitre. Oh, he showed up for Fonsie's wife's funeral. Married, birthed and buried all in the space of two calendar years. Who with a beatin' heart wouldn't? An' he showed up if he wanted something. An' he was very plausible then, as no doubt he is now. I often saw fifty pounds an' double goin' across this table. To good causes. Charity begins at home, how are yeh.' Brigit's eyes rose slowly up to Heaven.

A quartet of clocks called a halt to the confession.

She reached above the mantelpiece for her Rosary beads, kissed the cross and slid it into her apron pocket.

'Would yeh do me a favour and wind up his auld clocks before they stop entirely? I don't know what's come over himself this weather. Winding up was always such a religion with him.' She handed Muriel the keys. Set her winding tomorrow into the clocks. I'm off to me bed. I'm weary to me bones. That tired I sleep hangin' over a clothes line.' Brigit yawned loudly as she took the tilly lamp.

She hoped that she hadn't been too hard on the Bishop. But deep in her soul, she blamed him in some part for Fonsie's behaviour. The stark imagery came to Brigit. The disappearing act, the cut of him when he pitched up after the Bishop's party had only just departed. Ranting and raving about not being welcome in his own marriage. A stooge for the Bishop. She thought he was for Loman's mental institute that same night. She started her Rosary unsure of whether she was praying for her master's soul or his sanity.

Caught somewhere outside herself, Muriel sat stroking cool clean oilcloth. Soaking up familiar sounds and smells, she relaxed into the rhythm of the night. Sods of turf hissing and spitting out comforting smells. A cake of soda bread wrapped in white muslin resting on the

140

dresser. Fresh eggs laid out for the morning. Drowsily dreaming. Barclay, momentarily real, slides in beside her. Eyes black with desire burn into her soul. Blood and bones fill her brimful of him. The word is made flesh. She cradles her belly. As she dreams, hope, hopeless hope, bends and shapes her.

But circumstances had always conspired to curse Muriel Grey. Nature and nurture both, doubling her burden.

A father repulsed by his own wife replaces her with a daughter. Reviled, the mother watches as he pillages her child. Reigns a powerful pull over her. Falling short of his approval, the mother diminishes. The daughter miraculously grows. Ceaselessly bending to his will, she feeds his ego. Impotent, the mother finally concedes. Spaces and secrets separate mother and daughter until death takes a hand. And nature takes advantage of the vacuum and lets Barclay in.

This was an older story still. And Barclay has God on his side. Childish, charming, perilously eager to please, Muriel clings to him. Bursting with hope and practical innocence, she reveres him. Loves him more loyally than she loves her Father. A strikingly plain child, a condition constantly confirmed by her mother, she grows into a strikingly beautiful woman. Lacking only the confidence her small world has stolen.

Energetic and ambitious, the new Bishop of Dublin never misses a Sunday roast after her father's death. Courted royally by both mother and daughter. They cling passionately to every word and deed, take them to bed and wake up each morning with Barclay on their tongues, on their lips. Undivided attention gives him the chance to cross a forbidden line.

But his enthusiasm and drive are no match for her heightened expectations. What fevers him only frustrates her, until in time she takes the bull by the horn. And a child is conceived. Profoundly disturbed by the pregnancy, he turns his guilt on her and blames her for his mistake. Desperate for his approval, she tiptoes round his reason and welcomes his solution. Relieved, he watches her cover for his sins. Rests temporarily on his shaky laurels. Confession, contrition, absolution: he resolves never to sin again. But by then she's married and safely lodged in Leixlip.

'Barclay's sailing close to the wind again.' Her father's ghost commuted itself. *The difference between divulge and disclose is only the width of a Bishop's conscience.* Poring over Barkley's books, he's troubled. *He'll lose the mitre if they find our about the deposit box. Who else could keep these books? Who else would keep his secrets?* Careless, careless, he's calling Barclay.

141

Her father: she hadn't thought about her father in a long time. The thought troubled her. The child inside her moved. Heads or tails, she was never any the wiser. Sleep was closing round her. Turf light bounced off a batch of empty stout bottles. Harbingers of doom.

A key scraping round and round the heavy lock made her start.

Peloothered eyes rolling in his head, his suit smeared with the filth and stench of some public house, Fonsie staggered through the door. Grunting, snorting indecent insults.

'Take a drink with me, madam?' He pulled the cork from a bottle of stout and poured it unsteadily. Muriel froze. It wasn't a request, it was an order.

'To God what is God's. To Fonsie what is Fonsie's. It's a toast – a toast.'

She made to leave. She wasn't giving a drunk man her senses. But he was going to have his say.

'Yer astray in the head since the day nor hour of this marriage. An yeh have this poor unfortunate astray in the head too. Yer unnatural. Yeh couldn't even help the grievin' pass. Couldn't fill the gap.' His voice seemed to be coming from a demented place. 'I was conned, conned into this marriage. Led up the bridal path by the nose. No, no, by the Bishop.' His head drooped and swung from side to side under its own weight.

'Oh, I could curl your blood with revelations. But Fonsie Duggan's word's his bond. It's a secret, a sacred mystery, seal of confession on it. Shss... a mortal sin, only a Bishop can legally absolve it. I wish to hell I could break. Wasn't Jesus the wise man, never marryin'? Wasn't he wise' madam?'

'Loveless, friendless, wifeless. What are women for?' His mouth was slobbering; his reasoning was coming and going.

'Found meself a real woman for a shillin' in Fumble Alley. Serpent's prey. Curse a God on her. Oh, she'd have yeh on hot walls an' cold. Lies an' lust.' He dragged the slimy words along his sleeve.

Thick tongued. Muriel could only make out part of the clotted insults. Terror took hold of her. Her stomach was tightening and slackening. She thought she was going into her labour.

'Life for me now is made up of necessity.'

She tried to get past him, but he blocked her. Something carnal leeching behind his eyes sent a chill through her bones.

'Shame on yer soul. On yer soul, madam.

'Me day's mocked by parts of yesterday and bits of tomorrow. Compromise and cowardice.' The silence that followed this explosion was shorter than the previous outburst.

'It's taken the patience of a saint and no unsubstantial leap of faith not to cast yeh out on the street. Yiv turned the sanctity of me home into a sorry sordid place.' His eyelids were dropping; he was drifting in and out of sleep.

She waited for the sleep to deepen. With the weight of compromise on her back, she pulled herself up the stairs to bed.

In the early hours of the morning, still drunk, still shod, he stumbled and fell heavily beside her. She woke to find him hovering over her. Eyes begging without hope, a pickled vomit odour in her face. She retched as ice-cold hands fumbled under the sheets. Recoiling in horror, she tried to get away from him.

'Fonsie, in God's name, the baby,' she tried to reason.

'Whose baby?' The sour breath saturated her nostrils.

'I think you're confused.' She ripped the hand from her groin.

'I think, madam, you'll find it you who's confused.' Slow and slurred as a wound-down gramophone, the voice was menacing. 'I may in the recent past have been guilty of gross stupidity. But confusion, no.' She felt a throb of dread as he tore at buttoned trousers. 'I have conjugal rights that you' madam' have a duty to fulfil. Now you'll lie there and think of the roof over your head an' be grateful.'

Unleashing his anger, he mounted her like an animal. Writhing convulsively, his sticky mess spewed: stinking barren seed saturated her. Dry silent scream offered its dismal remedy. Her contempt was mute. When he finally fell off, she realised that the dry taste on her tongue was the sheet she was stuffing violently into her own mouth.

Brigit noted the dishevelled look on her Muriel's, the dilated pupils. She'd seen the wild look before. When night became mornin' and married couples appeared downstairs. At least, they were communicating. She thanked God for the small marcies. Himself would be down soon. Incapable of embarrassment. Never mind the auld retainer. The invisible serpent after its shameless pantomime. Requirin' a hearty breakfast, replenshin' his manliness.

She put her big pan on the range and cracked open fresh eggs. Herself would be wantin' a big feed too if the past missus was any indicator of the present.

Fifteen

Inching his way into the shade, Archbishop Ennis counted his blessings. In these, he included his full belly, a blessing he rightly attributed to his excellent cook. He also included his garden, his arboreal haven, where he should be today out enjoying the fresh air instead of being cooped up in his office.

He felt closer to God in his garden than in any cathedral in Ireland. In this particular climate, where every day was an uphill struggle with congregations and controversy and bull bishops. It was time to pull a few horns back into line. He turned his back to the sun and began his dictation.

The Archbishop's secretary kept his head low, took down all he heard as dictation, and offered the sun streaming in through the huge open window on his back up for the holy souls in Purgatory. Between blistering heat and the constant harping on and on about Doctor Noel Brown and the destabilisation that his crusade was having on the Church and State, he should surely get cartloads of the lost souls over the threshold and into Heaven this day.

'A creeping concern, which seems to be presenting itself with increasing vigour and regularity, is the widening social stance between Doctor Noel Brown and ourselves, and its deep moral consequence.'

The Archbishop began dictating another of his eternal documents to the Episcopal Committee. Long-finger letters, his secretary called these missives. The issues the Archbishop was addressing so passionately weren't due to be aired until the next Episcopal gathering in Maynooth. And that little jolly wasn't for at least six months. His secretary's own more creeping and current concern was the hurling match between the Dublin and Cork miners just up the road this evening.

'What set itself out as an irritant less than a year ago, is today, with gathering force and conviction, challenging the social and moral attitudes of friends and foes alike in Ireland. Specifically, the attitudes of women in the delicate areas of maternity and sexuality.

'These, my dear brothers in Christ, are dangerous times for Catholics and for the future of the Catholic Church in Ireland. To empower a public authority to educate women in regard to health is a folly. To provide women with gynaecological services that could or could not be used to control birth is fatal. To say nothing about the

144

laws of God and the rights of man. How far are we from abortion or euthanasia?

'This Doctor Brown worries me intensely. With his energetic socialisation of medicine, his shortsighted solutions. Everyone is against him but the public. Am I unique in thinking that we ignore this to our peril?

'A deluge of bilingual information is pouring out from the Department of Health. Cleverly illustrated half-page advertisements, in both national and provincial newspapers. And here, amongst my own brothers in Christ, we have seen little but lethargy and stale arrogance in combat.'

The Archbishop finished with a flourish of self-importance. And a worryingly high colour about the gills, his secretary noted.

His last letter that evening was addressed to his brother, a leading member of the Fianna Fail party. After suitable niceties, he went straight to the point.

'And a further blindness: amongst us, we have a magnetic Bishop in the form of the Bishop of Dublin, to whom peers and seniors alike appear to be giving too much credence.

'He worries me as much as the ethereal Noel Brown, but for differing reasons. Always an ambitious bishop, his ambition has recently turned inwards. There appears to me to be a new addition to this clamouring, the desire for reassurance and recognition. The distinction should be made to him that there are those who enter religion for the good of others and those who enter for the good of themselves. He appears to have confused his roles. And this, Dear brother, is the calibre of man that Rome sees fit to fight the driven Doctor Brown.

'I believe he is losing valuable ground. Explaining away blatant discrepancies in doctrine either side of the Irish Sea, as changing words for a changing world. It's nothing short of dogmatic suicide. Does he think or, worse, believe that Catholic congregations have the brains as well as the instincts of sheep? The days of bludgeoning blunderers are long since gone. The Catholic Church can't be seen to lose valuable, sacred ground.

'Maybe it's time the episcopate considered some hard facts. Am I not blue in the face preaching the weakness of idols both publicly and privately to each and every one of them? It's time the Bishop of Dublin was pulled back into line, and reminded that the Catholic Church is a body, made up of different men, of whom he is only one of many. And that whilst men change, the Church will always stay constant. And that is her strength.'

But even as the Archbishop wrote, he could sense the futility, feel the backslide. He was old. Men like Barclay O'Rourke, younger, powerful, more popular men were running the Church in Ireland. Had they ever handed over their guilty Bishop, the cowardly informant? Had any one of them had the gumption to come and speak to him about the whole unsavoury incident to seek his counsel? Had they hell.

Sixteen

A merciless sun blistered the pavement: the balls of Attracta's feet were burning. She wished with all her heart that she wasn't meeting Fatama and Concepta. Wished double that she didn't need the money for the abortion. Hands plunged like weights in her coat pocket, she waded through the mid-day shoppers in Moore Street. Fuming for being so stupid, for being no different from the rest of them.

Blather an' skite, the life blood of Moore Street flew over her troubled head.

'I know yeh ordered a dozen. Yeh, I know there's only eleven now. I threw one away for yeh. It was rotten.' Oranges and apples juggled between the banter. Stunning shoppers, summoning admirers. What would gladden her heart normally made her fit to spit blades today.

Fatama watched from the window of the public house. Concepta had been more than cute about this meeting with Attracta. Pregnancy, she suspected, was the problem. Nurse Flannagan and money the solution. She's thinkin' of goin' to England. She just needs the few bob for her fare. Concepta's decoy had doubled Fatama's resolve not to part with any cash. But it opened up the possibility of a mutually more beneficial arrangement.

She sipped at her whiskey. It was a sunny summer's day. She could afford to let the drama unfold. She hitched her top lip up to her nose, a habit she had developed over the years when she was studying someone closely.

Tawdry and potent, a trail of sexuality followed Attracta into the pub. Fatama knew it well, needed it in a girl if she was to make her the kind of money she once made herself. She was past teachin' auld dogs new tricks. She needed new blood in her stable. She suspected Concepta was short-changing her. Attracta Rafferty might as well be paid for what she was givin' away for free. She had a look that knew no boundaries. Cocky, selfish, comfortable in her skin. A mane of blonde hair. Come-to-bed eyes, taut tits, legs that went all the way up to her arse. Common, other women called it. But not men. If she had Attracta Rafferty working the streets of Dublin, she could retire in a year. Sitting on a fortune she was.

She felt the scrutiny of Fatama's eyes as the gabble and blather of Dublin accents assaulted her ears. A bizarre shriek rose from the crowd; Fatama's coarse sound brought attention. Fatama was a fucker.

A young boy brought over a round of drinks. Fatama paid. Terror filled Attracta's chest. Nel Rafferty would fillet her if she even had an inkling of the company she was keeping. Lie down with dogs and yeh end up with fleas. But beggars couldn't be choosers. And she was perilously close to begging. Time was ticking. She hoped the gin sluicing through her veins would bolster her confidence. It did precious little else for her last week. Cod liver oil, orange juice and gin – Concepta's concoction came back with a vengeance.

'Isn't this some weather all the same? It's hot enough to boil yer own water.' Fatama stretched out the young girl's terror.

It wasn't Attracta's first attempt at trying to raise the money, but it was her last. She couldn't put herself through much more of this humiliation. She gone to the pawnshop and made a holy show of herself. Telling Mortie Goodman that she'd have the money back to him in a week. Stuttering and stammering, making a pigs ear out of the empty promises. The eyes that nailed her lies to the floor had withered her will. The shift in circumstances didn't sit well on Attracta. Her pride suffered.

Fatama's eyes bored holes in her soul. She'll have her pound of flesh. Like a child's recitation, the warning ran round her head.

The hardest bitch in Dublin. Will yeh, won't yeh, will yeh, won't yeh. Well, yeh can keep yer money and stick it up yer tight arse. Don't make me beg. Poker faced, she didn't want Fatama to have any inkling of how desperate she was.

'I seen yeh hangin' outa the Butcher's young fellah.' She knew the same article had scarpered leaving a trail of debts, a bun in Attracta's oven. She began to relax into the disharmony.

'Red raw when's he's on heat, isn't he?' Nicotine poured in a steady stream from stained nostrils. 'Lusty Loins, they used to call his father. It isn't offa the side of the road he licked his longin's.' She played with Attracta's pride. 'He's more in common with the bulls he breeds than the cows he collects around Dublin.'

Attracta flushed. She couldn't find space to breathe, let alone beg. She wished with all her heart now that she had followed her own instincts and asked the Jewman. If that bearded baldly auld bollix doesn't get his money back, he'll take it in kind. In the glory hole: Concepta had told her.

She has me over her fat barrel. She eyed Fatama for too long.

'Yiv been in the wars, I hear – food poison. A dirty dose they say.'

148

'It's me belly. It's not been right since I started in Ballsbridge.' The practised lie tripped off her lips.

'Nothin' that gin or good dose of cod liver oil won't shift, I hope?' Callous eyes waited.

She stared at Fatama's hands. Five fortunes on every crooked finger. Any one of her rings would solve her problems, past, present and future.

Concepta swept in like a breath of fresh air. At last.

'Me an' me little whore's apprentice here are flattered by your company.' Fatama's sneer put Concepta firmly in her place. And Attracta too. They'd become far too friendly of late. Her jealousy surprised her.

'I don't suppose it's for the good of yer health yer sittin' here starin' at me, Attracta Rafferty.' She looked idly round the bar as she spoke.

'I was wonderin'? Is there any chance? What would yeh say to the lend of a loan?' Attracta fumbled with a procession of beginnings.

The silence that followed was excruciating. Concepta cringed. She'd never seen this side of Attracta. She wondered if she was all in it putting up with Fatama's shit-stirring. She's not stable since he's scarpered; not right in the head since his auld wan gave her short shift of the doorstep. It was terrible to think of her crawlin', but another to witness her crucified. Fatama was a cruel fucker when she had the upper hand.

Attracta's body slumped in the seat. Her sore head howled. If only the little bastard had owned up. Bookies, biddies, bad debts, the Mail boat. The turncoat. Every syllable stuck in her craw. Her coat fell open. If she'd planned it, it couldn't have been worse timing.

'Big diddies, round bellies, that's where the money's made.' Fatama's smile gained something in that moment.

Attracta could hardly bear the violence of the humiliation. If she hadn't been stuck between a rock an' a hard bitch, she'd have slung a drink in Fatama's leathery auld face, let it to soak up the sarcasm.

She would have bet her prized bonds Attracta Rafferty was too cute to be caught. In a way, she was disappointed with her. She saw the satisfaction that filled Fatama's face.

'Money is a pox, and love is a lie.' Did yeh ever hear that one, Attracta Rafferty?

Time was marching on. The lunchtime drinkers had come and gone. A few hard-chaws like themselves remained incarnate. Girding herself for another round before Fatama or her patience ran out. Attracta dug her nails hard into the palm of her hands. Feigning interest in Concepta and Fatama's yarns, she could hear herself laughing too long and too loud.

'I've a regular Friday nighter now, a rich man.' Concepta was humouring Fatama.

'How deh you know he's rich?' Attracta pretended she cared.

'She knows because I told her. When I get fed up rubbin' their auld relics up, I hand them over to her. It takes longer to rise them when they're auld. Fatama Fagan hasn't got that sort of time.'

'It doesn't take me long.' Concepta, smart-arsed, wasn't doing Attracta any favours.

Fatama caught her completely off the hop.

'You haven't said what yeah want from me, but I'll say what I want from you. The Butcher's Boy's scarpered and left yeh with a pain in yer belly. That's easy to solve. The way I see it, yeh haven't much choice. Yeh can be another beast of burden on Stretham Street with a babby in yer belly an' a blackguard on yer back, day and night.' Fatama spat resentment as she drained her glass. 'Or work for me and charge hard cash for the services yeh flingin' round so freely. Yeh can have the money yeh need to solve yer solution. An' yeh'll be workin for Fatama Fagan. Workin off yer arrears like yer little crony here. Yis might as well put all yer big buddyin' into business. A double act always pays more.'

Something between fright and flight took Attracta. She'd come looking for a solution but had ended up with an ultimatum.

In an attempt to claw back some credibility, she spluttered that the Butcher's Boy wasn't her only admirer. That she had a rich man in her life too. But she was going nowhere. Two painted and powdered faces looked pained at her strained lies.

Fatama turned on her. 'Yeh know the auld Dublin sayin'? It's a wise man that knows his own father. Let him fork out for that babby in yer belly then.'

She counted weeks frantically in her head. Counted them on her fingers just as she'd counted a hundred times. But this time the count fell into two camps. The Butcher's, and the Bishop's. Her armpits squelched with relief, and sweat ran freely down her back as her mind raced. They were both at it hammer an' tongs at the same time. Why hadn't she thought of it herself? Fatama was right.

'There now piss or get off the pot, Attracta Rafferty.'

The taunt backfired. From Fatama's mouth to Attracta's ear.

It wasn't a ready reckoner she needed. All she needed was an auld slapper like Fatama to figure out her future.

150

Seventeen

A band tightened round Fonsie's temples. He wished he could purge himself of these constant companions: anger and frustration. Jesus, how he hated Barclay O'Rourke. Hated him. For slipping the rug out from under his feet. For shackling him to a beautiful wife: a barren bed.

She stirred scalding hot tea and moved the breakfast cup out of harm's reach as she talked to the child. A light summer dress left her shoulders and neck modestly bare. Gentle and naked, his ear followed her voice up and down. There was softness, a grace, that went with her bearing. And for all the pride, there was an air of vulnerability. He could see the shape of the child inside her. Swollen in the darkness of the womb; waiting to come out into the light. Breasts straining, full to the brim. Madonna and child.

Conversation between them was limited but polite these days. All his wants and needs were addressed through Brigit. Arrangements set in stone. She stroked the child's head. A shaft of sunlight fell on her. The soft light on her skin tortured him. He had never referred to the incident since. Couldn't even think about that night now without crushing crucifying shame.

He nodded almost embarrassed when she asked him if he wanted a fresh cup of tea. It was always more difficult when Brigit was out. Awkward and strained.

Brigit was doing another novena. She'd seen a full moon shining through the kitchen window last week: it brought shocking bad luck. She had gone to the chapel every evening since. A seven-day novena. Where would she be without Brigit Murphy? She'd be on her knees now. Rosary beads flying through her fingers, whish-whishing wiles away. Weaving prayers around friends and foes. Curing all ails.

Muriel had never been tied to church or chapel. Her mother's fanaticism had seen to that. Her taste in art sealed it. The Agony of Christ, specially commissioned, hung high on the dining room wall. Good for neither the appetite nor the soul, her father used to whisper. Much good praying did her the night he raped her. It offered neither protection nor consolation. Agony had come back in battalions.

Where was God when she had found the nightdress? Torn at the neck, stiff at the hem, stark testimony to her torture. She should have burnt the obscene garment in the fire that ugly night. But she didn't have the energy after the ordeal. And when she had had the energy, she didn't have the strength to confront the evil. He'd never referred to the incident again. But he knew then, as sure as he knew now, that it had been rape. A full moon must have been shining through the glass window that fateful night.

Fonsie saw the chin rise. Pride was a big part of her problem, maybe both their problems. It was pride that separated them and pride that made her hang on the myth of Barclay. He wanted to reach a hand across the dead space, wanted to tell her how sorry he was, tell her that she was fooling herself. That Barclay O'Rourke was nobody's friend but his own.

But his fall from grace had pushed him even further to the sidelines of her life. She was unyielding in her requirements of him. Harsh realities and unspoken rules had established themselves both privately and publicly. He wished that things could be different. That they could put their energies into surviving. He opened his morning paper.

BISHOP SPEAKS OUT OF THE TOP OF HIS MITRE.

His relief was instant. He almost laughed out loud. At last, someone else was on his side. *You can fool some of the people some of the time but not all of the people all of the time.* The metaphor, mixed as it was, excited him more. For one holy moment, he didn't feel so alone, didn't feel so foolish.

As always in matters relating to the Bishop, Muriel focused with a concentration not lost on Fonsie. Holding the paper out like a trophy, he ensured that she had a clear view of the headlines. And he in turn a clear view of the turbulent emotions possessing her.

IRISH CATHOLICS AND BRITISH CATHOLICS – ANSWERABLE TO TWO DIFFERENT GODS?

His eyes fell greedily on every word. A surfeit of emotions overtook his pleasure. The bloodhounds are on his tail. I can smell the blood. I hope they crucify him. I hope he can begin to feel some of the humiliations I feel daily. Capillaries charged his face; his neck turned a deep purple.

Conscientious Catholics sin if they transgress against Catholic moral teaching. There is no such sanction attached to Catholic social teaching. If the Bishop of Dublin is claiming that the proposed Irish national health scheme is contrary to Catholic moral teaching, then let him stand up and be counted. But let him also stand up and condemn the British national health scheme in the North of Ireland in the same breath.

Muriel strained to read.

152

The women of Ireland might be martyrs to their men, but they aren't all fools to their Bishops. Supping deeply from his tea, Fonsie contemplated the delicious shift. Bringing children into the world was women's work. Decisions regarding such delicate matters should be left fairly and squarely in female quarters. Eager for confirmation, he read on.

This new Minister for Health is nearer the women's hearts than the Church thinks. All the clerical charisma in the country can't beat common sense.

And the sooner Rome gets that under their mitres, the nearer we'll all be to reality and Heaven. He sat back with a flourish. Barclay's torching released a flood of emotions in Fonsie. He wanted to share the running commentary going on inside his head. Wanted to have a conversation with someone who wanted to listen to him. Exhibiting more than a hint of satisfaction, he stood up from the table. Leaving the newspaper deliberately behind him.

Against the tide. Muriel read the editorial.

'When he changed a long-standing order from the *Independent* newspaper to the *Irish Times*, I should have know he'd changed his allegiance.' She spoke to the infant perched on the edge of her lap, continued reading in spite of the churning in her stomach.

A less than complementary photograph of Barclay was plastered across the front page. 'And Barclay never looked like this.' The boy's smiles reassured her.

In the Kingdom of the blind, only the Bishop of Dublin can see!

'Scurrilous.' The face looking innocently up at her registered the change of tone.

Powerful politicians, recognising that the Bishop of Dublin's power dwarfs their own in frightening multiples, court a dangerously out-of-control ego at their peril.

Muriel's mouth fell open. The article continued.

His promises are unlimited by reality. For him to question the right of the State to assume the responsibility of the education of mothers in motherhood is arrogance of the grossest human failing. And to postulate in the same breath the inevitability of contraception and abortion is ignorance of the highest order. His warning to a packed Adam and Eve's on the feast of the Holy Innocents needs closer scrutiny. To state that Doctor Noel Brown was interfering with the laws of God and nature, which in turn would lead to the ruination of Irish family life as we know it, is sinful. That his policies carry with them messages of a society out of control, and out of God's favour, is unforgivable.

153

Utterly confounded, Muriel read on. *Where did the Bishop of Dublin draw the line between Catholic social teaching and Catholic moral teaching? And how did the anomaly between the Catholic Church in Northern Ireland and the Catholic Church in the Republic sit so easily on religious shoulders? Could it be that the Reverent Fathers were singing from different hymn sheets?* Muriel's brow knitted. *Because if that were indeed the case, there was arrogance in the ignorance, and ignorance in the arrogance, that beggared belief.*

Muriel could virtually feel the vitriol of the final full stop through the paper. How could they get away with such an out-and-out attack on Barclay? Even in her advanced condition, she resolved there and then to support Barclay, publicly if necessary. She was in the act of burning the copy of the *Irish Times* when Brigit walked back in on her fury.

'Have you seen this morning's paper?' She could barely contain herself. 'Have you any idea what they're writing about our priests, our bishops? Holding them up to ridicule. Questioning their authority, inciting revolt amongst God-fearing people.'

Brigit had never seen her so animated before. She wondered what had incited such passion. Wondered too why a woman who rarely put foot or face across the chapel door had such fierce high regard for their clergy.

'As if we haven't enough troubles in the six counties. Making mischief, creating division with their odious comparisons; they are contemptible.' She beat the offending organ into the flame of the fire.

.'Don't be commentin' to me about the *Times*. Sure, yeh wouldn't expect to find anything less in that auld Protestant rag. Sayin' that, didn't I read the quarest stuff meself, in yesterday's *Independent*, a newspaper that should know better?' When Brigit eventually found her spectacles, she scoured the pages for the article. Deep in the heart of the *Independent*, she located the letter that had been troubling her.

'Written by a Jesuit no less.' Flat Kildare vowels marshalled Muriel.

If a free medical scheme were available to all and sundry, the standard of medical care available would be reduced to the levels of the ordinary dispensary patient. 'What class of condemnation is that of the ordinary man in the street? And what a damnation of our dispensary services. And the mentality of our foremost educators.'

Brigit's protestations and passions were all lost on Muriel. Bristling in defence of Barclay O' Rourke, she threw the gauntlet down to Brigit.

'There's a solidarity mass on Tuesday next in Maynooth. Organised by the Catholic Mothers Movement. The Bishop of Dublin is officiating. Would you like to accompany me?

The righteousness struck Brigit before the ridiculousness. 'The Catholic Mothers movement, how are yeh? God preserve us from religious fanatics.' Brigit's thoughts ran freely into her reply.

For one cold moment, Muriel remembered her mother. Her shiver was an automatic response.

'But given the present climate the attack on the Bishop, do you not feel obligated to make a stand?

'Barclay O'Rourke is big enough and bold enough to look after himself. He doesn't need God or man, never did and never will. It's that particular cause I have concerns about. In fifty years time, there'll be a new Pope. And a new petition for the beatification of Noel Brown. And they'll be expectin' us to forget all about the past and put proceeds to the same process.' Brigit exhausted her indignation.

***

By Tuesday morning, all of Muriel's dogmatism and most of her determination had deserted her. She was edgy. A feeling of uncertainty came over her as she sat into the car. She turned the key in the ignition, and the engine fired into life. She tried to slow her breathing down. She'd always made mistakes when she made decisions in haste.

Clenching the steering wheel, she proceeded to negotiate her way out of the narrow gates. She couldn't turn back now, not after all the fuss she'd made out of wanting the use of the car, not after all she had said about solidarity. Fonsie and Brigit watching at different windows were making matters worse.

Opening up the choke, the car stuttered and stalled. Jesus wept. Eventually, Muriel turned out on to the main street in Leixlip. White knuckled, she changed up and on through the gears. Maternity and madness blended in equal parts. Driving to and from Blessington had never been this much bother.

She caught sight of the hat cocked on the side of her head. Her hand unconsciously straightened the skirt of her dress. It was too late to turn back, to change. She was here to show him the strength of her love not the weakness.

She chastised her vanity, her superficiality. Tried to hoist fast fading convictions back up to their previous strength. She was on the edge of Maynooth before she knew it. Turning the sharp left corner that took her into the town, she could feel the wheels struggling in tar softened by the heat of the midsummer sun. Beads of sweat were forming on her top lip around her temples and hairline.

Maynooth was busier than on market day. More cars than she had ever expected lined the main street. The road that led directly to the College, where the Mass was being celebrated, was heaving with people. From time to time, heads turned and looked at the woman driver.

Muriel concentrated on finding a parking space as close to the College as possible. To her surprise, she found herself directed in through the main gate. She was directed to a parking spot that was a bit too high a profile for her liking. She rolled down the window and tried to convey her reservations but couldn't get her point past the enthusiasm of the young seminarian directing traffic.

'Invited guests, dignitaries or League?'

'League.' Her little white lie got her further and farther than she bargained for.

'Follow me this way.' An equally enthusiastic seminarian took her directly to the delegation of women waiting by the Church door. The energy racing through the women tightened her tension.

Muriel buried herself deep in the crowd, taking comfort from the cover, the constant shift and sway. In a moment out of real time, a priest was ushering half the crowd into a private room. The Bishop would like to meet some ordinary people. A thrill raced through the crowd. Feet barely touching the ground carried her along. A slipstream of obedience. Bells in the distance pealed out pure pleasure. Reverent tones moved them quickly along. Silence swollen by the sacredness of the invitation. In the splendour of the moment, the crowd parted involuntarily.

To her horror, she was at the front of the chosen fifty or so women. Blinding white silk vestments swished into the room. Yer Grace, yer Grace, a reverence of voices rose to a gentle crescendo. From every side, hands stretched over her shoulder. Jolted, she stumbled, her hand touching the shoulder of his garment. There was a ghostly pause as he half turned and saw her. His pectoral cross

156

encrusted with semi-precious stones glinting in the splintered sun. Blinkered between the past and present, Barclay saw none of the irony.

Straining fiercely to regain her balance, Muriel felt all of the horror.

He smiled edgily. A fly buzzed around his head.

'How clumsy of me.' Her heart pounded in the centre of her chest. High-pitched and tinny, her voice was unnaturally loud. She had forgotten just how tall he was, how stirring his eyes were.

He looked felt grossly uncomfortable speaking to a woman who was so blatantly pregnant.

'What a place to meet.' His voice was saying one thing, diamond-hard eyes another.

Thick-throated, shocked, her confidence spiralled downward into an almighty spin. They were about to move him on. Remove the nuisance.

'If you're ever passing the door.' Awkward, out of context as out of place, the timbre as awful as the timing. A pelt of perspiration covered her body. She tried to move back. Wedged in, the crowd wouldn't let her. He stared at her in astonishment. Embarrassment strained behind his eyes: love's fatal enemy communicated loud and clear to Muriel.

'We came prepared for a sacred service not a social invitation.' Nods and sounds of approval circled her. His secretary's eyes held hers hard. The smirk mortified.

The pressure pumping between her temples turned the moment red. Senseless shame smothered her. He waved a dismissive hand, addressed his insincerity to the crowd.

Expansive, radiant, he moved amongst the adoring mass, pressing flesh, promising prayers. Eager women elbowed and jostled her to the back of the crowd. She could feel the passion, smell the lust. Recognised the earlier energy that had carried her along for what it was.

Something raw struggled inside Muriel. She wasn't his ally. She was an indecent reminder of the past, here, present in a holy place. Tacit and real imports were becoming harder to ignore, reality gathering its own poignant weight.

In a fit of pique and rage, she headed back to Leixlip. It was time Barclay O'Rourke heard a piece of her troubled mind.

Eighteen

On the bus to Ballsbridge, Attracta fattened out the thinnest parts of her story. Slyly plumping up a state of hope. And why not? He should pay for his pleasure.

Down Harrington Street she saw the Loretto Convent. The Blessed Virgin cast in concrete gave her a stony stare. Jesus Mary and Joseph. Could we go any slower? The bus lurched. Huge wheels grappling with Sharp's Corner pushed and pulled her closer to him. The floor vibrated below her. She could feel herself getting sick and hot. Today of all days, yeh don't need to feel sick.

It was Wednesday, his visiting day. The day he used her excellent facilities. Availed of the tranquillity, the peace and quiet. His catch-up day he called it. His catch-me-up day, Attracta called it.

Oh Sacred Heart of Jesus, I place all my trust in Thee. The metered aspiration ran to the rhythm of the big diesel engine. Hope addressed to neither God ,or man temporarily allayed fear. She was desperate. Over in London, buying rugs to cover the old marble floor in the kitchen. Too cold on the old toes, you know. Ballsbridge bullshit. The grand accent in the seat behind her, a painful reminder, rankled.

Barclay and all his bullshit. The stentorian voice up on the pulpit blowing his trumpet. She'd heard him, only last week, larger than life. Fillin' Adam an' Eve's to the rafters. Fillin' it nearly as full as he filled my belly. She conjured the truth, put flesh to the lie.

And as he sowed, some fell by the wayside. She mimicked Barclay's homily to life. Some feckin' well did fall. Another bleedin' miracle. It's a holy day, Miss Rafferty. High days and holy days are as important as Sundays. The Visitation of the Blessed Virgin: a holy day of obligation to the rest of the faithful.

Hours off were better invested by Attracta. Dipping her fingers in the holy waters. Praying for a cure for her condition. Praying for blood. She was as mad as the batch of biddies reciting the Rosary under the picture of Our Lady. The one Fatama always checked her hair in. The one she often checked her own make-up in. For the Butcher's Boy. Caught now between the spirit and the flesh. Serves yeh right. She was mumbling. The man sitting beside her moved to another seat.

Her shoulders stiffened. The bus was stopping and starting.

Someone had to pay for the sum of Nurse Flannagan's favours. She touched her stomach; it didn't feel real. She couldn't feel anything. If only the one in the Coombe hadn't confirmed it. She slid her hand under her coat. The bus was on Pembroke Road now. Three more stops and she'd be at the site of her fate' three more hours and she'd seal it.

'Ballsbridge,' the bus conductor's voice bellowed up the stairs. It had happened in a hurry. She could feel her heart racing as she picked her way round and round the narrow steps of the bus. Here we go, child. The fearless and the frightened. She lifted her bag up and stepped off the bus into brilliant Ballsbridge sunshine.

She could see the conductor banging the bell twice. Ordering the driver to move off. She felt abandoned as the big bus pulled away. As abandoned as she'd felt the day she went out to look for him. Another painful scenario opened up in Attracta's head.

She'd gone looking for the Butcher's Boy. Gone out to his home in Lucan. Her face froze with humiliation.

Her courage had failed her then. But it wouldn't fail her today.

The big soft country woman she'd often see at Mass cut her in two with a look. A voice she'd never heard in the church had greeted her. He's not here. Harsh inflections had blocked every move. Her knees had gone from under her. What I have to say is private. It didn't get her across the door. She had been forced to present her predicament on the pavement. The woman wasn't listening. She'd heard it all before. Bigger and better put. Tall tales: telling little lies.

Black eyes had burnt holes in Attracta's soul. I don't know what your name is, but I know what your game is. Know a blackmailer when I see one. My son? She'd taken a step back, taken his name as if it were holy, wouldn't be seen with the likes of you, let alone lie with the likes of you. Now get off my doorstep and take yer filthy little scam to whatever back street in Dublin you crawled out of. Before I take a bull whip to you.

Bolted: beaten: back on the same bus. Back home before she began.

Dots of perspiration ran freely down either side of Attracta's face. She wouldn't be beaten twice. Fatama had hit the nail on the head. It was a wise man who knew his own father. So let the final fiddler pay the price. The Butcher, the Bishop, the Bishop, the Butcher. He loves me, he loves me not.

Taking liberty with the months, she'd shifted their positions. Sooner than she expected, the lie became seamless. Slowly but surely, she began to believe Barclay was the father. Seven days solid

159

rehearsal set the stage. Seven night's desperation, and the lie became flesh.

She turned the key in the latch. In the back door like a dirty shirt; she was getting giddy. A car engine backfiring out on the main road made her jump. He'd be here in half an hour.

She checked herself in a full-length mirror in the hall. She looked as if she had just had a dip in the public baths. The cashmere coat, the poor man's wardrobe, hot in summer, cold in winter. It covers sins not seasons. She put a lick of red lipstick on her mouth and coal-black mascara on her eyes. Piss holes in the snow, she disparaged the finished look. Maybe she'd let him have a last little fiddle before the sting. A frisson of energy shot head to heel.

His lunch was laid out on the dining room table. Starched linen covering the solid silver tray. She lifted the cloth and surveyed the offerings.

'Groanin with grub ... The mad auld cow's set a feed for five kings.'

Fig rolls and port gracefully laid out on a separate tray.

'Will I feed him before he fiddles or after?' Attracta stuffed a fig roll into her mouth. Taking the heavy glass stopper out of the decanter, she swigged the port by the neck. Down her gullet warm and sweet, it comforted and colluded.

Yer right there, Countess, who needs a glass when yeh have a mouth like Attracta Rafferty? The pantomime had begun.

'His favourites.' She had the Countess' voice off to a tee.

'His Grace's favourite.' Her fingers raced across the cloth, smoothing non-existing creases, tucking in corners, keeping his lunch fresh. Safe from fecker's fingers and fly's shit. Huffing and puffing in the same manner the Countess huffed and fussed. Revealing in her shameless pantomime, her hand slid another prized possession out from under the spotless cover. A sandwich dainty as the doily it was perched on. She held the crustless quarter up to the light and examined the contents.

'Exquisite. Pork, not a trace of fat. Such posh pig. I don't mind if I do, Countess. How kind of you to feed the Bishop's baby. How kind of you to correct me, Countess: the Bishop's bastard. I'm eating for ten this weather. God bless us is right, Countess. Maybe its twin Bishops, maybe triplets. Maybe yer right, Countess, maybe it's a batch of bloody Bishops. One sandwich is never enough. A pimple on an elephant's arse, one nut to a monkey.'

Her little finger ludicrously high, she examined the last of the crustless quarter. A grunt escaped from her chest.

160

'You know, you could be right, Countess. I could be least three months gone. At it hammer and tongs; sure, you know how it is yerself – time flies when you're enjoying the ride. Bet the Butcher's Boy by a neck. And a good neck too. Twice the speed. But half the stamina. Oh, there was no comparison Countess, you're so right. Still, the Butcher's Boy saw the benefits the Bishop had so freely bestowed. Broken in by a man for the boy. You beat me to it again. Better an old man's darling than a young man's fool. There's a lot to be said for that too, Countess. Better a young man's passion than an auld man's perversions. You just might have something there. Come to think of the capers: hands and hankies, sticky white hankies. She tucked the stiff linen napkin back in around the sandwiches. Concepta charges sixpence for a hand job, Jaysus wept is right, Countess. But it was too late when I told him. Too late for me.

It was deep into this maelstrom of madness and make believe that Barclay O'Rourke walked.

She had two hours. She didn't waste any time.

'Let me help yeh with yer coat.' She moved close to him. Closer to the lie she was about to tell him.

'Is it me or is it hot? She undid the top button of her blouse. Seductive, secret, she let him peep in. To improve the lie, she'd worn her stockings and the purple garters. And a black satin bra that had cost her a half crown on tick. Dressed for the kill.

Hands, eyes, lies, were all sucking him in. He was shocked at the instant effect she was having.

'I was thinkin' about yeh that much I forgot to put me knickers on.' She spun her erotic web around him.

His head rolled back. 'Attracta Rafferty, you're a tangler, a temptress, a terrible tease.' He let himself get lulled into the perfect moment. To a place far removed from the rigidity reality of his cold world. He began to see her in a different light still. Her nipples rubbing against her blouse, her breasts bigger, fuller than before. He fingered her blouse, another button came undone.

'Not here.' She slid along the wall.

'Don't open me up in public.' Syrupy sweet she was on him like a rash, sucking, licking, biting.

A huge vein pulsed in the side of his neck. He tried to ignore the surge of blood, the unruly member. But her hands were full of him. Teasing, testing, making him rise to the occasion.

'Close yer eyes.' She unbuttoned his trousers. There was never any of this pumpin' or pullin' on the Butcher's Boy. One crooked look at his trousers an' his cock was stiff as mischief' up like Nelson's Pillar. As high an' as hard too.

The ripple in her throat, the raw vigour, a wild tonic to him.

'God, yer a terrible trollop.'

'But I'm your trollop. Look now' A liquid voice bade him.

The room was turning on its axis.

'I never did anything so wild, so wilful, before.' There was no stopping him.

His hands were already full of her breasts, his tongue filling her mouth.

'Look what yer doin' to me.' Her voice was hoarse. His eyes feasted on her, on himself. His auld lad was like a stick of white puddin'. It was the best she could do. Her wrist was on fire from all the effort. His knee levered open her legs; he took her hand and rubbed it up and down. Lumpy, hairy grizzle. It was up, up her, up against the hall mirror, the glass cold on her arse.

She turned round and let him see. Pulling, pushing, she shoved him hard inside her.

'That's the girl, that's the girl, there now, now, oh my God'. He was spurting like a fountain. She was full to the brim of him.

A church bell struck a quarter past the hour. She had done the dirty deed. In less than an hour, she had got what she needed. Now she had to do the rest. She was seeing Nurse Flannagan on Friday night. All she wanted now was the money.

He'd barely buttoned up his trousers when the weeping and wailing began.

'Well, it wasn't the Immaculate Conception.' She brazened out the lie in Barclay's draining face. 'It might be due at Christmas, but I'm not the Blessed Virgin.'

Closer to Nurse Flannagan's solution than the Butcher Boy's location, Attracta battered away at the Bishop.

What difference did it make? They were both at it. Dippin' their dirty wicks. There's many's a slip between a woman an' her wits.

Consternation followed accusation. Madness followed badness. In her altered state, Attracta appeared possessed to him. Trapped, Barclay fought lake a bare-knuckle fighter.

'Don't try and tell me that I was the only one.' The *one* tore out of his throat. 'A servant girl from a filthy slum.' His nostrils fought for clean air. 'Who the hell would believe yeh? The likes of yeh are lethal. Let loose amongst God-fearing men. Breeding like rabbits. Blaming men. Discovering morals when yer backs are to the walls.'

With vaulting arrogance, he laid his shame and blame squarely on Attracta's shoulders.

'Well, that's a new tune outa an auld fiddle,' Attracta's rage erupted. 'Yeh weren't hummin' that when me back was to the wall. Or when yeh were full of champagne and had me over the kitchen table. Who the hell did yeh see in the mirror just now. Yeh were the first, mister, an yeh'll certainly be the last.'

Flummoxed, he stalled. The imagery of the memory disgusted him. It was weeks since he'd … months. Not since he'd seen Muriel in Maynooth, swollen up like a sow. No, no, he hadn't been inside her. Not all the way. Not until today. Hands and handkerchiefs.

He felt a throb of dread. He couldn't think straight. Maybe there was the odd occasion when she took him by surprise. Even then, he'd pulled out. Hadn't he? Frustration followed stonewalling rage. He scrabbled for clarity. Sins, secrets, sequences, mulched mercilessly in his gallbladder. Muriel first, now Attracta. Jesus, Jesus wept. Why had God burdened him with the appetite of a beast? Why, why, why?

A mad bull snorted and stomped before Attracta.

'You satanic bitch, you devil incarnate. No common whore, no walking occasion of sin, will bully or blackmail the Bishop of Dublin.' Bishopric flashing and fading before his eyes, he stood frozen at the altar of his misdemeanours.

'Whore, is that what I am? A walkin' occasion of sin, is that what I am?' Attracta's fist connected with a jutting jaw. His face contorted, colour crept towards his damp hairline.

'Now I have you, now by God I have you.' He grasped at straws.

'Yeh never said a truer word. Yiv had me and me likes for the very last time.' She spat her venom. 'Makin' rules for fools to follow, while you and your likes flaunt them. Well, I'm neither a fool nor a follower. And don't try and tell me that I was the only woman yeh ever had: it wasn't off the side of the road yeh licked yer lovemaking, mister.'

The consternation on Barclay's face lent its own class of victory. But winning a war of words didn't do Nurse Flannagan's sums. Attracta Rafferty knew that.

'If I were you, madam, I'd consider my position.' Menace coated every syllable. 'Before I set the Garda on you and have you slung into prison for slander.'

Terror hammered like nails in her head. The thought of prison terrified her. Her Grandfather Rafferty had landed up in prison for makin' whiskey. And it had killed him.

Barkley saw the switch. 'I suggest you tender your resignation to the Countess before I expose you for the bloody little blackmailer that you are. Don't ever try to pit your wits against the Bishop of Dublin. With the might of the Catholic Church at my back, you've lost before you ever begon. I'm a survivor, missy, people forget that at their peril. There's pure steel in my backbone; nobody, nothing, destroys Barclay O'Rourke.' He was half way out of the room and starting to get his Bishop's voice back.

Attracta had stumbled against the rock-hard secret society. But she'd only stumbled.

'Oh, I won't be goin' to any prison. It isn't called blackmail where I come from. In the Liberties, it's called mickey money. An' that mister is what you'll be payin' unless yeh want the whole of Dublin to know about yer vices.' Attracta clawed back the advantage.

A hidden spring at the back of her mind resurrected the moment. The whisper, the disturbance in her sister. The papers Gorette had found stuffed in the pocket of the apron she'd taken home to steep. Sketchy as it was, the memory came to the rescue. It wasn't much, but it might just be what she needed. She'd nothing to lose. Her adrenaline pumped. She remembered the letters she had found the day she was washing the skirting board behind the bookcase.

'Yer right about one thing. Satan does find work for idle hands to do. Let me tell ych what idle hands found in the study. Let me tell yeah about the filth the little servant from the filthy back streets found under the Countess' bookcase. Which will I start with – yer problem out in Leixlip or yer dirty prose?' She baited him enough to loosen his bowels and his purse.

His spirit shook. He'd searched high and low for those fucking notes.

She could smell the fear. Sensing victory, she jumped ahead.

'An' that brings us back to the beginnin'. One hundred pounds and the letters will be in yer hand and Attracta Rafferty will be on the mail boat on Friday.

But Barclay was way ahead of her. The two fifty pound notes burnt holes in his pocket. His winnings in the Phoenix Park. Twenty five to one on, in the six o'clock last night. Every penny would be cheap at half the price. But he had to be sure that this was the end of the matter.

It took him less than five minutes to come up with an answer. He'd have his money back a damn sight quicker than she'd have her character. Or freedom. And his reputation would be safeguarded too.

Who in their right minds would believe one word out of a common thief's mouth? All he had to do was ensure that the police lifted Attracta Rafferty before she arrived home. Secured in the back of a Black Mariah, and his money back safe in his pocket before she hit the Liberties.

The doorframe darkened. The Countess was on top of him before he saw her.

'I'm so pleased to find you still here. I was beginning to believe, Your Grace, that you were trying to avoid me.' Crucial to his plans, he played her along.

'Now, why wouldn't I wait for you?'

Her face unmasked, signed with hope. The air filled with potential. She blushed with shame.

Hinging at the waist, she searched for a bottle of vintage port in the back of her drink cabinet.

'You'll take a teeny tiny drink with me?' She plotted an unsteady course.

'I will indeed; how often do we get a chance to be on our own?' Overt flattery found its easy target.

Something deeply unsettling, something seminal, entered the air.

He held up his glass. The port slopped over the rim and down the front of his trousers. For more than a hideous moment, he thought she was going to help him clean them.

'How was bridge?'

'Bridge was boring.'

'Do you know, I haven't heard one word from my daughter in six months.'

The tangled web. Barclay's heart sank.

'She's her father's daughter. She has his looks, his temperament and obviously his bad blood. You're the only one who knows. You've the only one to hear my confession. I tried to do the decent thing. Tried to talk her into a Magdalene home. In the end, I gave her the princely sum of fifty pounds.' A moment's silence marked the vulgar admission. 'It was London I had in mind when I told her to lose herself and her bastard child, not Leixlip.'

Rhetoric was racing ahead of reality. Her determination to enlist his sympathy bordered on the obscene. Barclay moved swiftly to bring the ball back into his own arena.

'I understand your concerns, Countess. But I have an urgent matter to discuss with you. A more current matter.' The urgency in his voice cut through the foggy emotion.

'I'll ring for the girl; she can bring us some tea and sandwiches.' She needed to sober up.

'Miss Rafferty left over an hour ago.' An intense vigour lent its own brand of mischief. 'And speaking of Miss Rafferty, there's more to that little madam than meets the eye.' His opening gambit was lost to the Countess' incredulity.

He opened his mouth to speak but she beat him to it. 'Then I shall fetch the sandwiches myself.' Temper and greed doubled her speed.

She returned with a tray overflowing with food. Butter glistening on her chin; from time to time, the light caught it. There was something about the sight that rankled. Something basic. Something animal. We're revolting hybrids, half-human half-spirit. The reasoning distracted. Our spirits aspiring to godliness whilst our bodies aspire to earthiness. Bestial functions – intercourse, birthing, breasts feeding, pissing, shitting – all hallmarks. Unevolved stages of development: a long way from godliness, further still from spirituality.

Robust determination pulled Barclay back from the random reasoning, from the comfort of the temporary loophole.

'She's acquired a recklessness cockiness of late.'

Rigmaroles of rubbish were bouncing off his eardrums.

'Try as I might, I can neither map nor match her movements. She's as big a mystery to me as that other article of mine, Muriel.'

Held to ransom by an older terror, her sentence hung in mid air. The odd coupling had the most unsavoury effect on her. Her mind struggled with nugatory images. Patched and pasted, fleeting pictures spooled through her head. Negatives of Muriel and the Bishop, negatives of Attracta and the Bishop. Overt suspicion crossed and left the Countess' face.

Barclay observed the dangerous energy and realised in that instant that his solution would be in excellent hands. He allowed himself a sizeable gulp of port before he continued.

'I find myself in the unfortunate position of having to speak about Miss Rafferty.'

The Countess' own thoughts slowed, staggered to a halt. Leaning towards her, Barclay set the seed that would save his neck.

'Your servant has been behaving in a most unseeming manner towards me and my divine office.' He opened his eyes wide to declare his innocence. 'Neither is she beyond the odd leap of imagination.'

The Countess' chest swelled: the Bishop's confidante at last.

He allowed the full quota of silence for the suggestion to sink in.

'I, like you, Countess, in the beginning I made all the allowances for background and behaviour. But today things have gone too far. I'm saddened to tell you that quite a sizeable sum of money went missing from my coat pocket. Also some documents that are of a very delicate nature. They are the property of a priest who badly needs psychological ... ,' he allowed a sensitive second before he continued.

'Without breaking a confidence, how can I impress on you the delicate nature of this situation? It is of vital importance that we get the documents back. The money from the Sunday collection I will gladly replace out of my own pocket.'

The seriousness of the allegations effected instant sobriety.

'I've already contacted the Superintendent in the Bridewell. Sometimes we have to be cruel to be kind.'

The Countess' face filled with a sort of malevolent composure.

'How right you were Bishop. Only the harshest of institutions can help social and moral deviants.'

A sensation of calm spread through Barclay's body as he outlined his programme for the reformation of Attracta Rafferty.

Nineteen

Invigorated by energy she'd never known before, Muriel pulled her bedroom asunder.

A wardrobe she'd have thought twice about moving shot into its new location. Pulling a big feather bed into the centre of the room, she suffered little more than a shortness of breath. Cocking the mirrors on the dressing table at just the right angle, she managed to reflect badly needed light into the room. The new light, the warmth, the simple changes, pleased her.

When she was good and ready, she took the bedspread out. A whiff of Barclay caught her by surprise. She held her breath. Took it deep inside her.

'It's the hottest July on record. Ninety-seven they say it will rise teh today.' The exertion and heat puffed Brigit's acclamation out of all proportion.

'I'm rearranging the bedroom.'

"Well, if I can't beat yeh, I might as well join yeh.' A huge red face delivered the curtain line.

Muriel threw the bedspread high in the air and let it float gently over the bed. In all Brigit's time in service, she'd never seen anything so delicate. Apple green silk with a scattering of hand-embroidered roses

She wondered, as she looked around the sparse bedroom, if Muriel understood the duties of a married woman. If she knew the solid contribution that shunting himself to a spartan room at the end of the corridor was making to his contrariness.

Brigit threw a disparaging eye over the new arrangements. Not a trace of man in here and less of woman in his quarters. Leaving the nights to one side, the mornings must bring an awful reality. Wakin up in an empty bed, begod the hurt must double the indignity.

Muriel didn't like the clacking that was coming from the roof of Brigit's mouth. It always heralded trouble. She didn't want to hear about poor Mr Fonsie. Time would tell her long before and after Brigit what and if she ever wanted to know. Keeping her thoughts but not her temper to herself, she kicked the suitcase back under the bed.

Brigit wondered what else she'd kept in cold storage. What other secrets she kept under wraps. Youth was a terrible burden on the young. And young women could be hasty and foolish too.

'Would yeh not be better investin' all this energy in the back bedroom?'

She could hear the sharp intake of breath. But she took another leap of faith.

'Is a wife's place not beside her husband, Mam? Are children not better reared in a house of harmony?'

Silence hung like a firewall between the two women.

'Lord God, what me poor Mother and Father would have given to have had a room of their own, let alone a bed.'

Brigit slowed things up, but she didn't give up. Fonsie hadn't taken a drink for eight weeks at least. It deserved some recognition. Some class of gesture. Maybe not tonight or tomorrow night. Out and out Coventry was cold contribution in his condition. She battered away at Muriel's contrariness.

There was a season for everything, and now wasn't the season to be shoring and storing up soreness. If she did nothing else this day, she'd start a trickle to the thaw.

There were impasses in Muriel's personality, impulses too. Like that affair up in Maynooth two weeks ago. Makin an exhibit of herself. Remonstratin' with meself. Shootin' off in a stutterin' car. Back home again with the tail between the legs. Before the Mass started, never mind ended. An' after all the commotion, not a word to throw to a dog when she stepped back through the door. Given short shift by the Bishop, I'll bet me cap. The big Bishop, the big friendship, but that was another day's work.

Brigit huffed and puffed her doubts. She wondered, and not for the first time, if reality was playing as big a part in her head as it should. She watched Muriel's fingers flying up and down the length of the curtains, rail to floor, pulling and tugging, snapping old pleats into new places. It was all too frenetic, all too frantic for Brigit Murphy's liking.

'It's leavin' work not liftin' it yeh should be. Yer nearer yer time than yeh think. Yer like a hen on a hot griddle. Will yeh stop throwing furniture around, in God's name, before yeh swing the neck of that womb out of kilter turn an' that child in the wrong direction.'

'My private concerns are no concern of yours, Brigit. There are some things better left unsaid and others better left to rest. So if you'll excuse me, I'm won't be delaying you any further.' In a moment, she instantly regretted she blurted out her frustrations.

'I'm within' bawlin' distance if yeh need me.' She left, didn't take a blind bit of notice or an ounce of offence. Pregnant women,

169

unserviced men, dumb animals, all came under the same umbrella in Brigit's head.

There would be neither bawling nor calling today or the next or the next. Muriel was exactly ten days from her delivery date. She knew to the hour she'd conceived, and had calculated to the day when she'd give birth. She stroked the bedspread. Bold, he'd called her. What would she give to be bold with him now?

As she took the letter out from under her pillow, savage relief swept from her head to her toe. It had arrived three days after her abortive trip to Maynooth. She read and reread his letter. It was only by the grace of God that she hadn't fired off her deranged missive. It would have been the end of them. The ruination of him.

She ran her fingers over his signature, read the text thanking her for her solidarity and consideration, and wishing her all the best for the near future. Typed not hand-written. But it was written to her, not anyone else. She kissed the letter and slid it back under the pillow. Nothing about it struck her as calculating.

Pressing her fingers into the small of her back, she tried to knead away a tiny niggle. Maybe Brigit was right. Maybe she should try to rest.

She lay on the bedspread, soft silk caressing her fingers, her face. Burying her nose in the bedspread, she searched out remnants of him. Riotous smells and sensations flooded her. Hope surged in her veins. She wondered how many breaths she could steal before his smell faded. Her bladder brought an abrupt end to the romance. Lucid reality reigned as she struggled to get out of bed.

A walk before the sun gets too high in the sky might settle the agitation. A hen on a hot griddle: Brigit's bold words were nearer the bone than she would have believed. She was out and off at a gallop before Brigit could heckle or hinder her.

As the house faded into the distance, Muriel's frustrations and Brigit's dire warnings went with it. A sweet summer's day, full to bursting with all her yesterdays. Warm breezes at her back and a crystal blue sky swept her along. Long, low gurgles drew her eye to the swirling currents where the river Liffey met the Rye. Driftwood and spray tangling and tumbling in the sly currents unsettled her. Over the River Rye, down by the distillery. High above her head, coal-black jackdaws making an almighty racket. Behind high cast-iron gates dogs barked and bothered the stillness. Mid-morning in Leixlip, lazy and slow.

On up Captain's Hill, to Confey over the canal bridge, she stopped to take her bearings and her breath. A blue haze hung in the distant Dublin Mountains. She felt the great presence of the sun as it rose higher and higher, a basilica of fire. Days made up of other days. Soft heather beds, long lazy days and nights with Barclay. Her heart felt like a soft damaged place in the centre of her chest.

A young calf stared idly as she galloped by. Muriel was still walking an hour later, still smiling at the good of giving Brigit the slip, when a contraction that would make a mule kick a hole in an ironmonger's wall brought her to her to one knee. Grabbing hold of a low hanging branch, she scrambled to her feet and thanked God no one saw the slip. Turning quickly for home, she regretted with every step the long road ahead of her. Sweat pumped from every pore. *Well, that put the smile on the other side of yer face, miss.* She wished the voice in her head was beside her now.

Unfamiliar pain circling her back and belly tightened and released its grip. Taking deep breaths, Muriel tried to control mounting consternation. Struggling for composure, she counted, paced her way back to the village. *What in God's name got into yeh, way out in the sticks an' you so near yer time?* She could almost feel Brigit rounding on her.

The sun was climbing higher in the sky. The hottest July on record. She'd heard on the morning radio. Heard Brigit saying the same thing. But she hadn't listened. Sweat ran freely down her face. She'd never known heat like this. Hot, peppery pain hurtled out another leveller. Strength born of desperation kept her knees from buckling under her.

The crown of the Captain's Hill appeared in the distance. The whispered thanks to God as she covered the level ground that led to her descent. A couple of locals passed. Head high, eyes straight ahead, she ignored their concerned looks. Walk, breath, walk, breath, walk, she half said, half sang the incantation.

Delving deep inside herself, she strove to stay calm. The steep gradient of the hill pulled like splints on her shins as she made her descent. Mistaking the pain, she believed that it too was part of the punishing process. She'd have to contact Barclay. He'd be as anxious as she was now.

Her heart racing with a hope that wouldn't come to pass, she caught sight of the main street. Turning right: seconds, seconds, she had the house in her sights. Air shot out of her lungs with relief. Breathing erratically, she was felled by another almighty burst of pain. She tried to ignore the length and depth of it. The front door in full view now, waves of relief swept her along. Ten steps, nine steps, eight, seven, six, she counted maniacally.

But somewhere between Komiskey's and her own house, she lost the battle. Gushing water saturated her knickers. Puddles and scalding tears circled her feet. The world crowded and empty as she squatted above her shame. Groping for a nearby windowsill, she tried scrambling to her feet. But gravity held her down tight. Haunched over her secret she felt a peculiar sort of confinement. Eyes stuck out on stalks stared down at her, staring up at all that bad luck and broken sky. Mute spies. Every breath had the sweet scent of scandal. The privacy she put so much store on dissolving before mortified eyes.

'Get out of her way.' Imperious voices, the Teeny Tinys, were music to Muriel's ears. *Someone fetch the Widah Fay*; flat Kildare vowels rose from the belly of the crowd. Flanking her, the tiny women hauled her to her feet. Half holding, half carrying, they took her across her own door.

But nothing could cover her shame. The back of her skirt, soaking, stuck fast to her thighs, her backside; she'd never live it down. Searing pain put pay to what was left of her pride. Someone was trying to rip her pelvis in two; pulsing, peppery pain was setting fire to her private parts.

Here, here, Brigit's voice registered no assurance. *In here; put her into my bed.* She was pushing open a door off the kitchen, leading the calamity into a tidy little bedroom. A makeshift mirror leaning causally at the foot of Brigit's bed fell flat on its face and shattered into smithereens. Muriel's misery reflected in jagged shapes. Irish Art, soft voices whispered, as fingers whipped jigsaws of glass out of harm's way.

'Now out, out to hell's gates and let me look after me mistress. Has anyone told Doctor?' Brigit put no store in the Widow Fay, less still on the same lady's midwifery skills.

'Can no one stop this pain?' Muriel's lower parts were molten and seared. She heard her own voice above the bedlam.

Out of the corner of her eye, Brigit spotted the wide-eyed child.

'Maybe one of yis would have the decency to look after that babby.' *Jack, Jack* – the Teeny Tinys led the startled child away.

With a modicum of order restored, Brigit set about making Muriel comfortable. 'Now, if we keep our heads, we might just have all this done and dusted by the time the cavalry arrives.' She knew the Widow Fay would be in no hurry to cross her door. Not after the last debacle. And by the time they'd dredged the local doctor up off the golf course, the worst would be over.

'I've seen me mother, God rest her worthy soul, do this more times than I've had hot dinners, and not a bother on her,' Brigit lied.

It was beyond her why any woman would subject herself to such terror. And in her mother's case, again and again. It was like some awful conspiracy, a terrible trick played on one woman by another. Wouldn't yeh think one would warn the other? Still, if the truth got out, I suppose that would be the end of the human race. She'd spoken the whole of the last sentence out loud, unbeknownst to herself, as she poured cold water into a bowl beside Muriel's head.

'Could yeh have picked a hotter day to bring this child into the world?' Brigit's constant blather reassured Muriel.

'It's only a suggestion, Mam, but me mother did a lot better on all fours. Maybe if yeh knelt, yeh'd be more comfortable.'

In the absence of better advice, Muriel did as Brigit said. And for a while it seemed sound. Water wrung from a cool clean flannel, running down the sides of the enamel bowl, made comforting sounds. Brigit's big hands stroking her back' mopping her clammy brow' kept a kind of calm Muriel couldn't feel herself. Burst upon burst of pains swarmed round her stomach and lower back.

'Where's the bloody doctor?' Terror curdled every word. 'Surely he can give me something for this God-awful agony.'

'Stop fighting the pain,' Brigit countered the protests.

White-knuckled, Muriel gripped the iron bedstead.

Brigit put one hand at the bottom of her belly and one to the small of her back and rocked her pelvis.

'Easy an' slow, easy an' slow. Go with it, sway with it, pray with it.' She mouthed the well-worn phrases as she mastered the well-worn practice.

'It won't be long now. Yer at the Jesus, Mary and Holy Saint Joseph stage.' Brigit hoped she'd read the signs right. The energy was rising, the calm before the storm was right. Help her, dear Jesus, help her now.

Don't snatch another woman from this house. She prayed silently as Muriel panted and pleaded for mercy. The broken mirror and all its bad luck revisited Brigit Murphy in a thousand pieces. Don't let me ever face that nightmare again.

A scream that would split stones shattered her prayer.

'The worst is over now, a stor.' A bulge she prayed earnestly was the baby's head ballooned. A flash: the breech birth that killed her last mistress flooded Brigit's brain. She prayed as she'd never prayed before.

'Wait, wait a sacred minute.'

173

Timing was the essential trick now. She'd heard the same instructions on countless crucial occasions before. And could only guess now it was a better sighting of the head they were waiting for. She'd learnt more at the foot of her mother's bed than she'd bargained for. Suddenly, the head presented again. A head of black hair.

'Push now. In God's name. Push, push – as if all the bats in Hell were comin' after yeh.' Brigit's voice filled the tiny room.

Molten heat ripped Muriel's legs apart. Screams of terror, cries of triumph, broke in one breath. As evening's cardinal red light flooded the bedroom, Lily Rose's cries of birth filled the air.

Triumphant silence reigned complete before either woman spoke.

The commotion of Fonsie arriving, doctor and midwife in tow, took the timeless moment.

'She's beautiful,' Brigit choked. 'And the head of curls on her. Black as the Earl of Hell's waistcoat. No wonder yeh were killed with heartburn.' She was as excited as if she had given birth herself.

'Mr Fonsie's comin down the hall.' Brigit straightened herself up. 'The proud father himself.'

'Fonsie's not her father Brigit. The Bishop of Dublin is the father.' With monstrous pride, Muriel's voice pronounced the sentence.

Brigit's face clouded with confusion. Riotous silence separated the two women in that desperate moment.

'God between us and all harm, Madam.' She couldn't look at Muriel as she made the sign of the Cross. 'Would yeah hould yer whist.' Birth, like death, plays strange tricks on people's minds.

Brigit Murphy had reached the limits of her natural understanding.

'She's rantin', Sir, rawmaishin', sufferin' from exhaustion.' Winking her assurances, Brigit faced Fonsie. 'Congratulations, Sir, you've a child. An, a finer daughter yeh never saw this side of the River Liffey.'

Twenty

The Angelus bells peeled over the Liffey swell. Attracta Rafferty woke with a start. The strange surroundings confusing her. The row with the Bishop brought her back with a bump. She shook with terror and relief. She'd left Ballsbridge before midnight. Managed to break one of the notes in the Kiser Pass. The Garda would have asked her less. She told the barman that the Countess needed the nagan of whiskey, and to mind his own business.

With the waxy notes stuffed in the toes of her shoes, she knew her way by a roundabout means to Concepta's. You could never be too careful in the Liberties. They saw more than they heard, and heard more than they saw. Telltales and thieves.

Attracta slid out of bed, put the kettle on and checked the shoes. There was enough money here to end one way of life and start a new one. She took a sneaky look at Concepta, sound asleep. The night shift's a killer was all she'd said when she'd found her waiting at two on the doorstep. She didn't tell her how much money. Not the whole story. Just that her rich fellah had come up trumps. This time tomorrow the dirty deed would be done.

It would have been impossible to go home. Her Ma was like a dog with a bone. Watchin', weighin' off every move she made this weather. If she got even a sniff of what she was about to do, there'd be no need for an abortion.

A chill ran through her. It would be all over bar the shoutin' by this time tehmarah. She'd be back in Ballsbridge in the morning. And no one would be any the wiser. Concepta was as sound as a bell. She didn't talk and she didn't tell. Without evidence, they'd be doubting themselves, never mind Attracta Rafferty, before the summer was out.

Concepta and the children were starting to stir. 'Irish twins' they called them in the Liberties, nine months and five minutes between them. Without Nurse Flannagan, there would have been four; Concepta had sounded very cut and dried.

'Seein' as your foot's stuck to the floor, I'll do a couple of tricks this afternoon.' Concepta had hit the floor running. 'Fatama will be expectin' her cut tonight. And that young fellah there needs shoes. If his feet doesn't stop growin', I'll be takin' him to a blacksmith' won't I son? Every word was filled with pride. This one's different.

Her youngest son was staring at Attracta with eyes the size of saucers.

'His Da came in on a foreign ship, Portareekin I think it was, I do lose track. Between Russians, Americans, Spaniards and the French, sure me head does be in a bigger spin than me hole. She looked distinctly puzzled at the child. I'm nearly sure he was Portareekin. He was small and skinny anyway. With the help of God, he'll be cheaper to shoe and feed.'

'Bejaysus you deserve a medal for services rendered to foreign legions. And style.' Attracta had given Concepta the blouse she'd worn last night.

'Jaysus, it's holy show. No brassier, no buttons, no hook an' eyes, no drawers. Just the raw material. She bellowed as she shook her diddies in Attracta's face.'

Attracta heard herself laughing. That was Concepta for yeh, no please thanks or kiss me arse.

'There's an American ship waitin' in the Liffey Basin an' here's me wastin' good workin' time. Neither time nor tides waits for Concepta.' She left Attracta, with her foot, as she put it, stuck fast to the floor.

'Missus down under will be up by eight. I'll meet yeh outside of Adam an' Eve's.' It's a good walk and we'll need time for a jar. I'll be thirsty and you'll be terrified.' Concepta hadn't left her with any illusions.

The afternoon was agonisingly slow. Nervous energy was dispersed in fits and starts, checking children were all right, checking that the money was still in the same place, still safe. Attracta opened a window to try and let in some air.

Glorious sunshine flooded the pavements, with children playing hopscotch swinging free as birds from lampposts. A day God must have ordained especially for himself. Ninety-seven degrees, the hottest July on record. The wireless was describing scenes from the Phoenix Park and Stephen's Green. People swimming on Dollymount Strand, picnicking and sunbathing. Attracta wished she was outside, wished with all her heart she was a child again. She didn't have a choice; she couldn't be seen in the Liberties. There was nothin' like reality to ruin a God-sent day.

She tried hard not to look at the clock, yet all she seemed to see was time. The day dragged on, and not a breath of air circulated round the small flat. The children became fractious in the heat and confinement. She gave them the milk Concepta had left for their tea hours too early. Two Guinness bottles with big rubber titties stuck

176

on the necks. Brown milk, as brown as the babbies that trailed after her.

She held the youngest in her arms. Her own breasts tingled as she fed him. The toddler snuggled in beside. Like a young calf sucking till the bottle was dry till he was sucking thin air. Married life with a little family snug around her would be lovely. Reality struck hard. Why oh, why, did yeh run out on me? Her stomach was in uproar.

At around five, the children settled. She sat in the stillness and waited. From time to time, terror would strike at the very heart of her. She looked at the children curled up like a couple of spoons on Concepta's bed. Overcome with exhaustion, she lay in beside them. After all the stress of the past week, she fell into a deep sleep.

The two children were stirring. She woke with a start, immediately awake. Ten to eight – they'd been asleep for hours. She raced down the hall to the lavatory. Both ends spewed at the same time. Empty as a shell. Splashed her face with a drop of cold water and pulled on her coat. Hot or not, she wasn't exposing herself.

She rearranged the money. Fifty in one shoe, two tenners in the other. And twenty in her bra. *Yer sittin' on a fortune*; she slid a waxy ten pound note under each diddy.

She put a couple of quid in a jug on Concepta's mantelpiece. She told her she'd see her all right after tonight, but there was only so much yeh could do for Concepta, she owed money the length and breath of Dublin. Cash or couch, she'd heard her with her own two ears doing a deal with the Jewman.

The woman from downstairs was busying herself with the two children. She wasn't worried about them sleeping; they'd keep her company – some nights were longer than others. She'd given Attracta a knowing nod.

Again and again, she checked that she had everything. Money, handbag, the key to the latch in Ballsbridge: it was all there, all still where she'd left it. She'd be back in her own little room soon, God willing. It wouldn't be long now

Money, handbag, keys, coat; she tapped pockets, repeated the words. Fear ran through the aspirations. She took the shortcut through Adam and Eve's. Sodality banners flew from every pew. Flying the flag for the faithful. She couldn't look at the Blessed Virgin or the baby Jesus snug in her arms as she bolted through the candlelit church.

'Shortcut me arse.' The tips of her fingers were frizzing. Queer energy raced through her body. She felt distinctly queasy. It was fifteen minutes past eight. Concepta was late. Auld wans in and out of Sodality were givin her the evil eye. Stuck out like a running sore on the Money Mile.

'Fuck off an' mind yer own business, yeh dirty-minded auld bitch.' She put the heart crossways on one old woman staring absent-mindedly at her. She could see Concepta in the distance.

'Where the fuck were you?' She was like a bag of weasels. 'Fukkn' auld biddies starin' an' glarin'; they tink I'm on the fukkn' game.'

'Well, what did yeh expect when yeh stood on my spot. The shoe's on the other foot now.'

Concepta was already hot; she didn't need any more bother or shite. There was only so much strain a body could put up with. She had friction burns she'd fucked that many sailors. She hadn't seen Fonsie for two months. She was doublin' up tryin to make up the loss. Money she'd spent, lent and owed. She wasn't takin' any more shite off anyone tehday.

They walked for ten minutes before either spoke again.

Attracta was weak with hunger and fright. Acid churning in her stomach was shooting up her neck. 'How far more do we have to go?'

'Sir John Rodgerson's Quay.' Concepta didn't know the exact location. It was always winter when she got caught, always winter.

'It's a moveable service. It can be any one of four houses. There'll be a light in an upstairs lav to show which house she's workin'. She flicks it on an' off so we'll keep our eyes well peeled nearer the time.'

She didn't tell her, daren't tell her, that if the coast wasn't clear, if there was a whiff of the law, there'd be no Nurse Flannagan tonight or the next night, or the next. She'd had to come on four consecutive nights herself the last time she was doctored.

Attracta didn't seem to grasp that the service they were after wasn't exactly legal. That they all could end up in Mountjoy for a very long time if any one of them was caught. She was moanin' and groanin' like the riggin' on a ship.

'It's about five minutes further on.' She'd have said anything by now to shut her up. They were outside Tim Tighe's, the pub she used as her marker. She could make out the outline of the houses from where they were standing now. It was ten, maybe fifteen, minutes further on. She wasn't taking another step until she had a drink inside her.

There wasn't sight nor light to be seen in any of the windows. In the derelict houses, any sign of light would stick out like a soar thumb. She'd sit near a window; she'd have as good a view from there as she would from here.

'We'll have a jar in here before we go any further. It's where I go meself before I...' She didn't finish the sentence. 'Steady the auld nerves. Another half hour an' it will be as black as the hole of Calcutta down these docks.' She could see the fear of God in Attracta's eyes. There was no point tellin' her there was no light in the window yet.

She bought Concepta a pint of Guinness. A Club Orange and a couple of bag of Tayto crisps for herself.

'Take advice from a fool, get yerself some mother's ruin. It'll be easier on the eye an' the belly as it shoots back up yer gullet.' Concepta took full advantage of Attracta's ignorance.

She drank the orange like a drowning man.

'Take it easy there. Yeh can stuff yer belly tehmarah. Tenight, all yeh need in it is somethin' to adjust the attitude.'

'It's too fukkn' serious for to be drunk. I intend bein' in the full of me faculties.'

Attracta had started on her second bag of crisps.

'Suit yerself. Yeh can stuff yerself there like a Galway goose for all I care. But yeh'll be spray-paintin' the docksides of Dublin before the night's out.'

'The pot callin the kettle black. Yed think yeh had a hallow leg the way you lower the black stuff.'

Concepta shrugged. There was no use talking to Attracta – she should know that of old.

'Well, yeh know me and the black stuff; white is nice, but black is hard to better. More length an' strength.' She licked froth of her top lip, relishing the tease as much as the taste. 'And they can go all night.' She elbowed Attracta.

'Yer a rare tulip.' For a second, there was a sliver of relief. 'Yeh'll never know how much I miss yeh livin' in Ballsbridge.

'Who gave yeh the money in anyway? Is he really famous?'

Safe in the knowledge that Concepta would believe it was a lie, Attracta told the truth.

'The Bishop of Dublin himself is financin' this dark and dirty expedition down the Dublin docks.'

'Up the pole. I thought you were as safe as nun's knickers.' Concepta twirled the last of her Guinness round and round her glass.

'Oh go on, rub salt into the womb.'

'Anyway...' She took a sly look over Attracta's shoulder. A light flickered in the distance. She wasn't sure whether it was Nurse

Flannagan's window or not. She stood up in a hurry, wiped a ring of froth with the back of her hand and licked the surplus clean.

'When we go in, keep yer mouth shut. Let me do the introductions. Just do as she tells yeh. No questions, no tempers. This one's tricky; she's as likely to leave as she is to stay. She makes and breaks her own rules. There was a time she'd do yeh up teh twenty-eight weeks. But things got a bit sticky there a while back: the Garda nearly caught her. So she's cut it down to twenty.

'And if yeh try it on with her, lie about how far yiv gone, she'll up an' leave yeh bleed to death.' The drink was oiling Concepta's tonsils.

Attracta followed her out the door in stunned silence. It was all getting a bit close for camaraderie.

'She a quare hawk. With a set of top teeth splayin' out of her mouth, she could ate an apple through a hole in a wall. Try not to look to close when she comes at yeh.'

'She drips somethin' as innocent as holy water on a cloth an' holds it over yer face. It smells disgustin' but it takes care of yer faculties.' Setting the scene as they approached.

Attracta was feeling distinctly uncomfortably.

Concepta was relishing her new role. For once, it wasn't her on the wrong end of the stick. 'Don't look at the ting she sticks in yeh; its like the number ten knittin' needle only with a crochet hook on its head. It'd shift shite out of constipated men. It shifts the shite out of me ... every time.' She nodded and shook her head at the same time.

Attracta couldn't get the air to the bottom of her lungs.

'An' another ting. She scarpers as soon as she's done the dirty deed. I'll be outside the door. Yeh'll be dopey, but I'll carry yeh.'

She noticed that Attracta never asked how she fared herself in the same circumstances.

'She doesn't even carry a bag in case the Garda's id be watchin'.'

'Where does she keep the, yeh know, tools?,' Attracta asked in spite of herself.

'Everytin' she needs is stashed in the linin' of the big black coat she wears. Dr Death she looks like when she swishes in.'

The blood drained from Attracta's face. She wasn't sure which she feared more now – Concepta full of the drink or Nurse Flannagan's service.

'I do hate wakin' up there on me own. One time I saw a rat lookin' me right in the eye.' Concepta was turning the screw.

'Well, it's as dark as its goin' to get. Where's this fukkn' light?' There was a determination in her voice.

Clouds, bruised black and blue, threatened everything on the Dublin docks.

'It comes and it goes; she can't leave it on all the time.'

'Jaysus, if we don't stop soon, we'll be off the edge.' The fear in Attracta's fingers had invaded the nerves of her face and neck. She felt unnatural.

They walked on and on. Watching waiting for the signal.

A ship the size of O'Connell Street lolled in the basin of the Liffey. 'What about it? Let's stow away. Leave behind all the hurt and shite, the gloomy streets, the doom and desolation. Steal away; come on, Attracta, can yeh imagine it? Sometimes I see the ships, sailin' down the river easy and slow, out into the open sea, anchors up, chains off, set free.' Concepta stood to salute her dream.

Attracta stopped: for a split second let something of that breath of freedom take her. Two black sailors smoking on the deck whistled, long and slow. Concepta waved up at them as if they were two respectable women out for their Sunday stroll.

Something cold gripped Attracta's soul as she scoured the landings for light. On her right, huge houses four, five, stories high stood out against a black Dublin skyline. In their time, houses of some standing, but now all that was left were charred remains. Vertical tombstones. She shivered. To her left, a black tide crashed against the dock wall. Seagulls screeched for something to scavenge. They'd walked pasted three, maybe four, of the houses before they saw the dim bulb flicker on an upstairs landing.

Attracta waited for her eyes to adjust to a deeper dark. Stopping for a second, she took a deep breath, then took the dingy stairs two at a time. A shredded sack hanging off a low ceiling shrouded her view. Alien smells clung to her nostrils and stuck at the back to her throat.

She thought she felt the stairs swaying. 'Are these stairs safe?' Her voice sounded small.

'Its on'e natural to want to run.' Concepta knew exactly how she felt.

'It's only natural to run from something unnatural.' Attracta pushed on in spite of her own words.

'Yeh'll be relived of yer burden by the mornin'. Keep that fixed in the front of yer mind.'

She knew Concepta was right. She couldn't wake up one more morning and experience the terror she'd been experiencing every day and every night for the past six weeks.

Stains, some fresh, some stale, splattered the bockety stairs.

'Jesus, Mary and Joseph.' The third flight of stairs shifted under Attracta's feet. Rooted to the first landing, she put her hand out to steady herself, felt the wall moving further away.

'Keep yer voice down, and yer eye out for rats.' Concepta was racing ahead.

Attracta doubted rats would stoop so low.

'Come on, for Christ's sake; she won't wait around.'

She could hear her own feet dragging. 'Wait, wait, Concepta; does it hurt?'

'Not as much as the Butcher's Boy.' She could have slit her own throat but the words were already out.

It happened in a hurry. A low-watt bulb immediately to her right lit the scene of her fate.

A tall, thin-faced woman was standing in the middle of a bare room. Yellowed teeth overshot a bottom jaw. A shock of wiry grey hair lent a further derangement. Never trust bony women – they're not even good to themselves. Attracta's brain worked furiously as it tried to unravel a tangle of messages.

Lifeless eyes neither met nor greeted Concepta. Crisps, lemonade, chundered around Attracta's stomach. A late seagull's forsaken cry put the fear of God into both young girls.

'This is me friend that I told yeh about.' They huddled unnaturally close.

'Has she got the money?' The register was merciless.

She slipped the note into the lining of her coat. Never taking her eyes off Attracta.

Concepta left her to Nurse Flannagan, a bare bulb, a bare table.

Half her face hidden behind a white mask, a black coat hanging on a bony back: a haunted ghost.

'I'll leave yis an' love yis as God left the Jews.'

She was waving goodbye to Attracta as if she was leaving her at a hooley. The Butcher's Boy was waving goodbye too. She never felt so lonely.

Nobody spoke.

In the corner of the derelict room, a torture tap dripped and stopped, dripped and stopped. It'll be all over soon bar the shoutin': Attracta tried to stop herself vomiting up a fusty wall. A stained sink dangled on bent copper pipes.

From deep in the lining of the coat, Nurse Flannagan produced a small glass bottle. The watery concoction dripping into a soft cloth made Attracta's eyes smart. New smells and tastes were hitting the back of her throat: sick smells, dispensary smells. She was fighting hard to catch her breath. She'd never experienced terror on this scale before.

Tipping her chin, Nurse Flannagan signalled Attracta up on the table. Guts and gizzards tangled and turned as she climbed up.

There was nothing to lie on, no pillow, no sheet. The hard wood bit into her back her shoulder blades: on the hard table again, for him, not with him this time.

The loud silence behind her amplified her fears.

Nausea was coming in waves. She wished she'd listened to Concepta, that she hadn't eaten the Tayto. Rubber gloves slapping on to hands terrorised her.

'Take your knickers off.' A long tongue automatically licked a lower lip.

Terrified, trusting, doing what she was told. Knickers dangling on one ankle. Thin fingers placing an aluminium basin beside her. In the cracked ceiling over her head, a naked bulb offered less light than hope. Attracta closed her eyes and prayed.

The clang of metal landing in the bowl made her head swivel. A needle with a hook like a harpoon filled the dish. Concepta's words were taking form before her eyes. The skin on the back of her skull crawled. The smell coming in off the Liffey mingled with an older smell. A familiar smell. The contents of her stomach rose up and hit the back of her tonsils.

Nurse Flannagan bent over her. In one hand a square of damp cloth, in the other the grappling hook. Ramrod straight: never designed to go round soft bends. Attracta's knees were slapping like fleshy symbols.

Jaw clenched in some kind of maniacal rage all set to pick over the remains. 'Hold your legs open.' The spitty command spliced the thick air.

Suddenly an obedient child, Attracta did what she was told.

Preying eyes protruded from the gauze mask. Vomit filled her mouth.

A berserk shriek rang out in Attracta's head. At the speed of fork lightening, she was off the table.

'Fukkn' grim reaper.' She kicked the wrist so hard she thought she heard the bone crack. An aluminium basin crashed to the floor. Attracta saw the needle shiver as it impaled itself in a blackened board.

'Yeh filthy auld bitch, are yeh tryin to kill me?,' she screamed as she lunged at her.

'Yeh disgustin' peltful of shite.' Fists flew and flayed as she fought for her life.

Concepta pulled her off, still kicking, still screaming abuse.

'Get me outa here before I catch somethin' contagious.' She was hissing, snarling like an alley cat.

Concepta was still screaming. Trying to drag her by the hair of her head out on to the landing. In the row and the ructions Attracta spat hard in Nurse Flannagan's face. A split second was all it took to retrieve the Bishop's money; as Nurse Flannagan fought with the spit, she didn't feel Attracta's hand sliding into her pocket.

'Fukkn' butcher's sidekick.' Attracta screamed with relief as the rat-eaten curtain dragged back over her wet brow. Stairs and landings swinging and swaying beneath her feet.

'Yer not just fukkn' yer own chances, yer fukkn' mine.' Concepta jumped stairs two three at a time.

Survival flooded Attracta's veins. She shot through the door out on to a soaking wet dockside.

'It's only yer first time. Wait until yer caught over and over again. Yeh'll be as desperate and as grateful as the rest of us.' Gasping for air, Concepta jumped puddles and potholes trying to keep pace.

Attracta felt a length of freedom inside her.

'Let's get to fuck out of this Go-forsaken place; it's not fit for shite or scagulls.'

Near the lights of the city, the contents of her stomach rose up and savagely split some unfortunate's pot of geraniums straight down the middle. Till God called her, she could never remember how far down the docks or what door Concepta took her through that night. But she never forgot the cold or the evil in Nurse Flannagan's rooms.

'The money. The fukkn' money,' Concepta's lament echoed the length of the Dublin docks.

'Keep runnin', the wages of sin are safe in me knickers.'

Twenty-one

It was midday before she left Concepta's. The morning saw them better friends than the night before. The money too: ten pounds she'd told her, and ten pounds she'd split. The promise of a fiver, getting lenders off her back, bought Concepta.

Blistering sun was lifting tarred roads, trapping fleas and flies on the journey home. If Jemser wasn't in, she'd tell about the babby. She saw the Black Mariah and wondered who the Garda were lifting. She wouldn't have to wait long to find out; gossip would be spilling on to the streets, rounding every corner.

The silence worried her more than the stares. She thought someone had committed murder as she crept round and round the well of the stairs. Climbing higher, she could see that the Garda were on her landing. She knew deep in her waters it had something to do with the Raffertys.

Stray whispers followed her as she made her way slowly down the hall. *It's Jemser, the bousey. I heard it was Attracta. No, it's the eldest youngfellah; he has her heart broke. Remember the caper with the Rosary beads – the nuns are still waitin' for the money.* Speculation spouted from every mouth and door.

The flat was wide open. From inside, she could hear her Mother pleading.

'She's never done anytin' criminal in her life, Sergeant. Yeh can search every shaggin sock an' shoe in the house, heel and toe.' Young ones, wide eyed, were stuck to Nel Rafferty's side. 'She's a pain in the arse, but she's not a thief.'

The scalding in Attracta's bowels was gazumping the morning sickness. She didn't know where the young Garda sprang from. He flung her, face first, against a pealing wall, frisked her, found the money, and was marching her at high speed through a stunned crowd before she saw her mother's face.

The case against her couldn't be clearer cut. And with some of the evidence in their possession, there'd be no denying the plain truth, the sergeant told her as they bundled her into the crowded Black Mariah and drove to the Bridewell. The stench in the back of the van was as much her own fear as the prisoners surrounding her. The squabbling and swearing silenced any protest she might have to make.

185

Last in, she was first out of the prison van. Up before the Superintendent before the woman behind had time to tell her what was going to happen.

'Just listen; don't aggravate them or they'll keep yeh here for a month before they charge yeh,' she had time to warn her.

More then one hundred pounds had been stolen from the Bishop of Dublin's wallet. His Grace had spoken personally to the Superintendent in the Bridewell. There were further allegations of interfering with the Holy See's mail and attempted blackmail on the back of it.

That his Garda had failed to find any written material was a headache to the desk Sergeant; that the only printed word they saw was used as tablecloths and toilet paper was no surprise at all. The likes of the Raffertys only knew how to leech off the State and steal. His eyes told Attracta what he couldn't be bothered to communicate verbally. He would deal with the more disgusting but equally serious crime first.

'The Sunday collection.' The desk sergeant's revulsion was tangible. She couldn't get a word in edgeways. 'The poor of Dublin's hard-earned wages.' He spoke low and slow, each breath invested with loathing and finality. 'I hope they lock you up and throw away the key.'

The young guard she was standing beside nodded along viciously to every word.

'I didn't steal a penny of that money,' she pleaded to the dead eyes and deaf ears of the desk sergeant.

'Attracta Rafferty, I'm charging you with the offence of...'

She hit the floor of the charge room before the offence was fully read. When she came to, she was lying on a thin board with a pissy, hairy blanket at her feet.

'We can shift prisoners 12 and 13 to Mountjoy.'

An eye peeping through a small hole appeared to be talking about her and an auld tinker woman, lying drunk as a skunk opposite her.

She prayed fervently to Saint Jude that she was having a nightmare. I still have the babby in me belly. I didn't do anything wrong. Please, please, Jesus, Mary and Holy Saint Joseph, Michael the Archangel. I'll Christen the babby. I'll bring it to Mass. I'll do anything you want me to do for the rest of me life, but don't send me to prison.

The auld tinker turned her arse to Attracta and farted loudly. It was hours before anybody came back. She was sick, thirsty and hungry. But she didn't utter a word.

'Shift yer arse, yer on the move.' The young guard who'd accompanied her to the police station swung a hefty kick at the tinker's backside.' You, yeh scabby little thief, get over to the wall and wait in line till I say yeh can move.' Hope fading faster than reality, Attracta did exactly as he said. She didn't know what hour of the day or night it was, and she didn't dare ask.

The women either side of her looked as tired and confused as she was herself. She could see the sergeant who had charged her speaking on the phone. 'Stick 12 and 13 back in the holding cell.' He held his hand over the mouthpiece as he gave his order. The sound of a big heavy key turning behind her made her jump.

'Don't let them see yer frightened; they does luv dat.' The tinker had come to life quickly.

'Why have they locked us back up?' Attracta swallowed hard.

'They could be full up in Mountjoy. They might be movin' us on to another prison. They might just feel like puttin' the fear of God into yeh. Who the hell knows what happens in dees boyos' heads or when they gets their mouldy auld hands on yeh.

'But I'll tell yeh one thing that's not two, a dead cock doesn't crow, so no matter what's said or done, keep yer head well down and yer mouth shut tight. Her matter-of-factness was as consoling as her farting.

Twenty-two dry and hungry hours passed before Attracta heard her fate. And at that, the hindrance came from the least likely quarter. The Countess, dressed for a funeral, hat, gloves, Reverent Mother shoes, was holding court in her cell.

'My God, Miss Rafferty, did we not do enough for you? Were we not generous in the extreme? How can we ever change conditions for the poor when the poor won't change themselves? To think that I harboured a thief. Watered, fed and financed under my own roof. And to interfere with the sanctity of the Sunday collection is not just the sin of stealing but the sin of deprivation as well.

'And as for your stupidity and allegations, I won't even grace them with fresh air. You are either bad or very mad. That the Bishop realises it's the latter, is the mark of a very special man. To say that I'm disappointed would be an understatement. I'm filled to bursting with disgust, and humiliation at what I have been sent to say.

'The Bishop of Dublin, in his greatness, has bestowed on me the humble task of gifting you your freedom. In his magnanimity, he has seen fit to forgive you and to request that all charges against you be dropped. In essence, to save you from the horrors of prison, but not from yourself. In his wisdom, he has suggested that a doctor for the criminally insane examines you. He is,' – the Countess touched her breast bone – 'as great a visionary as he is a benefactor. I can hardly think for veneration.'

Attracta waited for the swelling in the Countess' chest to subside. As the full weight of her commuted sentence began to sink in, she unleashed a gospel of defiance. Hard eyes met across a filthy police cell.

'Well, let me enlighten you about your Bishop's medicinal lies, vision and generosity. He's a cheat, a traitor an' a fornicator.' The sentence slipped off her tongue as easily as it slipped off Nel's. 'He gave me that money. I didn't rob him.'

Locked in with Attracta's wrath and a very alert tinker woman who had her back against the door, the Countess had nowhere to hide.

'An', will I tell yeh why I needed the money? Or where I was last night? I was with Nurse Flannagan. That's right, the grim reaper herself, to rid me of his child. And he knew exactly what I wanted that money for.' Attracta slanted the truth to a slither of itself.

'And to make double-sure, he gave me two times what I needed. Oh, he's generous all right, yer benefactor Bishop. Why don't yeh ask him about the bit he keeps well out of the way in Leixlip. Or the filth he scribbles when you think he's supposed to be workin' up in yer booklined office.'

Blood drained from the Countess. Muriel and Attracta's faces coupled up like Siamese twins.

'I wasn't the only one accommodatin' His Grace.'

'Enough, that's quite enough, Miss Rafferty.' Her voice split the tinker's eardrums.

A new impotence took control of the Countess. Something sore challenged her memory. Barclay wearing different faces. A lying laugh, a tease, a wink: Muriel, Attracta, Attracta, Muriel. This strange scene, unsolicited, staged itself again. More substance than shadow this time, the truth presented with biblical clarity.

Overt flattery, sublime deception, Barclay O'Rourke the lie that told the truth. As the Countess reeled out of the police station, she took more than her torment with her.

She passed Jemser on the station steps. Neither, in their anxiety, saw the other.

Like a raging bull, Jemser Rafferty ranted, refused to let the desk sergeant speak until he had had his say.

'The Raffertys were many things in their day: highwaymen, IRA men, philanderers, blackguards. One of us, God save us, was even in the Garda. But robbers we never were; thievin' was never in our blood or bones.'

He put his arm around Attracta and led her past a line of dejected souls. 'Come on home, child, because Jemser Rafferty knows when he smells a rat. Even when it's dressed up in clerical garb.

'Yer problem, sergeant, is yis judge yerselves by lookin' down on them below, instead of lookin' up at them above – it's an elementary mistake, an' in yer ignorance, yeh might be forgiven.' Jemser left the sergeant in the charge room with a flea in his ear.

'What are yeh goin' to say to the neighbours, Da? I didn't disgraced yeh, but who'll believe me now.'

'When the neighbours put food on Jemser Rafferty's table, Jemser he'll put explanations in their mouths. Now, put yer head in the air and behave like the true soldier that I know yeh are.' They walked out of the Bridewell in bright Dublin sunshine.

'There's another thing, Da.' She took a deep breath, told him she was pregnant.

'Did yeh think after thirteen of our own we didn't know?'

'What did me Ma say?'

'She said, God's good, what he takes with one hand he gives back with another.'

Attracta stared at him in incredulity.

'Not a word of a lie, that's what yer Mother said. Now, let's get in here into the shade and get ourselves a couple a glass a Guinness before they run out in the drought.' He took her by the elbow and led her into O'Dwyer's.'

Attracta Rafferty never knew the strength of Jemser's love till that day.

Twenty-two

Had the devil himself taken a contract out on her soul? Had he, in all his malevolence, forced her on to this path of pain and deception? Muriel Grey couldn't have been in any more pain.

Barclay's jaded promises were displaying little more than the signs of old age. He hadn't come near his daughter. Her birth acknowledged with an air of officialdom that was heartbreaking. Calculating callousness had plunged Muriel into ever-deeper despair. Fonsie, for all his failings, had contacted both Barclay and the Countess. That her mother had displayed fewer manners than interest had surprised her.

She stayed up in her bedroom for hours on end swallowing indecision and tears. Brigit listened, watched her move round like the walking dead. Bothered and bewildered, neither here nor there. Half dressed for day, half dressed for night, not dressed for either.

'I can't.' She'd hand the newborn infant back. Day after day, the act broke Brigit's heart in a thousand different smithereens.

Seeking solace in the cloak of darkness, Muriel would drift in and out of sleep. But the dark had an agenda of its own. Deep in her soul, withered demons chattered noisily about sins and secrets. Her mother's vitriol, Barclay's filth, seeped off their tongues.

Pregnant – pregnant! You stupid slut. A woman's unclean loins made to pleasure a man's parts. Spools of evil spun round her heart. *And you – you little trollop – couldn't wait till you lifted your skirt. Tight as a drum, I'll hammer me way inside, come in her slithery sewer.* It was often morning before sleep in earnest relieved her.

'Listen to me, Mam. I don't want to know what's pullin' yeh asunder. I'm more concerned with puttin' yeh back together again. Brigit had rocked her as she'd wept and wailed through the thick and thin end of her torture. 'Just listen an' try an' hear what I have to say,' she'd shush and sooth. 'To cling to a dream when it has lost its magic is to condemn yerself to madness.'

Brigit had never acknowledged Muriel's fate, she never would. But she couldn't ignore the turmoil of the consequences.

When cajoling, porridge, penicillin soup, novenas, Mass and Confey honey didn't shift her, Brigit took a firmer hand in piloting the proceedings.

'What yer sufferin' from, Mam, is distress not disease.' Brigit walked into the bedroom early one morning, flung open the curtains and opened up windows. Let fresh air and fortune throw some badly needed light on a dismal situation. 'What can't be cured must be endured,' she started her homily. 'Harness the hurt. Offer it up as a sacrifice so that this child will never suffer what you're suffering. Make it the price you had to pay for her to be spared.'

Brigit still wasn't sure whether Muriel's moroseness was based on a real or an imagined fate. So she plumbed her prescription for sanity straight down the middle.

'The moment suffering finds a meaning, it strengthens instead of strangles. It's a natural law. Be worthy of your suffering, Mam; carry it with pride. You'll grow spiritually and you'll be free. Before long, you'll rise, and this little sweetheart will feel the wind beneath her wings.'

She handed Muriel her daughter, waited quietly while she put her gently to her breast. It wasn't an instant cure, but it was a remedy.

Slowly but surely, it began to take effect. Real or imagined. One morning, Muriel summoned Brigit and told her that Lily had looked her straight in the eye, and in that blinding instant she had understood the secret of life. It was an epiphany, the call of the soul. Not the dull gross voices that had been misleading her for years; this was the love her heart yearned for. A mother's love, the highest love of all, she had explained to a very perplexed Brigit.

From that day forth, she took the bad days with the good. Soldiering along bravely, offering her suffering, her pain. With all her emotions centred on Lily, hopeless hope slowly started to recede. If Brigit was right, she told herself, the painful apprenticeship might be worth it.

The rite of passage brought a host of new possibilities. The possibility to be free, to be master of her own destiny.

But the respite was temporary. Dread wasn't finished with either women yet.

Brigit thanked God daily for the breakthrough. And whereas before she couldn't get her to go near the child, now couldn't get her to put her down.

Muriel held her daughter close, gave her one more hug before she lay her down in her pram.

'Let her stretch her little spine. A child gets sore from too much handlin'.' Brigit was like a clucking hen.

Lily, Lily Rose; she whispered her name. Rolled the silky syllables round her tongue as she draped the high pram with soft white muslin. Protecting her daughter from insects. And cats.

'Feckin' cats. Pull that muslin tight as tuppence so they can't get near her face.'

Brigit checked and checked again the cat net. Muriel took the bucket she'd abandoned and continued to feed the two hungry goats. They had more than earned their keep these days; between keeping the grass down and producing enough milk to feed Jack and Lily, they had become blessings in disguise.

An Indian summer lengthened days and doubled Muriel's pleasure. She didn't know why the baby had brought such peace and serenity. But she knew that she was healing a very private and complex grief. Barclay had lost his iron grip on her soul.

She was more shocked at her absence of shock than she was at the changes she was daily experiencing. She'd started to feel secure in herself. To believe that Lily Rose was a mosaic: a host of hope, beauty, joy and peace. The best of them all fused into one. Radiating a magic and energy, Lily coloured and cured everything around her. She was the rainbow that brightened Muriel's dark sky. She was all she'd ever needed. And Fonsie too.

Lily effortlessly took possession of Fonsie's heart the day she bestowed on him the gift of her first smile. His love and approval were both permanently sealed. He was delighted and relieved to see how much Muriel included Jack in all her wonder. 'Leixlip Lily' she was teaching Jack to call his sister, and Leixlip Lily he was mastering, and matching.

The children were weaving their own particular magic on the household. Fonsie, sober long before Lily was born, was beguiled with the harmony they were doubly distributing.

Domestic help was his suggestion. And Brigit hadn't protested. The heavy laundry was now collected and delivered back in pristine condition once a week. A young girl was organised to walk the children. 'The Black Mariah' Brigit called the pram as it would disappear up the street with Jack sitting like a lord on the special little seat that Muriel had ordered from Brown Thomas.

The changes lightened the domestic load. Allowed the women time to get on with their own likes and needs. Brigit was starting to look her sixty years instead of seventy. And Muriel was beginning to dress and feel like a woman again. The visual changes alone were pleasing to Fonsie's eye. The chaos was being challenged, if not quite conquered.

Somehow in the midst of these changes, a gardener appeared on the scene. Whether this contribution was inspired by the nanny goats or in spite of them, Muriel never knew. His addition to the household staff was making a valid contribution. The garden fast became an extension of the kitchen. Flowers bloomed all around them; fruit bushes, trees, blossomed and ripened.

In the glorious sunshine of late August and September, Muriel ate outside with Jack and the baby at every available opportunity. Fonsie would often join them. She was surprised to find him easy company. He would come and go with the minimum of fuss. Pleasantly relaxed when he was around; often when he didn't appear, she'd find herself wondering where he was. It was as mysterious to her as her contentment.

'She'll be nut brown like her brother by the time the summer is out.' Brigit turned Lily round and set her pram to the sun again. 'She's lucky she had her mother's complexion. Protestant skin we do call it in these parts. Yellah Protestant skin.'

'She must be a throwback,' Muriel humoured her.

'Begod, between the goats and McGinty, the garden will be ready for prizes soon.' Brigit thought all her prayers were being answered at once.

It had been another beautiful day, a day made up of other days. A soft knock at the door brought bounty to the harmony.

'It's a caution what's to be found lurkin' in the bushes at the end of the day.' McGinty laid a basket of freshly cut rhubarb and blackberries on the kitchen table. 'There's an apple tree at the edge of the river, and I'll ate me hat if it isn't bobbin' with cookers by September.' It was all music to Brigit's ears. Fresh produce for her larder.

'This place is getting more productive by the minute.' She was washing and weighing, laying out sparkling jam jars as Muriel took herself and two tired children up the stairs to bed.

Rhubarb and blackberries were starting to simmer; the smell, twisting and turning, percolated into every bedroom as she prepared the children for bed. 'There'll be custard and rhubarb tart; blackberry jam potted and laid up for the autumn, all labelled and sorted by high noon tomorrow.'

Jack listened earnestly as he sucked on a bottle of warm goats milk and honey. He lay in his cot across the landing, never taking his eyes off her as she prepared Lily for bed. Cupping handfuls of warm soapy water over her daughter's head and shoulders, she washed the soft baby skin with the tips of her fingers. Tiny as a doll. She had her infant bathed and fed in no time.

She was surprised at the similarities between the two children. Both had the yellow Protestant skin: so boldly named. And if Lily finished as she started, they would both have the same silky black hair. Black as the earl of Hell's waistcoat, Brigit had announced the moment she was born. And here we were, eight weeks later, and not a hair on her head had altered.

It was quite extraordinary to Muriel that there wasn't a trace of Barclay O'Rourke to be found in her daughter. Not a trace of his red hair or his abundance of freckles. She thanked God for the small mercy. As Barclay had become older, the freckles looked more like a rustic map than the sprinkling of angels' blessing he had been so fond of describing. His hair she would have had no complaints about. It changed with the seasons and was truly the crowning glory. At the drop of a hat, he'd boast about it.

Muriel yawned as she pulled a comb through her own hair. It seemed longer and stronger since the birth. She just might get it cut into a bob when she was in Dublin. She just might do that. The grandfather clock in the hall chimed. Ten to nine, Lily and Jack were sound asleep. She tucked a blanket in at Jack's back: the days might be warm but the nights could be cold. And he always woke with the cold.

She turned down her bed. If the wind was in the right direction, she could get four or five hours before Lily woke for her next feed. A full moon cut like a dagger through the top right-hand pane. Wands of slanting moonlight cast a halo into Lily's crib. A full moon seen through a glass window brings shocking bad luck, Brigit's pishoguery irked. Slivers of fear inserted themselves into Muriel's spirit. She got back out of bed and drew the curtains in spite of her dislike of superstition.

On the far side of the street, a billboard creaked: Barclay's face swayed in the light evening breeze. In an unguarded moment, she faced eyes. Strangely unmoved, she read the caption below the jutting chin. Conflict and consciences.

Was she more accustomed to his absence than she understood? Had she lost him by degrees. First his presence, then his pretence, his sounds, his smells. Maybe he'd just faded away until there was nothing left. Had the spirit that had so generously brought gifts of light and love lost its power? She drew the curtains tight and banished the moon and its mischief to limbo.

In deep sleep, a more sinister portent gripped her. Wild and unkempt, her mother was screaming and cursing at Barclay. The harsh reality that divided mother and daughter dramatically altered. She was running too, her mother, but her legs were heavy and slow in motion. Curse, curse, curse of hell on him, the curse of hell on

194

him; syllables choked and spat out of her mother's throat and chest. The agony behind her eyes turning the room red, coagulated into pools of revenge. Her arms were reaching out, she was calling trying to calm, comfort, her mother. But all she heard was silence coming out of her mouth.

Someone was knocking frantically. Knock, knock, knock; the beat impeccably timed to her terror. Her bedroom door swung open. Fonsie standing at the foot of her bed. In her confusion, she thought he was part of the dream.

'I was knocking.' His face was as white as a sheet.

She jumped out of bed, whipped Lily out from her cot.

'It's your Mother.' A strange kind of relief washed over her.

***

'I don't think she's long left.' A square-fronted sister met Fonsie and Muriel at the nurse's station. 'She picked a good day to meet her Maker, the feast of the Triumph of the Cross.' The embodiment of starched calm led them into the darkened room.

Four candles, sentinels of death, stood around the eerie room. It looked like a bedroom and felt like a chapel. She'd never seen her mother in bed before. She felt embarrassed seeing her dressed for private in a public place. Her lips were blue, her eyes half closed, her breathing shallow.

'We've called a priest.' Piety coated every syllable.

'You can talk to her; she'll know you're here. It seems to have been a stroke. She'd been very agitated since she arrived. We're loath to give patients any medication before the priest has seen them. You never know what the dying need to get off their chests. Your mother's troubled. Take your time, talk gently, she may find some solace in your being here. Sometimes the dying need permission to die.' She left the room, in silence.

'Mother, it's Muriel.' Her solicitation sounded false. Words fought and faded on her mother's lips, her eyes flickering in the hopelessness of the moment. Numb and still, Muriel sat in the timeless warp.

From time to time, her mother struggled to communicate. In a room luminous with pain, the terror of death strangely mimicked to life the terror of birth. Unwilling participants trapped in an alien space, the slothful night crawled over old and familiar hurts. Fonsie

195

had been and gone and come back again with hot tea and her coat. Witness to the failed attempts, witness to both women's turmoil.

Like a priest hearing confession, Muriel was close enough to touch her mother's face. Her frustration took her beyond rage. She resented this selfish intrusion into her new world, could hardly contain her anger.

As in everything, Mother, your timing is impeccably off. Like the one and only time I could have spent a whole weekend away with Barclay O'Rourke. Remember ... you had one of your turns then, too. I should be at home now with my daughter. Oh pardon me, Mother, Lily Rose – or did she slip your mind as conveniently as your own daughter? Or was her birth as inconvenient as your death is for me?

She had hated her mother then as she hated her now. Hated this mockery, this filial falseness, this excruciating last act. She just wanted it to be over. Wanted her mother to be out of the way; out of her life; as much as her mother had wanted her out of hers. She wanted to be back in the world of Lily and lightness. As far away as possible from this descent into darkness.

'She can't die in peace until she's told you what's troubling her.' The nun returned the unbridled stare.

'She was brought in this evening. Her gardener found her slumped over the kitchen table.' Between prognosis, past and present, the Countess would struggle to communicate. Once, Muriel thought she'd said handbag. But she kept her composure; she didn't want her mother's vanity added to the confusion.

Without warning, 'handbag' sounded again in a crystal voice. With strength born of desperation, her mother half rose in the bed. Gasping, greedy for air, she finally make her dying request clear.

As Muriel opened the envelope, her mother visibly and audibly surrendered herself to death.

Muriel felt the blow in her chest. Death had a fist.

Like a cesspool, the contents of his filthy letter swirled before her eyes. In her hand, the root cause of her mother's distress shook violently. Barclay's letters so disingenuously posted to the Countess' home by Attracta. Face frozen with revulsion and shame, Muriel bolted from the bedside. Stumbling down long corridors, Fonsie fast on her heels. A convulsion of horror seized her. Crude technicolour augmented her rage.

The evidence in the body of the text was irrefutable. Ruthless, unarguable, the case cruelly, callously, set out before her eyes.

And oh so obscenely. Muriel vomited profusely and in agony.

Duplicity flooded her system, cruelty her arteries. Her veins, her capillaries, charged with the poison. Brutal inarticulate words forging a passage round her brain. Her blood in revolt, she wandered miles of empty streets until she found herself back in her old home. Fonsie beside her. Her fists, her teeth, clenched convulsively as she made her way up the stairs. Rage constantly augmenting her agony. Barclay copulating as casually as a stray dog with a servant girl in her father's study, her mother's bed. Inebriated by betrayal, filled with a loathing that would radically change her. Afforded a freedom in which morality was of complete irrelevance, revenge a God-given right.

But the hurt would have to be lanced first and a poultice applied to Muriel's festering wounds before she was ready to do battle with her Bishop.

***

Winter saw out summer. In a surfeit of sorrow, Muriel saw neither. The hopes and dreams that had so recently buttressed her behaviour were diminishing with frightening alacrity. She ached to calm the turmoil in her chest. Longed to turn back the clock. But death and the obscene letter had connived to put pay to her trial expedition into reality.

'Try and get some sleep. You're like the walkin' dead. Another drop of goats milk won't hinder Leixlip Lily here; indeed it might help.' Brigit hoped the sleep would get Muriel out of her arrears. Like snakes and ladders, she was back at the beginning. She had lost the coordinates to cope. She was exhausted. Brigit thanked God for Fonsie's forbearance, his diligence, his silent strength.

Even in death, her mother had left no peace. Heaped on top of her hurt, the reality haunted Muriel. You learn more by subtraction than addition. The awful truth scratched on the back of the most offensive of his letters in her mother's hand taunted Muriel: in places, the pen had torn right through the paper. Not a work of sympathy or empathy, just the ruthless epilogue etched on the back of the explicit letters.

It was Fonsie who had eventually taken them out of her hand. Gently, the same way he'd led her like a ghost at her own funeral from her mother's house. The same silent and systematic way he was sorting out the affairs of her mother's estate.

197

His patience, his peaceful countenance, was playing no small part in these painful proceedings. And his bravery. *Roll with the punches, don't freeze or fight them. It only prolongs the bout, prolongs the agony. Do as I tell you, it might be more painful but it will be over much more quickly.* He hadn't bolted or balked in the face of her fury or the perimeters of her madness.

Night after night, as Fonsie's car pulled into the yard, she'd put out the light. She didn't have the interest or the energy to make decisions.

He spent weeks sorting and sifting through the house in Ballsbridge. Every morning, when things at home were as settled as they could be, he made the thirty-mile round trip. His daily pilgrimage.

A veritable repository, the ice-cold house daily delivered a rush of new bile to Fonsie. Tripwires took him back into seminaries, to scenes of disgrace and defrocking. Dried out holy water fonts hung in every room. The all-seeing eyes of the Sacred Heart of Jesus tracking his every move. Above the mantelpiece in the kitchen, a sharp-nosed Pope looked pious and pleased every time he passed. Statues of saints plastered up against bedroom and bathroom walls. The house resembled more a tacky church souvenir shop than a home.

Idolatry. Muriel had sent symbols and long-suffering saints crashing ceremoniously into one another on that pitiful night. Spinning and flying, her mother's devotional objects lay cracked and broken at her feet. Back in this tainted place again, she seemed to reabsorb the querulous odour of deceit. Reliving, relaying the terror, the tackiness, the filth, of the pornography.

Fonsie was lucky he didn't have to take her out in a straitjacket. Determined never to let her set her foot inside the place again, he worked tirelessly through the estate. It would be locked up and sold as soon as was humanly possible.

Day after dog-tired day, the same disconnected scene confronted Fonsie. Mountains of unopened mail and unpaid bills covered the Countess' writing bureau. Documents, newspapers, books, magazines littered every drawer, every cupboard, in the house. For a woman who was so involved in everyone else's affairs, she'd paid little or no attention to her own, Muriel had enlightened him.

In stark contrast, her husband's affairs were in meticulous order. Left to the same fate as her own paperwork, the Countess had managed by default to leave them alone. It was in seeking the order necessary to finalise the estate, to keep his promise to Muriel, that

Fonsie stumbled on the two sets of accounts that would radically change the course of his life. And make no small contribution to Muriel's sanity. Fortune, if not fate, was about to play its hand in their respective futures.

Muriel tiptoed over to her daughter's cot. Lily Rose was just stirring. Her crimson face, as crumpled and confused as the day she was born, looked up at Muriel. Stretching tiny arms that didn't quite clear the top of her head, she arched her back and yawned.

'Six months old and sleeping the night. Nanny's milk and mammy's milk.' Muriel picked her up gently carried her back up to a warm bed. *Now this little body mighten mend yeh, Mam, but she'll heal yeah*; Brigit's wonderful words filled her full of hope and healing. Again and again, she'd put the baby to her breast. Muriel wondered where Brigit Murphy got her faith from, where Fonsie Duggan got his compassion.

Truth comes in multiple choices. Brigit had battered away her malaise. Locutions, locations, situations, but when you're blind its hard to see. *Your problem, Mam, is your lettin' the heart have the run of human affairs. The head's the man yeh need to take charge. The head will out-run the heart on every occasion.*

Cold, lucid reality – drip, drip, drip – fed daily into her soul until the dam inside her chest had finally burst. And again Brigit was there, holding her, asking no questions, telling no lies. Just reading all the signs, talking quietly when she had something to say. 'Have yer dreams by all means, but don't let yer dreams have you. When the tales you've been told are no more than an ordinary lie, it's time to call a halt.'

Some lessons were hard earned. Convictions held deep inside Muriel rose to the surface. What she once held sacred as a consecration, she now saw as nothing more than a desecration.

'I swear before Almighty God and all that's holy in this house, if it takes all of my strength and the rest of my life, I'll right this obscene wrong.' She stood beside Lily Rose's bed as she swore the vow.

Twenty-three

She shoved the grubby envelope over to Attracta. The dark brown stain looked like dried blood to her eye. It made less sense to Concepta than it did to Attracta that the Butcher's Boy had chosen to post the letter to her house.

He was living in digs with ten other paddies. He'd enclosed a ten bob note for the baby. He'd send more when he could afford it. Working as a boner in a meat factory. The long hard hours wasn't as well paid as they had all bragged and blowed about in the boozers. He missed Dublin, the shop and the crack. Concepta had never seen Attracta in such a state. There was no forwarding address on the letter. Just a short note, the money and a Liverpool postmark.

'If I could only get me hands on the boat fare, I could go and find him,' she'd sobbed on Concepta's kitchen table.

'Liverpool is bigger than Ireland. Besides, when he wants yeh, he'll send for yeh. When he writes again, he'll write where he lives.' She'd tried to call a halt to Attracta's gallop.

'Maybe I'll go in anyway. Get out from under Nel's feet and nose. Yeh can't fart in here but every fekker knows what yeh had for yer breakfast.'

'Maybe yeh ought to tink once and tink twice about the way he left yeh in the first place,' Concepta cautioned her. 'Yeh haven't got a pot to piss in, yer head's hurtin', yer back's broken. Before yeh go off at half cock, yeh need to get yerself sorted.'

'There's too many of yer likes beggin' on the streets of England. You ask Fatama. She might be an auld whoremaster an' a miserable auld shite, but even Fatama couldn't cut it in England. They ate their young over there.' Concepta plugged away on Fatama's behalf.

'There's plenty of work in Dublin, yeh only have to give me the nod. There's no need for yeh to be skint or beholdin' to anybody.'

Attracta couldn't understand why the Butcher's Boy had taken such a long time to write. On bad days, she didn't know why he bothered at all. It was nine months since he bolted. Three since the babby was born. And she'd been broke before and after.

Concepta was way ahead of her. Someone was leaning on him. Probably the father, and certainly the mother. Billy Atkins could be a hard bastard but he always was a man of conscience. And she knew for a fact that Jemser and Nel made a point of parading the new babby past and into the shop at the drop of a hat. It had even been suggested in some quarters that a couple or more parcels of mutton were slid across the counter. One or two auld wans had mentioned money, but Concepta could see little evidence of such money on Attracta.

'I can't stay at home much longer. God knows, Jemser and Nel in their own ways are as good as gold to me. The babby is as welcome as the flowers of May. A replacement for the one Nel lost. Sure, yeh can see the way it's paraded up and down the streets of Dublin. There's never a cross word of blame or shame. But we're swingin' from the rafters already.

'An' how long will I be on a housin' list? Who in the housin' is goin' to give a sinner like me a flat? There's five of us on the brew now. And the rest on the breadline. I'm bet and broke. Nel does her best with a bad lot. If anything, she's better than before. Able to stretch the few bob further and further. But if I never see another bit of mutton or marrowbone or tripe, it will be centuries too soon. I'm an ungrateful bitch an, a miserable burden. Me name is a black as a boot all over Dublin.'

'Why don't yeh stay here for a while? I know I'm only down the road. But the change will be as good as a rest.'

She'd been around at Concepta's for three weeks when Nel arrived in a fluster. Brandishing a letter, she could hardly speak from the exertion and excitement.

'I opened it for yeh. I thought it might be important. Gorette was at work; it took meself and Jemser over an hour to figure out the grandiose scrawl. I'll read it out. Yeh know what yer like with the joindy-up writin'.'

'What in the name of Jaysus could the Countess' daughter want with yeh?'

She was all fingers and thumbs as she pulled the stiff velum paper out of the envelope. 'To discuss a matter of importance.' All Nel's Ps and Qs were in the right places. 'To right a wrong stumbled upon in the wake of the Countess' death. Jaysus, she's comin' to see us,' Nel heightened the drama.

'Right a wrong?' Attracta saw pound signs. Saw her ticket to Liverpool floating before her eyes.

'Pack up yer few bits love an' come on home. There's no use lettin' the likes of these people seein' yeh out of yer natural environment. Yeh wouldn't want to give the wrong impression. Let them think yeh were livin in the lap of luxury.'

It was far from luxury they were. Attracta looked around her. Concepta and her two children, herself and the babby, all squeezed into eight square feet. There wasn't enough room to swing a cat let alone its kittens.

'We'll have the place bulgin' with kids when she comes. Let her see how the other half live. There just might just be somethin' in this for the Raffertys. God helps dem dat helps demselves, so lets get crackin'. We'll borrow Concepta's children on the day – add a bit of colour and confusion.' Nel led the little expedition back home.

She did exactly as Nel said. Set a scene for sore eyes and suckers. There was great talk of new housing schemes just outside Dublin. It was always a good move to play your trump cards when someone of importance was in the vicinity. Yeh never knew what position or pull people had.

So a royal reception of Raffertys would be part of the greeting party. And maybe a few runners in as well. The Reillys up the hall were always good for doublin' up confusion. She got Gorette to rustle them up and be on standby on the occasion of the visit. Two heads were better than one, and Gorette's head was better than ten.

Nel asked Mrs Mooney next door if she could speak to the important lady in her place when the going got too tough. Where neither chick nor child would disturb her. The neighbour said a key would be hanging just inside the knocker. Herself and her husband would be at work, so there was no need to worry about bein' disturbed or overheard. The traps were baited and set for Muriel's visit.

***

The evening was cool. Damp sicknesses hung in the air. A hundred bright eyes were watching as Muriel stepped into Stretham Street. TB, weather, Brigit had lamented the smog that rifled Dublin in the spring of '48: God protect us from the gasworks and Guinness' polluters an' pollution. Muriel could see smell her concerns. All around her, overbearing buildings ruptured the smoke-grey skyline. Floor upon of floor of red brick. Vertical villages, she'd heard Fonsie call them; he wasn't far off the mark.

Through corporation windows, tightly stacked human shapes revealed themselves. Regulated light broke through narrow slits at the end of each hallway. Lavatories, she didn't wonder. Powdery facades showered tiny hails of crumbling brick on pavements as she passed. Weeds sprung from cracks in casements. A teeming mass peopled this hell-hole, this prescription for epidemics.

Doctor Noel Brown had been castigated for his impertinence and interference. How could anything survive such a miserable measure of architecture? How could anything alive thrive in this a place?

And this black hole, this illustrious pit, is where a Prince of the Church sees fit to rear a child. Where the Countess thought she could cure a conglomerate of conditions. Force-feed her daily diet of invisible miracles and madness.

Something slipped and slid inside Muriel's stomach. Broken sticks beat buckled bicycle wheels nosily over cobbled stones. The noise was astounding. She slumped momentarily. Her head seemed full of contradictory voices. All having their say, all clamouring. Children showed less than passing interest as she side-stepped their games. Laughing, livid-red faces, shouting and smiling, snarling. None of them wore a coat on this damp, drizzly evening. She was over dressed, under par.

She ducked ropes swinging high and low from street lampposts. Alien smells stuck like paste to the back of her throat. She'd left it late to benefit from the cover of dusk. Maybe too late.

A steady trickle of light was beginning to appear in upstairs rooms. On ground level, she could see directly into some of them. A sprinkle of yellow and orange varying in brightness seeped through windows. Women and girls noisily, busily, seeing to children and men's needs by gaslight.

A curiosity began crystallising inside her. Her senses sharpened. Everything here seemed more intensified. Every scene more defined. There was more life, more living, more love, crammed between these teeming walls. More fight in the fight, more sin in the sex, than the stifled, sanitised existence that lay just a few miles north of the city.

Nearer the bone, something more compelling gripped Muriel's guts. Had Barclay walked these streets? Talked his way into their hearts, heads, beds? Used his position to lord it over them, lie under them, to do the dirty deed? Who would think to question the philanthropic priest? Who would dare challenge him?

With a start, Muriel realised she was standing staring through the doorway of an equally bewildered family. A wave of fatigue swamped her. But this part of the sequel had to be attended to. She pressed on. Without quite knowing how, she was on Attracta's landing.

Ten different people pointed her towards the Raffertys. A door flung open and wide, revealing two rooms. Thronged full to the gills of children and women, mostly. It wasn't until Jemser welcomed her that she noticed the small, thin man. More suited to saddle a horse than a wife. The image was lost to the ructions. She'd never seen so many bodies in one space. It was physically impossible to accommodate the basic needs of all these people in two rooms.

Attracta bided her time, kept her powder dry. The tangled web was winding itself round and round again. But this time, she wouldn't be the one to be caught.

Muriel watched the chaos develop into a slow dance. Caginess and caution replacing energy and urgency. Contingents of children moving in contrary circles. A woman sitting by a low fire, a child in her lap, rocking. Eyes critical as a clucking hen, watching, waiting for time or Muriel to make the next move. Jemser handing out mugs of tea. Turning the cracked side away, she drank the sweet, watery concoction. A beauty, eyes colour-blasted by hurt and deceit – no more than a child herself – was holding a red-headed baby. Strong as a bullock, the bones build spit of him.

The child had taken its toll on the emaciated body. Arms flailing, lungs bursting with frustration, the baby, Barclay's baby, was trying to satisfy itself at Attracta's skinny breast. Breasts he'd had the best of, sucked and swollen himself at time and time again. In the stillness of her mind, she saw with resounding clarity, the living consequences. How his unfathomable act of cruelty had connected them all. Barclay, Attracta, herself, Lily. And this red-headed boy, Paul, called after one of the Apostles.

In this blinding instant, Barclay's betrayal reached treacherous levels. She believed her duty in this portent of dark forces was to break the mould. To redress the recurring fault. He'd pay dearly for the full force of his destruction. She'd have the warrant for his dethronement in her hand before she left this Stratham Street tonight.

Quick to calculate the odds, Attracta engaged Muriel's need with energy all of her own. In the relative calm and quiet of the next-door neighbour's, the plot unfurled itself. Attracta began to see a pattern of events unfolding before her.

Christmas might have come and gone, but there was still a fat goose to be had. If there was a chance anything could be salvaged from the mess, she was in, she was more than prepared to play the part. The injured party, galvanised, inebriated, resurrected the lie. She was relieved to find that all Muriel was interested in was revenge. Justice, Muriel called it, but her eyes told a different tale.

Marching bluntly into the past, Attracta pillaged the present to provide for the future. After a few crudely engineered moments, she hacked the remains of the Bishop to bits with a clear conscience.

'Every cripple has his own way of walkin' and I'm no exception. I put dem letters in an envelope and posted them to the Countess. To make sure an' double sure that she knew that I wasn't the one tellin' the lies. D'yeh know what they were goin' to do to me? Have yeh any idea what kind of madness your mother an' the Bishop of Dublin were hatchin'? A fukkn' mental institution, a mental institution for the rest of me natural life. Prison would have been a holiday camp by comparison.

'Pure evil was at the bottom of that plan. Pure evil. I'm not sayin' I was a saint' because I wasn't. But bejaysus – a mental home! But God works in strange ways. I put dem letters in me pocket when I was tidyin'. Forgot all about dem and brought dem home to the Liberties by mistake. An' here's the rub. If yer mother hadn't sent the Raffertys out to school so diligently every morning, our Gorette here would never have been able to read.'

'The dismissive, defamatory and downright filth that the letters contained.' The quiet young girl looking intently at Muriel stole the show. Gorette Rafferty put the nail finely and succinctly into the Bishop of Dublin's coffin.

With a fifty pound note in their sights, it took more energy than eloquence to extract Muriel's pound of flesh.

Not short of creative function, Attracta performed her final pirouette.

I, ATTRACTA RAFFERTY, DO FAITHFULLY SWEAR THAT THE BABY I GAVE BIRTH TO ON THE 17TH OF NOVEMBER 1947 IN THE CITY OF DUBLIN IS THE SON OF BARCLAY O'ROURKE, THE BISHOP OF DUBLIN.

After two hours, several attempts and not a few bucks and fucks, Muriel finally left with the affidavit that she'd come for.

Attracta Rafferty felt fully justified as she swore the lie on Fonsie Duggan's headed paper.

Twenty-four

Help, like hindrance, came from the most unlikely quarters. Fonsie Duggan would never have given a second thought to a key left in his safe hands if he hadn't seen for himself the fates of the two very different women.

So while Muriel garnered evidence for her kangaroo court, Fonsie focused on the sharper end. He didn't care much for dramatic scenes: he knew the clergy only too well, knew their's wasn't a confrontational game. But he knew figures, and he knew falsifying when he saw it. He knew how plan and how to be patient.

Through the autumn and winter, Fonsie trawled convoluted, creative accounting systems that would try and test consummate accountants. Researched column upon column of figures found and unfounded.

The fine-tooth comb system wasn't difficult, but it was painstaking. Comparing the true sets of figures with the false lent impetus to the intrigue. Periodically, Fonsie would marvel at the fusion of her father's fortitude and his own need for retribution. Alternately pondering the curious coincidence that would be Barclay's undoing. He spent long nights checking obscure entries. Probing the weaknesses and the strengths of the second set of accounts was crucial to his plan.

By spring, Fonsie was ready to involve Muriel. His timing was as perfect as his plan. She wasn't just open to reasoning, she was primed. He listened carefully, voiced his concerns, but he didn't dismiss her. She wanted her pound of flesh, wanted her day in court. Fonsie Duggan didn't believe in revenge: he believed in planning, evidence and rock-solid alibis.

Her plan, more dramatic in nature than his, would need to be meticulously timed and rehearsed. In short, he told Muriel it needed more work. He offered the benefit of his experience but requested that she extended him the courtesy of one more week.

'You take him out by the heart if that's your desire. I intend to take him out just below the belt. To hit him where the hurt is infinitely more measurable. And publicly accountable.

'What I need now is your full attention and cooperation. I've thought long and hard about what I'm about to say and what I'm about to do. I've witnessed your humiliation, both private and public. Had my own share of sorrow and sadness.' It was the one

206

and only reference he'd ever made to his own grief. She had never given it a thought before this moment; it was something she now regretted. 'And this is how I propose to balance the hypocritical equation.'

It had taken over two hours for Fonsie to furnish his final solution. A slow smile spread across Muriel's face as the plan unravelled.

'Different bulls, different measures,' he'd said when he finally finished. Brigit would have been proud of such a prophetic line.

The confabs and configurations of conversations that were taking place in Mr Fonsie's office were mighty. Brigit was less curious than relieved. She'd seen highs and lows in marriages. But never the intimacy of intrigue. Thick as thieves. The glue that was binding them together was strong. She blessed herself, and said the Joyful Mystery a day early.

***

Muriel was all dressed up. The comings and goings this morning were as big a mystery as the Rosary. Brigit thanked God for His mercies, both riddlesome and real, as she monitored the proceedings and processions. Her dressed like the queen of Sheba and himself still talkin' ten to the dozen to her as she started the motor car up. She'd never seen Fonsie so animated. Or earnest!

The big black diamond on the sleeve of Muriel's coat was another curiosity to Brigit Murphy. A public sign of grief she'd seen little of in private. Grievin' grabs people in different ways and at different times. She chastised herself and waved back at Muriel as she pulled out of the yard.

But the black diamond on the arm of Muriel's coat wasn't a mark of respect for her mother's death. It was a distraction, a topic of conversation for the bank manager in Blessington. It would allow her to slip coyly from one role to another. A curious man by nature, the manager's need to know was easily sated by titbits of inside and outside information. Anticipating all of this and more, Muriel turned his weakness into her strength.

Brigit, in her innocence, had given her just the nugget of information she needed. A letter from her sister had been the source of the good fortune. As close to the horse's mouth as she once was herself, she didn't doubt the validity of the contents.

These were the kinds of thought she allowed herself as she drove the twenty miles or more to Wicklow. Random thoughts and road signs. Fonsie had made her memorise the road signs as well as taking a map. Stop if you need to read the map. We can't afford any diversions. But she didn't need to consult the map. She knew the route. Leixlip, Lucan, Clondalkin, Tallagh Baltinglass, Blessington. All the signposts pointed her in the right direction. She was outside the bank in Blessington at one minute to ten.

At the appointed hour, Muriel stepped into the cool, hard granite bank.

'It isn't often enough we have the pleasure of your company these days.'

The manager in the Royal Bank lit up like Guy Fawkes as Muriel was ushered into his office. Between the black patch on her arm and the wedding ring on her hand, there was no shortage of commiseration and congratulations.

'Mr Duggan of Leixlip. Well, I'll be praised.' The manager, who had always had a soft spot himself for Muriel, lamented as much as congratulated her. 'We are more than familiar with Mr Duggan in these premises. Though, like your good self, we never saw enough of him. And who could wonder? Now that he's married again, and a father again, I don't suppose he can find the time to fit us in.' The long haul of sentiment permeated syntax and sentence alike.

After a suitable silence, he talked about the Bishop's robbery. She shook her head sagely. Sadly, she was more than familiar with the ins and outs of it. The Sunday takings, she repeated after him as if it were her own contribution. Indeed, the ever-anxious manager was as eager to confide as he was to disclose. That his brother, the Superintendent in the Bridewell, the station where the young woman was taken, was still eulogising about the generosity and spirituality of the Bishop. Can you imagine having it in you?

He forged ahead of his unfortunate simile. Powers of forgiveness and discernment gifted in abundance to one man. He deplored his own shortfalls, the failings of mere mortals. The shocking lack of remorse of the young whippersnapper, the bald cheek of the bold brat, more than doubled the Bishop's magnanimity, in his humble opinion. He'd flushed as he gushed his admiration.

His yap-yap-yapping was turning into a big porridge of sounds. Muriel could feel the thin sheen of sweat forming on her top lip. Her heart was thumping so loudly she actually thought he might hear it; so shook was she at talk of Attracta Rafferty. For more than an ugly moment, the letters floated before her mind's eye. Words welded into her brain gave a new edge to her urgency. She steadied herself and waited for the clamouring in her chest to subside before she threw in the winning nugget.

'Speaking of mere mortals.' Pooling all her survival skills, she leaned conspiratorially.' Between you and me and these four walls, our brilliant Bishop is on the move.'

She took her time utilising the fullness of the bank manager's greed for gossip, his need for power.

'Rome.' She let her eyes do the work.

'A Cardinal's seat.' He almost imploded with satisfaction.

'He has of course given permission to tell your good self. No, no, I haven't heard who will be the next Bishop of Dublin. He'll be visiting within the fortnight. No doubt you will be one of the first to hear who his replacement is. Until then, not a word to a soul.'

His head nearly bobbed off his shoulders, he was doing so much nodding and agreeing.

'And that brings me to the purpose of my visit here.' She tapped the soft document case. Still reeling from the confidence, he was way ahead of her when she announced her intention to deposit documents into Barclay's safety deposit box.

'He'd be here himself, but you can only begin to imagine the hectic schedule.' She inclined her head, gilded the moment.

It was too easy. Currents of her confidences led her through the body of the bank. Into the bowels. Beaming, whispering, unctuous courtier. The cast-iron door was already propped open. The key to the inner door was on a chain in his inside pocket. He held the set up to the light and chose the third one. The inner door sprung open. He flicked on the electric light in the windowless room, bowed and left her to her own devices.

It was déjà vu. Nothing had changed. Exactly as she remembered. Cardboard boxes laid casually on the floor. Shelves stacked high and low with leather, wood and tin boxes. Private affairs, boxed safe and sound in the vaults of the bank. To her surprise, the Vatican's boxes were still in the same place, Italian inscriptions on their sides and front. The same haul of gold coins, she didn't wonder. The spoils of war, bigger and bulkier, were secured by locks and chains. She thanked God she didn't have to loot them. She didn't need God's bankers after her!

In light of his impending role, Barclay's box, alongside the Holy Sees, seemed somehow befitting. A thick lair of dust suggested his box hadn't been opened in a long time. Muriel listened for footsteps, and checked that no one was watching, before she took the key so fortuitously entrusted to Fonsie from inside the document case. For a sublime moment, she saw Leixlip Lily's smile. She opened the deposit box, slowly relishing the wholeness of the moment. Concentrating her energies, she began shoving bundles of used notes, all large denominations, into her shoulder bag. It didn't look like much, but she was certain there was several thousand.

Four large white certificates at the bottom of the box were strange to her. 'Swiss Government Bonds' arched in bold print across the top of large sums of Swiss Francs. The size and shape of the tough, waxy paper made it look fake. A lot of foreign money in the wake of the war wasn't worth the paper it was written on. Witness the Vatican's solid gold; she talked to herself as she put the bonds back.

It wasn't until she was about to lock the box that she thought they might be of some interest to Fonsie. That they might just shed some light on the audit trail that he was finding so frustrating.

Fonsie had winked as he put her through her paces. Carry this document case. It will lend an air of importance to the deposit you're supposed to be making. Wear a loose-fitting coat and under it strap a shopping bag round your shoulder. Fill it quickly and quietly with the cash. And leave with a reverent look on your face. A look that says a matter of grave importance has been entrusted to me and has been attended to.

It wasn't the first time that Muriel found his wink attractive. She had made one small adjustment to the plan. She'd tell him when she was home and dry about the little deposit she had left behind in the bank for Barclay.

Don't bring any notice on yourself. Don't let the engine flood. She waved at the bank manager, face like a full moon in a fog as she turned the key in the ignition. Easing out the choke, she pulled smoothly away from the kerb. She noticed that her hands were shaking as she held the steering wheel.

The car lurched and spluttered in the middle of Blessington. Pushing the choke gently back in, all fingers and thumbs, Muriel swung round the broad sweep of the road. Trying hard to look calm and collected, she found second gear and settled the high pitch of the engine and her nerves down. She had to grit her teeth to kill the grin as the local guard saluted her. Nice and easy, she slid the gear stick into third, put the choke fully home and made good her escape.

She wondered how much money she'd stolen. Time enough to look at what you've got when you get back to Leixlip, Fonsie had drilled her.

She squeezed the bag under her coat; it sat snug on her hip like a holster. It felt thin, but money was like that – deceptive. She didn't have to calculate too hard to know that she had just helped herself to a king's ransom. She'd put at least ten bundles of red and purple notes into her bag. Assuming that notes bundled together were all of the same value, it was an elegant reward. Fonsie had spent weeks poured over Barclay's accounts, and if that figure alone was right, she was harbouring a fortune under her coat.

She'd never experienced anything like the surges of adrenaline. She'd taken some chances with Barclay O'Rourke in her time, but robbing a bank under Fonsie Duggan's meticulous directions took her to another level. I do believe, Muriel Grey, that you've just pulled off your first heist. Your next performance will be more public, but it will be just as thrilling and warranted.

Fonsie's face was as white as a sheet when she emptied the contents of her bag on to the desk.

'My good God, I knew he had stashed away a fortune, but until I saw the bearer bonds, I didn't realise it was five fortunes. He still hadn't finished counting the cash; the figure as it stood was fifteen thousand pounds.

It was past midnight by the time they had checked and double-checked. The final sun was forty-two thousand pounds. Ten thousand in cash and thirty-two thousand in bearer bonds. Until the dust settles, we'll let it lie on deposit in a bank in the Isle of Man. I keep a client account there. I've had sizeable lodgements there before, and I suppose I'll have sizeable lodgements there again. They won't blink an eyeball at Swiss Bonds or the size of the cash deposit.

'It's bullet-proof; we're bullet-proof. If he opens his mouth, he puts himself in prison on ten different counts of forging, falsifying, embezzlement. To say nothing of falling off his Cardinal's throne.' That wink again – it was getting better and better. She felt at tiny flutter in the bottom of her stomach. The length, breadth and depth of the sting was slowly dawning on Muriel.

'These figures in the second set of books, the ones that took so long to find and so long to figure out, confirmed a long-held suspicion of mine that Barclay was on the fiddle. Avoidance or evasion, the entire evidence well documented. Look at the accounts, windfalls, bequests, huge sums of money, but no record of their whereabouts. The bearer bonds ended the audit trail. I knew there had to be more money somewhere. Then, like a rabbit out of the hat, you produced the missing pieces of the puzzle.'

Fonsie shoved the thin copybook across the desk. 'And these accounts, these meticulous entries, signed by your father and sealed by the bold Bishop himself, condemn him. Double entries in his own indomitable hand, in black and white; Barclay O'Rourke, the author of his own downfall.'

'And these,' Muriel ran her finger over the two very distinctive signatures, 'would have been at my father's insistence. He was the stickler for rules even when the procedures weren't strictly legal.'

'Well in the face of the evidence, God bless your father's forbearance, that's all I can say.' Fonsie put down his pen.

'We could buy half of Ireland with this kind of money.'

'Or we could make a huge donation to Noel Brown's campaign and double the dose of punishment.' Fonsie's eyes danced with mischief.

'Only the Gods dish out such charity.' Muriel's heart was pounds lighter.

Giddy with exuberance and expectation, they made their way up to bed.

'Leixlip Lily, he may never have recognised you, but after today he'll never forget you,' Muriel talked to the sleeping baby as the new moon peeped and pasted the window.

'I left your photograph and birth certificate in his safety deposit box. Today the retribution was private. On Wednesday, may God be my witness, it will be very public.'

Twenty-five

'I know it's late, Your Grace, but the grand woman said it was personal, and urgent.' His secretary failed, as he always failed, to impress Archbishop Ennis. It was ten o'clock at night.

Muriel had waited until the eve of the Convention in Maynooth to deliver the letter. One of the most exciting days in the Church's calendar. Muriel knew just how painful this ethical straitjacket would be for Archbishop Ennis.

He knew as soon as his silver knife slit the envelope open that trouble was its content.

Sadistic and disgusting, these notes are self-defamatory. Do what you will with them. I want them neither in my possession nor on my conscience. No doubt the author's hand, Barclay O'Rourke's hand, will be as familiar to you as it is to me.

The Archbishop slammed his fist on the desk. His loss was for credibility not words. Barclay O'Rourke. I should have followed my hunch and confronted him eighteen months ago. Should have listened when that auld menace Maggie Murphy tried to show me the note: the steamy incident. Dithering whilst that bucking eejit preached and punched pulpits the length and breath of Ireland: the bounden duty of Catholics to copy their Bishops by word and by deed.

But he must temper his desire for retaliation. The public announcement was eminent. The private one already a fait accompli. The Cardinal's seat was already filled as far as Rome was concerned. The climate couldn't be more sensitive, both inside and outside the Church. The women of Ireland were on the turn. The Mother and Child act had done the Catholic Church more harm than good. A scandal of this magnitude could set the Church back a century.

Archbishop Enis replaced the telephone receiver that he was holding in his hand. The telephone wire wasn't secure. Nothing was safe in the whispering corridors. Even as he dithered, the Council of Bishops was assembling. This evening, Maynooth would have started celebrating the candidate for Rome.

Hamstrung by compromise he sought counsel in the secrecy, and safety, of the confessional.

Twenty-six

She was impressed and just a little amazed at how systematically she had set about Barclay's downfall. If she had been religious, she might just have thought that God was on her side.

She felt no guilt about the money. On the contrary. The added burden of Attracta had served to double the pleasure of her reward. And her resolve. He had been infinitely more calculating, more brutal. He'd callously stolen their dreams, their youth, their virginity. Pleasured himself liberally at the cost of their future. It would have been cheap at half the price.

She sealed the letter and sat it on the desk. It would be hand-delivered the night before the Conference, timed to cause the maximum of embarrassment and allow the minimum of manoeuvres.

Fonsie was sitting in the car waiting for her. Today would conclude the dress rehearsals.

She could hear the echo of her own footsteps in the corridors of Maynooth. The solid steel tips on the heels of her shoes clattered the stone hallway. Maybe softer heels on the day, he'd suggested. She'd agreed. That's what trial runs were all about.

Afternoon sun shone in through high, leaded windows. Hitting the back of their shoulders, sharpening shadows on polished stone floors. No man had bent his back in three to achieve this high shine. Walls two-feet thick kept reality outside with the cold. Priests passed, nodded. Went unperturbed about ecclesiastical matters. No one stopped to question the well-dressed man and woman they would all so eagerly and ably recall later.

Her smile trailed into silence. Calm and ordered, they proceeded to the auditorium where Wednesday's convention would be held. How could he be so sure? These are ancient institutions: they don't change their formats or formations. Careful and contrary. It's their strength and their weakness. She had no doubts then.

'All ready for the convention?' Fonsie's bare-faced cheek amused as much as it confirmed.

'Just a few finishing touches.' An overeager student hurried into the auditorium. She allowed herself a smile.

'Nobody will take a blind bit of notice of you. The young girls from the convent were always in and out like fiddler's elbows typing theses. You don't look a day older than any one of them.'

'Flattery?'

'Fact,' he'd said on that Sunday afternoon's reconnoitre.

'Fact: and just a little flattery.'

'So I'll get my day in court?' They walked on.

'Robbing banks, casing Catholic colleges: what will be left to entertain us?' She broke the silence.

'Be careful, don't get giddy. Not yet.'

You'd be amazed how liberty and equality gazump cowardice and compromise. That was the answer she made him when he questioned her strength.

For him, the journey was less than comfortable. A cathartic communication with the past. But integral to the planning, it had to be done. She must walk these whispering corridors alone on Wednesday. Arrive at her destination unchallenged.

He wished he had her courage. To confront the past, confound the future. He had surprised himself when he'd started to talk. Pierced with sorrow, punctuated with sadness, he'd left no stone unturned. He'd shocked himself when he felt tears running freely down his face.

'The announcement will be made on the twelfth of the month, up there in Maynooth.' Brigit had made the unwitting disclosure. Muriel had checked and double-checked the details as surreptitiously as she could.

'Sure, me sister knows what he has for his breakfast,' Brigit added for good measure, having described in minute detail the plans for the party back in Drumcondra afterwards. The expensive material he'd chosen himself. The increased waist measurements, the size, the style of the orders flying off daily to the convent in New Bridge. For vestments and robes, sandals, shoes, silk socks, skull caps, scarlet cummerbunds, soutanes with the thousands of split-pea-sized buttons he'd be wanting for the big promotion to Rome. Muriel's fake naivety had doubled Brigit's contribution.

Wednesday had come more quickly than Fonsie would have liked. With a strange mixture of reluctance and pride, Fonsie watched her as she lifted her knees gracefully into the taxi. Lineaments less than two weeks old were now sound and structured certainties. Her speech was good. If she delivered it with a quarter of the aplomb with which she'd delivered it to him, she'd be nothing short of brilliant.

Barclay O'Rourke was about to be stripped. The last vestiges of pride as doomed as his fortune. It was an inconvertible fact. He was out of her heart, out of her head. She was about to get him out of her bones.

Attracta Rafferty, she'd winked at him just before she left: three hundred pounds wouldn't go amiss. The shoe could have so easily been on the other foot. He opened his chequebook – a draft for five hundred pounds was already drawn up. She'd pursed her lips, a little habit he noticed she displayed when she was pleased. He didn't show her the draft for Concepta: some things were private. He waited a full fifteen minutes before he followed her.

She had made the taxi turn right out of Leixlip and head towards Dublin. Just in case Brigit was at the window watching. When all was said and done, she wouldn't want her to know she had played any hand or part in Barclay's downfall.

'Off to Dublin again. Twice in the one week. Where de yeh get yer energy? Yiv an eye for the style and the figure too now, I'll say that for yeh.' Brigit had made her do two full twirls before she'd let her go out of the door.

The taxi-driver swung the steering wheel round with renewed vigour. Turned a full circle back towards Maynooth. 'We might as well go backwards as forwards.' He'd looked in the mirror for some class of explanation. She smiled, made him none the wiser.

'It's the only decent road in Kildare. Sure, nothin' but the best for the Princes of the Church. With our lives in their hands, I suppose it's wise to get them here in one piece.' His running commentary had cut her journey in half.

Wednesday had come more slowly though than she had wanted. The day of reckoning. The day the fiddler must pay the price. Publicly.

'Soft rain, thank God.' The porter at the main gates tipped his cap as he waved the taxi through. They drove up the short concrete drive that had been laid straight to the main doors. Lush green pastures well stocked with Aberdeen Angus and Short Horn grazing either side.

You'll have three minutes, no more, before they lynch you: Fonsie's warning recalled. *Please listen carefully: they'll show you no mercy. Timing is everything. Say your piece by all means, but get out before they realise you're stolen a march on them.* She'd promised him she wouldn't outstay her welcome. That she'd stick strictly to the rehearsed script and the allotted time.

Heavy ornate doors led her directly into the great hall; Christ crucified, cut deep in the hard wood. Built on the backs and the pennies of the poor, she could almost hear Brigit. Wands of slanting light slung shadows and shrouded shapes before her. Uncharacteristic insouciance took her further down the hallowed halls. Instinct and suspicion turned to mild curiosity and acceptance as she passed priests and nuns alike. From cloistered doors *sotto voce* voices. Men making decisions secretly and behind closed doors. Holding women's sanity in their manicured hands.

She was a world away from Stretham Street, miles still from the overcrowding, the sight of barefoot children, the stench of emaciated beggars. How could these worldly sybarites in all conscience and consciousness kneel before their God? Fonsie's proposed donation to Noel Brown's campaign was doubling its appeal.

Don't be distracted. Eyes straight ahead, concentration, determination, are your allies. She focused as she retraced last Sunday's steps. Past the same oil-painted cardinals – the gallery of rouges. Under the auspices of saints and scholars, she turned the sharp left-hand corner down the finishing straits. She could hear a few rasps and coughs, clearing of chests, chairs scraping wooden floors. A general settling down as she made her final approach. Comforting rituals before the resumption of the afternoon session.

A young seminarian was sitting at a small table just outside the theatre door reading the office. She didn't hesitate, met the challenge in his eyes until it had passed and stepped into the crowded auditorium. A surge of adrenaline propelled her up the podium steps. Like obedient schoolchildren, they sat looking up at her.

'Good afternoon, gentlemen.' Poised, Muriel looked out at the sea of barbered heads.

'Spiritual violence.' She paused. No instinct told her what to do, no tradition what she ought to feel. Charged with unconscious voltage, she thumped the lectern. 'Bear with me, gentlemen. Walk in my shoes; exercise this unscheduled item.'

A sea of bewildered faces stared up at her. In a voice that she didn't recognise as her own, she began.

'When we are no longer able to change the situation, we are challenged to change ourselves. To transform personal tragedy into triumph.' She paused, waited as they waited for her.

Then the deafening harangue defied the panelled room.

'I'm difficult now I've grown thorns on my tongue.' The clock on the back wall was ticking. 'But after holding, in rank, this chest full of emotions for months, years, I have to speak out.

'Not that I wasn't part of the sin that led to this ignorant place. But I didn't know how potent first love was: so I at least can plead innocence. But you...' She looked Barclay straight in the eye. His horror had a renovate effect on her.

'You took full advantage of my innocence. Played with my fate. It wasn't just some unfortunate parcelling of destines that took us to this barren place. You took my innocence in your soulless hands and abused it.' All around her, cardinals and bishops cringed and curled their toes.

Terror bit viciously into Barclay O'Rourke. The transition from libertine to liar was incarnate.

Unsure of whether they were being spoken too or at, the confraternity amazingly continued to give her her quarter.

'And bless me, Father, but I have one more sin to confess.' She addressed Barclay O'Rourke directly. 'In the best possible interpretation of the Bible, I've extracted an eye for an eye.'

Not sure whether his interests were best served by staying or going, Barclay hesitated. He was lost.

'I've taken the money from Blessington.' The last drop of the blood in Barclay's face drained with his dignity and greed. 'Yes, yes.' Her voice reached new highs, people started to rise.

'Oh, I wasn't greedy, I just took the pittance you'd put away for a rainy day. Compensated myself, and the young servant girl you so callously impregnated in my mother's bed. Secured a life for her, a home more befitting a Bishop's son than the one guaranteed in a tenement in Dublin.'

Whether it was the mention of the pregnancy or the money, the shock was electric. The shuffling stopped. In the distance, a cock crowed. A sea of red skull caps swam before her eyes. Unfettered by their stature or stares, she lowered her voice, finished what she'd come to say.

'As for your daughter; our daughter. Well, have no fears, Bishop, or should I call you Cardinal, she'll live in Leixlip as you planned. But in a style more befitting the daughter of a Prince of the Church.'

Fonsie was standing in the doorway. His temptation to cheer was overwhelming.

Every betrayal has its perfect moment. As Barclay O'Rourke sat pole-axed beneath the podium, Muriel Grey had hers.

Lightning Source UK Ltd.
Milton Keynes UK
29 August 2009

143208UK00001B/27/P